Mouth to Mouth

Lilith turned to go, and hesitated. That should have warned him, but it wasn't until she looked back over her shoulder and he saw the mischievous gleam in her eyes that Hugh realized her intent. He didn't have time to make a decision or protest. Between one moment and the next, Lilith was bending down and covering his mouth with hers. Anticipating a forceful kiss, Hugh began to resist, but his tension drained away when he felt the difference in her touch. She'd done this before, but never so gently. Her hands remained at her sides; with light pressure, she ran her tongue across his bottom lip. Lilith exhaled softly in pleasure and her breath filled his mouth with heat. And he was the one who reached up, clasping her nape to pull her more tightly against him—he who sought her tongue with his, suddenly starving for the taste of her. How did she affect him so deeply, and after so long? He had no defense against it now . . .

DEMON ANGEL

meljean Brook

BERKLEY SENSATION, NEW YORK

THE BERKLEY PUBLISHING GROUP
Published by the Penguin Group
Penguin Group (USA) Inc.
375 Hudson Street, New York, New York 10014, USA

Penguin Group (Canada), 90 Eglinton Avenue East, Suite 700, Toronto, Ontario M4P 2Y3, Canada
(a division of Pearson Penguin Canada Inc.)
Penguin Books Ltd., 80 Strand, London WC2R 0RL, England
Penguin Group Ireland, 25 St. Stephen's Green, Dublin 2, Ireland (a division of Penguin Books Ltd.)
Penguin Group (Australia), 250 Camberwell Road, Camberwell, Victoria 3124, Australia
(a division of Pearson Australia Group Pty. Ltd.)
Penguin Books India Pvt. Ltd., 11 Community Centre, Panchsheel Park, New Delhi—110 017, India
Penguin Group (NZ), Cnr. Airborne and Rosedale Roads, Albany, Auckland 1310, New Zealand
(a division of Pearson New Zealand Ltd.)
Penguin Books (South Africa) (Pty.) Ltd., 24 Sturdee Avenue, Rosebank, Johannesburg 2196,
South Africa

Penguin Books Ltd., Registered Offices: 80 Strand, London WC2R 0RL, England

This is a work of fiction. Names, characters, places, and incidents either are the product of the author's imagination or are used fictitiously, and any resemblance to actual persons, living or dead, business establishments, events, or locales is entirely coincidental. The publisher does not have any control over and does not assume any responsibility for author or third-party websites or their content.

DEMON ANGEL

A Berkley Sensation Book / published by arrangement with the author

PRINTING HISTORY
Berkley Sensation mass-market edition / January 2007

Copyright © 2007 by Melissa Khan.
Excerpt from *Demon Moon* copyright © 2007 by Melissa Khan.
Cover illustration by Franco Accornero.
Cover design by Lesley Worrell.
Interior text design by Laura Corless.

ISBN: 978-0-425-21347-6

BERKLEY SENSATION®
Berkley Sensation Books are published by The Berkley Publishing Group,
a division of Penguin Group (USA) Inc.,
375 Hudson Street, New York, New York 10014.
BERKLEY SENSATION is a registered trademark of Penguin Group (USA) Inc.
The "B" design is a trademark belonging to Penguin Group (USA) Inc.

PRINTED IN THE UNITED STATES OF AMERICA

10 9 8 7 6 5 4 3 2

With all of my thanks to Echo, Megan, and my in-laws, for watching the tot. To Soojee and Maili, for helping me along. To Kat, for being there every single step of the way.

And with my utmost gratitude to my editor, Cindy Hwang, who likes men in tights and women in bustiers as much as I do.

A million times, thank you.

PART 1

CHAPTER I

county essex, england

october 1217

The road lay enshrouded in mist. Though Hugh had traveled
through this area many a time—as a squire accompanying
Robert d'Aulnoy to Colchester, and once as a knight fleeing to
the sea and seeking passage to Normandy—the familiar verdant
landscape receded under the fog as it smudged groves of trees
into vague shadows, erasing distance and detail with unrelenting gray.

The fog lay across the road, but could not obscure it. If not
for a well-worn track, Hugh would have been forced to wait; the
river ran too close to venture forward blindly, and his cargo was
too precious to risk. But in the soft, illusory mist, the ancient
road proved a solid guide as it unwound below him. Hugh
watched fine gray tendrils eddying around his gelding's legs,
and each step pushed them into a swirling dance.

The ring of hooves against stone, the murmurs of the servants, and the wooden creak of the countess's wagon seemed

more insistent with nothing but the ground to look upon. He glanced back at the sun once; poised like a dull, silver coin, it shed weak light that turned gray to white, but failed to penetrate or burn away the thick vapor.

"Will we lose our way, Sir Hugh?"

Hugh turned in his saddle, reined his mount to the side and waited for the wagon to draw even with him. Lady Isabel had ordered the curtains tied open to better watch their progress—though there was not much to see. The countess's silks, weaved through with metallic threads, failed to shine as brightly as she'd no doubt intended them. Even the golden curls peeking from beneath her filet seemed subdued. Though she had dressed in her finest raiment for the final day of their journey and the reunion with her husband, Hugh detected neither excitement nor pleasure in her expression. And despite her question, nor did she appear concerned that the fog might delay them; her countenance remained as sweetly demure as ever.

"Nay, my lady, so long as we do not stray from the road." The perfection of her cheek drew his gaze; younger even than he was, she possessed flawless skin unmarked by time or labor. His hands flexed in his gauntlets, and he felt the rasp of calluses against leather. He'd earned them protecting her—in constant *preparation* to protect her, and to serve d'Aulnoy.

"Are we near Fordham Castle?"

"If not for the mist, we could see it." Hugh pointed to the northeast. "Do you notice the incline of the road? We are approaching the ridge on which the first Earl of Essex built the castle."

The countess glanced down, as if searching for evidence of the gradual rise. Her servants did not need to see: they would feel it in the ache in their legs.

"Are we near the ruins, Sir Hugh?"

He dipped his head in confirmation. The remains of a Roman settlement marked the beginning of d'Aulnoy's holdings. "We shall come upon them soon. They lie a short distance from the road, however; we may not see them through the fog."

One of the countess's ladies-in-waiting leaned forward. "The thieves' den you spoke of, Isabel? Is it true, Sir Hugh, that we shall be set upon by bandits hiding among the ruins?"

The young countess blushed delicately; but Hugh had realized long ago the serene demeanor she affected in the courts and before her subjects hid a fanciful imagination, and it did not surprise him to learn she had been spinning tales to her ladies in private.

Would that he could blame his own yearnings on his age, but seventeen was long past time for fancy.

"Indeed, my lady. An ideal spot for an ambush it is," he said solemnly. In truth, lovers were more likely to be discovered between the deteriorating walls than outlaws. "Fear not, however; you are well protected against their villainy." He waved behind them, indicating the two knights who rode at the tail of their train and the foot soldiers. "I shall return you unharmed to your husband within hours."

The lady offered him a soft smile. "You have fulfilled your promise well, Sir Hugh. My husband shall be pleased, and I will request that he rewards you accordingly."

Surprised by her compliment, and trusting that the pale light and his helm masked the betraying heat in his cheeks, he bowed and said, "Serving you these two years has been its own reward, my lady."

He immediately regretted the triteness of his response, but she blushed and sat back against her cushions. She slanted him a glance wrought by delight and longing before she looked away, regaining her serenity. A low murmur from one of her attendants was followed by a burst of giggles from inside the wagon; Lady Isabel's mouth curved into a small, sad smile.

Contemplation of her expression suddenly felt like treason. Urging his horse forward, Hugh took lead again.

Despite the countess's promise of reward, he doubted d'Aulnoy would greet him with riches or lands. Hugh had been raised in the baron's castle and had acted as his squire for years; but the Earl of Essex could ill afford to bestow valuables upon a poor, unconnected knight, regardless of his affection for Hugh. The baron would have to strengthen his political alliances and repair whatever damage Lackland had wrought on his properties during his siege and afterwards.

And Hugh's service surely paled in comparison to those knights who'd been at d'Aulnoy's side during those desperate hours against the king. Protecting a child bride, however commendable, would not shine as brightly nor as immediately in d'Aulnoy's mind.

The shadow of the ruins appeared on the left, and he gratefully turned his attention to them. Though pleased their journey had been without incident, Hugh wished it hadn't provided him so much time to reflect on his uncertain future upon his return to Fordham Castle. And, despite his assurances of safety, it would be foolish not to be wary as they passed; in two years and under chaotic rule, a lovers' hideaway could easily turn into a site of ambush.

Centuries of pilfering for materials had left the walls partially intact. At least three buildings had stood beside the road; Hugh had examined them on previous trips and knew the layout well. The two closest to the roadway had been stripped almost down to the foundations, leaving a knee-high wall of masonry. The one behind retained its height, though the ceiling had long since fallen in. Columns lay broken into heavy cylinders at the entrance; it was generally accepted that it had been a temple, though to whom—or what—Hugh had never learned.

His gaze skimmed over the low walls, and he looked past them toward the temple, but could not discern the barest outline.

"Oh!" One of the women cried out, and he turned. The ladies' faces crowded the wagon's window. "I do hope the thief who steals the jewels from my kirtle is a handsome one!"

Their laughter trilled from the wagon, and Hugh allowed himself a smile before facing forward again. Spurring his horse on, he cast one last glance toward the ruins.

A figure in crimson rose from the ground behind the nearest wall and darted into the mist surrounding the temple.

Hugh blinked, certain he'd imagined it and mistook shadow for human. Nothing could move with such speed, not hind nor hound, but the ladies' shrill screams confirmed he had not been the only one to have seen it. He drew his sword and peered blindly into the fog. Was the person alone, or did the ruins conceal a party lying in wait?

Despite his attempt to calm himself, Hugh's pulse quickened until his heart pounded into a galloping beat. From behind him came a flurry of activity as servants and soldiers formed a defensive ring around the countess's litter. A few murmurs from Lady Isabel quieted the other women, and silence fell over the group, save for the jingle of mail and thud of hooves as Georges de Rouen rode to Hugh's side.

"You saw?" Hugh asked in a low voice.

"A female, richly dressed." The knight shouldered the crossbow that usually lay slung across his back and slid a bolt into the shelf. The Church frowned upon the weapon, but Hugh had not argued its presence for this journey. "You know this area best; what are your thoughts?"

A woman? Hugh had not been able to determine shape from his brief glimpse, but he trusted Georges's assessment. The older man's eye was unparalleled, whereas to Hugh, objects appeared blurred until he came within fifteen or twenty feet of them.

"Though the ladies would make this place a site of villainous infamy, the only sin I have encountered here is that of fornication." He met Georges's laughing gaze with his own before he sobered and added, "But women, even those fearing discovery of an assignation, cannot run so fast as she. An arrow from a bow couldn't have caught her."

Georges nodded thoughtfully and looked into the mist. "Should we suspect a trick? A cloak tied to a string? Or did the fog distort our vision and give her the illusion of quickness?"

"I know not." With a frustrated sigh, he glanced back at the litter. But for Lady Isabel, fear pinched the women's expressions. The countess watched him with calm, steady attention, trust shining in her eyes.

Hugh's gut tightened. "I will go," he said without thought. "If thieves wait, I shall flush them out before they can cause harm."

Georges's eyebrows rose, disappearing behind the brow of his helm. "Do you wish to prove your mettle, there are more worthy opponents than outlaws. Let us go on; they would be foolish to attack a party as well armed as ours." A smile tugged at the corners of his mouth. "Of course, perhaps a jaunt into the mist would allow you to end this journey with an act of courage."

Noting the knight's wry tone, Hugh reddened. Was his attachment to the countess so obvious? And, apparently, harmless—Georges seemed to view Hugh's feelings with amusement rather than concern of infidelity or disloyalty.

"Go on, boy," Georges urged quietly. "Had we been in danger, they would already be upon us. And I doubt the lady we saw belongs to a band of thieves. More likely, you shall find her lover's braies left behind in his haste to escape." He raised his voice and cried, "Rout them, my brave lad! I shall cover your backside!"

Hugh lowered his head to hide his embarrassment and

laughter, but obediently kicked his horse into motion. Once off
the road, the gelding picked his way between the foundations
and discarded stone of the nearest buildings, his steps muffled
by the soft clay and thick grass.

At the temple's southwest corner, he paused and glanced behind him. Fog masked both road and travelers. The trepidation
roused by the woman's appearance had faded during his conversation with Georges, but now, isolated from sight, his tension returned. If he and Georges had mistaken their safety, Hugh's
display of bravery could endanger them all. Holding his sword
at ready, he circled the temple walls, keeping their solid bulk on
his left. Even should someone hide within the temple, he could
not attack Hugh through the thickness of the masonry. Though
perhaps by climbing the rough, rectangular stones . . . Hugh
stole a glance upward, almost expecting to see a horde of thieves
peering over the walls. No one. He grinned in self-reproach,
chided himself for his nervousness, and approached the temple
entrance. His horse skirted around the fallen columns. His ap-
prehension eased into confidence when his first glimpse into the
interior revealed it to be empty. But as he urged the gelding past
the threshold, a moan sounded from the southeast corner.

Pivoting his horse with pressure from legs and reins, Hugh
backed his mount against the opposite wall. He hefted his
sword in warning, and his vision quickly adjusted to the dim
light inside . . . there. A man stood by the—

Hugh's eyes widened and he barely contained the laughter
that threatened to erupt from him.

Sir William Mandeville. D'Aulnoy's seneschal had not
changed in two years, though Hugh had never seen him
stretched as he was now: his hands tied over his head, his hose
bunched around his spindly, white ankles. His partner had left
him with the hem of his surcoat resting atop his erect rod and
trailing down either side, exposing his ballocks and inner
thighs. A woolen scarf covered his eyes, but couldn't disguise
the rigid cast of his ruddy features, nor his rage and fear as he
cried out, "Who is there? I hear the footsteps of your horse! Reveal yourself, coward! You dare look upon me in secrecy?"

The query cut through Hugh's amusement; silently, he
watched the man struggle against his bonds. A part of him enjoyed the seneschal's humiliation; he well knew Mandeville's
temper and pride, had been a target of the cruelty lingering be-

neath his words and actions. Mandeville was a fine seneschal, but should he realize Hugh had seen him in such a state, he would make Hugh's position in the castle unbearable.

As his status could not survive Mandeville's hatred, Hugh swallowed the response that rose in his throat, along with the temptation to declare himself the owner of this bit of power over the knight.

The gelding shifted uneasily beneath him, as if in response to Hugh's tension. There was nothing to do here—nothing to report. With a press of his heels, Hugh guided him back the temple's entrance. Once outside, he drew on the reins, closed his eyes, and breathed deeply the clean, thick air. A trembling had taken hold of his hands, and his sword rattled against the wooden scabbard as he sheathed it.

Shame and temptation shook him equally. If he had been older, more secure of his position, would he have taken advantage of the seneschal's weakness? Undoubtedly. But such an action would have been foolhardy; no matter how he wanted it, how it burned bitterly in his gut, he must act in a manner that would ensure his future. He must curb his tongue. He must act with honor—even though Mandeville rarely did the same.

"A rather disappointing display of cowardice, Sir Pup."

A woman stood by the gelding's head, stroking the horse's broad cheek. Though her words had been spoken softly, Hugh startled, and her lips tilted into a secretive smile as she looked him over. Her gaze finally rose to meet his, her eyes dark and amused.

He quickly recovered his composure, but the quick beat of his heart did not immediately ease. Had he been so distracted that she'd been able to sidle up to him undetected? How did she move so swiftly, so silently?

Like she, he kept his voice low so as not to be overheard by Mandeville. "Cowardice, my lady?"

For indeed, her clothing declared her such. Her scarlet cloak was thrown back, revealing an overdress of fine black. She wore no cap over her dark hair, though it was parted and bound as severely as any other lady's. No beauty was she, but broadbeamed and flat-featured, like an ill-tempered cow.

Yet her eyes sparkled with wit and vivacity, as if she would not be contained by her lackluster features, and demureness were a sin.

"Yes, cowardice. Imagine the power you could wield over

him had you the courage to grasp it." Her expression challenged him to take offense. When he made no response, she stepped forward and traced her fingers over his hand, still clenched around the hilt of his sword. Her skin was warm—hot—despite the cool air. "You shook with desire, Sir Hugh. Could it be I'm mistaken, and you have not been aroused by the opportunity to secure a better position within Fordham? If you threatened to bring each member of your party into the temple so they may be shocked and decry his perversity, do you not think he would honor your every request?"

Her breasts pressed against his leg. His chausses prevented direct contact, but the pressure of her soft, generous curves drew his eyes. Though a moment ago he had not noted any immodesty in her dress, he realized naught hid the upper swell her bosom, and creamy flesh mounded over her neckline. Hugh stared down into the depths of her cleavage and swallowed, finally remembering to reply.

" 'Honor' is not a word I would associate with profiting from a man's humiliation."

Her laugh set the mounds a-jiggling. He hastily returned his gaze to her face, and she said, "Do not pretend you aren't tempted, honor or no. I am sorely tempted to expose him, and I'm the one who tied him there."

Aye, he could easily imagine this woman, with her wicked eyes, binding Sir William and teasing him into the state Hugh had seen. Who was she? She'd known his name, his destination, yet Hugh was certain they'd never met. "If you wish his humiliation, then you must know Sir William well," he said.

Her grin revealed sharp, white teeth—unexpectedly perfect teeth for someone of her apparent age. "Indeed. Although the position you found him in is a far better indicator of how well I know him." She smoothed her palm over the back of his ankle, unprotected by armor. The heat of her fingers burned through his hose and boots. He shifted his foot in the stirrup. Her breasts heaved upward with the movement, and her hand slid up the length of his calf, hugging his leg against her.

Trapped by a fine pair of bubbies. Choking back a laugh, he said, "You have me at a disadvantage, my lady, for you know far more than I."

An unfathomable emotion flickered in her dark eyes. Just as quickly, it disappeared and her amusement shone bright again.

"An innocent, are you?" Her fingernails tickled the back of his knee, and she smiled when he drew in a sharp breath. "Then perhaps we should make a bargain, and even our playing fields? What would you like?"

"Your name."

A harmless request, but unease skittered down his spine as she drew back, her expression triumphant. "A name is nothing, Sir Hugh. Agreed. 'Tis Lilith." Surprise fluttered across his features. Before he could respond to the unusual name, or demand a family and connection, she pursed her lips and added, "And I should like you to announce your presence to Sir William."

He began shaking his head, and her smile grew disdainful. "Or shall you betray our bargain and your honor?"

Lilith struggled to keep her scorn on her bovine features when all she wanted was to bang her head repeatedly against the temple's rock wall. Stupid, to try casting aspersions on his honor or courage in order to generate a heated, thoughtless response. She'd done so earlier, and he had regarded her as calmly as he did now.

Did she never learn? Or had she become so used to men of Mandeville's ilk—proud, vain, cruel men—that she'd become a creature of habit? True, she'd become bored in her old role, and seized the opportunity to corrupt an innocent when Lucifer had offered it, but she hadn't expected innocence to present a challenge.

Nor had she expected the challenge to be so pleasant to look upon. A pity this innocent was not hers—still, that would not prevent her from playing with him.

"Honor?" he echoed, his eyebrows raised in disbelief. Oh, those were fine brows. Even a demon could not find an imperfection in them, though she might try. Like dark mahogany, they matched the hair that curled soft as a cherub's, barely visible beneath his helm. Thick lashes framed clear, azure eyes. At an age between adolescence and maturity, his cheeks and jawline curved gently, as if his face were too youthful for angles. "What you ask is hardly in fair exchange for what you deemed 'nothing.'"

"My good sir, the terms of the bargain are equal! I gave you my name . . . and you have only to give yours to Sir William."

A smile seemed to threaten the corners of his mouth. "The

consequences are uneven. Name another—worth nothing—and I will leave you to your assignation and return to my party."

She affected a pout. She'd been listening to those waiting on the road, but Hugh's absence had not yet caused them significant worry. Much longer, however, and they would come after him. "Perhaps they already begin to search for you," she lied easily. "Your resistance will be for naught, and they will all look upon Sir William. I heard the ladies laughing earlier—will they laugh the louder for his prick being exposed to their gaze?"

"Not one lady," Hugh said beneath his breath, but Lilith had no trouble discerning his words.

"Ah, aye," she said. "Lady Isabel. She is far too kind a creature to laugh at another's misfortune. And she would not think the better of you for being the procurer of their amusement. Does her opinion matter so much?"

To her frustration, she could not read his face, and he had unusually strong shields for one so young—as if he often hid his thoughts even from himself. But the granite voice with which he replied gave her the answer she sought. "Name your side of the bargain, lady."

"A kiss." He looked at her with surprise, and she arched a brow. "'Tis nothing but a meeting of lips. It only has meaning when there is love or a promise involved, and there is neither between us."

"It should not be given without love or promise," he said, but his gaze fell to her lips.

"So idealistic." She grinned and slid her tongue over her teeth. "I should love to corrupt you."

A chuckle rumbled from him as he leaned over. "I promise I would not be worth the effort."

She had to rise on her toes to meet his lips. They were firm and cool beneath hers, and he did not immediately pull away, but neither did he deepen the kiss. She felt his tension—as if he expected her to take the kiss farther, and both feared and hoped she would.

Oh, to choose between desire and fear. Her instincts cried for her to take his mouth fully, to subject him to a sensual on-slaught, to play on his fear—but her instincts had guided her wrongly with him before. And so she decided to both assuage his fear and deny his desire by ending the kiss.

She nipped gently at his bottom lip and his mouth opened.

The beat of his heart skipped and increased, drumming loud in her ears. Pleased by his involuntary response, she stepped away to gauge his reaction. He blinked and straightened, his cheeks flooding with color.

"I see you make a habit of only taking a man so far," he said ruefully.

Had he said it in any other tone, it would have been a condemnation of her as a cock-tease. Instead, he made sport of himself.

"Only as far as they will," she replied; for truthfully, she could not act contrary to a human's free will.

"Perhaps you mistook mine."

She pushed the absurdly pleased rush of emotion away, and wondered if she should feel insulted that he suggested she'd misread him. "I think not."

"I've never pitied Sir William before this day." He smiled as he delivered the backward compliment, then bowed. "My lady."

Lilith seized the reins beneath his horse's chin before he could turn away. He frowned.

"Do you not realize the women will speak of your brave venture into the ruins after they reach the castle?" The words tripped from her mouth. "Mandeville will discover who saw him thus."

Hugh nodded solemnly, his beautiful mouth tightening. "Of course I have realized, my lady. But the dishonor of his reaction—should it be dishonorable—will belong to him alone. I will not compound it by threats or humiliation."

She narrowed her eyes and studied him. How foolish to set himself up for the punishment Mandeville would undoubtedly deliver when its avoidance could so easily be had. Then inspiration struck: he had already made one bargain. It should be easy to convince him into another. "I will enter into another agreement with you, Sir Hugh. You undoubtedly want Sir William to have no knowledge of your seeing him—I can guarantee that."

"How?"

She lowered her lashes. "Come now, you do not think I will reveal my secrets?"

"I think you have already revealed them." His gaze fell to her chest.

She did not need to feign her laughter. When it faded, she asked, "What say you?" He had little choice but to accept her offer; he must know that.

"What shall you ask in return?"

She hid the triumph that shot through her. "I do not yet know, but it shall be an equal favor." When he hesitated, she pressed, "Have we a bargain, Sir Hugh?"

He gave a short nod. "We do. I'm in your debt, my lady."

He did not sound as though he relished that knowledge—all the more reason for her to enjoy it. She lowered her lids to hide the glee that boiled within her. Her nape burned as his stare fell upon her like a hot iron prodding for lies. He doubted his judgment in making the bargain, and did not trust her—but he would not renege. Of that she was certain.

She folded her hands demurely over her midriff to prevent herself from rubbing them together in anticipation. " 'Tis nothing, Sir Hugh."

❧

Lilith watched as the mist swallowed Hugh's mounted form, listened to the laughing, nervous coos of greeting from the women. All but one woman—Lilith paid particular attention to that lady's relieved sigh.

Ah, but this was almost too easy.

The rough slide of rope against stone recalled Sir William to her. Gathering up her skirts, she skipped into the temple.

He turned his head, blindly following her trampling path. "Marie?"

"Aye, 'tis I," she sang and danced into a spin. His hesitation pleased her, as did his fear.

"You ran, and I was seen." She felt his shame roll into rage. He shook his head as if to dislodge the blindfold. "Untie me!"

Her good humor dropped from her like a shroud. "You were not seen," she lied, observing his angry struggles with distaste. Whilst she waited at the castle, she had chosen him to play with, to pass the time, but it seemed little worth it now.

"I heard—"

"A horse."

"Without rider?" he scoffed. "You are both slut and liar."

"Oh, I am more than that," she murmured, settling herself lightly upon a fallen column. Perched as she was, he might have discerned something of her true nature—but, blindfold or no, such as Sir William had no discernment. It had served her so well over the centuries: those she had manipulated saw nothing beyond themselves.

She sighed as he roared for her to untie him. Destroying him would have been a sweet pleasure, if a rather worthless one. Unless Sir William had a dramatic turnabout in his nature, he was destined for Hell; anything she did would only accelerate his damnation. One such as Hugh, however, or the baron, or Isabel—their temptation and damnation would add a soul not already doomed.

She touched her lips, ignoring Sir William's increasingly furious demands. If she did this well, perhaps she could tempt all three. Such a coup—and on her first attempt in this role!— should win her some reward. And Hugh would make a fine companion, with his beauty and his absurd mix of practicality and idealism. He could entertain her for a time, perhaps even a century or two. Beneath her fingers, her mouth curved into a frown. Of course, Lucifer would not allow him to retain his beauty, as she had not been able to keep hers. Nor would his innocence survive the descent and torture Below.

"—IMMEDIATELY! Do you hear me, Marie? Marie!" As if her silence had made him fear she'd left him again, he repeated her name with a hint of uncertainty.

She eyed his flaccid penis, then leaned forward and collected a long, slender branch from the floor of the temple, where she'd dropped it after a similar encounter a sennight earlier. It had left satisfactory stripes across his arse, she remembered. "Have you finished bellowing?"

A poke to his testicles sent the heavy sac swinging. He gasped in pain—but not too much, she noted, as his cock began to fatten. "Marie?"

That ridiculous name. She lifted the tip of his burgeoning penis with the switch, balanced its length along the wooden shaft. Studied the blind little eye.

And because there was no one to see, she let herself be Lilith. Her constricting clothing vanished. The shift from human to demon form was instantaneous, a shiver of newly crimson skin and a ripple of muscle. Black, membranous wings sprouted from her back; she stretched them wide, debating whether to push the transformation further. No one would appreciate the effect of fangs, forked tongue and claws, so she grew them for her own pleasure and imagined William's reaction if he saw her this way.

His screams would be as music to her pointed ears.

But she'd made a bargain with Hugh, and so she must create a different tune. She had to fulfill the terms of her agreement; as with human free will, it must be honored. She was unused to bargaining—her slip with the name, allowing Hugh to ask for her real name instead of what she was 'called'—had been a mistake, but not an irreparable one. Bargaining wasn't usually part of her repertoire when tormenting murderers and rapists, but a skill she still had to learn. In a hundred years, she'd be a master—but for now, she would do what she could.

Lowering the stick, she fastidiously wiped the tip on the ground. She didn't need pain to get her point across.

Her tongue would do quite nicely.

CHAPTER 2

The celebratory mood that swept over the castle slowly faded as the day wore on, and though Hugh was greeted with exclamations and felicitations for his successful return, these were soon replaced by the duties life demanded, conversations became shorter, men more ready to excuse themselves from Hugh's recounting of the journey.

Robert had claimed his wife and kept her by his side throughout the day, her ladies-in-waiting settled themselves and set about their work, and Hugh found himself in the bailey, standing beside Georges and watching the squires' fencing practice. Though Hugh knew many of the squires well and was of the same age, he couldn't ignore the separation that seemed between them now. More than two years, it was the separation of rank and position—one that, judging by the glances he'd received, many of them felt he had not deserved.

"When do you return to Anjou?"

"A fortnight, perhaps; the court should like me to report that the lady is settled well," Georges said. "The boy should plant his feet less firmly."

Hugh nodded as a squire failed to give against his opponent's blow and was knocked to the ground. Beyond the field, a figure rode through the gate, and Hugh stiffened. Mandeville.

Lilith did not seem to be with him—but no, likely they'd have arranged to return as if separately.

"The lady in crimson," Georges said softly. He was looking in the opposite direction, and Hugh turned to see Lilith striding across the bailey. She saw him at the same moment and smiled boldly, redirecting her steps on line with him and Georges.

Georges rested his hands on the hilt of his sword, as if casually, but Hugh had known him long enough to sense the tension and readiness within the older man. He had barely a moment to wonder at it before Lilith reached them.

"Sir Hugh." He bowed, and as he rose noticed her sudden rigidity. Her hand clenched at her side. Her smile was brittle. "And—?"

Realizing that she stared at Georges, he quickly made the introduction. "Sir Georges mentored me during my time in the Angevin court," he added.

Her head tilted, her eyes narrowed. "Indeed."

"Indeed," Georges echoed.

Awkwardly, unsure of how to explain her when he knew only her Christian name and nothing of her connections, Hugh continued, "And this is the lady, Lil—"

"I am Marie de Lille," she said smoothly. "Recently come from Rochester Castle."

Hugh nodded; likely, she'd been a part of the household before the siege and had been shuffled between distant relatives after the castle had changed hands. Unmarried, brash, unremarkable in face and form—she would be a difficult fit in many ladies' circles. He eyed her rich clothing; she must have some form of support, and he doubted it was the generosity of other women.

She slanted him an amused glance, as if she could read his thoughts, and his cheeks heated. He was almost thankful when Sir William interrupted them.

"I see you are returned, pup." His gaze ran between Lilith and Hugh, hot with anger.

Hugh fought to keep his dislike from his expression. "I am."

"And you returned on the same worthless nag you borrowed ere you left," Mandeville said.

Hugh felt the insult. A horseless knight was one of little

value, a burden to his lord. "He was too worthless to eat, and so I rode him," he said.

"For two years? Tourneys are not outlawed in France, yet you've not earned arms nor mount."

Lilith stood with her hands behind her back, rocking back and forth from heels to toes as if enjoying the tension immensely. "Why is it, Sir Hugh, that you have armor but no arms?" He flushed, but she only pursed her lips and allowed her eyes to run the length of his form. "I have heard speak of a young man—an exceedingly young man—knighted the evening before the barons met Lackland at Runnymede. And of how d'Aulnoy gave him his own suit of mail, feeling the deepest affection for him."

Hugh shrugged, trying to control his embarrassment. "He'd had another made for him; it no longer fit him, but it did me."

"Aye, he grew too fat," Lilith said bluntly. "But you have grown in those two years, for you've had to split the links at the shoulders."

She couldn't have known that, since he'd removed the heavy armor soon after arriving at the castle, but she'd seen him wearing the mail. It was impossible to pretend he'd not met her at the temple now. Mandeville's face mottled with his rage; Georges stared at her without expression.

"I had plenty of time to practice," Hugh said quietly. "I expanded."

Her eyes glittered with humor. Tapping her finger against her bottom lip, she continued, "But Sir William thinks you should have been making your fortune in tournaments. Yet you did not enter even a one, and so you own nothing of a knight's belongings but a poorly mended bit of armor. Even your horse was loaned to you for the mission only." A sly look entered her gaze. "But I suppose it would have been difficult to protect the countess had you jaunted off to every tourney."

"Aye," Hugh said, suddenly baffled. Was she making sport of him or defending him? "Many men die in the tournaments, and I couldn't fulfill my duties injured or dead."

"So you let yourself grow soft in the courts?"

"He has said he expanded in practice," Lilith said to Mandeville with a touch of exasperation. "Sir Georges mentored him."

"Aye?" He gave the older man a dismissive look.

"You are welcome to try his arm," Georges said.

A bit of glee lit the seneschal's face. "Are you game, pup? Want a bit of practice?"

Hugh grinned, a cold, confident expression that belied the angry resignation in his gut. "Of course."

❧

Lilith leaned against the wall next to Georges, her hands behind her back. In her fists, she clutched the sword she had called in from her invisible cache of weapons, and hid its length between skirts and stone.

Unfortunate she couldn't make it appear in the center of his chest instead of in her hand.

"You reek, Guardian," she said for his ears only.

"You did not notice my odor at the ruins earlier."

That he was right annoyed her. "You sent him in, knowing I was there." She glanced away from the field, where Hugh and William circled, each holding swords with blunted edges. Though he'd adopted the appearance of a man long past his youth, this close he couldn't hide what he was from her. Michael—the Doyen, leader of the Guardians, sworn to protect humans from such as she.

Except he had never killed her as he did other demons; she knew why, and the reason made her bold and angry. "You should no longer be so careless with innocents around me." Unlike Lilith, Michael did not take his eyes from the combatants on the field, as if he did not consider her a threat. "You thought he would distract me from my mission," she guessed.

"He has."

She smiled. "He is but part of my plan. Surely you've seen how he looks at the countess? And she him?"

"It means nothing; he will not do what you think."

"Of course he will." She returned her attention back to the combatants. William fell back, unable to withstand the onslaught of Hugh's speed and quickness. Easy to admire the play of strength and agility in his body. "You've trained him well, for a human."

He cast her a disapproving glance. "You are not so different from him."

She let her eyes glow red for the briefest moment. "I am."

He stared at her, seeming to pierce inside her until she had to look away. "This new role is not for you, Lilith. The old one, where you played the Fury and acted in the name of vengeance sat more easily upon you."

She laughed. "I grew bored, and that role wore thin. Damning souls for the armies Below will be much more rewarding." She looked at Hugh, who had finally managed to win and gave an exaggerated lick of her lips. "Much more rewarding."

"I will not allow you the same leniency in this new role, Lilith," he warned.

"My sword is ready."

"Your soul is not," he said. When she waved a dismissive hand, he continued, "You are not the first of your kind, the halflings, to attempt this role. They all failed." She felt him study the stony line of her face. "How many are left, Lilith?"

Only five. Sick dread tightened her belly, and she forced it and the image of the frozen faces away. *She* would not renege on her bargain.

"Perhaps if you succeed in this, the Morningstar will make more of your kind. Perhaps he'll include you in the making of them. Instead of collecting souls, you'll simply have to persuade men into blood sacrifice. How would that role suit you? I wager no better than this one."

Her mouth firmed, but she was distracted as, on the field, Mandeville was forced to his knees. The fine tremor in Hugh's arms, his stranglehold on the handle of the sword suddenly fascinated her. "Look," she said. "He shakes with the desire to strike the seneschal again, and the effort it takes him to hold back. All for a bit of practice. Think you not I can break him, bring that forth in a manner so destructive it will tear him apart?"

"Aye, he bends to temptation," Georges said. "But he will not break. You know naught of good men, Lilith."

Unsettling, that a Guardian said what she'd thought to herself upon meeting the young knight. And, indeed, Hugh was pulling back from Mandeville now—the danger had passed.

"I know I should like to kill *you*," she said sweetly. "And he has already entered into a bargain."

No surprise on Georges's face; of course not, he would have heard its making from his post on the road. "Will you not release him?"

She answered with her laughter. Entering a bargain didn't

endanger its participants' souls, but failing to complete it did. A human could release himself from a bargain in which neither of the terms had been fulfilled, or only the human's part completed—and a demon was bound up to that point. But once a demon had fulfilled its part, only she could release the human.

And she had completed her part.

He sighed, and she clenched her jaw against his disappointment. She should not feel it.

"I leave this evening," he said.

Her brows rose, mocking. "To search for your sword?" All knew he'd lost that great weapon a millennium before.

"A nosferatu, in the northern part of the isle."

Anticipation of a hunt boiled through her, but she forced it away. She could not chase after nosferatu *and* work on the baron and countess.

The Doyen smiled. "Aye, this new role chafes already, does it not?"

And she could only seethe, for Hugh's return to their side prevented her the last word.

❧

"I do not think you've fulfilled your side of the bargain," Hugh said, unable to hide his amusement. Flicking a glance at Mandeville's seat upon the dais, he found the seneschal watching them. "He glowers at me like death. 'Tis fortunate my lord has forbidden weapons in the great hall, or I fear I would be one of the courses, skewered and laid out on the table."

Lilith turned to see, her eyes narrowing as she took in the seneschal's expression. Hugh watched her stare him down with a touch of amazement; Mandeville looked away, his face flushed and with not a tiny bit of fear.

She glanced back at Hugh, her chin raised at a haughty angle. "Death," she said, "would never cower before me."

"I should like to learn that trick," he murmured. "Though I'm certain I wouldn't like to do what it was that made him fear you so."

"His fear will turn to anger soon enough," she said. "As for the matter of our bargain, I did as you asked. He has no idea that you saw him."

He sliced her a doubtful glance.

She laughed. "You must allow that I had little to work with;

tales of your jaunt into the ruins have already spread through the castle. I had to include that into my tale, or he would find me out for a liar."

"What was your story?"

Her mischievous gaze held his. "That I encountered you outside the temple, enticed you from your horse, and allowed you under my skirts."

He paused with a bit of lamb halfway to his mouth, his eyes widening. "Nay," he said, choking on a horrified laugh.

"Indeed." She grinned. "And I explained that your horse wandered into the temple, and then out between the time I first took you into my mouth and you spent your seed within me."

A groan rose within him, accompanied by a rush of heat, but he couldn't stop laughing. "Nay," he repeated, and dropped his head into his hands. He peered through his fingers. "Please tell me that you jest."

"I'm in earnest." She dipped her fingers into her goblet, lifted them to trace wine over her lips. "And when you had left me, I returned inside the temple and explained to him that you had left me so well used that I did not feel like finishing with him. That, in comparison to your great length, youth, and virility, there was little reason for me to continue with him. He was so distracted by such a thought, that all his anger turned to me and the idea of his having been seen by a stranger fled."

Hugh held himself very still, his laughter dying. "The aim of our bargain was to keep myself from his anger; you have merely transferred it from one reason to another."

She blinked slowly, like a cat full of canary. "I fulfilled the terms of the bargain."

And he was in the same predicament he had tried to avoid. Bewilderment and a sense of betrayal stalked his emotions, though he did not know why. He could not find anger within him at her, though—he had himself to blame. He should not have trusted her.

"Aye, you did," he agreed. "And I owe you a lie. Perhaps I should call you a beauty."

He immediately regretted such cruelty, but it was as if she didn't feel it. "Nay," she said, her eyes leveled on his face. For the first time, he could detect no hint of amusement, or mischief. "I will let you know when I need the lie."

Nodding stiffly, he turned back to his food, began eating

with his full attention. He felt her gaze upon him, though. Trying to ignore it became impossible, and when he finally gave in, he found her grinning at him.

He couldn't resist. She was wicked, terrible—and the most intriguing person he'd met. Perhaps he was too easily led astray by sin, too eager to enter into bargains and let his curiosity get the better of his judgment, but for now, he would allow it. "How did you know me?"

"At the temple?" At his nod, her grin widened. "Sir William spoke of you often. 'The foundling pup favored by the baron.' That is what he calls you: Sir Pup." She looked him up and down. "I knew who you were, not only because the castle was expecting your and the countess's return, but because of your youth. And your beauty; Sir William is not the only one to talk."

He blushed, and she looked upon it as if his embarrassment were a present solely for her.

"Though Essex does not seem to favor you so much now," she said softly. Hugh's gaze dropped to the table. It was true; a coolness had descended between, though he knew not the reason. "Perhaps he has realized that knighting a boy in his fifteenth year could be perceived as a display of weakness, more than strength. How many were knighted that day?"

A smile touched his mouth. "All who had earned it and had the means to procure their armor and arms." Hugh had not been one of them, and he was three years younger than any other. "You think it a weakness, to arrive with a large retinue of knighted men?"

"It is when the soldiers are boys, and the knighting an obvious attempt to bolster his numbers. It reeks of desperation. Perhaps you have become a symbol of that failure to d'Aulnoy—he lost his holdings for a year and a half. His display of strength was apparently not great enough to keep the king at bay." She smiled suddenly. "But perhaps an advantageous marriage will change your luck. Amongst the ladies, there is naught but gossip of the handsome knight who has finally returned."

Hugh glanced down the length of the table, uncomfortable with this talk of what he had—and what he did not—and met the interested gaze of several women. A few puzzled looks as well, as they glanced past him to Lilith. He quickly dropped his gaze again; he should not be sitting with her—he had not the importance. But, upon meeting him within the hall she had insisted he serve her, and he'd not wanted to cause a scene by refusing. And, he forced himself to admit, he still resented that Mandeville had put him in his place in the courtyard.

A capon sliced easily under his knife, and he laid several choice pieces upon Lilith's trencher. " 'Tis unfortunate they do naught but gossip."

"And which one would you have do more?" Though neither her expression nor tone betrayed her amusement, he felt it and could not resist smiling in return. "Behind you sits the youngest daughter of the sheriff of Chelmsford, and I have heard her speak of your eyes, bright blue as the afternoon sky. She is exceedingly comely, is she not?"

"Aye, but her poetry lacks originality."

"Her father is rich."

He stole a look over his shoulder, grinning. "Aye? Perhaps her singing will compensate for her poor verse-making."

"A fine voice can give life to dull lyrics," Lilith nodded, her eyes sparkling. "And she will sound lovely in bed, even if her movements put you to sleep before the song is spent."

Hugh choked, coughing until his laughter cleared his throat. "Has a man ever dared fall asleep before you?"

"Only very brave and very stupid men." She placed a small bit of roasted apple daintily on her tongue. "But I'll admit my singing is not particularly fine."

"Just exceptionally loud?"

"Aye, loud." She tilted her head, and her gaze dropped to his lap. "And I have mastered the appropriate instruments."

Her words inspired an image that heated his blood, and he was grateful for the table, hiding the effects of it. His breath hitched, and her gaze met his; knowledge and temptation burned in the dark depths of her eyes. Remembering Sir William's situation, some of the wicked bravado that had allowed him to equal her in the conversation deserted him.

As if sensing his withdrawal, she frowned. "Come now, Sir Hugh. Do not disappoint me."

"I do not mean to, my lady," he said, his voice rueful. "But I'm unused to such conversation with a woman."

"You were enjoying it."

"Aye."

A page set the new course before them, allowing Hugh a moment to gather himself—though it was not a lonely moment, for he felt Lilith examining his face as if she could discern every thought that passed through his mind.

"Perhaps that is the difficulty," he said when the boy had moved down the table. "I should not take pleasure in such a discussion. 'Tis . . . unseemly."

She regarded him in silence for a moment. "I frighten you."

A flush reddened his skin. She was laughing at him, and after a moment of wrestling with his masculine pride, he allowed himself the same. "Aye, my lady. I would not like to end up tied to a wall—but I think your conversation and the temptation you offer may lead there."

"Such frank conversation arouses you?"

His face burned. "Aye."

"Is it so terrible to be aroused?"

He nodded, and took a sip of wine, hoping that it would soothe his suddenly parched mouth.

"Then we should turn our conversation to a different topic," she said. "What non-arousing subjects did you and the countess speak of when you fled to Anjou? And in the two years during? For certain, you never discussed anything that wasn't perfectly innocent. What could have filled your thoughts two years ago? The decision of the Lateran Council, forbidding clerics from issuing an order of execution? Forbidding them to bless the water and hot iron used in torture?" She nodded, her lips tilted in amusement. "Such would be fine conversation between a lady and a knight."

"We spoke of the barons' rebellion," he said slowly, certain it was true but unable to remember her position aside from the demure support of her husband. Pleasantries, such as *I am certain my lord will prevail* and *I trust my lord will do what is right* had fallen from her lips many a time, with no indication that she possessed a real understanding of the rebellion. At the time, he had found her unquestioning support a sign of true love and devotion; now he wondered if she had simply been so young the situation had bewildered her, and his own youth had hidden her lack of understanding.

"And what did you say of the barons' rebellion?" Lilith did not seem interested in his answer; she pushed her food around with her fingers, and Hugh noted absently that aside from a few tiny bites, she had not consumed much at all. Hardly enough to maintain her bulk. Perhaps she was a woman who had meals sent to her later, when no one could observe her gluttony.

But no, that did not fit. He could not imagine her hiding any sin. She flaunted her faults.

He might as well flaunt his. In a low voice, he said, "I thought they should have dragged Lackland to a platform and hanged him."

Her head jerked up, and she stared at him in surprise. "You *said* such to her?"

"Nay." He glanced up at the dais, where Lady Isabel sat next to her husband, smiling sweetly at him. D'Aulnoy appeared utterly enraptured by his young bride. "But his tyranny should have been halted with more than a document that he had no intention of honoring."

"He was forced into signing," Lilith said. "By barons who had only their own interests at heart."

"Better the interests of many be served than the selfishness of one. His wars would have taken all, from all."

Lilith lifted a shoulder. "He was king. The barons' duty was to serve him." She slid a sliver of capon into her mouth.

"He was king. His duty was to serve and protect his subjects."

Licking a trail of almond milk from her bottom lip, she raised an eyebrow, her expression one of obvious doubt. "So, if a ruler is selfish his subjects may remove him from his throne?"

"Aye," he said. "And if there is no other course to remove a tyrant, then what other option but death?"

She smiled. "You are bloodthirsty, demanding the head of a king whose offenses are not truly terrible. I think you must carry the opinions of your liege, for were you older, you would know what Lackland did was not truly tyranny."

He flushed. Had he not thought the same thing of Lady Isabel a moment ago—that she was too young for understanding? True, the countess was a woman and should not have a head for such things, but he was only two years her senior.

"And who determines his selfishness? Those who benefit from his removal?" She waved a hand at the dais. "A boy rules now," she continued. "There can be no more selfish creature than a child. And he is hardly competent but for those around him . . . who happened to advise the return of Essex's holdings. Do you approve of his leadership because you benefit from it as well?"

His color deepened. Did she twist his words to suggest that he would execute a boy king? That his acceptance of an incompetent ruler was only because he'd been able to return to Fordham Castle? "If a ruler is just, whether it be due to advisors or no, then all benefit, and his removal will not be necessary or called for."

Her laugh took on a brittle edge, as if echoing against something hard and hollow within her. "The Morningstar and his followers are a primary example contrary to that statement, I think."

"That was their evil, not His," he said.

"Ah, but who created them?" She pushed her trencher forward. Her dark gaze seemed lit with inner fire. "He must have known what would happen and allowed it. Is the evil theirs, or His? Why give the individual free will, then punish them for the wrong decisions, when He must know the wrong decisions will be made? Is everything a test?" Lilith's eyelids lowered. "We all fail."

Hugh stared at her, his stomach twisting into a knot at such blasphemy. "The mother who has lost her babe asks the same question. Why allow such a thing to happen, and innocence to be lost? 'Tis not a new question, but one we do not need to ask. If He planned it, it must be right. There are many questions I could ask, many laments: why was I not born into a noble family, but a foundling? Why are those without honor or piety rewarded now? I don't question, but accept what I've been given and make the best of it, and trust that we receive our due in time."

"Then you shall sing with the angels in no time at all," Lilith said.

He frowned at her sarcasm. "I don't pretend to be without flaw. None of us are."

"Except, of course, your Lady Isabel."

How had the conversation delved into this? He ran his hand through his hair, strove for something lighter. "She snores in her sleep." She pursed her lips, and he hastily added, "I know because I was guarding her, not because I made a habit of sleeping near her."

"She desired otherwise."

He shook his head, rejecting her claim.

"Aye," Lilith said. "And how could she not? Look at her husband: powerful, but thrice her age and nothing to desire."

"He is a good man," Hugh protested.

"You think that matters to a girl such as she? In ten years, she will become a powerful woman in her own right. She is not a silly girl, but she is a fanciful one at times. Tell me, Sir Hugh: in the Angevin court, did you hear the songs of the troubadour, the tales of the beautiful maidens and their loyal knights? Don't you think she spun you into her dreams? What is that popular one? About the knight in the cart who abases himself for love of a married lady? Who saves her by crossing a bridge of swords? Who bleeds when he breaks through the bars of her bedchamber to have her?"

"Nay," he managed. "She knows her duty."

"Aye, duty. Her mind does, but does her heart?" Her gaze pierced him. "And what of yours? If a tournament were held tomorrow, and she asked you to do your worst and to wear her favor, would you?" Her voice lowered further, and he strained to hear her, though part of him rebelled against her words. "No one would think anything of it; her husband would not fight, for he is too aged, and it would seem natural for her to pick you in his stead. But the two of you would know the significance behind such a choice. If she asked, would you lower yourself before her to prove your devotion, like the knight in the cart? Would you give your life, your good name, and your soul for the adoration of a woman who will never be yours, and who, within ten years, will have lost the innocence you so cherish in her?"

"My life, my good name—aye," he breathed, and it was as if she had pulled that exhalation from him. "But not my soul. She would not ask for it."

"She asks for it with each longing glance she fails to hide," Lilith said.

"And what do you ask? With your wicked words and your suggestions? What is it you want from me?"

She held his eyes over the rim of her cup. "The same as Isabel."

CHAPTER 3

Even in the dead of night, the castle never quieted; always a noise intruded, from human and animal. Lilith lay between the daughter of the Chelmsford sheriff and Colchester's youngest sister, staring at the ceiling and counting lines of wood grain until she thought she might go mad from it. She could hear Isabel's snores, and she grinned into the darkness, thinking of Hugh. The baron's breathing was low and deep, though an hour ago he had been straining and grunting over Isabel, punctuating his groans with murmurs of love and devotion.

Love. A human weakness, easily confused with lust. And when it was true and fierce, as Robert's love for his wife was fierce, its strength was the perfect tool for destruction.

She should have been taking this opportunity to enter his dreams, as she had the past few weeks, planting suggestions of Isabel's betrayal. Should have been sending erotic images of the young knight to the countess. Should have sought out Hugh's mind, suggested ambition and adultery.

But she did not.

The Chelmsford girl rolled in her sleep, pressing against Lilith's breasts. With a shove, Lilith pushed her off the pallet, biting her lips against a laugh when she heard the thump. She regretted it when she was forced to close her eyes and feign sleep as the girl crawled back into the bed and snuggled against her side, shivering, and she waited interminably for her to fall back into slumber.

It was intolerable, having to live among them, pretending to sleep and eat when the food was tasteless, sleep impossible, and dreams far from her. She ached with boredom, reduced to staving it off with petty pleasures. Certainly, it had been relieved for a few moments during supper with Hugh, but now it fell upon her again like a hair shirt, itching and scratching until she thought she might scream from inactivity.

Finally, unable to bear it a moment longer, she slipped from the bed.

The floor was freezing beneath her bare feet, but she paid no attention, focusing on the sounds outside the castle. Mandeville had assigned Hugh to castle guard, and she doubted the seneschal would have given him a cozy spot within the keep or the newly built garrison at the front gate.

She stepped silently through the hall, avoiding the benches topped with sleeping knights and servants. A couple rutted in the shadows of the spiral stairwell, and she gave them barely a glance as she passed them.

The curtain wall surrounding the inner bailey still held evidence of John's siege; though d'Aulnoy had begun repairs and added fortifications, the masonry was patterned with jagged holes and uneven pilings. A half-moon shed pale light across the scene, though she did not need it to illuminate her way. She waited a moment, sniffing the air, until a thread of scent led her to the tower that joined the south and west walls. She climbed the stairs and found Hugh asleep, his back against the parapet, his chin hanging against his chest. His helm lay next to him, and he'd wrapped his arms around himself as if cold mail could warm him.

He stirred. She had formed no real plan when she'd sought him, and she had but a moment to decide to appear as Marie or Isabel—and though sense and purpose demanded Isabel, her vanity overwhelmed them and she remained Marie.

Hugh looked up, scrubbing his hands over his face and squinting against the darkness. She knew the moment he saw her. He rose awkwardly to his feet, still half-asleep, his arms and legs at odds with his intention to stand.

"And this is how you guard your lord and his lady?" she chided, and though her tone was light, he flushed. She sent the heavens an exasperated sigh. "Truly, I don't care should the walls fall down around them."

Hugh smiled drowsily. Tapping his heel against the battered stone, he said, "'Tis possible they will."

She pretended to examine them. "They would not even hold a man tied."

"Is that why you ventured into the cold night?" He gave a short laugh and hunkered down again, as if respect to a lady must only go so far against frigid air, and rubbed his hands together. "Sir William has a much more comfortable alcove than I."

"I could warm you." She caught his hands in hers, held them clasped between her palms. His shivers eased as her heat enveloped him.

"Aye, my lady," he said. For a moment she thought he was agreeing to something more, and unfamiliar lust twisted in her belly. "You burn like hellfire, and I fear you would reduce me to ashes."

"I do. I would." She lifted his hand, slipped his forefinger into her mouth. He drew in a sharp breath between his teeth, and she straddled him, seating herself in the cradle created by his raised knees and body. Her skirts settled over his legs like a blanket, her skin radiating heat through her clothes. "Shall we bargain?"

A low, tortured groan escaped him, rumbling against her chest. "God, no."

She laughed but persevered. "I'll keep you warm."

"And I will owe you doubly? A lie and . . . a kindness?"

Rocking against his arousal with a wicked smile, she said, "'Tis not kindness I offer you, but pleasure. Or temptation. Or pain, depending on how you take it."

"To me, it would be comfort and warmth only," he replied, then pulled back to stare at her face as if intrigued. "What would bring comfort to a woman such as you? What would be kind?"

She stilled. Felt her mask of amusement slip. He must have seen her—desperation? Regret? She dared not name them, even to herself. "Naught you can give."

"Who could? Mandeville?—but no, you have already rejected him," he said with a smile, gently prodding deeper. "The baron, or one like him? To offer you power and riches? Success . . . but in what?"

"No man or woman," she said, her eyes on her fingers as they traced his throat. "He who does not cower."

He watched her, as if trying to determine whether she spoke truth or merely toyed with him. "The bargain cannot be struck," he said with regret. "Though I would offer kindness, it seems equality in this exchange is impossible."

"And would you take the temptation if I were like Isabel? Beautiful and pure?" Her voice challenged him, sought to call him a liar.

"If you were like Lady Isabel, you would be married," he said. "And it would be a betrayal of fealty to my lord and God. Will you betray your liege in return? To whom do you owe loyalty, that it would be equal?"

She remained silent for a moment. "Do not be kind to me," she said finally.

§

The stone floor was hard and cold beneath him—the harder and colder for having had Lilith's softness and heat and then losing them. As the ache of arousal slowly subsided, Hugh realized himself a halfwit. What was he, that an eager woman sat upon his lap and he spoke of *kindness*?

He would have called her back, but she'd disappeared into the darkness, and he daren't alert the castle to their activity by making noise or seeking her out.

Pushing to his feet with a frustrated sigh, he tucked his hands into his underarms and stepped to look over the wall. The bailey was empty, save for outbuildings and—

A man crossed the distance between keep and wall, and for a moment Hugh thought it was Mandeville, searching for revenge upon Hugh for what he thought had taken place at the ruins. The dread of such a meeting was neatly cut off as the figure came closer and he recognized Georges—and seconds later, a figure swooped down from the top of the keep, landed facing the knight, and folded great, membranous wings.

The impulse to raise the hue and cry warred with his disbelief, his doubt that he was seeing aright. The creature was no taller than Georges, apart from the wings that rose above its head. It stood with its back to Hugh, and though the wings hid most of its form, he caught brief glimpses of long, dark hair, the elegant curve of feminine hips and waist, and strong, lean legs. Georges did not move to defend himself, and after a moment, in which it seemed he and the creature spoke, it disappeared into the night with a powerful flap of its wings.

Georges looked up, and Hugh thought his gaze settled directly on him—or perhaps his destination had always been to Hugh's post—for he continued walking toward the wall.

He must have been mistaken. He *must* have been. But try as he might, Hugh could not convince himself an owl or a falcon had deceived him for something else·in the darkness. Hugh's hand settled upon his sword hilt as Georges climbed the wall steps, and he was reminded of the older knight's stance upon meeting Lilith in the courtyard earlier.

"I do not see everything clearly," Hugh said as Georges stepped onto the allure. "But my confusion cannot be blamed on poor vision this time."

The moon silvered the older man's hair and face, lending a marble cast to his features. "Will you skewer me for your confusion?"

Though Hugh could not remember sliding it from the sheath, he stood with weapon drawn. An ignoble reaction toward one who had mentored him well for two years, perhaps, but he found trust difficult to recall over memory of the creature. "Do you leave me no other choice, I will. If you tell me other than the truth."

"Truth is not always a choice," Georges said.

Hugh smiled thinly. "Then I shall choose whether to believe you."

He spread his hands wide, palms upturned, but Hugh did not relax his defensive stance. "Aye, I can not force you to believe," he agreed, irony tingeing his voice. "Nor will most of what I tell you require more belief than you already have."

"What of my patience?"

"Of that, you have an excess." Frowning, Georges dropped his arms back to his sides. "After Morningstar led his revolt on Heaven, he and his conspirators vowed to complete the fall of mankind."

Startled by the shift of tone and subject, Hugh lowered his sword fractionally. "Aye."

"Though the seraphim were sent to Earth, to interact with

men and protect them against the demons' manipulations, they could not be as men. Before long, humans began to look upon the seraphim as gods themselves."

"Their idolatry incurring His wrath?" Hugh guessed, his mouth twisting. "Surely you don't think I will believe—"

"No." Georges's voice swelled and took on a melodic cadence. More than a rejection of Hugh's doubt, it surprised him into—*commanded*—silence. "Stirring Morningstar's jealousy. His former brethren worshipped by men? He could not tolerate it. He rose up, better prepared by time and experience of the first battle, and led his demons into a second. With him were the creatures he'd created of Hell and Chaos, hounds born of sin and death and darkness, whose bite proved fatal for the seraphim. The first defense against the demons' attack failed, and the seraphim protecting Earth fell. The second phalanx from Above arrived quickly enough, but they had to take care— even though Morningstar did not—for a full-scale battle between Heaven and Hell should not take place on Earth."

It would tear apart and destroy those they sought to protect from the demons, Hugh realized, trying to imagine such an event.

"Morningstar chose his arena well," Georges continued. "For though the seraphim managed to destroy many of the hounds and their demon handlers, their ranks were badly damaged due to the care they took to keep the fighting away from the human sphere. But they pressed onward, and seemed almost to prevail until Morningstar brought in a wyrm. The seraphim fell back against the terrible dragon, attempted to regroup, but were scattered."

It was preposterous, shockingly blasphemous. Hugh turned away, but Georges's story followed him, weaving it in a voice as deep and compelling as the most talented troubadour.

"But it was impossible to keep such a battle from the ears of men, and many rushed to join the fight."

Hugh closed his eyes. "Only to be slaughtered, surely."

"Neither demons nor angels have leave to take human life."

"As dictated by God?" he guessed, swinging back to Georges. "After his revolt, why would Satan agree to such terms? How could killing a human be worse?" As the words left his mouth, he felt a rush of shame and horror that he had asked the question in earnest, as if it were a truth to be sought.

"Free will and life are the two gifts bestowed upon humanity which may not be compromised." Humor flitted over Georges's face. "And as few men will bring injury upon themselves, the demons could not hurt them."

Questions flooded Hugh's mind, but the image of Sir William bound and awaiting Lilith rushed to the fore. He gave a short laugh, and the answering smile on Georges's lips told him the older man divined his thoughts. "Aye, some do will it upon themselves," he said, sobering. Perhaps the man *could* see within his mind.

But if Georges did, he gave no indication that he recognized Hugh's suspicions. His gaze, though directed at Hugh, seemed far beyond him. "The men could do little against the demons, for they had neither the strength nor speed to combat them effectively. But the army of human foes distracted them, scattered them, as the dragon had the seraphim. And one man, finding himself alone against the wyrm, managed to defeat it with a strike to the heart."

Of course—Saint George and the dragon. Hugh had heard this tale from the time he'd been a lad. "Do not forget to include the virgin, *Georges*," he said, his mockery little disguising his anger. Young he might be, but rarely a fool. "The king's daughter, a sacrifice to the dragon, saved moments before it devoured her."

"That is a later story," Georges replied. "And I failed to save her."

Hugh shook his head in disgust. "You are mad." But his breath drew fast and tight, and he could not erase the image of the winged creature from his mind. If Georges was mad, then Hugh must be equally.

"And what of that?" he said, gesturing with his sword to the bailey. "A demon, was it? Or a dragon come to devour the castle?"

Georges did not answer him directly; he stepped to the parapet and looked over the side. There was naught to see. This side of the castle faced the valley, and everything below the ridge lay in shadow. "The ruins here, in Greece and Rome—we heard many a tale from the Crusaders and traveling knights while in the Angevin court, did we not? Of their magnificent structures, and the wonder of a society that could produce that beauty. That ours is a poor and corrupt society in comparison, succored on the last remnants of their greatness."

"That is what they claim," Hugh said impatiently. "If not for the degeneracy of men, it would still be standing, not a rotting memory."

Georges shook his head, turned to lean against the parapet, his arms crossed loosely over his chest. "Men are no more evil—or better—than they were then. Nor has the number of demons, sent to tempt and lead men astray, dwindled. But that second battle made apparent to those Above that the seraphim, in all their power, could not relate to men, nor protect them, without being worshipped themselves. And men could not be blamed for that— the seraphim were too different, too . . . *inhuman*; they could not pass, even in a human guise. Likewise, so the demons are too inhuman for one who knows how to look—for one who knows that he needs to look. And so to gain an advantage, those Above created the Guardians: men and women given angelic powers, enabling them to defend against the demons, but who remained men and women. The one who destroyed the dragon was the first made, and he was given the task of choosing others to join him."

Hugh's laughter rang out over the bailey, echoing against the stone and returning, the angry edge worn off by disbelief. "I suppose you are here to recruit me then? What shall be my test? To kill the demon in our midst?"

"That is not how it is done." His eyes darkening, Georges said, "You saw that demon, and you still reject the truth I have told you."

"Aye, because demons are well known—but men who are as angels, and take the name of Guardian? 'Tis profane."

Georges stared at him for a moment, and then his face softened with the slightest of smiles. "I told her you would bend, but not break—I was mistaken: in some things, you don't even bend."

"Does she think to unbalance me?" Hugh did not need to ask whom Georges was speaking of. *If one knew how to look;* it had not taken him long to think of all he'd seen since his return to Fordham Castle. There was Lilith, who moved with uncommon swiftness. Who bargained for kisses and lies. Who indulged men's perversity. "Is that what you spoke of? How she intends to corrupt me?"

Georges's eyebrows rose. "Nay. Indeed, if there has been an unbalancing, it has been hers. She informed me that she would do no work upon you, and focus on her true target."

"Isabel." Hugh breathed the name, dread tightening his

throat. "Why did you not kill this demon, if you are one of these Guardians?"

"Ah, and now you charge me with failing in duties you do not believe in."

Frustration, worry for Lady Isabel, fear—aye, fear, though he hated to admit to it—forced the words that burst from him. "You have given me nothing to believe! Only an impossible, blasphemous tale!"

Georges's transformation was so swift that once again Hugh doubted his eyes. Then he accepted, and fell back; his breath rushed from him, and he stumbled, landing hard upon the stone walkway, his spine jarring from the impact.

The knight stood before him, but no longer Georges. With close-cropped dark hair and features that seemed sculpted in bronze, wings of black feathers, and a body garbed in a loose, flowing garment that draped over one shoulder and gathered at the waist, he appeared an ageless warrior, terrible and deadly in his beauty. His eyes glinted like obsidian. "Do you see?"

"Aye," Hugh whispered, sweating as if with sudden sickness, his stomach balled into a tight knot. His fingers automatically rose to his forehead, but he paused, uncertain. "Who are you?"

"Michael."

Unable to comprehend, Hugh looked away. His hand fell to his side. The stone pressed cold and hard against his back, but now he welcomed its solidity. Michael: the same name as the archangel, but the man before him claimed to have been human once. Did he also lay claim to the deeds that had been ascribed to that other, greater being? And if such an illustrious figure appeared before him, what manner of creature had Hugh seen speaking to Michael? Lucifer, in the guise of a woman? "The demon. Was it the Deceiver?"

He transformed back into Georges and proffered his hand, but Hugh could no longer see his friend in that skin. He stood without help, refusing to lean against the parapet though the trembling in his legs demanded it.

"Nay. Though the name fits her, in her fashion." Michael's arm dropped to his side. "Many things from Above and Below are not as they seem. You must learn that appearances are almost always deceiving."

A wry smile curved Hugh's lips as his gaze skimmed over his mentor's changeable form. "I am well taught."

CHAPTER 4

The castle readied for evening's entertainment. Servants folded tables and pushed them from the center of the great hall. Conversation accompanied the scrape of wooden benches against the floor as they were shoved and carried toward the perimeter of the room. Lamplight flickered, lit each corner and crevice, and danced over the ceiling's great polished arch.

In the minstrel's gallery, a player struck a discordant note on his pipe, a short, piercing shriek that drew attention and laughter from the ladies gathered near the screen's passage.

Hugh looked toward the group in time to see Lilith slipping away from the women, threading her way through the hall and disappearing behind the dais.

Hesitating but for a moment, he moved to intercept her. He used the opposite entrance into the family chambers; his departure would not go unnoticed, but it was unlikely any observer would associate his leaving through one door with Lilith's exit through another.

The partition separating d'Aulnoy's rooms from the hall did little to muffle the noise, and the chambers were dimly lit. Hugh waited for his eyes to adjust, uncertain of her direction.

Instinct drove him through the archway that led to the newel stairs. Isabel's bower was on the floor above the chambers—and it was there that Lilith had managed to avoid Hugh for nearly a sennight.

Hugh paused on the first riser; darkness filled the stairwell. Below, the faint glow of the torch lit the flight from the lower floors. It flickered against the curving stone near his feet, but didn't penetrate the shadows above.

The air was laden with a thick, acrid odor, the heavy scent of a flame recently snuffed.

He pulled his eating knife from his belt and briefly wished for his sword—but perhaps it was better this way. If someone should come upon him, he could more easily hide his dagger than sheathe a larger weapon.

His back pressed to the cold stone, he presented as small a target as possible. The newel stairs had been designed with defense in mind, spiraling so that the person ascending, with a weapon in his right hand, would leave his body open to attack. *No need to fear attack,* he reminded himself; though he'd not seen Michael since that night on the wall walk, he'd reviewed the conversation in his mind countless times, and had accepted the Guardian's declaration that humans could not be harmed by demons. For if it were not true, wouldn't they have destroyed mankind, and murdered every last man, woman, and child?

True or not, he took the stairs with care, and his need for caution seemed verified when he reached the torch; the head was still hot under his questing fingers.

He lurched up the next step, into cobwebs that tickled his cheeks and nose. He brushed them away impatiently; Lilith was expecting him, or she wouldn't have extinguished—

His heart caught, skipped.

For as long as he'd been in the castle—as a young page, carrying items up and down these stairs—the passageways had been kept scrupulously clean.

Not cobwebs. Hair. Automatically, he glanced upward and felt the strands sliding over his face again. He grabbed them, gave a sharp tug.

His pull met resistance, and a brief hiss of pain was followed by a scrambling noise, like claws against stone.

Lilith's voice came from the darkness above him. "You think to take that sticker to my flesh and devour me?"

Though unnerved to realize she could see his knife when he might as well have been blind, he shook his head and blithely raised the blade. "I think to take a trophy."

The edge sliced through the strands held taut between them. Released from the strain, the cut ends curled soft in his palm, and he wondered at his daring. Why did he bait her when he knew what she was?

"Is it not the custom to take a trophy *after* the opponent is defeated? Are you so confident that, because a kiss was easily attained, my heart will be easily opened as well?"

He felt her amusement, imagined the white flash of her grin. Hefting his knife, he said softly, " 'Tis long enough to open any heart."

"No man lives who does not think his blade long enough."

He smiled despite himself. Tucking the dagger and the hair into his belt, he tried to gauge her position by the sound of her voice, the angle of the hair he'd cut. Did she lay on the upper curve of the stair, leaning over? "Why are you here, when the rest of the castle revels in music and acrobatics?"

"I left a kerchief half-embroidered in the bower, and I must finish my work." She did not disguise her mockery. "I could ask the same of you, but I know your answer."

"And what would it be?"

The unexpected touch of her finger against his lips made him draw a sharp breath. He reached for her hand but could not find it, and lowered his arms to his sides rather than flail about in the dark.

"You desire my companionship," she said lightly. "For I have been required by Lady Isabel to embroider and sew and gossip the last sennight, and you've had no one with whom you can speak. Aye, for Sir Georges has absented himself, has he not? And everyone else looks at you askance—as if tales and rumors had been spread, naming you mad." Her voice dropped to a whisper. "I have heard you spoke to Father Geoffrey about a demon in our midst."

Could she see the flush that rose over his neck? He had visited the priest, confessed what he'd seen; Hugh did not blame the man for doubting him. "He did not see; he could not believe what I had to tell him, but called it a nightmare."

"Perhaps the good father is correct." Her breath skimmed over his forehead, teasing the ends of his hair and sending a shiver over his skin. Where was she? He wasn't certain he wanted to know the answer. The sudden image rose of her hanging above him like a bat, and he shoved it away. She must want his fear, would likely feed on it. "A nightmare—brought about by frustration. I left abruptly that evening. If I had stayed, perhaps you would not have these notions of demons in the castle."

Remembrance of her weight, her warmth made him ache. "My flesh and my eyes are weak, my lady," he said, "but my mind is not."

Her lips brushed his eyelashes, and he felt a soft exhalation against his cheek. He leaned into the contact. As if surprised, she drew back.

Did she expect him to retreat, then? He had no intention of playing to her expectations.

"What do you think you know, Sir Pup?"

"That a woman came to me with the intention of leading me like an animal to her bidding."

"Whatever you think my sins might be, I assure you I have never done *that* with an animal."

He bit back his laughter, shaking his head. How did she so easily manage to amuse and distract him? "A horse, a dog, oxen—all are led by the foremost part. You thought to lead me by mine."

The slight thump as she landed on the stairs in front of him and sudden waft of displaced air were his only indication of her movement before her palm covered his burgeoning arousal. "Indeed, a woman has but to touch it and it swells to better fill her grip. I daresay it was made for this."

"A man is not an animal." His throat closed on a groan, and he had to clear it before continuing. "After you left, I saw you—"

He broke off, sweat breaking over his skin as she placed his hand on her breast. Bare, it burned like fire under his fingers, her nipple tight beneath his palm. "Then a woman must be led by these," she said.

Heat rushed through him, and he ground his teeth against the ache of his erection. Acting on the lust she created in him—or running from it—would both serve her purpose; he could neither give in nor flee. Steeling his resolve to act contrary to her expectations, he gently pinched the tip of her breast and pulled.

She gasped and fell against his chest, his hand caught between them. He echoed her earlier mocking tone. "Apparently *you* can be led thus." Letting go her nipple, he traced his fingers along the underside of her breast. He cupped his hand; she filled his palm, but barely. Certainly not as much as Marie's generous proportions had suggested. The beat of her heart thrummed against his fingertips. "But I find most women are led by what is beneath."

Her chest rose and fell in a quick, ragged breath, and she wrenched herself from his embrace. He let her go, listened to the scratch of claw and stone. Her voice came from above again, laced with bitterness. "Only when she is a fool." As if with great effort, humor returned to her tone and she added, "Fortunately, there are many women willing to think with their hearts, and it makes them as brainless as their tits."

"And there are many demons willing to take advantage of them." Hugh crossed his arms over his chest, leaned back against the wall, and let the cold stone ease the heat she had built within him. "After you left me, I saw you in the courtyard with Michael."

She did not reply; music and voices from the hall filled the air between them. He wished for a light that he could see her expression, discover what lay behind the darkness. She wore neither clothes nor the form of Marie, but he did not think she looked as she had in the courtyard, either. She'd not had wings when she'd been in his arms.

"Will you not try to convince me it was a nightmare? Or pretend to have no knowledge of that which I speak?"

"I'm not a priest, nor do I have need for lies." She paused as he burst into laughter, and she joined in after a moment. "Why are you not afraid of me? It is extraordinarily vexing."

He smiled broadly. "I was told you cannot do me harm."

"Michael." The name was followed by a hiss of displeasure. "And you believed him?"

Recognizing her question for what it was—an attempt to fuel uncertainty—he shrugged and said, "Difficult to refute the evidence I saw."

His casual tone held no indication of the doubts and thoughts that had plagued him over the week, the sickness that roiled within him as he'd forced himself to accept a different version of truth than he'd known. How easy it would have been to take Father Geoffrey's explanation, to call it a nightmare. How many times had he almost convinced himself that he'd heard incorrectly, that he'd experienced an hour of madness?

But he could not. He'd *seen* the demon—Lilith—and Michael's miraculous transformation into a thing of terrible beauty and power.

"Evidence? A figure in a night-filled courtyard?" She drew a sudden breath. "Your certainty is not because you saw *me*—he showed you what he was."

"Aye."

Her snort of laughter echoed through the passageway. "You trusted his *appearance*?"

Sparks flew above his head. He ducked, belatedly realizing that she'd only scratched the stones with her fingernails. She did it again, and in the flash of light he saw her: a lithe, strong figure clinging to the spiraling stairs with her feet, her black hair trailing toward the floor. Another flash, and her wings spanned the width of the stairwell; horns smooth as polished jet curled from forehead to ears. Fangs gleamed over her lips.

Darkness again. He blinked away the spots that crawled behind his eyes, willed away his unease. "You have a mummer's dramatic flair. Perhaps the entertainers in the hall could apprentice you."

She laughed and struck the wall; the sparks landed on the resinous torchhead and caught. The tiny flames slowly climbed higher.

He turned back toward her and froze.

She stood on the stairs, though he'd not heard her movement. Her face was Lady Isabel's, as was the blond hair tumbling down her back. Naked skin appeared golden in the dim light. White, feathery wings waved behind her, stirring the air around them.

"I must concede that I understand your fascination with the lady," she said. "I like her myself. Though nothing surprising passes her lips, everything she says is charming. Packaged in such innocence, 'tis hard to resist, is it not?"

He swallowed hard, backed up onto the next riser. There was nothing angelic in her smile.

"Shall we bargain?"

$

To Lilith's surprise, he halted his retreat. The corners of his mouth quirked into a smile, but she could not read the emotion behind it. Whether amusement or self-deprecation, it did not please her. Could the man do nothing she predicted? He did not drive himself mad questioning what he'd seen, nor was he weakened by self-doubt and fear. He should have been fleeing—or falling prostrate, overcome with desire for the body she'd assumed.

She deliberately embodied his fantasy, his ideal. Chivalry and his code of honor should have repulsed him; his love for Isabel should have drawn him near. Yet he smiled and remained where he was.

Frustration fueled her next words. "Or shall I simply make you beg?"

"If I beg, it shall be of my own volition, not forced by a demon."

His smile widened, and she had no trouble deciphering his triumph; she pursed her lips and studied him, trying to maintain her annoyance. Michael must have told him that his free will would be honored.

That the Guardian had told Hugh anything at all settled uneasily in her chest; she'd thought Michael had been protecting Hugh, but if he'd revealed all, 'twas possible he considered the young knight a candidate for the transformation.

She shook herself. She should not care if Hugh sacrificed his life. A woman led by her heart could be called foolish; a demon who did the same courted Punishment.

But the tightness the thought of his death created beneath her breast did not quickly fade.

His gaze narrowed upon her face, as if weighing her response and calculating his. Unusual, that he was so calm, that he sought ways to thwart her, and tried to remain little influenced by his emotions. She'd let herself be discovered before, but—if not full of anger and fear—men typically became sycophants, courting her power in hopes of securing their own. They'd never presented this challenge, nor gazed upon her as if he were her equal.

"What manner of men are you accustomed to, that you anticipate so few responses from them: lust, anger or fear?"

Though she could have screamed in frustration at his acumen when he should have been terrified beyond reason, she fixed her smile and ran her fingers over the pale skin on her hip. "I'm not accustomed to men who have as little drive between their legs as a eunuch."

The corners of his eyes crinkled with laughter, though he did not give it sound.

She bit her lip to keep from letting loose her own. Cerberus's balls, could the man not take offense at anything? Would he twist every insult to find the humor in it? He looked exceedingly young, unrepentantly so, like a boy caught stealing a pasty from the kitchens and who licked his fingers during the scolding.

"You know your beauty," she said. "If you give me neither lust, anger, nor fear, would you indulge me and reveal a hidden vanity?"

He flushed with embarrassment, but did not protest her claim. He did not even suffer from false modesty—and she should not be charmed by it. Yet she delighted in the blush that heated his cheeks. She could have told herself she found pleasure in his discomfort, but such would have been a lie. She simply took pleasure in provoking a reaction that he couldn't hide behind calculation and calm.

Smiling, he said, "I have a bargain to offer, my lady."

Her eyes widened, and her hands flexed convulsively at her sides. Her tongue seemed heavy in her mouth, and she was slow to respond. "A bargain," she echoed finally.

"Truth for truth."

To enter willingly into a bargain, knowing . . . She laughed silently. Too certain of himself, he was. 'Twas not physical vanity that she could exploit, but his intellectual vanity. His conviction that he would not succumb to her, that he could remain separate from their dealings. Did he think to play with the demon's tools and not be worked on in return?

Only fair that she should warn him.

She didn't.

She pretended doubt. "Truth for truth? You get the better bargain. My truth is valuable to you, whereas yours is nothing to me."

He raised a brow and smiled again, as if amused by her lie. Aye, he was too certain—but not without insight. A combination of imprudent bravery and cleverness.

"Truth for truth," she agreed.

He grinned as if she'd fallen into a web of his making rather than the reverse and took her hand in his. She allowed him to lead her up the stairs, circling round and round, feeling uncharacteristically dizzy and out of sorts—and excited, as if she were a girl following her lover to a hideaway. She stifled the urge to transform so her appearance would fit the sudden playfulness that overcame her: into a maid with a circlet of flowers in her hair and white gown, trailing velvet ribbons. What would he think, should he look behind him?

Bemused by the fancy that took hold—resenting that bemusement—she became the demon. At the click of talons against the stone steps, he glanced back. The crimson glow from her eyes limned his features; his lips tightened, but he did not let go her hand. He continued up and up, allowing her touch though her fingers ended in claws, her wingtip scraped the wall beside them, and her form declared her a monster.

What would bring comfort to a woman such as you? What would be kind?

She blinked away that memory, absurdly grateful when they reached the top and entered the tower chamber. Moonlight spilled weakly through the shutters, illuminating the family's private chapel. Using the pale light to navigate, he led her to a cushioned bench on the far wall.

"Father Geoffrey is in the hall," he said with a lift of his brows. "Despite the Lateran Council's rulings that suggest they avoid such entertainments."

Pursing her lips, she glanced from him to the bench.

He answered her wordless query with a laugh and a shake of his head. "The stairs are much too uncomfortable. It would be torture seeking truth there."

"For you," she said. "The stairs suited me well."

"Perhaps I could apply an iron rod to your skin during the questioning and make it equally torturous."

Her gaze dropped to his groin.

"The priests forbid that as much as possible, too," he said as he sat down. Leaning back, he crossed his ankles and linked his hands behind his head.

'Twas a pose without easy defense; was it designed to lower hers?

Unwilling to relinquish whatever unease her demon form created in him—and it must, no matter his relaxed posture—she hopped onto a stout table and perched, her knees against her chest.

His eyes widened and he looked away from her.

Her sultry chuckle drew his gaze back. He swallowed convulsively.

"You expose yourself, my lady." His throat worked again. Abandoning his careless posture, he leaned forward and rested his elbows on his knees and pressed his head into his hands. "I'm only a man. Take pity." 'Twas a sound between a laugh and a croak.

The note of arousal under his tortured plea, and the bulge that had risen beneath his hose soothed her pride; she relented and called in a hose and tunic that matched his.

"Now we are equal," she said.

His shoulders shook, and he gestured to his lap. "I don't see you with this problem, my lady."

"I'm not willing to grow one for the bargain," she said, brushing a long black curl from her forehead and tucking it behind one of her horns. Trouble was, she did feel the arousal that their exchange had risen within her. A liquid heat and velvet tightness that settled in her breasts and belly.

Bedroom games were a tool, a method of persuasion and power, or even pain. There was only the chase, the corruption, the attainment of souls. Only bargains and negotiations. A demon might take pleasure in those results, but not for herself.

Never for herself.

"What truth do you need?"

If he was surprised by her abrupt question, that the humor had faded completely from her voice, he did not give evidence of it. His eyes met hers levelly, their blue depths silvery in the moonlight.

"As Isabel, you assumed a pleasing shape. Why do you not always?"

'Twas not the question she had expected, and there were too many answers to offer. She gave the simplest one. "The measure of a man cannot be taken by beauty; all love it, and treat it with reverence—even though, aye, it also inspires jealousy and lust." Her lips twisted. "But the plain, the ugly, the poor and lowly? Easy to forget them, or to abuse them."

He nodded slowly, his gaze thoughtful. "But is it not easier to corrupt with jealousy and lust when you are beautiful? Is that what you tried to do to me?"

"Tried?" she echoed, brows raised high. "If not lust that you felt on the allure a sennight ago—if not lust that rose your cock-stand here, then what? Surely you don't think *this* form pleasing? You gave not a thought to beauty. No man does when faced with tits and a lifted skirt."

He pinched the bridge of his nose. "Perhaps that is true of some men, but not all." She snorted derisively, and his grin flashed. "But what of your vanity? As a demon, surely you indulge every sin. Do you not crave beauty for yourself?"

She stared at him, tracing his features. Craved? Surely it was too weak a word, when his question made her feel as if a knot unraveled beneath her breastbone, loosening skeins of emotion and drawing them through her body. She recognized anger, despair; she grasped at those threads and held them tight.

"Aye," she said, and dropped from her perch. His nostrils flared, as if sensing danger and preparing to run. But he wouldn't, would he? He would stay, certain he knew enough to be safe. Certain he knew enough to handle her, when she hardly knew herself.

"Lilith." Did he say her name as a warning as she stalked toward him? Hard to determine, when the beating of her heart pounded in her ears.

Foolish of her, to hear it at all.

CHAPTER 5

It did not speak well of his morality that a woman—nay, a demon—could take a monstrous form, clothe herself in masculine garb, and he failed to summon disgust and horror.

Uncertainty, aye—but even that faded as she seemed to rein in the tension that had overtaken her. She crouched before him, her face level with his.

Falling through the shutter, the silvery moonlight touched her features, washing away color and emphasizing shadow, and leaving him unable to distinguish the obsidian horns from the midnight of her hair. She no longer smiled, and her fangs were hidden behind full lips.

Strange, that shadows revealed what light had not. A widow's peak framed her high, smooth forehead, and her brows formed elegant arches above the ebony depths of her eyes. Her cheekbones were angular, instead of broad and round as Marie's had been. This was also beauty; not delicate and ethereal as Lady Isabel's was, but strong and fierce.

And yet it must be a pale reflection of what she'd been before Morningstar's rebellion.

"I have answered your questions, Sir Pup. Now I would have

your truth," she said, her voice a soft slither, silk drawn across stone.

How easily he could imagine that whisper warmed by arousal. He resisted the urge to shift in his seat, remembering the ease with which she had brought him to readiness. His erection had subsided, but desire remained. "I do not believe I've received my part in its entirety."

Her eyes narrowed, but he raised his fingers to her lips, preventing her reply. His calluses rasped against her skin, and he felt the tremor that shook her as he disarmed her with a touch.

He'd noted the same reaction in the stairwell, when he'd taken her hand, but had put the notion of her temporary weakness aside, blaming it on fancy. Had it ever occurred to him to consider the weaknesses of demons, he would not have imagined one susceptible to a simple touch. 'Twas a bizarre realization, that he had power over her. Surely after the wonders of Heaven and terrors of Hell, nothing human could impress her.

Nor would he have imagined that his fascination for her would give her equal sway over him.

"It must be forbidden," he mused, before he could explore the extent of that power. Was he master of himself enough to stop before a touch became a caress, or more? "A punishment, to deny beauty to those who had once been nearest its source."

She shrugged, but the intensity of her gaze belied the casual gesture. " 'Tis true the rebels were transformed when they were cast down, but they are not prevented from resembling spirits of light by *Him*."

"Who then?" Her hands slipped over his thighs, as if to distract him; he stiffened, but did not stop her until she reached the knife at his waist. He wrapped his fingers around her wrists, holding her still.

Huffing out an impatient breath, she tugged her hands from his grip. "You have seen what happens when subjects forget their place, and think themselves equal to a ruler. They make demands, threaten war, force him to acknowledge rights and sign charters."

She sat back on her heels, and tapped the point of his dagger against her chin.

When had she stolen it? She'd had only a second's opportunity, and the theft had been so light he had not felt it. She grinned, and he dipped his head in acknowledgment of her skill. "So long as you do not steal the throne, aye?"

"Aye." She slowly retracted her horns and fangs. Unable to suppress his curiosity, he reached up and felt the smooth protuberance above her left temple as it flattened and disappeared. He brushed his thumb across her hairline. No lump remained, only silky red skin edged by soft curls.

His voice was low, rough. "Is this your true form?"

He met her gaze for a breathless moment before she slapped his hand away. "Nay," she said flatly. She stood and took a step back, crossing her arms over her chest. "Your truth: Why did you enter into this bargain?"

He clenched his fingers, welcomed the stinging pain. "Because I cannot be near you without forgetting my intentions and transforming into an imbecile."

"You cannot blame a demon for that." Her lips pursed. "I daresay you must have always been an imbecile."

"Aye," he agreed. "I must be, else I would have followed my first instinct upon discovering your nature."

"To slay me?"

"Aye." He eyed her warily, wishing her countenance revealed her thoughts, but her posture was a study of indifference.

"You would have found that difficult. If you wish to test my sword, however—"

"Nay," he said. "I have no inclination to fight a woman who possesses the speed of the wind itself."

"You fear defeat?"

He considered her wording. "I don't see the wisdom of entering into a fight in which victory is impossible."

"So you think to engage a different sort of battle? To outwit me with this bargain?"

"Surely a mere man cannot use a demon's bargain to his own ends. In the years you've lived, your wit must have been honed to perfection."

She gave a reluctant laugh. "You seek to flatter me."

He did. "Do you fear flattery, my lady?"

"Am I too weak to resist the compliment to my vanity, and thereby incur Lucifer's wrath?" She smiled, as if delighted he would try such a tactic. "I think not. Your pretty words are naught to me, and the risk is only yours."

"Mine?" He shook his head. " 'Tis flattery, but is also truth. I don't admire your intentions, or your methods—there is little risk that I would use them. I could never be as you are."

"Nay," she said, her eyes flaring red. "You risk engaging my vanity so strongly that I would cleave myself to you for the remainder of your life, begging for bits of kindness from your lips, tormenting you when you do not offer them."

The censure in her voice made him flush, reminding him that he had been the one to follow her from the hall. True, he had some effect on her, but she had not sought his company as he had hers. Had not Michael told him that she'd said she was done with him?

"I want to know my role in this," he said suddenly. "That is why I made this bargain."

Her lids lowered. "What conceit convinces you that you are involved at all?"

"Though he must have known what you were, Michael encouraged me into those ruins," Hugh said. "Of my feelings for the lady, you make something of nothing. I have been included—of my own will at times—but also unwittingly. Included by a demon, which should not surprise me; if I were to commit evil I would use any tool available. But Michael, who is an instrument of Heaven—"

He broke off, realizing that his voice had risen and anger coursed through him like fire. Struggling to contain it, he abandoned the seat, striding across the small room to the opposite window and throwing open the shutters. The cool air did not ease his sudden choleric temper.

"*Formans lucem et creans tenebras.*" Did his voice shake? He rested his elbows on the stone sill and lowered his head into his hands. "There must be something good in what you do, even if it is only to try men's hearts, to make them earn their place with God. There must be a reason that I'm drawn to you, even if it is only so that I resist. But I no longer know what is truth, or what to believe."

"There can be no light without darkness," he heard her say quietly, as if to herself.

He laughed shortly, bitterly. "And that *you* say something similar makes me doubt it the more."

From beside him came a flash of moonlight against steel, the clang of metal against stone. He spun around, tensed for her attack, but she'd only slammed his knife onto the sill. "You think Michael led you like a lamb to the slaughter?" A mocking smile curved her lips. "You are no lamb, Sir Pup. I do naught but sow the seeds that have already been planted: jealousy, lust, and greed." Her gaze skimmed the length of his rigid form. "Wrath."

His hand clamped down over hers, and he pried his knife from her fingers. The knowledge that she *let* him take it made his stomach tighten: were all in the castle acting by her leave? Was everything dictated by the whims of these demons and Guardians?

Her brows lifted, and she nodded toward the weapon. "Would you use that on me now?"

Nay, he could not defeat her with it. Its threat held no sway.

She stood close; he could feel the warmth of her body, the brush of her exhalation against his skin. She was tall, her lips only inches from his.

'Twas no effort to close the distance between them, to fist his hand in her hair and seal her mouth with his. Did her lips part in surprise or protest? Surely not encouragement, for there was no kindness in the way he tasted her, none of the gentleness with which he had touched her before. He'd meant to use those against her, but lust fueled him the moment her lips met his.

Her mouth was hot, and she tasted like cream and subtle, exotic spice. He delved more deeply, and she lightly suckled his tongue in return—a sweet, delicious pull that conflagrated the ache into exquisitely painful arousal. He pushed her against the wall, pressing his length tightly against her.

She'd spoken true; there was nothing innocent in him, in the ache that spread through him as she opened herself to his kiss. Would that he could blame his desire on her, on her temptation and wiles, but it was his own.

A shudder ran through him, and she laughed softly into his mouth.

He stepped back, shaken. He would have turned away but for the hint of sympathy in her dark eyes, the clenching of her jaw that told him, despite her laughter, she was not unaffected.

His breath came sharply. "Can you not leave us? If our sins lead us to destruction, why do you need to help them along?"

"I have a role to play, and I must play it. Humans have the luxury of free will; demons do not, for a singular choice made long ago."

"I cannot accept that," he said quietly.

"'Tis not for you to accept."

He wanted to grasp at her explanation as a way to exonerate her, but could not. She enjoyed what she did; he'd seen her amusement at human folly, the pleasure she took in exposing their flaws. Whether she thought she had a choice did not signify as much as her willingness to accede to her role. "Why does Michael not kill you?"

"Because there are many things worse than I stalking the night and preying on man." She transformed suddenly, into a pale, hairless creature. Towered over him, her ears ending in points, fangs protruding over thin red lips. "Those who abstained from choosing a side in the First Battle were cursed with a bloodthirst and an intolerance to daylight. The nosferatu can kill humans, and they follow none of the Rules set down for Guardians and demons; Michael hunts one now." She watched him for a moment, as if searching for signs of fear, then sighed and regained her form.

He frowned, shook his head. "But the presence of other— worse—creatures is not reason to let you live. Is he allowing you to play out your role? An acknowledgment of light allowing—needing—the dark?"

"Nay." A shadow moved across her features. " 'Tis guilt."

"For what—"

"You venture beyond the boundaries of our bargain, Sir Pup," she said. Then her voice softened, and she added playfully, "Unless you wish to enter into another?"

Did he? Perhaps his desire to do so was an indication that he shouldn't. He could little trust himself near her. Shaking his head, he walked back toward the bench, but did not sit down.

"I cannot conceive a way to stop you," he said. "If I pursue the truth with Father Geoffrey, I will soon be called mad." He glanced at her beseechingly. She had remained by the window; with moonlight behind her, he could only discern her silhouette and the eerie scarlet glow of her eyes. "Is there no way to appeal to the part of you that must yearn for goodness, the part of you that once called itself angelic?" She did not respond, and he wondered if he could trust any answer she gave; if truth were no longer required by the bargain, would she speak it? *Could* she speak it? Or did acknowledgment of life before a demon's fall from Heaven resemble vanity—did Lucifer consider both an insult to his rule?

"I was never a denizen Above," she finally said.

He did not mistake the bitter humor in her voice. "What are you?"

"I sprang fully formed from Lucifer's head." Once, he would have immediately dismissed such a statement as fantasy—no longer. But he could not determine from her tone if her claim was a jest, and she gave him no opportunity to ask. "I'm one of his plans—a failed one. His daughter, conceived of a brilliant idea, embodied in a worthless form."

"And you intend to prove your worth by damning us? Does that not approach ambition? Surely he forbids that as well as vanity."

She laughed and hopped onto the sill in an easy, lithe movement, folding herself into the window's small space. "You do not understand; Lucifer always speaks with doubled tongue, and always has a plan."

"To what end?" But no matter what else he'd learned—had to relearn—he did not think Lucifer's nature would change.

"To gather souls for his armies Below. To torture them. To bring Hell onto Earth and to rule the world of man." She waved her hand, a gesture that encompassed the castle around them—casually, as if what she suggested had little import.

He resisted the urge to leap forward, to pull her back into the room as she leaned out the window. His hands clenched into fists at his sides. "Do not come near me again if you wish to succeed; I will defeat you, one way or another."

Her eyes dimmed. "You will try," she said quietly and fell over the side.

His heart dropped to his stomach though he knew she was not in danger—knew before he heard the flap of giant wings and saw the figure that flew past the window.

The sound of the entertainment in the hall faintly reached his ears; he did not rejoin them, but made his way through the darkness of the stairs, blindly spiraling down.

Thinking of a demon who was both monster and woman—and neither.

❦

The end came swiftly, as it always did.

Sitting atop the peaked roof of the keep's southwest tower, Lilith watched Isabel venture across the bailey. The lady's head was down, her hood up, and she'd dressed in a washerwoman's clothing as a disguise.

That had been Isabel's idea, inspired by some troubadour's tale. Lilith would have preferred that Isabel march through the bailey in her fine gown, leaving no doubt to her identity, but she had to appreciate the girl's ingenuity. In the darkness, no one bothered to look past the rags, and the lady reached the wall steps unmolested.

Isabel would have to be quick; from within the keep, Lilith heard the suspicious note in d'Aulnoy's voice as he inquired of his wife's whereabouts.

She wrapped her arms around herself to make a smaller silhouette, though none but Hugh would look for her in that spot. And if someone caught a glimpse of her outline, they would never think it a demon come to observe the results of her labor.

Isabel's betrayal. A husband's jealous rage. A knight's folly. None immediately damning, but the events of this night would eat at their souls, twist them into something . . . unclean.

Lilith knew the feeling well.

Though she wasn't cold, she scrubbed her hands over her arms. The wait for Isabel to climb the stairs to the allure seemed interminable.

Was this all there was to this new role? Waiting? Endlessly waiting and living among them, letting their humanity seep into her with a touch or a word of kindness?

Far better, what she had been before. The targets were already damned, and she had only to secure their souls by arranging their deaths. If they committed suicide or were executed before they could repent, they were hers.

But it would take many years before Hugh would be hers— and there was always the chance he wouldn't be destroyed by this, just as Isabel or Robert could make peace with their betrayal and rage.

That was if they ever did anything to make peace with. She tried to laugh at herself, her impatience—Lucifer must have known this waiting would seem like punishment.

She tried to laugh, but she could not look away from Hugh.

He had not yet noticed Isabel's approach. Leaning with his elbows on the parapet, he looked out over the valley, his head bent. Thinking of a way to thwart her, most likely. It should have made her smile, but she could see the invisible weight that lay across the line of his shoulders.

Ridiculous, that she should want to ease it. That she would have traded herself for Isabel at that moment. That she yearned to appear before him—not as the demon, Marie or Isabel, but as she'd been once, before she was Lilith.

But that was forbidden, as was the envy rising in her heart as Isabel lay her hand on his forearm.

Hugh turned, saw the woman beside him, and did exactly as Lilith had known he would: he assumed it was a demon, come to torment him.

And now Lilith laughed softly, bitterly, because she realized had Isabel *not* worn the commoner's garb, Hugh might have paused. For there were reasons a lady might be on the allure with a knight, and he might have waited until he was certain 'twas not a demon. But, given his belief that Isabel was all purity and innocence, he could not conceive of her betrayal. Could not imagine she would appear before him wearing deception.

"Isabel," he said with enough sarcasm and disrespect that the lady hesitated.

But she did not lack courage, and bolstered by weeks of Lilith's encouragement, did not retreat. Her words poured forth in a rush, a declaration of love and devotion, of fate and fancy.

Lilith heard the lady's nervousness, the effort it took for her to say those words; Hugh heard a demon playacting.

"You have come to pledge yourself to me?" he asked, affecting surprise, but with an unmistakable edge of anger beneath.

Isabel mistook it—for passion or something else, Lilith couldn't say. "Aye." Suddenly shy, she lowered her head and stared at his hands. "If you would have me."

"If I would have you?" he echoed, then laughed. "I would die to have you. And then, perhaps—if Robert would oblige us—we could marry." His voice deepened, exuding a lazy sensuality. Lilith's skin seemed to tighten and prickle; he intended that voice for her, and it promised heat and a slick tangle of limbs.

And it promised violence. The sensuality was a thin veneer; he was furious.

Isabel raised her face, tears glittering in her eyes. "I do not think we will be allowed to consecrate our love with vows."

"Nay!" His eyes widened dramatically, and he grasped her

hands, pulled her against him. "Perhaps we could kill him then. As a widow, you'll need a new husband." He ground his hips against hers, and Isabel gasped, tried to tear herself away. "We could consecrate our love every night."

"I . . . I do not think—" Sudden fear broke her voice.

"Come now, my lady. Let us seal our promise of love with a kiss. 'Tis nothing, a kiss. All of this is nothing."

The last was said bitterly, and the ache that had threatened beneath Lilith's breast bloomed into full. Hugh kissed Isabel hard, ignoring the beating of her fists on his shoulders.

Lilith looked away, her throat tight. It might have been a good plan, if he meant to punish Lilith with such a kiss. If he meant to hurt the demon who'd proved susceptible to his touch.

In the courtyard below, d'Aulnoy and Mandeville began a slow, deliberate trek toward the tower post. Their swords were sheathed at their hips, and she could hear the weapons' soft swaying with every step they took. The baron radiated jealousy and disbelief, Mandeville cold satisfaction.

Aye, she had sown the seeds well. *Wait*, Lilith thought, but couldn't give voice to the word. *You are fools to have listened to me.*

Isabel's frightened gasp sounded loud as a scream, and Lilith shot to her feet as Hugh bent the lady over the parapet. But he did not toss her to the ground; his hand pushed her skirts up, his fingers roughly sought her femininity. Isabel sobbed as he shoved himself against her.

"If he throws her over the wall, thinking she is you, her death will be more than you planned. Is this what you wanted?"

Lilith startled and tore her eyes away from the scene; Michael stood next to her. "Aye," she whispered, but she shuddered as she looked back.

Hugh had stopped as if frozen, staring down at the woman in his arms. At the tears streaking her cheeks.

"I think you lie," Michael said.

"Isabel? My lady? Nay." Hugh groaned the denial, staggering away from the countess. The lady collapsed in a heap. He stared at his hands, at the glistening moisture on his fingers. "Oh, God help me."

Lilith sprouted her wings, but Michael clamped his hand over her shoulder before she could jump from her perch. "You cannot interfere."

She halted, her breath coming in sharp pants. "You can."

He shook his head.

"You *won't*." She called in her sword. Robert was running up the stairs ahead of Mandeville.

"It is too late," Michael said. "Are you not proud of what you've done, Lilith?"

It was not only me, she thought, but could not voice her automatic response. Not when 'twas obvious that, had she not interfered, human thought would never have become action. Not when Hugh pleaded for help.

But did she help him, Lucifer would have no mercy.

Perhaps d'Aulnoy would. She wavered and waited again. Her success depended on the baron's rage, but perhaps he could forgive what met his eyes as he climbed onto the wall walk.

Though his expression was tormented, Hugh straightened and stood with squared shoulders as the baron took in the scene, as he recognized the lady in the washerwoman's rags. Lilith recalled Hugh's description of d'Aulnoy: *He is a good man.* Would he see the clothing, understand what Isabel had tried to hide? Would he think she sobbed from Hugh's rejection of her adulterous advances?

Indeed, the confusion on the baron's face gave Lilith hope.

"My lady," the earl said, his voice tight. "Can you explain why you are dressed thus?"

No mistaking the guilt that trembled over her features. She took a deep, shuddering breath, wiped the tears from her cheeks. Aye, no weakling she. Lilith wanted to slap her. "I sought Sir Hugh's company and did not want to be noticed."

D'Aulnoy flinched as if struck. "For what purpose?" It was clear he yearned for any answer than the one he suspected, but Lilith knew Isabel would not be other than honest.

Lilith glanced at Hugh; he stood rigidly, but his gaze was not on the baron or young countess, but directed atop the keep. At her.

Lie, she urged him silently. *Convince him she seduced you but you resisted. You owe me a lie.*

A half-smile curved Hugh's mouth, and he spoke before Isabel could answer. "I took advantage of the friendship my lady and I cultivated while in France, my lord. Then I brought her up here—nay, forced her here—with a threat on your life. She attempts to protect you by claiming this was of her own volition."

Isabel shook her head. "Nay! Only after I came did you threaten—"

"Do you see?" Hugh laughed. "Marie de Lille and I have been planning to reach this moment; we were so successful that, even now, Isabel worries that you will challenge me for daring to force my touch upon her and fall before my sword."

"What madness is this?" Lilith whispered.

Michael's smile could have been carved from stone. "He is saving his lord and his lady from your scheming. Rape, treason, and murder? Justifiably punishable offenses. The baron will feel no guilt after, and the lady will eventually make peace with her part in this—for *obviously*, 'twas all a terrible plan of Hugh's and yours from the beginning. He believes he is saving their souls."

"I can smell her sweetness on my hands," Hugh continued. "She is ripe for the pluck—"

D'Aulnoy's fist shot out, catching Hugh's jaw and knocking him back against the parapet.

His hand rested upon his sword hilt, but he did not draw his weapon. He turned to his wife, his chest heaving. "My lady, is what he says true? Did he touch you with force? Did he threaten my life? Did another lady convince you to come here?"

Isabel looked from her husband to Hugh; he clung to the low wall, clearly dazed. "Aye, but—"

"Take his sword, William. And his mail. 'Twas an honor he never deserved."

He was stripped of his rank. Lilith sank onto her haunches, letting her relief ease the tension that had held her motionless. He would be exiled, then, as had many of the barons who had been called traitors to their liege.

"We are even, demon," Hugh muttered; no one but she and Michael could have heard it.

Lilith's mouth fell open. "He has defeated me." She began shaking with laughter. "And he has fulfilled his bargain in the doing: a lie for a lie."

Perfectly equal lies, spun of half-truths that held no advantage in the telling. Unable to stop her grin, her expression a reflection of disbelief and admiration, she hid her face so Michael would not see it and triumph.

"Nay, do not look away." Michael's voice was sharp in her ear. Searing pain tore through her scalp as he jerked her head up by her hair. "Witness the results."

Furious, she transformed, her horns sprouting from her temples and stabbing through his wrist.

He did not make a sound, but encircled her with his arms and drew her hard against him. It was like being crushed by a boulder. "Open your eyes and *witness*!"

Unable to move, she stopped struggling. What did he speak of—what was left to observe? It was over, she had failed. On the wall walk, Robert tucked Isabel close and led her toward the stairs as Mandeville roughly stripped Hugh of his hauberk.

The baron descended the steps, and said over his shoulder, "Put down the faithless dog, William. Now, and quietly: the heart as he tried to take mine, then the head for his traitorous thoughts."

There was no pleasure, only grim duty in Mandeville's expression. "Aye, my lord."

Isabel made a sound of protest, cut off as Robert shook her with barely restrained violence. "Had he gone further, I would do it myself. Be grateful your youth and inexperience does not put his blood on my hands, and that he didn't get far enough to put a babe in your belly."

Michael's arms tightened, though Lilith hadn't struggled. "Watch."

She tried to sound as if it did not matter. "Hugh has beaten Mandeville before."

"Do you think Hugh means to fight?" His laugh was cold.

She hated martyrs. "Foolish. How can he be so foolish?" If he ran, he might escape. He was young, strong—much faster than Mandeville.

Michael clapped a hand over her mouth. "Do not interfere."

Her heart pounded and she began fighting in earnest against Michael's hold as Hugh rose to his feet. His chest was bare, and despite the lean strength of him, to Lilith he seemed utterly defenseless.

Why were men built so weakly? What chance did they have against steel or fangs?

She heard Isabel's weeping as the lady walked across the bailey under the protection of her husband's arm. Did the sound of her tears reach Hugh's ears? Was he glad for them, that the woman he'd sacrificed himself for wept for him? Was it any comfort?

"I am sorry, pup." Mandeville's voice shook. "I cannot think what evil took you."

Michael said into her ear, "Look; though he had no love for Hugh, it is not easy to execute a man."

Hugh raised his head. He must see the burning of her eyes. Could he see that she was held back, that her feet scrabbled for purchase on the roof as she tried to escape Michael—or did he only see that demonic glow?

"Was a woman."

"Always is." Mandeville's short laugh held a note of hysteria. "I cannot do this if you do not close your eyes, pup."

"Perhaps you can still win," Michael said. "Will surely be a mortal wound, but if Mandeville does not have the stomach to take his head, you'll have time to transform him. *If* you gather the blood, perform the ritual, and call for Lucifer to make his bargain."

Lilith froze.

Hugh bowed his head, closed his eyes: a kindness for the man who would kill him.

A scream of denial built in her throat. Mandeville whispered a prayer for forgiveness, and his blade struck true, slicing into Hugh's heart.

Michael released her.

She dove, arrowing toward the allure as Hugh fell to his knees, clutching his chest. Mandeville raised his sword over Hugh's exposed neck.

The blade cut deep into her shoulder, but she scooped Hugh into her arms with nary a break in movement. With a terrified shout, Mandeville pulled his sword from her flesh. Lilith hissed and lashed out with her foot, hard enough to numb his hand, knocking the weapon from his fingers.

"He's mine," she growled. Nodding frantically, emitting a stream of high-pitched whimpers, he scrambled toward the stairs; she was airborne again before he reached them.

Hugh's skin was cool and slick with sweat, his muscles bunching as he convulsed with silent, heaving coughs. Blood pumped from his wound and streamed in pulsing rivulets over his chest, pooling on his abdomen. With a small, sobbing breath, she lifted his knees higher, cradling him tight against her so as not to lose any of the precious fluid.

Imbecile. But she couldn't say it aloud, not when her throat burned with acrid fear. What was she doing? Even if the transformation was successful, even if Hugh agreed to his terms,

Lucifer would not forgive her part in this. Would not forget that 'twas not cruelty that drove her, but something . . . human.

His back arched violently; she fought to regain her balance, angling her wings as he nearly broke from her embrace. Head thrown back, cords on his neck straining, he began shuddering; there was nothing beautiful in it, and she should have gloried in the ugliness that death ravaged upon him, but she could not.

"He's mine," she said again, but instead of anger, desperation laced her voice.

And she knew death would not cower before anger or care for desperation.

It was only seconds until they reached the temple ruins. She landed amongst the fallen stones, holding him against her. His shudders began to weaken, and for a terrible moment, she couldn't remember the markings needed for the ritual. She had not thought of it in so long, had made herself avoid the memory.

But 'twas not something she could truly forget.

She shifted into the body that had been forbidden her, and a single glance at the designs on her skin brought it back. The one between her breasts—her name—would be different than his, but she could use her body as a guide to creating Hugh's new life.

She laid him on the ground, reforming her wings and sliding the membranous tissue beneath him to catch the blood. They'd removed his sword, but his dagger was still in its sheath; she pulled it out.

The convulsions had ceased, and she could not hear the beating of his torn heart.

Her mind blanked. The point of the blade hovered over his chest as she tried to think of a name—any name would do, any name, but it had to be quick. The name did not matter: she could be Marie or Lilith or Isabel and . . .

Her vision blurred.

He would not be the same. How could he not lose his humanity if he became what she was? Even if his beauty remained, would there be anything left of him? Did anything remain of her?

The knife trembled in her hand.

"Hugh," she whispered.

And then spoke another name, knowing that it sealed her fate.

❧

He heard a voice, though it seemed far away. His chest burned, but the pain was easing to numbness. He was colder than he could ever remember being.

Seemed the greatest effort he'd ever made, to open his eyes.

Though darkness edged his vision, he did not mistake the loveliness of the face staring down into his, the outline of wings behind her. The realization of what she was took his last breath.

"Angel." His hand lifted, and he touched her face. It was oddly familiar, yet he was certain he'd not known her. Surely he could not have forgotten this beauty.

Her skin was warm, so warm.

Her eyes widened, and he tried to memorize the display of emotions sweeping across her exquisite features. Sadness . . . grim amusement . . . regret.

"Nay," she said softly, "not me."

She caught his hand, clasped his palm to her cheek when his strength failed. Her touch, her warmth, her face slowly faded.

When she spoke again, her voice surprised him. "Will you take him? Is it not what you planned?"

Hugh tried to answer, was relieved when he was saved the effort by another. Georges? "You could not have done what was required, Lilith. It is not a failure that you tried but you could not carry it through." He paused. "He will punish you for this."

She laughed bitterly. "Do you invite me to Caelum then and give me asylum? Do you transform me to Guardian?"

Hugh knew the silence she received in response was telling, but could not remember why it meant something.

"I do not have that power," Georges said finally. "I am sorry, Lilith."

Her fingers clenched on his; Hugh tried to squeeze back reassuringly, but he couldn't offer even that small comfort. Her voice softened, but lost none of its bitter edge. "What did you think would happen when you manipulated me to this point? Are you satisfied upon proving that I can be—" She broke off, and her tone was devoid of emotion when she continued. "Don't pretend to concern yourself about my welfare, Michael. You must be glad to be rid of me."

"Not in this manner."

What manner? Hugh wanted to ask, but the darkness was closing in. Beneath him, the ground began to rumble; the air reeked of sulphur. Fear crashed through him as he realized the demons of Hell were coming to collect him. He braced himself against the inevitable pain.

He felt the faint touch of the angel's lips to his—then she was gone, leaving him bereft, seeing and feeling nothing.

And then all he could see was light.

CHAPTER 6

caelum

1217

Hugh looked around him with perfect vision. Caelum, a city of marble, with spires that streaked into a brilliant sky, must be as Heaven itself. And it was more than Hugh could have dreamed. Even the Crusaders, with tales of temples and ruins, of societies great—without corruption—could not have imagined such beauty.

The stories of the holy wars, of knights who had brought glory to His throne, had fueled his dreams as a boy; here, in Caelum, surely only the angels were closer to His purpose. This must be what he'd been born for—and what was worth dying for. He would serve for eternity and could think of no better fate.

His blood still sang from the transformation. Beside him, Georges . . . no, Michael—waited silently. He must be accustomed to this awesome display; Hugh was certain he never could be.

Guardians milled about—men and women, some with wings, some in human garb, some nude—and he searched the faces for the one who had come to him, saved him.

And did not see her.

"Where is she?" He blushed as Michael raised his brows. Would the Doyen think his intentions toward the woman were impure? But still, he asked, "My angel."

Michael did not reply.

Hugh swallowed, looked at the ground. Pure, clean—no dirt nor rot. " 'Twas Lilith?"

"Aye."

How could it be? Except that there must be good in her, must be something within her that resisted the demon. "Can she be saved?" Did he not owe it to her to try?

Michael studied him with obsidian eyes. "I cannot save her."

Hugh nodded. If a place such as Caelum could exist, then it was surely possible to save a demon. "Then I will."

the pit

The floor was wet, but Lilith did not let herself think of what she might be lying upon. So long as she could remain still, she was content.

But as with all things Below, contentment was denied. Tremors rocked her surroundings at regular intervals, and she was tossed against items solid and soft, alive and . . . not alive.

It was some time before she heard the whimpering, before she recognized what the warm, squirmy thing that huddled next to her must be. Her fingers explored the coarse fur, scratched the pointed ears; she laughed as its tongues licked her hand eagerly in response.

She could not see it. Though a demon's eyes made darkness visible, they had been taken; she would need time to regenerate them. And as she tried to pet it with her other hand and could not, when the tremors jarred her and phantom pains tingled in her limbs, she was glad she couldn't see what had been done to her.

They had left her tongue—not out of kindness, but because they knew she would still taste the metallic liquid slide of blood, though none remained in her mouth. Clever of them, to return her sense of taste for the Punishment. Would a symbol be missing from her skin, or a new one added?

But it mattered little when she could not see them. "And what could you have done, pup, that would bring you here?"

Chuffing softly, it nudged her hand, neck and shoulder with its cold noses.

"I see," she said. "You are far too friendly for a hellhound. They will try to take that out of you."

It broke into a chorus of frightened barks as the room shook; something crashed against the wall and shattered, raining debris.

She pulled it against her, protecting the small body with hers. "Might take them a while to return to our Punishments. 'Tis war out there, and they have no time to concern themselves with torturing the likes of us. I did not think Belial had it in him to challenge Lucifer, but it seems he did. Which outcome shall we hope for?"

One of its heads whined and another growled; she nodded her agreement. "No good for us, either way." She sucked in a lungful of the foul, sulphuric air. No need for her to breathe except to provide a medium for speech, but she liked the rhythm of it, the push and pull—and stinking air was better than drowning in blood. She measured time in those breaths.

No surprise she'd lost track of it years—decades—ago.

"Perhaps you'll be full grown before they return for us," she mused. "If so, you'll not have much to fear from them. Your bite is death for a demon, and they'd likely not risk it just to teach you a lesson." She felt it startle and back away from her and laughed. "You are not a threat to me: I'm but a halfling. Only those of the original orders—demons, angels, nosferatu—have aught to fear from you; and if you did not have power over them, they would not need to subdue you. If they come—"

Another tremor; she buried her face in his fur and waited for it to pass. Pain streaked through her as the room shifted. Its whimpers matched hers.

It was nearly two hours before she roused herself, remembered what she had been going to tell him. "If they come, there are ways to endure. Aye, you might be slightly mad by the end, but it is much easier to endure without *full* sanity."

His sharp, pointed bark made her laugh again. "Not revenge,

though I do dream of that. Revenge is not enough to sustain yourself. You must look forward to something." She stroked his coat, and it grew silky under her touch. Pleasure rushed through her; most often, hellhounds protected themselves with barbed, poisonous hairs or venom-tipped spikes. "You might imagine a field of werehares, I suppose, or pettings without cease." Two of his heads were snuggling into the crook of her neck, but he lifted the other and studied her.

Realizing she could see him—not well, but it was vision— she grinned. "You're as ugly as your father. I often take his name in vain . . . or, rather, his male bits. I suppose you come from those bits."

He panted, tongue lolling, and seemed to return her grin as his lips drew back against sharp, gleaming teeth.

"Aye, I heal quickly. Though they'll take it all again soon, I suppose." She sighed, and he gave a questioning whimper and a doubled growl. "How do *I* endure? I anticipate the end, of course. When I can return to Earth and resume my duties. Though I doubt it will be the same role; I failed spectacularly. Lucifer was . . . displeased with my performance." The pup might have laughed at such an understatement; Lilith wasn't certain. Her voice softened as she admitted, "I look forward to seeing him again. His eyes are the same color as I've always imagined Caelum's sky. He must still be training there; he will train for one hundred years. There are endless Scrolls to read, did you know? There is naught like that here; Lucifer adores ignorance." She frowned. "But perhaps the century has passed? Perhaps he has already returned to Earth and is slaying demons and quietly dispensing moral advice to humans."

She lay still for a moment. A scrabbling on the floor next to them was followed by a squeak. Calling in her sword, she twisted and stabbed, and the wyrmrat squealed and wriggled at the blade's end. She tossed it to the pup.

"I would very much like to see what I've made; he will be entertaining. And that is all he will be. Whatever Punishment the victor in this war comes up with will surely rid me of any of those human emotions that got me into this mess," she said, and tried to persuade herself that she spoke true. The pup's three heads stopped tearing into the rat, and in unison gave her a doubtful look. She laughed, rolled over, and stood up. "Oh, I'll make his life a living hell, of course. What do you take me for?"

Lille, France

August 1389

The scent of the nosferatu was strong; it nearly overwhelmed Hugh's senses. Though his Enthrallment upon first returning to Earth had not lasted for long, still there were moments when the sights and sounds of Earth overtook him, made him doubt he was seeing and hearing aright.

Such it was for a man who'd been given the ability of an angel; it did not rest easy.

There—a furtive movement. The nosferatu's pale skin glowed bright beneath the moonlight, and its psychic reek permeated the village. How many had it murdered? The odor of blood was thick in the night air.

However many it had killed, it would not take another.

Hugh made the vow, then cursed when a woman came out from one of the small dwellings at the edge of the village. Her gray hair and sagging form revealed her age, her slow walk her frailty. But blood was blood to the nosferatu; did not matter the source, old or young.

And she was a temptation the nosferatu couldn't resist.

It darted from behind a tree, soundless over the ground. Hugh called in his sword, created a suit of armor over his body and moved to intercept him. He barely had time to shove the woman out of the creature's path before engaging him.

The nosferatu did not have much skill with his weapon; it was as if he had not used it for centuries. Still, he was strong, quick—it took all of Hugh's concentration to match each of its blows.

But the killing stroke did not come from his sword. His eyes widened as the creature's head was lopped off in front of him, rolling across the ground to stop at his feet. The old woman?

His heart skipped—no frail woman that. The nosferatu's psychic odor disappeared with its death, and he could smell, feel, taste the demon before him. Had he not guarded this part of the country because of its small connection to her?

"Lilith," he breathed. "I have looked for you."

Her eyes began to glow, that eerie scarlet he'd not been able to forget. She shed the old woman's form, became the demon he remembered from the castle tower—and attacked him.

Laughing. How could he be laughing as her sword clashed

against his faster, ever faster? Yet she was, too—perhaps it was madness that had taken them both.

He tripped. And she was on him, a whirlwind of teeth and wings and naked crimson skin. She could have killed him but she kissed him. He stiffened beneath her, unprepared for the onslaught of lust and pleasure. Like Enthrallment, but from one source. Then pain, as her fangs cut his lip—and she scrambled off him, put the point of her sword to his throat, wiped her mouth with her free hand.

For a moment she stood, her chest heaving; then her gaze fell to his suit of armor. "I see you have made something of yourself, Sir Pup." Her teeth flashed as she smiled. "Though you shine so brightly you could be a target for a blind woman."

He flushed. The armor had been the first thing he'd created, when he'd learned how to make clothing for himself, to dress with a thought. The polished metal did shine, aye—but as befitted a soldier from Caelum. "Or an old woman."

"Aye." Her grin widened. "To change one's shape is a fine trick, is it not—yet you do not use it for yourself. You appear as ridiculously young as ever. Or perhaps you have not mastered the ability?"

"I have." But he had no need for deception, as she did. His natural form was not terrible to look upon.

Though it was difficult to think it terrible when her form was so strong—so appealing.

"And what of your Gift—have you yet received it?" Her head tilted as she studied him. "I have heard a Guardian's unique power reflects him as he was in life. Perhaps your Gift shall be the ability to leave a man's prick limp and useless. For certain you never succumbed to the temptations of the flesh while human." Her sword rattled over his armor as she trailed the tip from throat to groin.

"My Gift has not come upon me," he admitted, then stiffened as she slid the sharp point into the armor's vulnerable joint between his torso and thigh. Beneath the metal, blood trickled over his hip. "Will you slay me now?"

Her brows rose. "Slay you? I made you."

"Aye," he said. "Strange that you did."

Her sword vanished, and her eyes narrowed on his face. "Not strange at all, Sir Pup. I have paid for, but have not yet gotten the use of you."

He rose to his feet. "What purpose could I serve for a demon—except that I could slay you?"

"I'm not likely to ask for that," she said.

"Then let me save you."

She stared at him for a long moment, then burst into laughter. "Oh, you cannot save such as me. And I serve a better purpose than you."

He frowned. "You cannot believe that."

Pointing toward one of the small wooden huts, she said, "In there sleeps a man who murdered his brother and his brother's wife so that he could have a bit more barley for supper. I am his mother—though she died ten years ago. I harangue him day and night, until his guilt will drive him to confess, or take his own life. What do you plan to do, to make certain he pays for his crime?"

He could do naught. "This is why Michael did not slay you. You provide justice we cannot."

She smiled slightly. "There are more reasons than that. Will you stop me, Guardian?"

"It is my duty," he said. "Those condemned souls feed Lucifer's armies Below; perhaps if you do not kill them, they will repent. Given time, a murderer can become a saint. So, aye, I will stop you."

She grinned in full. "You can try." Turning, she began to walk away.

"Lilith," he said. The amused glow of her eyes as she looked over her shoulder made his body tighten. "Thank you for giving me this."

Her amusement faded. "Don't thank me yet, Sir Pup. It wears thin."

wallachia

november 1461

It should not have shamed her that he saw her this way.

She did not look at him as he got her down, and rolled away from him when he would have held her and offered comfort.

And she willed herself to heal quickly, so that she would not look weak.

Hugh did not appear weak—not in that gleaming armor. Giant wings sprouted from his back; she was not accustomed to seeing him wear them, but they had been necessary for him to reach her. He was beautiful and did she look much longer, she would begin to weave silly dreams around him. She closed her eyes, rested her cheek on the snowy ground.

He lowered to his heels next to her. "I sought you tonight, but I did not think I would find this. Who was it?" No mistaking the rage in his voice.

She would have replied, but he would have known the lie. When she was healed, she could tell him whatever she pleased. But her shields were not strong enough yet.

Then his Gift hit her, forcing truth. "Demons." Her laughter was hard, bitter. "You use it against me when I am like this and cannot resist?"

"Belial's?" He sighed when she remained silent. "Lilith, please."

Her body did not pain her as much now, and it did not hurt when he used his Gift, but still the admission came through clenched teeth. "Azzael. One of Lucifer's lieutenants." And she had to continue when he asked the reason, "I was sickened by the Impaler's offering to Lucifer. The prince courts my father's power and invited us to witness it. My father was not pleased by my response." Release, and she quickly asked, "Why did you seek me?"

He hesitated but for a moment. "I cannot kill Prince Vlad; but if anyone deserves the justice you offer, it is he."

She laughed and shook her head. "I do not think he has a conscience to work upon." Opening her eyes, she looked up at him. "I could not anyway. Humans have proved unreliable allies in the past, but my father tries again—attempting to gain Earthly power by pulling a prince into his service."

"That is what this series of massacres has been? Vlad courts him for vanity, power—immortality? But for the last, he could not have them and still serve."

"Aye." She smiled, but it held no humor. "And he will not succeed. He values himself too highly or lacks sufficient belief in Lucifer's power. He sacrifices others, never himself—all that he makes is display. A worthless, bloody display; but one that Lucifer enjoys, even if Vlad fails to offer that ultimate sacrifice." She sighed. "Either way, Lucifer surrounds him with his lieutenants, who protect him. I would be no more successful than you even should I try. And did I try, this punishment would be nothing in comparison."

He nodded, bowed his head. "*This* is a tyrant."

"Aye." Sitting up was possible now, and she folded her legs beneath her so her eyes would be level on his. What had it taken him to approach her, ask this favor?

"And there is naught I can do to stop him." Resignation, anger in that statement. His armor disappeared. A brief flash of naked skin, before he covered it with a brown robe, such as those she'd seen in monasteries.

Surprised, she touched the coarse material. "What is this?"

"Humility. To remind myself that I serve." He remained still for a few moments, then his fingers brushed her face. "What will save you, Lilith?"

"Do not ask me," she said. "For I also have to serve."

He sighed, and then his mouth drew into a tight line. "Where is Azzael now?"

"In Vlad's fortress." Studying his features was no hardship, and she looked long before she said, "If you kill him, do not say it was on my behalf. I dare not revenge myself; I will owe you."

"No, Lilith." His voice was cold. "You owe me nothing."

She lifted her brows. "I thought we'd established that 'nothing' is a kiss."

Finally, warmth in that blue gaze. But she called in her sword; though it was nothing, better to have him earn it.

london, england

september 1666

Lilith found Hugh atop St. Paul's Cathedral, standing on the roof and staring out over the city.

"Even you cannot stop its approach," she said, landing lightly beside him.

He gave a half-smile. Soot covered his skin; the edges of his robe had been singed through. "Aye, it will burn." Flaming debris fell around them; none had yet caught on the peaked iron roof, but it would not be long before the timbered scaffolding would. The recent restoration would be for naught. He slanted her a curious glance. "You have not yet drawn your sword."

"I have decided it will be far more entertaining to watch you attempt to maintain your countenance in anticipation of my attack," she said. A buttress arced from tower to roof; she hopped onto it and perched. The air around them shimmered with heat. To the southwest, St. Andrew's-by-the-Wardrobe collapsed in an eruption of smoke and fire. "It cannot be a surprise if I immediately engage or kiss you *every* time. I should hate to become a bore."

"You could not be that."

She grinned, but it faded as she turned to study his expression. Exasperation, humor—she was accustomed to seeing those. Not the careful scrutiny he subjected her to now, as if he were trying to probe her mind's darkest recesses.

"Is it thus Below?"

She searched his eyes, but could not see the purpose behind the question. No reason not to answer, though. "In part. Rivers and lakes aflame." She waved her hand toward the Thames. "But our cities do not burn. Nor are they constructed of wood, and infested with a plague-ridden population. Perhaps," she mused, "this destruction will be of some benefit; purify the city of that which keeps it corrupted, diseased." She raised her amused gaze to his. "Below, we are the plague, and cannot be purified by fire."

He did not laugh. "Aye, it might release it from corruption. But at what cost?"

Acrid air filled her lungs as she drew a sharp breath. Did he ever think of aught but saving her? She pretended to misunderstand him. "The cost will not be dear; how many did you and your students save this night? When they make a history of these days, will it not be with amazement that more did not perish?"

"I saw you carrying children from their homes," he said quietly.

Grateful for her red skin and the orange glow of the fire that hid her embarrassment, she grinned and said, "It is difficult to tempt people who are not living. I fully intend to return later, and lead them to eternal damnation." Pursing her lips, she added, "Only do not tell Lucifer. He will not like that explanation, and would have preferred death and grief. I do not think he would consider it a service."

He shook his head. "I imagine not. Why do you still serve him?"

The question and the powerful thrust of his Gift took her unawares; she dug her claws into the buttress and held herself still. But his attack struck when her resistance was low, and she could not stop the words from tumbling from her mouth. "I am bound by my bargain."

He froze. "A bargain?"

"Yes," she hissed. Her sword glinted in her hand. "I will kill you if you do that again."

His lips tilted, but the smile held no warmth. "You will try. Why do you need a bargain to serve?"

Again that wave of power; she was prepared and leapt forward. His blade met hers, but he never halted the flow of his Gift. Impossible to fight *and* resist it—it was likely what he'd planned, to provoke her so that she was so busy with her weapon she could guard neither her mind nor her tongue.

Only him—why did *he* have to be Gifted with truth, the one thing that could destroy her? She had to hide it even from herself; if she failed in her bargain, her Punishment would be more terrible than any Lucifer had given her before. And it would be an eternal Punishment, not simply a hundred and fifty years of torture.

She transferred her strength to her shields, and fell.

His body was heavy atop hers as he held her down on the steep roof, his sword at her throat. His Gift smashed into her mental defenses, and she gasped as she felt them begin to crumble. *No, no.* She lifted her hips, trying to dislodge, trying to arouse—but there was no hardness in him except of muscle and bone.

There hadn't been since he'd become a Guardian—since she'd been able to test through the flimsy barrier of his monk's robe. Why would there be, now that he knew what it meant to be a demon? Yet still she tried to distract him with touch; once, it had been her weapon against her—but with his Gift, one he no longer needed.

"Tell me. The others put him on the throne Below, swore their fealty. But you say you were never an angel—that, like the hellhounds, Lucifer created you; you should have no obligation to serve. Yet you do."

Her scream was of anger and fear. Desperation. She called in her heaviest sword. It was impossible to bring it from her cache directly into another body, or anywhere but empty space—she had to hold it separate from other objects. Yet she could place it a hundred feet into the air, directly above him.

Any lower and it would not have enough force from the fall. It would likely pin them together in death, but she would be fighting . . . if she did not fight it would be a betrayal of her service.

He must have heard the whistle of air across the sharpened blade; he rolled, taking her with him. Not fast enough; it sliced her side as it embedded deep into the softening roof.

His face whitened beneath the mask of soot, his skin drawing tight. His left hand still pinned her wrists, but he vanished his sword to staunch the flow of blood with his right. "Lilith?"

She laughed, though the metallic scent filled her lungs and she'd rather have vomited. Yet another weakness, this sickness. That he saw her this way was worse than the injury. He created a length of linen cloth, held it against the wound.

Why must he be kind? It made her more vulnerable than truth, than blood.

His Gift surrounded her with unrelenting force; combined with his gentle touch, she was defenseless. "Aye, I was created by him. I serve through the bargain—but I must serve, regardless," she said. "There has to be one who reigns: to enforce the Rules, to administer Punishment or destroy any demons who think to deny humans their free will, or to bring death to them."

"Aye, one must lead. But why not Belial?"

She laughed again, bitterly. "He would be no different, though he promises much. He says we would all rule, and it would be equal; but that is a lie. It may be better to reign in Hell, but only one truly can—the rest serve. And I am bound to Lucifer."

"What happens if Belial wins the throne?"

"I will be destroyed, as have the rest of my caste." Surely Belial would not tolerate the presence of a halfling; their creation was Lucifer's evil, a corruption of the demon race. She closed her eyes, and Hugh finally relented. The crackling roar of the fire grew ever closer; the southern part of the roof was aflame. "Do not ask me these things, Hugh. There is nothing that can save me."

"That is a lie," he said quietly. Her wound had healed, and he vanished the cloth. He stood, pulled her to her feet. "You will not tell me."

She smiled bleakly. "I cannot tell you."

"And that is truth." He sighed, ran his hand through his hair. "I have something for you."

Her gaze dropped, and she forced humor into her voice. "Do you?"

With the tips of his fingers, he tilted her chin up. "Nay, it isn't that. I know you could not enjoy that; demons do not feel what humans and Guardians do. You only tease me to torment me."

She looked away, out over the glowing sky darkened by smoke. The roof beneath their feet was hot, melting; the interior of the cathedral must be burning. "Yes."

He was silent for a moment, then he said, "I found this in a library; I did not think it so wrong to take it. It would have been destroyed had I not." A bound quarto volume appeared in his hands. "It is Marlowe's *Doctor Faustus*."

Her heart thundered. "You would give this to me?"

"You haunted him mercilessly. As you did Milton, playing his amanuensis after his eyesight failed. Shakespeare and Donne. There was hardly a poet or playwright in the last century you did not torment with your stories." His gaze pierced her. "Why?"

She couldn't tell him she was the last halfling left. Impossible to say that her destruction weighed upon her with every passing year, her inevitable frozen end. And so she only laughed and said a partial truth, so that he would not ask again. "I seek a second immortality; I'm too greedy to settle for only one." She affected a pout. "Yet they always twist it, make it a male demon or villain . . . or Lucifer. Their quills and the printing press erase my sex, remove my identity, and destroy me more efficiently than a sword."

There, a true smile from him. "Will you take it?"

They staggered as the roof buckled and caved; a hole opened yards from where they stood. Flames shot up, sparks showered down around them. Yes, it was much like Below. What would Lucifer do, should she have such a gift in her possession? She wouldn't be able to hide it, or excuse it. It was not a theft—was not something she could cover with a lie.

She clenched her hands by her sides, tempered her shields, and forced the words through the tightness in her throat. "No. I want nothing so worthless."

His features hardened, and his gaze dropped to the book. He slid his palm reverently over the tooled leather cover.

Then he tossed it into the fiery pit beside them and walked away.

Lake geneva, switzerland

june 1816

"This must certainly be the lowest point to which a Guardian has ever descended."

Hugh felt Lilith's amused gaze, her psychic scent before she spoke. No, she no longer hid from him when she approached. So much easier when she had; he did not have to conceal his eagerness to see her when he'd no idea if she'd appear. But this waiting she forced upon him now, the anticipation—it was its own torment.

He did not take his eyes from the scene before him. Frustration spilled from her before she closed herself away.

Yet her frustration could be nothing like his.

He stood stiffly, willed his heart to keep its steady beat, his body its indifference—all the more difficult with the soft moans that surrounded them, the cries of pleasure.

"It is a vampire?" She tilted her head to better see through the window.

He gave a short nod.

"It is the one from Derbyshire? The one we helped create?" Surprise in her voice now, laughter. "I know he is extraordinarily handsome, but I cannot believe you would follow him from England for that."

"No." He had to fight his smile.

"Why do you watch him fuck her?"

Hugh closed his eyes. Cold. He needed to be cold. "He will feed. There have been deaths in this region; I know not if they are vampire or nosferatu."

"Likely nosferatu," Lilith said. "I hunted one in these mountains only last month; I came searching for poets and found a bloodsucker. They have become bolder of late. I think they tire of their solitary exile and centuries hidden in caves." She paused. "Do you see how he kisses her thigh? Will he bite her there, do you think? Or simply feast from her? Do Guardians feast so splendidly in the halls of Caelum?"

Her voice had deepened, as if in arousal. But it could not be; impossible for demons to feel such. Only a trick to lower his defenses.

Concentrate on the nosferatu. "You have become too reckless, fighting them alone."

"They are stupid. Ignorant."

He could not keep himself from turning, from lifting his hand to brush her throat with the backs of his fingers. Her crimson skin burned under his—a warning, and one he should heed.

His hand fell back to his side. "Stupid also to allow one close enough to rip out your throat, without certainty we would make it back to a Healer in time."

"It cannot be as stupid as turning your back on a demon when Michael's sword is within reach; had your fledgling student not been near, I'd have had your head and the Doyen's sword to present to Lucifer." Her glowing scarlet gaze held his. "And I didn't *allow* it. I fought. It was service, even had I been killed."

His heart clenched in his chest, and he returned his attention to the bed, the darkened room. "You are correct," he said softly. "I am the greater fool."

A scream came through the glass, but it was not of pain. A name.

"Colin," Lilith echoed, a smile in her voice. "I remember his vanity well. I believe had I ever called him beautiful, he would have done anything I asked."

"Yes," he said, but his gaze went to the cloth that the vampire had draped over his lover's mirror. Did he hate so much what he'd become, or did something else haunt him? Guilt?

"Are you here to slay him for taking her blood?"

He shook his head. "He is not nosferatu; there is human in him. I will not begrudge him survival, so long as he is not cruel. So long as he does not kill."

Her silence stretched the air between them, until she said, "I have been cruel. You may not have been a voyeur outside my window, but you know I have been so."

"Only with their consent," he said, betraying nothing of his jealousy, his despair. Keeping his indifference firmly in place. "But a vampire does not have to honor a human's free will."

"Nor do I a Guardian's," she said softly, her breath in his ear. He'd not heard her move. "He is inside her now, taking her blood; she wills it, and he brings her only pleasure. Are you satisfied?"

"Aye."

Quick as thought, her hand was beneath his robe, gripping

him, stroking him. It took all his strength to keep his body from responding. Sweat broke over his brow. He could not think. Only hold his defenses . . . they could not hold long.

Lilith's patience ran out more quickly.

With a sound of disgust, she turned away. Hugh ground his teeth together to keep from dropping his glamours, showing her the truth of it. From hauling her back, burying himself within her.

Losing himself within her.

"You swore to your student that you would protect the vampire, yet you contemplate his execution?"

How had she known of his promise? Had she listened in doorways after Ramsdell had Fallen? It was several moments before he had the ability to say, "Yes." He glanced at her; her mouth was set, her eyes flaring with anger.

"You would break your vow?"

"Yes," he said quietly. "If he cannot be saved. If his bloodthirst overwhelms his humanity."

"I will kill him now." Her sword appeared in her hand, a hard smile on her lips. "It shall bring me pleasure to finally rid the world of all bloodsuckers, half-human or no."

"No, Lilith." He laid his hand on her arm. She looked down at it. "As long as he is not cruel, not a murderer—I will not break my vow." And he could not keep the rest from hanging unspoken between them. *Even for you.*

She grinned suddenly, and said, "A vampire's life is nothing. Shall we bargain? A kiss, and I'll promise not to kill him."

It was impossible not to agree; she would be bound by the bargain, and it was a small price to help secure his vow. Perhaps it was what saved the vampire that night, and those that followed; but as her lips touched his, he felt his destruction bearing down upon him.

When had the price of saving her become his soul?

new orleans, louisiana

august 1857

The moonlight cast long shadows across the graveyard; stone angels guarded houses for the dead, locked in endless prayer.

They'd have been better served protecting the living.

Lilith darted between granite tombs, her taloned feet silent over the red clay. It clumped between her toes; she paused and shook it off as she listened.

The thick perfume of magnolias hung in the humid air, and the cicadas chirped their annoying tune. A psychic probe revealed nothing. No sign of the Guardian she'd followed here, or the human Selah had been protecting.

Her breath hissed out between her teeth. Most humans wouldn't have been able to hide their minds from her, but this young man had much to conceal—from those humans around him, and that which he attempted to hide from himself lest it rage inside him.

He'd do well to release some of that anger.

Lilith's focus narrowed. There—a heartbeat, a low, quick breath. She called in her sword.

Selah leapt out from behind a low wall, a tall blond figure in a white gown. Not to fight; she held the young man in her arms. His dark form was in stark contrast to her pale skin and wings. She raced toward a tomb, his slim arms clinging around her neck. Hardly older than fourteen, but of age to decide his future.

With a triumphant laugh, Lilith gave chase. The Guardian was a fledgling, only recently returned to Earth after a century of training in Caelum. Lilith would have her skewered before—

Oh, fuck. The tomb opened; Selah and her charge fled into the dark interior. Hugh closed the heavy stone door and stood in front of it, his arms crossed over his chest.

He caught her wrist before she could bring her blade down on his head. She took hold of the neck of his robe and whirled, slammed him back against granite. The tomb shivered under the impact.

Her eyes shone red across his skin. Her fingers wrapped around his throat. "She's your student?"

"Yes." He stared down at her, his gaze hooded. "Let him be, Lilith."

She snarled, her lips drawing back over her fangs. "Give him to me. You cannot save him; he will not leave of his free will. Not without his mother."

"No. But driving him to murder will not save either of them."

"It *is* justice. He is free, but his mother is not." Her hand tightened; Hugh didn't flinch. "Do you know what her owner does?"

With barely a thought, Lilith shifted. Her black hair became an artful tumble of auburn ringlets; her breeches widened into hoops and skirts. Ridiculous trappings, in a ridiculous society.

She pressed her lips to his cheek; her slim white hand covered his flaccid cock through his robe. "Service me, boy. I should like to ride upon you—you are nothing but a beast. An animal." Her slow drawl dripped with bitter honey. "And if you do not . . ." Her gaze rose to Hugh's. "The threat depends upon her mood: one day, his mother's back is stripped of its skin by a whip; the next, she is sold to a plantation upriver."

"If he kills her, he will have a noose around his neck and his mother would still suffer—perhaps still beaten and sold. That is not justice."

"And what is your alternative?"

His fists clenched; his mouth hardened, and she briefly felt his psychic despair before he closed his mind to her.

It was answer enough: there was nothing.

"Poor Guardian. So limited in your options; so long as he will not leave, you cannot force him to go."

Her tongue traced his lips; Hugh did not react. Not even a twitch from his limp flesh. She vanished her skirts and rammed her knee into the offending organ. His mouth opened on a pained grunt, and she swept inside.

For an instant, he responded with gentle suction, his palms rising to cup her jaw—and then he shoved her away.

Lilith grinned and wiped her lips with the back of her hand. "Let me have him. You know you would like to kill her yourself; I will convince him to do it."

He watched her with cold eyes. "You will try." Stepping aside, he opened the tomb.

Her brows drew together; Selah was not inside. Nor was Lilith's target. There was only one entrance, and they'd stood in front of it. "What kind of trick is this?"

"No trick," Hugh said softly. "We leave such methods to you. We will both be protecting him, Lilith—and we will convince him to go. His mother does not believe she owns herself; once we persuade her of that and she acknowledges her free will, we shall take them both to the North."

"So he will flee, and his abuser shall never pay . . . and you will let him be used in the meantime?"

"It is unfortunate, but aye. I must."

"'Unfortunate'?" Hilarity rolled from her, high-pitched and wild. "Just as losing an eye is unfortunate?"

"For a Guardian, losing an eye is nothing at all. It regenerates."

She searched for any humor accompanying the statement, and found none. It did not surprise her; she had not heard him laugh for two hundred years.

Hers had become increasingly desperate.

Her amusement faded; a strange lethargy took its place. She could not even make the effort to fly—she perched on a nearby tomb, and watched him walk away. It was hard not to admire his form; even in that endlessly youthful body, he had powerful shoulders and a strong back.

She should have stabbed him through it.

London, England

october 1945

Despite the early morning sun, London lay drab and tattered, like an old woman abed in a ragged dark cloak. The wartime blackout had ended; electricity hadn't yet been restored to this part of the city, but still the mortar-pocked townhouse was closed and shuttered.

Hugh was not surprised; the vampire inside didn't need the light. The front door opened easily—the lock had been broken. The rooms were bare but for the cracking plaster, rubble and dust. A broken portrait frame lay empty near the fireplace in the front parlor; the marble mantel had been removed.

A tortured moan drifted down the stairwell, ripe with pain—and human. A wet, wheezing cough followed it. The scent of blood permeated the air: the human's, and the rich, heavy odor of a vampire's.

Colin's.

Hugh frowned as he moved toward the stairs, automatically transforming the suit he'd worn on the street into his woolen robe. The vampire had never managed to create more of his kind; each attempt had ended in death. Did Colin try again?

The risers screeched under his weight; the carpets had been ripped away, the wood left to dry. As if disturbed by the sound, a shower of debris rained down from the vaulted ceiling.

Hugh froze; the building had been damaged, but it was not so shoddily constructed. His sword appeared in his hand. "You promised you would not kill him," he said softly.

Lilith dropped from above; the banister splintered beneath her boots, but did not collapse. Her wings snapped wide. "This house reeks of sickness and blood," she hissed. Her weapon glinted at her thigh. "I tire of both."

So did Hugh. "Then you ought not to be here; if you have sought me in hopes of finding relief from them, you must be disappointed." He turned, continued on to the next step.

Her sword pressed against his throat; he knocked it away with a dismissive swipe of his blade.

The psychic blaze of anger hit him before she did. His steel shattered under the force of her blow. Hugh called in a second sword, blocked a thrust that would have torn through his heart. He spun; his heel slammed into her jaw.

Lilith crashed through the banister; the foyer wall crumpled around the shape of her body before she slid to the floor. Blood streamed over her chin, splattered at her feet along with a small chunk of flesh.

She'd bitten through her tongue.

His gut roiling, Hugh watched her spit into her hand, her body heaving, and waited for her second attack. It didn't come. She stared up at him, her narrowed gaze radiating crimson heat.

Then her attention shifted, moved past his shoulder. Surprise etched a line between her brows.

"How marvelous! A demon is struck dumb by my countenance," Colin said. The vampire stood at the head of the stairs; his slim sword gleamed as sharply as his smile. "How fortunate that you do not need a tongue to appreciate it." He glanced at Hugh; his mouth dropped open in exaggerated shock. "Good God, now *I* am speechless. I daresay that robe is a greater sin than any she could imagine."

"I rather doubt it," Hugh said. His face was without expression as he took in the vampire's appearance; the dark suit and vest were perfectly pressed, but his blond hair was disheveled as if he'd just risen from his bed. Never before had he seen Colin with a strand out of place. Tall, slender—but paler than their last meeting, and his skin tautly drawn. "Have you had trouble feeding?"

"No. The London vampire community is . . . difficult, but there are war widows and shell-shocked soldiers enough, and I shall soon return to San Francisco." With an elegant wave of his hand that included both Lilith and Hugh, Colin gestured for them to follow. "Since you are come, I may as well take this opportunity to hunt. I am drained," he said as he entered a room. "I prefer not to pass the day in hunger, but I do not like to leave him alone."

Unlike the rest of the house, these quarters had not been stripped of their furnishings—or the suite had been redecorated. An old man lay sleeping fitfully on the bed; his breath rattled in his lungs.

Lilith strode to the window, threw open the shutters, and leaned against the sill. Fresh air flooded the room, and daylight fell across the occupant of the bed and the vampire. Colin slanted her an amused glance before stepping out of the sun's path.

"Tuberculosis?" Hugh frowned; bloodstained metal bowls and yellow tubing cluttered the top of a nightstand. "You have been providing him with transfusions?"

"Yes. He'd not have survived the journey from California without it. His family is in Hartington; I hope to travel with him to Derbyshire tonight. They asked that he be with them when it took him."

Hugh nodded. A human could be transformed into a vampire if he was drained of blood, and then drank vampire or nosferatu blood; transfusions offered strength, and if applied to an injury, could speed healing—but the effects were not permanent. "Who is he?"

"My valet," Colin said. "The fourth Winters. Unfortunately, his niece has no desire to take his place. I'll have to learn to comb my hair, I suppose."

"In San Francisco?" No surprise then that he'd not been able to locate the vampire for more than four decades.

"Yes, but I shall not give you my direction." The vampire grinned. "Protecting me should be a challenge."

"I found you easily enough merely passing through London," Hugh said.

"Yes." Colin retrieved a black umbrella from a stand near the door and propped it casually against his shoulder. "But you knew very well that my family has owned this property for generations. It shall not be so easy in the future, for I've every intention of discarding it. Shiftless ruffians have scrambled through it from kitchens to attic, and the house is hardly livable with their boiled-wool stench about." With a shudder, he left the room.

"He does not use the shade," Lilith murmured. She looked out over the square; Hugh joined her at the window and watched as Colin strolled across the street. He glanced up at them, his golden hair brilliant in the sunlight. "He should be afire by now—and he should be in the daysleep."

"Yes," Hugh said. "He should." The vampire disappeared; if they hadn't been Guardian and demon, they'd not have seen him move.

"A vampire cannot run so quickly." She pushed away from the window, began a circle of the room. "Not even one who is nosferatu-born. And despite his vanity, there is not a mirror to be found."

"There is not."

Her lips curved. "Has he taken Stoker's tale deeply to heart, and convinced himself he has no reflection?"

"I believe," Hugh said, "Stoker met Colin, and added that detail to his tale. Or perhaps he merely heard rumors; Colin did not abandon Society until the turn of the century."

"How extraordinary. And how pitiable—a creature as beautiful as he, unable to see it." The hard crimson shine of her eyes told Hugh she did not pity Colin at all. "He is entertaining; I rather like him. And I am pleased by his cruelty; it alleviates the dissatisfaction my promise brings me now."

"His cruelty?"

"What else can it be, when one prolongs the suffering of another?"

His jaw hardened. "You twist it, Lilith. Colin is quite capable of cruelty, but he is not in this."

Her head tilted as she studied him; she slid her forked tongue over her teeth. "And is it not selfish of the family to extend it so that they may say their farewells? It is not to give this dying man comfort, but to gratify their grief and weakness. If they cared for him more than of themselves, they would let him die. No," she amended sharply, holding up her hand when Hugh took a step toward her, "they would kill him, and stop his pain. There is nothing left on Earth for him to do but suffer. Waiting only draws it out unbearably."

Numbness slid over him, brittle, icy crystals beneath his skin. "Perhaps you ought to remain here, and try to convince Colin of it."

"Perhaps. I have not the time, however, nor the desire to wait and play nursemaid until he returns. I've had enough of that role." She shifted, took on face and body of a Japanese woman in a nurse's uniform. "I saw your Guardians trying to use their healing Gifts among the humans in the hospitals. They were useless, but they continued to try."

Aye, it must have been useless. A Guardian—even the Doyen—could not heal damage humans inflicted upon each other, whether it was with a sword or a destructive weapon of war and its resulting radiation sickness. Michael would have no better luck healing the consumption that took Winters in this bed. "Why were you there?"

"For my pleasure, of course," she said, and slipped back into her red skin. "There is nothing quite like the flesh falling from bones outside of Hell, and we do not get any children Below."

Her shields had not slipped, but he read her lie. How easy it was; for centuries, he had been able to determine truth from lie with the lightest psychic touch—now he no longer needed that touch. Forcing truth, however, still required his Gift.

But he did not use it; he could imagine all too well what had happened: Lucifer had once again determined she should enjoy the humans' suffering—and what he deemed a delight would be as punishment to her.

"You did not save any of them," she said softly. "Nor any in the camps, or the trenches, or in the firebombing—"

"I could not save them," Hugh bit out. "I cannot stop them if they kill one another of their free will." He swallowed past the bitterness in his throat. "What will save you?"

Her face was rigid. "Not one such as you. Not a coward who ties his own worthless hands." She turned, leapt out the window.

Coldness worked its way through him; he'd not known his heart could still beat when frozen.

That had been truth.

CHAPTER 7

The bridge shuddered against the gusting wind; Lilith dragged her sodden hair out of her eyes and decided that if Thaddeus White didn't jump to his death soon, she would push him.

After weeks of whispering suggestions of suicide into his sleep, and twice as long listening to his whining declarations of misunderstood genius, her patience was at an end. The satisfaction of his splattering against the highway below would almost be worth the inevitable Punishment killing a human would bring.

Almost.

He whimpered and turned away from the edge. Lilith fought the urge to roll her eyes and let them glow bright red instead. The effect wasn't as startling as it had been before horror films had inured the American population to monsters and demons, but it was still impressive.

So were the membranous wings and crimson skin she'd chosen to shift into during this assignment. Her face was her own, but when she saw him wavering yet again, she adopted the features of his first victim.

"The police—they suspect, they know," she said. A hint of impatience threaded through her voice, but she doubted he noticed: he was transfixed by her appearance.

She tucked in the grin that pulled at her mouth; this tactic was one of her best, and she'd employed it often over the weeks with him. He fancied himself in love with his prey, and her ability to mimic each of them had alternately frightened, overjoyed and enraged him—and had reinforced his delusions of godlike impunity. He thought of Lilith as a manifestation of his work, a sign of his imminent triumph over the rest of humanity.

She played on that now.

"They'll take that away, lock you up and keep you from me forever—but you can join me." Lilith shifted into another woman and another. "You can join *us*. And those pigs will never touch you. You'll have beaten them."

He gave a greedy, self-satisfied smile and looked down at the wet concrete as if it held glorious reward.

Lilith shed the dead woman's likeness and angled her wings to keep the worst of the rain off her head. It wouldn't be long now; her father would have another soul for his army, and she would be one step closer to regaining his confidence. She'd had a succession of failures, but this time she'd performed her duty and composed Thaddeus's suicide with skill and style.

So why wasn't she taking pleasure in the result?

If there is going to be a result. She frowned as Thaddeus paused yet again. For a man who killed others so easily, he apparently considered his own life—and death—valuable. But his wavering kept her from what would likely have been an unsettling self-analysis, and relief slipped under annoyance.

"Why do you hesitate, my love?" she said and grimaced. The *my love* was overdoing it—certainly none of his victims had ever called him that.

Thaddeus didn't seem to notice; he stared at the highway below, and his voice held an awestruck tremble. "There's . . . an angel waiting for me," he said and dived.

"*An ang*—oh, for fuck's sake!" Lilith leapt atop the railing just as the figure below—bewinged and dressed in a monk's robes—caught Thaddeus.

Hugh.

Though he obviously did his best to cushion Thaddeus's fall, the impact of the thirty-foot drop into Hugh's arms knocked the human unconscious. Which, in Lilith's opinion, was splendid—there would be no need to worry about the serial killer witnessing something he shouldn't. He'd have a nasty case of whiplash and a few unexplained bruises, but he'd remain unaware of her—and Hugh's—true nature and his brush with *real* immortality.

Her sword materialized in her hand, and her blood thrummed in anticipation of battle.

This was something she could take pleasure in.

She couldn't subdue her delighted grin, but she disguised it by affecting a cry of outrage. "This is the last time you interfere, Guardian!"

A flash of lightning accompanied the declaration, and her grin broke through. The more theatrical the confrontation, the better—and it looked as though nature was cooperating in the drama.

Thunder cracked and rumbled as she waited for his response. Hugh tilted his head back to stare at her for a long, silent moment, and she greedily searched his features for a hint of regard. It usually lurked in the silky line of his bottom lip, in the crinkle at the corner of his eyes.

Disappointment and anger settled in her chest when she could find no warmth in his expression, only the somber mask he used to hide his emotions. Her breath hissed through her teeth. Why did he always resist her? Why must he—

"It is the last time," he agreed quietly.

His tone startled her out of her anger. She considered deliberately misinterpreting his words, taking them as a challenge, but the weariness in his voice was too unfamiliar—and too unnerving—to disregard.

Hugh didn't sound tired, but *exhausted,* as if something within him had burned out. A chill that had nothing to do with the rain sheeting upon them rushed under her skin.

Her eyes dimmed, her sword lowered a fraction of an inch. "Why?"

He glanced down at the man in his arms when Thaddeus shifted and groaned. "I have decided to Fall," he said, and carried Thaddeus beneath the bridge.

She stared unseeing at the place he'd been standing, felt the nausea rise in her throat. *Falling.* For a Guardian, it meant a reversal of his transformation. A release from his duty and a renunciation of his role.

It meant that he would travel a path she could no longer ambush.

It took her a moment to recognize the cause of the yawning, hollow ache in her stomach: Pain. Loss. It only took another moment for her to twist it into something she could understand and use.

Rage.

She didn't remember jumping, but she must have remembered to break her fall with her wings; she landed silently on the concrete highway, her muscles coiled and ready. Thaddeus lay on the incline on the side of the roadway—Hugh was gone. A growl rumbled up from her chest. Opening her senses, she focused her anger into a searching sweep of the area. He wouldn't have left Thaddeus alone with her, couldn't have gone too far.

"I *made* you!" she shouted into the dark. Her voice echoed in the concrete barrel of the overpass; knowing he could use the noise to cover his attack, she ground her teeth together and delivered her threat with quiet intensity. "I'm the reason you aren't a stinking, rotting corpse, and you think to become human again? I'll see you dead before I allow it."

A whisper of movement. Instinct and skill proved too slow; he caught the wrist of her sword arm and bent it around, holding it immobile at her side. He yanked her back, trapping her wings between them and dragging her to the shoulder of the highway. Sharp, cold steel pressed against her throat.

"I should have killed you in Lille."

She felt the difference in the rasp of his voice into her ear, the tension in the taut form behind her: exhaustion, yes—but also something deeper, darker. A shiver ripped through her, and it was answered by a tremor in his hands, his breath.

"You're on the edge," she realized. Jealousy dug its claws into her chest, and she welcomed the pain it brought. What—who—had managed to shatter his control, brought this heat from ice?

It should be enough that he came to me, even if it was only to kill me. But it wasn't enough—she didn't like to settle. Humans could be happy with half of something; she could not.

She arched her back and ignored the pinch at the base of her throat where his sword cut into her, the warm liquid slide of her lifeblood. "Are you to finish this, then?"

She didn't think he would—didn't think he *could*.

He inhaled sharply, and she knew he scented the blood by the way his grip shifted on his sword, easing its pressure without removing its threat. "I've already gone over and back again," he said.

But not all the way back. If he had, she wouldn't be able to feel death still burning within him. And then the import of his statement sank in. She vanished her wings and turned in his arms to look at him in surprise, unmindful of the blade he held against the side of her neck.

Hugh slew demons and nosferatu with barely a thought; something else—someone else—must have pushed him to this point.

"You killed a Guardian?" Unimaginable. Whereas demons might destroy each other, the Guardians practically oozed brotherly love and kindness. It was disgusting, really. A wicked grin tugged at her lips. "Was it Michael? Because I'd love to see the golden boy's head on a pikestaff."

His gaze dropped to her throat. She was certain the wound had already healed, and the rain had washed most of the blood away. Only a faint stickiness remained. "It was a human."

"Don't be ridiculous," she said it automatically, because it *was* ridiculous, impossible; she could understand his being driven to kill a Guardian—applaud it, even. But he'd never slain her—as he should have—and so she could hardly believe he would have murdered a human. No matter the provocation.

But Hugh never lied—and only moments before she had been certain he would kill her. It seemed inconceivable, but perhaps, after endless years of sameness, something within him had truly changed.

Rain dripped from his lashes; she'd once thought his eyes must be the same blue as the sky in Caelum, and the only bit of that sacred place she would ever have. Now they were dark, and reminded her of the frozen faces Below, the blue of the tormented and the damned.

"I became you," he said.

Fear scrambled up her spine. She covered it with a laugh and tried to pull her hands from his grip. He held her fast. Pausing, pretending to submit to his strength, she said lightly, "You became me? If you'd wanted my body that much, you know you could have had it."

A mistake. She realized it immediately, but it was too late. She should have fought him; he was different, but she wasn't: she had responded as she always had, expecting him to rebuff her suggestive playfulness.

And this Hugh used her hesitation—and her weakness—against her.

He leaned forward. "I became you," he repeated softly. "I didn't put the gun to his head, but I used my Gift against him and he did it himself. He couldn't face the truth, and he pulled the trigger." His lips were a breath from hers, and the gentleness in his voice—from him, whom she'd fought and fought for so long—disoriented her; he wrapped her in his Gift before his words registered.

He'd used it against her before. He'd compelled truth and taken information, but it had always been in focused bursts of power—never this sweet persuasion that seemed to wind through her and steal her resistance.

Because your resistance is a lie, her mind whispered.

She caught the thread of that truth, used it to steady herself. Of course it was a lie; she was a demon. Demons were nothing if not brilliant liars.

And truth was not a tool used solely by those Above.

"So? That was his failing, not yours," she said, and tilted her head to indicate Thaddeus's prone form. Hugh's gaze didn't stray from her face, as she'd hoped. Relaxing her sword arm, she continued, "Truth is a weapon that can be easily twisted. If humans believe in something strongly enough, it can be used against them. It becomes a truth."

"No, that is delusion."

She smiled and shifted her weight to her left leg. "Perhaps. Is there a difference?"

"Yes." Sliding his hand from her wrist to the hilt of her sword, he pried the weapon from her fingers. She let him have it; she had others, and her hand was unencumbered now.

He'd used gentleness and seduction as part of his artillery; so could she. She threaded her fingers into the hair at the nape of his neck and pulled his mouth closer to hers. He smelled of damp wool and warm skin, a disturbingly human scent.

But he wasn't human yet. Wouldn't be. Her hand itched to call in her second blade, but she wanted—needed—more from him first.

He cupped her chin; his palm was rain-wet and cool. His thumb brushed her lower lip. "Your role is your delusion, Lilith."

She laughed and shook her head. "The outside is an illusion, Hugh, but the role is true. It's essential."

He took his sword from her neck, and his arm dropped to his side. "Why?"

Her eyes narrowed. He wasn't asking because he didn't know, but because he wanted her to say it. But for what purpose? Her blade appeared on a thought, heavy in her hand, hidden behind his back.

"Because—" Her throat closed, and she felt his Gift strangle her answer. She tried again and couldn't produce anything but a choked, whistling exhalation.

As if his exhaustion had finally taken him over, he rested his forehead against hers. "I know what you want to say: *There is no light without darkness.* That is the lie, Lilith. One of many. You must see it. Neither Guardians nor demons have a place in this modern world."

"No—"

He halted her denial with the soft press of his lips against hers.

This was almost what she'd been waiting for—a touch, given without coercion. Simply Hugh, without having to steal a kiss or bargain him into it. Nearly eight hundred years of wanting, and now she could finish what she'd begun.

But she lost her grip on her sword. Her arms were weak, her chest tight. Her breath burned her lungs.

"Lilith," he said. His hand moved between them, and the pressure beneath her breast became screaming pain.

She didn't need to look down at the hilt protruding from her chest to know he'd cut through her heart. She'd waited too long; but then, she'd always been greedy. She'd always let human emotions dictate her actions; it was no surprise that failing had brought her end.

He slid the sword out and held her securely against him. She couldn't maintain her glamours, and she felt him shudder when he recognized the pale, naked woman in his arms. He smiled and pushed her hair away from her face with his bloodstained hand. His voice was laced with sadness, but not regret.

"So my angel was always under there."

It hurt to laugh, to shake her head, but she did both. *Not me,* she'd told him the last time he'd seen her this way. It had been the truth, yet he had persisted in holding onto the illusion that she could be something she wasn't.

"I am sorry I cowered for so long, Lilith."

She tucked her face into the warmth of his neck. Hell must be nearing; the raindrops splashing against her cheeks burned her skin. No . . . no. The oceans Below were of fire, but not salt. No, do not weep—this was not Hell, but release. But she had no breath to tell him. She closed her eyes, and there was silence.

It did not last.

PART 2

PART 2

CHAPTER 8

san francisco

may 2007

The rain had not let up.

Hugh leaned against the wall, staring through the water-streaked windowpane to the darkened street below. His skin prickled as his warm perspiration slowly dried in the cool room. He'd pulled on a T-shirt to top his pajama bottoms when he'd finished his reps, but the thin cotton did little to ward off the chill.

Just as the exercise had done nothing but delay the inevitable. It had certainly not kept the thoughts that plagued him at bay.

He turned away from the window; nothing was out there. Not now, anyway. It was considered a quiet neighborhood, and four in the morning was one of the few times it matched the description and was truly quiet.

How long would it last?

Amidst the pile of sheets and blankets, Emilia woke, stretching her paws to accompany a long, feline yawn.

He shouldn't have been so grateful for the distraction. "I

doubt very much that you'll be hunting today," he told her. San Francisco's generally mild weather had been temperamental of late; instead of fog, the city had been covered with heavy rain clouds. Nearly every day for the past month, Hugh had taken his morning and afternoon runs surrounded by cold and wet. "The forecast was incorrect. For all their technology, men are no better at predicting the future than the crofter and his gouty leg."

She lifted her head and glared as if to chastise him for his inane conversation, then launched into a rolling purr—designed, no doubt, to lure him back into the bed so that she could take advantage of his body heat.

"You have been sleeping well without it for the past two hours." His feet had warmed the floor where he'd been standing, but the floorboards were cold as he crossed the room. The mattress gave under his weight as he sat, and he scratched her ears fondly when she crawled into his lap. Her claws pricked his skin as she kneaded his leg in appreciation.

There was always a price for kindness.

For cruelty, too, he thought, though the ones who paid it were often not the same as those who paid for kindness.

Sighing, he picked up a slip of paper from his nightstand. Nightmares of his cruelty—kindness?—had left the phantom odor of blood and dirt on his hands; perhaps it was better not to be left to his thoughts in the midst of silence. Better he could not sleep.

And it was not the sort of call one made during the daylight hours. Nor was it a call Hugh wanted to make, but he found himself dialing.

The slip of paper he held had an address written beneath the phone number. Perhaps it was cowardly to ask this way. But it would be foolish to delay longer in order to visit in person, particularly as Hugh did not know who he would find there. *What* he might find.

But there was no mistaking Colin's voice when he answered. "Savitri Murray. What a delightfully mixed-up ethnicity you must have, and how delightfully foxed you must be to ring the wrong number at four in the morning. I must confess, I love nothing so much as exotic women who drink excessively."

Hugh pinched the bridge of his nose and rested his elbows on his knees. Caller ID. Careless, to have forgotten that Colin might trace the call back to Savi. He wanted her to remain completely distant from the vampire. But it was done; the rest should be done quickly, as well.

"I am—unfortunately—sober," he said.

Silence reigned for a moment.

"Hugh. You must have seen the news footage of the fire at the club."

"Yes," Hugh said. Emilia jumped down and twined between his legs. Absently, he reached down and rubbed beneath her chin. Her soft purr eased some of his tension, made the question less difficult to ask. "Do you require assistance?"

An edge of astonishment sharpened the vampire's laugh. "Do I want you to fulfill the vow you made two hundred years ago and try to protect me against the horde of nosferatu that has descended upon the city?"

Hugh's breathing stilled. A horde? Was it that dire, or did Colin exaggerate? Difficult to determine truth without seeing the person; he preferred to observe faces, expressions—not to guess from tone and inflection. "Do you need help? Or protection?"

"No."

Strange, to feel disappointed in Colin's answer when it was the one he'd hoped for. Ridiculous, that his urge to offer the strength of his sword dwelt so long on his tongue. It was for the best; the only weapons he owned now were a pair of decorative Japanese swords Savi had given him years before. He scrubbed his hand over his face. Forced himself to remember the last time he'd seen his sword: buried hilt-deep within the Earth, the handle left exposed to mark Lilith's gravesite.

Did she rest easy?

His stomach clenched, but his voice remained even. "Very well. Good evening, Colin."

"Good eve—ah, hell." Colin's formality broke. "Are you well? Who is Savitri? Is she beautiful? Have you become entrenched in suburbia, lost your boyish charm and half your hair?"

Hugh grinned despite himself. "Yes. Good-bye, Colin."

"We should speak," Colin said quickly.

"Of things past? I think not."

"Things past have a way of presenting themselves in the present." He paused, and his voice lightened. "Well, that was a bloody awkward way of saying: I have much to tell you. Meet with me tomorrow. During the day, if you no longer trust me;

I'll not likely chase you into the sun if you need escape. Bring your Savitri, and we'll have lunch."

"Better to protect her from creatures such as you." Hugh shook his head, smiling.

"Beautiful? Sartorially exquisite? Witty? Aye, creatures such as I are a menace indeed."

"Dangerous." Hugh pushed away the temptation to meet with Colin; it would do him no good to revisit the past, to reenter a world he was no longer a part of. His curiosity was just another symptom of the restlessness that burned within him of late.

But was it curiosity or sense when Savi might be in danger—not from Colin, but from the nosferatu? Why not gather information from this source? "Have there been any human deaths?"

"Only vampire," Colin said. "They seem intent on exterminating us. There were seventy or so at the club; the community elders thought there would be safety in a group."

Hugh nodded slowly. It wasn't surprising; in the last hundred years, as the nosferatu neared extinction, the creatures had been unable to endure the combined insult of the destruction of their kind and its corrupted continuation in the diluted, human form. They had begun killing their vampiric offspring, and the vampires had little protection against the stronger, older nosferatu. But as the number of nosferatu decreased, the danger to vampires had been slight.

Until now.

"What protection have you?"

Colin seemed to choke. "A dog."

Hugh frowned. "Colin—"

"I'll explain tomorrow. After six? You choose the location."

Withholding information was an old bargaining tactic, and one Hugh had always been susceptible to. "No."

"She'll kill me, but it's time you knew." *She?* The vampire forged ahead before Hugh could question him. "Oh, and Hugh—I read your book."

The dial tone cut Colin off mid-laugh.

Hugh slowly replaced the phone. Emilia licked her paw and stared up at him. "A menace," he told her, feeling a bit as if he'd fought three invisible demons and come out the loser. Miraculously alive, and unsure of what the hell had happened.

A light knock at his door was followed by Savi opening it and poking her head through. "I heard your voice, and broke in," she said. They kept the door connecting her upstairs apartment to his house unlocked, but she always insisted on making her visits sound like a crime. Her way, Hugh assumed, of adding excitement to a rather tame living arrangement—a tame *life*. "The team in Mumbai just finished the code on the update. Since you're awake, want to play? I need a beta tester."

He groaned and dragged his hand through his hair. "No."

"No fun." She pretended to pout, but her quick eyes focused on the paper in his hand. "Did the number reach who you thought? Were you speaking with him?"

"Yes. Thank you." He crumpled it, and tossed it into the garbage bin, then picked up his glasses from the nightstand. He slipped them on, grateful that her presence would keep him from dwelling on his conversation with Colin—and the reason he'd been awake to begin with.

She shrugged and stepped half inside the room, leaning against the doorjamb. Her short black hair had lost some of its spike, but otherwise she looked fresh, alert. "I'm always up for a quasi-legal search of government databases." She cocked her head. "The London address you had was fifty years old. I went into the IRS records—followed that trail from Ramsdell Pharmaceuticals. The grandson is the major shareholder now, but it was like the same man . . . don't give me that big brother look. You may have only asked for contact info, but you *know* I'm nosy. So it's your fault."

He only stared at her.

She grinned. "Food then? I'll meet you downstairs; I have to burn the new version onto a disc first. And then you can watch me as I kick the demons' asses. And they're bigger and badder than ever."

❧

Bigger and badder than ever. Hugh rewound the video, paused as the camera panned across the crowd. The fire flickered across the features of those who had gathered to watch Polidori's burn, but only two faces had caught Hugh's attention the night before.

To the casual observer, they would only have seemed to be large men who had taken body modification to an extreme. It was not unheard of—particularly in the Goth community—to have undergone cosmetic surgery that lightened the skin to such a degree, pointed the ears and removed any trace of hair. Fangs could be dentures, or implants. Their appearance might be remarked upon, remembered, but no one would assume they were truly inhuman—particularly outside a club famous for its vampiric theme. Very few knew the vampires inside had often been real, but even those humans who might have known would be hard-pressed to tell the difference between a vampire and a human in costume.

Not so the nosferatu. Along with an inability to shift form, they had long been denied the ability to move through society without their physicality exposing them to human disgust and revulsion. But now, in a culture where plastic fangs could be purchased at a local drugstore, their difference was noticed—but accepted.

What a blessing it must seem to them, an era in which they could walk amongst humans without facing pitchforks and burning torches.

And how dangerous it was for man.

Hugh frowned, studying the screen. The nosferatu should have been dead. That one nosferatu could have gone unnoticed and unchallenged for any amount of time seemed impossible— and yet there were two, standing in a crowd of humans as if they feared neither notice nor challenge.

Where were the Guardians? Or, at the very least, the demons who should have hunted and killed their former brethren?

"You're looking at those freaks again? You've developed an obsession." Savi dumped a plate of chips onto the oversized ottoman that served as a coffee table, then crossed over to the entertainment center and pulled a disc from the pocket of her loose pajama pants. "Do you mind if I . . . ?" She tilted her head toward the game console.

He thumbed off the recorder. "Go ahead." There weren't answers to be found, anyway. Only questions.

Savi pushed her chair closer to the television, and Hugh obligingly shoved the ottoman alongside it. She flopped into the deep cushion and crossed her legs beneath her, wires trailing across the floor. "Ah," she sighed, and scooped up salsa with a chip. "A game and munchies. My life is excellent."

The smile that had formed as he'd watched her settle into her gaming ritual faded, and he suddenly could not tolerate the idea of sitting, of being still. He pushed to his feet, but she stopped him from leaving with a wave of her slim brown arm.

"You have to see this new opening sequence. The First Battle." Angels and demons warred against the backdrop of the cosmos; Hugh didn't watch. With her back to him, Savi wouldn't see and feel slighted by his inattention, the way he restlessly skimmed his gaze over the room, searching for something— anything—out of place so that he'd have an excuse to move. But everything was in meticulous order; nothing cluttered the end tables or shelves, and the Spartan furnishings had clean lines. Except for Savi's chair, there were no pillows or loose cushions to straighten. He'd chosen them for that reason; he disliked the smothering, sinking sensation of too-soft furniture, but now it left him with nothing to keep him occupied.

"Cool, yeah?"

He glanced up as the scene faded to black. "Nicely done."

She chattered on about the features of the game, but trying to drum up matching enthusiasm proved impossible. His perfunctory responses didn't satisfy her; after a few minutes, she gave an exasperated sigh and fell into silence. Her fingers jabbed at the control buttons, and the demon slayer on-screen whirled in a dizzying pirouette, swords and fists flashing through the air.

Except for practice, it had never been that choreographed. Battles had been fierce, quick. Never a dance. The only sparring with that much give-and-take had been verbal.

And with Lilith, often playful. Sensual.

For a moment, the yawning darkness within him seemed to open wide and swallow him whole.

On leaden feet, he forced himself to walk across the room toward the floor-to-ceiling bookshelves lining the far wall. Like the rest of his house, his books were neatly arranged, but there would be something to distract him, to keep his mind busy even if his body was not.

But it was not the books that ultimately drew him.

He'd placed the swords Savi had given him on display beside the shelves and had barely looked at them since. Seventeen years old and a devoted manga fan, she'd thought them the perfect gift when he'd received his doctorate. He glanced back, at her complete involvement in the game, at her character's choice of weapons. Smiling, he stroked his fingers over the hardwood sheath of the longer sword.

It was lighter than he'd expected. His broadsword had been brutish in comparison to the elegance of this blade. The katana had a thicker handle—to his surprise, it allowed for easier handling. A looser grip and greater maneuverability. Not effective against mail or plating, but for drawing and slicing flesh. He rotated it in his hand: excellent balance, and the air fairly whistled around the razor-sharp edge.

He eyed the shorter sword. Perfect for defense, for blocking a blow from an opponent while keeping the advantage of the longer sword on the leading side. And in close quarters, better for a disemboweling slice, or a strike to the heart.

"Where did you learn that?"

His hand stilled, and he realized he'd been absently spinning the sword. He slid it back into its sheath with a dismissive snap.

"It's nothing."

"You were twirling it. Really quickly. Did you just happen to run across Ninja 101 at Berkeley?"

Normally he enjoyed her sarcasm. Normally he would have insisted he didn't *twirl* anything. And though she didn't deserve it, he couldn't keep the ice from his voice as he repeated, "It's nothing."

Her face hardened. "Fine."

He replaced the sword with more force than necessary. They'd be useless against the nosferatu anyway. Difficult to disembowel a creature that moved more quickly than a human could see.

"By the way, Nani's pissed at you." From her tone, he could hear the *too*. Her felt her gaze burning into the rigid line of his back, but he didn't turn. She added in Hindi, " 'Ungrateful, worthless boy! More interested in his books and his papers. If he insists on making such a long day at work, he should have become a doctor as I instructed him!' "

He had to chuckle at her perfect imitation of her grandmother, and some of his unreasonable coldness faded. Turning, he leaned against the shelves and crossed his arms over his chest. She never remained angry for long, at anyone or anything; indeed, she looked at him now with a mixture of amusement and concern.

"You're lucky she then launched into another tirade about my dropping out of college, and I didn't get a chance to tell her the truth."

"Which is?" he asked softly.

"You don't sleep. You get up within hours of going to bed and have since I moved in six months ago. I hear you."

He stiffened. "You hear . . . what?"

"Your damn gym is right beneath my office. Three o'clock: *clank, clank, clank*. Five o'clock, I hear you leave to run." She snorted. "Imagine Nani's reaction if I told her it wasn't just work, but that you spent five hours a day deliberately driving yourself to exhaustion."

He bit back a sigh of relief, and the moment's fear that he'd been crying out during the nightmares. "I sleep."

She looked pointedly at the clock on the VCR. "I'm up because much of the development team is half a world away. You have classes to teach in four hours; unlike me, you don't make up for it during the day. So what's your excuse? Chronic insomnia?"

"I'm fine." It was almost a growl.

"You're not." Her mouth firmed, and she began counting off his flaws on her fingers. "You're withdrawn. Moody. Cold. Granted, not as cold as when—"

She broke off, and his stomach sank. "Savi—"

"In the hospital, and the two years after I got out, you remember? Except with Nani and me, you were the coldest bastard I'd ever seen. And while Nani and I loved you—adored the boy who'd come from nowhere to help us out in that awful time, who spoke Hindi and every other language anyone spoke—everyone else thought you were an emotionless psychopath." She raised her hand when he would have interrupted. "I was only nine, but I *remember*. And I don't want you to be that again."

His eyes stung. Dipping his head, he rubbed the back of his neck, unsure of how to respond.

She saved him. "And now that I know you have ninja skills, I definitely don't want you to be a psychopath."

He laughed, but found he couldn't assuage her fears. The restlessness within him did not abate, and he would not make promises he couldn't keep.

Instead, he approached her, touched his lips to her forehead. "I'll try."

She blinked quickly, gave a watery smile. "Do, or do not. There is no—"

"God," he groaned before she could finish. "No more. I'll try."

"But you're going running now." She drew back to look at him. "Aren't you?"

"I have to." He clenched his teeth, wishing he could lie more easily to her. A glance at the window and the darkness outside made him pause. "But I'll wait until dawn. And try to sleep."

CHAPTER 9

For two thousand years, the night had been her ally.

Men's fears ran shallow in the dark, made their souls easier to manipulate with whispers and dreams. Lilith had learned to use its inky face to mask her own; deception had become her sword, her shield.

But there were others who'd known the darkness longer than she had, and the night betrayed her in favor of an older acquaintance: the nosferatu.

The night, Lilith decided, was a bitch. A bloodsucking, hellhound-whelping bitch. And she was going to enjoy tearing out the hearts of the two bloodsucking, night-loving nosferatu in hungry pursuit behind her.

That is, she was going to enjoy it *if* she survived.

The line of trees surrounding Lake Merced blurred as she ran; she couldn't outpace the creatures behind her, but as long as she maintained some distance she could plan her defense and try to think of a way to gain an advantage.

Unfortunately, the nosferatu had superior strength and speed, and they knew it. Delight tinged their psychic scent: her flight pleased them, allowed them to play a malevolent game of cat and mouse.

Nude, hairless, seven-foot-tall cats, against a halfling demon mouse.

Lilith let them play; she benefited from the extra time afforded her. With every step, she learned more about them. The smaller nosferatu seemed just as interested in upstaging his companion as chasing her. The tempo of his gait increased in spurts, as if he occasionally needed to overtake the other nosferatu, to prove his power like a peacock flaunting his feathers.

She could use that against them, if she could only find the right stage for the confrontation.

Turning down a lightly used path, she sprinted away from the lakeside, toward the municipal golf course. It had closed hours ago, and little danger existed that a human might see her demonic form. The open fairways wouldn't hide her from her pursuers, but without the distraction of the obstacles in the wooded area that kept them marginally occupied, they might reveal more of the rivalry—and weaknesses—between them.

Odd, that they were together at all. She'd never heard of a nosferatu paired with another. Not that she minded; nosferatu-slaying was one of her few remaining pleasures, though an infrequent one of late. She hadn't seen a bloodsucker in almost a decade. And though she'd returned to San Francisco that afternoon and found the city reeking of nosferatu, she hadn't anticipated finding one in plain sight. It hadn't been necessary to track him; she'd been flying over the park, spotted his poor attempt at traveling furtively from shadow to shadow and dived into her attack.

The appearance of the second nosferatu had been an unpleasant surprise. Unprepared, outclassed, she'd run.

It was humiliating.

She reached the seventeenth fairway seconds before the nosferatu and streaked down its length. The instinct to materialize her wings and escape by air grew insistent, but she ignored the impulse—flying limited her maneuverability. She concentrated on the sounds her pursuers made instead, on the flavors of their psyches.

The first one—the peacock—radiated confidence. Unconcerned about losing his quarry, he chased her for the pleasure of it. He did not fear her. Good. She'd take him out first, before he could learn differently. But the effort would leave her open to attack from the second, whose focus hadn't deteriorated. Though he thirsted for the kill, he remained cautious.

Leaping across a bunker, she landed hard and veered right. Her boots flung divots from the carefully manicured green as she ran up the slope toward the clubhouse. Behind her, she heard one of them slip on the rain-soaked grass.

Idiots.

But bless their worthless souls—she hadn't been this exhilarated in years: her heart pounded, excitement hummed along her skin. For the past six months she'd been stuck in a podunk town in Oregon, infiltrating a Satanic cult and gathering evidence against the leaders. Their eventual arrests had taken place without a single shot being fired; a travesty, in Lilith's opinion. All that time—all that *paperwork*—and no shoot-out.

Unfortunately, the past sixteen years had followed the same pattern as the last half-year. If the nosferatu didn't kill her, boredom soon would.

God, but her life was shit.

Had she not needed to hear the nosferatu's progress, she would have laughed aloud at how far she'd descended since the last time she'd died: from a low-ranking, oft-thwarted demon; to a chicken- and goat-sacrificing government lackey; to a bloodsucker's snack on a putting green.

She wasn't afraid of death, but she would have preferred to avoid a pathetic end *this* time.

It was Hugh's fault she'd come to this. If he'd cut off her head instead of tenderly wrapping her body and burying her, she'd have been free—not fleeing from white, naked creatures who had likely spent every year since Creation in a cave.

Hugh. He probably had a paunch, thinning hair, a vapid blond cheerleader wife, and ten fat kids by now. When she finished with the nosferatu, she was going to find his address and spend the rest of his life tormenting him. No need to wait for her father to call in her debt; for once, she'd be proactive. Hugh had wanted her to move into the modern era? She'd proactively stick her modern FBI-issue pistol up his ass and tell him to dance.

The image broke her control, and she was shaking with laughter when she reached the clubhouse. Backing up against the side of the building to protect her rear, she called in her weapons and waited for the nosferatu.

Judging by the way they slowed in their approach, they hadn't expected to find her giggling hysterically. Most of their prey probably screamed in terror or cried for mercy.

Lilith was tired of terror and sick of mercy.

Peacock halted fewer than ten feet from her, grinning. His fangs glistened in the moonlight. For a moment Lilith was tempted to show her own, but shifted to her human form instead. The peacock underestimated her; she might as well capitalize on his assumption and appear as weak as possible.

The other nosferatu was not fooled. Unlike Peacock, who disregarded the sword in her right hand, he carefully approached Lilith on her left. Did he not recognize the gun in that hand, or just not fear it? After all, a bullet couldn't decapitate him, nor rend his heart in half.

"Did you think to escape us, little demon?" Peacock asked, his English absurdly over-enunciated. He strutted back and forth, chest puffed out, and his exaggerated musculature rippled with each step. He apparently hadn't been out of his cave very long; Lilith hoped the same was true of his companion. "Look, Mondiel, how the halfling threatens us with her steel."

Not just steel. Lilith's laughter slipped away, and she repressed her triumphant grin. Ignorant bloodsuckers.

Mondiel materialized his weapon, a bronze battle-axe. Ancient, but just as efficient as her blade. "Silence, Pandibar." A simple command in the Old Language; it could be an indication of his unfamiliarity with English, or a tactical decision. He might think she lacked fluency in the angelic tongue.

He would be wrong.

"Pandibar?" she echoed in the same language, lacing the name with scorn. "My father has spoken of you. How you cowered behind a frozen mountain on Pluto until the victor was declared in the battle between the demon army and the angel horde. How you, wormlike, slunk back to the Throne and declared your fealty. How you sobbed when He cursed you and the others who abstained from taking a side in that war." She pointed her gun at Mondiel, and felt no reaction in his psychic scent. "Mondiel's name is not mocked Below, but we all laugh at Pandibar the Worm."

"You lie!"

"Do I?" She did, and the blinding rage that filled him was exactly the response she'd wanted. Now, to blind his companion.

She squeezed off two shots. Mondiel fell to his knees, howling and clutching at his eyes. Pandibar swung around in surprise and disbelief, vulnerable for an instant, and she scythed his head from his shoulders.

Moonlight flashed against bronze. Dropping to a crouch just as Mondiel's axe sliced the air above her, she twisted, stabbed upward.

And missed. She felt her blade cut through flesh, saw the line of blood appear on his chest, vivid against his pale skin—but steel hit bone and was deflected away from the creature's heart.

Oh, fuck.

His foot shot out, caught her chin. Luckily, it was only a glancing blow; even so, her head snapped back and pain shot through her jaw and neck. Rolling with the momentum to keep his next kick from taking her skull off, she barely avoided the swing of his axe. It dug into the ground an inch from her left shoulder. Too close.

She levered her legs under her, tried to push herself upright, but his foot slammed down on the wrist of her sword arm, pinning it against the grass. His hand clamped around her throat, fingernails cutting deep. Her gun slipped from her fingers.

Mondiel's face twisted into a snarl, revealing his canines. His eyes had partially regenerated; glassy white orbs reflected her moonlit face. This was the end, then. Again. She thought she'd be angry, mortified, but instead a fierce pleasure rose.

Lucifer wouldn't be able to revive her after this. Nosferatu tore their demon and Guardian adversaries apart. Finally, escape from her role. The nosferatu would thwart Lucifer and his plans for her, as she'd never been able to.

Mondiel paused, stiffened. "The Morningstar? Your father?" His hand flexed on her neck with crushing pressure.

Lilith's eyes burned. Morningstar—the name by which Mondiel would have known her father before the First Battle. Had he arrived just in time to 'save' her, to keep his plot alive?

But no . . . Mondiel did not look around; his focus remained intent on her face. She realized she must have been projecting her final thoughts, that Mondiel must have picked the name from her mind.

"You are not one of Belial's, but Lucifer's?" The nosferatu ground his foot against her wrist, snapping bone. Lilith dropped her sword, stifling a cry of pain. Her left hand fisted in grass, tore it from its roots. She'd suffered worse than this in silence; she'd not break now. "Did the Betrayer send one of his halflings to kill us? Does he betray again?"

His furious questions barely registered, but the brush of her hand against hot metal did. The gun barrel, still retaining the heat from the two shots she'd fired. She grasped, clutched, until its familiar weight rested in her palm.

Suddenly, with hope in her hand, death didn't seem as agreeable. She'd only have one chance—a slim chance—but she'd take it.

"Are you Morningstar's? Are his promises made with doubled tongue?" His blind eyes bored into hers, reminding her for a moment of a poet who'd said her fate and her role were fixed, unchangeable—and of Hugh, certain that the poet had been wrong. Hugh, who'd cut her heart in half.

One bullet might not do the same, but surely ten would.

Cerberus's balls, this was going to hurt.

She slipped the gun between them, pressed it hard against his breastbone, and pulled the trigger in rapid succession, changing the angle slightly with each shot. As the first bullet whipped through his chest, he tore her throat out. The third, he dug his fingernails into her abdomen, burrowed under her ribs toward her heart. The eighth, he shuddered, fell dead atop her.

She quickly pushed him off to keep his blood from mixing with hers. Her body screamed at the movement; light-headed, too numb to triumph, she curled into a ball and waited for her body to heal itself.

It'd better do it quickly. Morning neared, and the maintenance crew would arrive soon. Finding her like this would be bad enough; seeing the nosferatu might have irreparable consequences. Though their bodies turned to ash at the touch of the sun, she couldn't depend on their remaining undiscovered until then.

She lay with her eyes closed and dragged a wet breath through her regenerating windpipe. The rush of cool air into her damaged lungs felt like heaven. Her gut slowly knitted back together; in a few minutes, she'd be able to move without her insides falling out.

Lucky that Mondiel had been distracted by her connection to Lucifer. Why had he assumed she'd been one of Belial's demons? The war between Lucifer and Belial for supremacy over Hell had raged for eight centuries, but both sides hunted the nosferatu with equal fervor and hatred.

The rumble of a diesel engine brought a halt to her uneasy contemplation. Staggering to her feet, she vanished her sword and gun. Nothing could be done about the blood; the nosferatu's would be destroyed by the sun, but hers wouldn't—and it would make her sick to carry it in her mental cache. It would be found, investigated, but remain a mystery.

Next time, she promised herself, she'd have more firepower. She'd pull out an Uzi, and the nosferatu would never get near her.

A self-deprecating grin tilted her lips as she hoisted each nosferatu up, her arms wrapped around their waists. She lied even to herself: she'd never give up hand-to-hand combat—she enjoyed it too much, and only rarely had circumstances been so dire.

She'd been fortunate the bloodsuckers had been ignorant of modern weaponry, but she couldn't depend on it again.

And she had no doubt she'd soon be fighting more. With the death of Mondiel and Pandibar, the psychic stink should have dissipated. Instead, it surrounded her, coming from the city in waves and pulses as if previously shielded bloodsuckers were opening their minds and reaching out for their dead companions.

Six months away, and her city had become infested.

Her unease multiplied. Had the nosferatu, like those Below, decided to infiltrate human society and live among them? Why hadn't the city's demons and Guardians sought them out, killed them before now?

She jogged across the golf course, the nosferatu bouncing limply at her sides. She'd dump their bodies in the lake, and then return to her apartment and clean herself up.

She might find the answers she wanted at work; if anyone would know the reasons behind this infestation, it would be her boss. Her grin twisted into a snarl.

God, but she hated her day job.

CHAPTER 10

ASAC Bradshaw's office reflected its occupant all too well: bland and tasteless. The Assistant Special Agent in Charge of the San Francisco Division of the FBI, Bradshaw was also careful, precise, intelligent—and completely unaware that his immediate superior, SAC Smith, happened to be one of Lucifer's lieutenants.

And although Lilith suspected that Bradshaw thought her a nutcase, she knew he had no idea how far from normal she actually was.

He listened silently as she gave her account of the Oregon arrests, steepling his chocolate brown fingers as if in deep contemplation. More likely, he was trying to think of a way to take her badge. He'd quietly opposed her methods and assignments since she'd been transferred to the San Francisco office ten years ago, suspecting their legality and her reliability.

With good reason, too. Lilith didn't hesitate to manipulate evidence when the truth couldn't be proven through usual means. With demons and vampires involved, truth and lies became distorted; she created an official version that was as authentic as possible.

She doubted that Bradshaw would appreciate hearing that the head of the cult had been a rogue demon posing as a god; Lucifer had taken exception to the rogue's arrogance, and SAC Smith had given her the assignment. She'd had only to capture and take the demon to one of the Gates leading Below, but bringing down the human part of the cult legitimized Lilith's presence there.

Why Lucifer didn't just send a horde of demons in and take out the rogue, she could only guess. Perhaps he enjoyed playing according to human rules, and then bending them to his purposes; perhaps it gave him pleasure to infiltrate and act through human institutions.

And perhaps he just relished the knowledge of how much Lilith despised it.

In any case, the favoritism and leeway shown her by SAC Smith hadn't earned her any friends in the division—not that she needed or wanted any. But she would have appreciated avoiding the type of bullshit she was being forced to endure now.

Still, when Bradshaw closed the case folder and didn't run through his typical piercing questions in an attempt to locate flaws in her report, she was almost disappointed. She'd created some truly spectacular lies; it was a pity her brilliance would be wasted, accepted without a single argument.

What he said instead was better. "I don't like you, Agent Milton."

She stared at him expressionlessly a moment, delighted by the unexpected admission. How she loved it when humans were honest. "I'm sorry to hear that, sir," she said. "I shall make acquiring your respect my sole endeavor from this point forth."

In a twisted way, he already had her respect—not that she'd let him know that. His insight and determination to do right reminded her of Hugh, though Bradshaw lacked the underlying passion that had drawn her so powerfully to the knight. Bradshaw presented her a pale substitute, but it was, at times, an entertaining and challenging one.

He tapped the folder against his desktop, contemplating her wordlessly. "Just so we understand one another," he finally said and passed the file back to her.

Her smile was genuine. "I think we always have, sir." Tucking the folder beneath her arm, she stood.

"You've put in for time off this afternoon?"

She couldn't tell him that she wanted a chance to backtrack the nosferatu's trail through the park and would rather do it during the daytime. "Yes, sir. I have no current investigations, and during my absence my personal affairs—"

"It's been approved." He waved off her explanation.

Lilith snapped her mouth closed, disappointed that another lie had gone to waste.

"Thank you, sir. Good day, sir." She clapped her heels together and saluted because it amused her and left him shaking his head in disapproval.

Feeling quite jolly, she paused at the front desk, inquired after SAC Smith, and heard the same reply she'd been given all morning: he was in a meeting, and taking neither calls nor appointments.

The prick. Unfortunately, she couldn't determine the veracity of it; his office and the conference room had been soundproofed, even against hearing as acute as hers, and his psychic blocks were impenetrable.

Oh, well. She had other ways of finding out information about the nosferatu.

❦

"Hey, Dr. C! Dr. Castleford!"

Hugh tested the padlock to make certain his bike was secure, then looked up, squinting against the bright morning sun. Jason Willis jogged toward him, holding his neon orange board shorts up at the waist, his book bag swinging against his hip.

"Dr. C. What's . . . up?" Too winded to say more, he dropped his bag to the ground. It landed with a solid thump. His freckles had been nearly lost amidst a deep tan, and Hugh wondered where he'd managed to take in so much sun since the last time he'd seen him.

Hugh glanced at the sky. "I was just thinking that gouty legs make fine barometers, after all." Accustomed to the look Jason gave him—at one time or another, almost all of his students stared at him with similar expressions on their faces—he paid it no mind and unbuckled his pack from the bike frame. Slinging it over his shoulder, he nodded toward Jason's overstuffed bag. "My office hours are in ten minutes, but I won't make you carry it back to the Humanities building. I haven't seen you in class lately."

"Yeah, well, that's what I was coming to see you about." Worrying the beaded leather thong around his neck, he explained, "My mom lost her job, and I've been working odd hours at the video store; that's why I've been gone a lot. But my schedule's worked out, so I wanted to make sure I could still catch up."

The kid was a terrible liar.

Hugh sat down on a bench, slipped off the elastic he'd used to keep his pant leg from catching the bike chain, and considered his options. Though he no longer had his Gift, centuries of being able to feel truth, to force it, had left him with the ability to read it in the most accomplished of liars. Jason, though he clearly wanted Hugh to believe what he'd said, was barely an amateur in comparison to the demons he'd known.

But pressing Jason for the reason behind the lie wouldn't serve a useful purpose; no matter the cause of the absences, if he thought he could make up the work, Hugh wouldn't prevent him from doing so.

He wouldn't make it easy for him, though. "You still have your syllabus?"

Jason nodded, clearly relieved by Hugh's response.

"Catch up within two weeks; and by the end of the semester I want two extra journals. Next week's paper should be on time."

"I will." With a mixture of chagrin and relief, he hiked up his shorts again and leaned over to grab his bag. "Thanks, Dr. C."

He wouldn't be feeling quite so grateful once he realized how much work he'd have to do over the next two weeks. "My pleasure," Hugh said, and waited until Jason backed up a step before adding, "In the future, when you decide to take a vacation in the middle of the term, you'd do well to e-mail your professors first."

"Oh, man." His blush at odds with his grin, Jason began walking backward. "Did Ian tell you?"

Hugh shook his head. "I haven't been to Auntie's in a month or so."

"You gonna be there tomorrow?"

"Yes." After Savi's outburst that morning, it seemed the best way to mollify both women. Auntie would appreciate the visit, and Savi could hardly call him withdrawn if he sought the company available at the restaurant.

"Where tomorrow?" A tall blonde sidled up to Jason. Tanned, athletic; Hugh would wager anything it hadn't just been surfing that had pulled Jason from classes. They shared a long, deep kiss, and Hugh grinned as he finished unrolling his cuff.

Had he ever been that young?

"We were talking about playing DemonSlayer at Auntie's," Jason told her after she released him.

"That card game you tried to teach me?"

Jason turned to Hugh. "I couldn't teach her."

"I like the video game, but the other . . ." She flashed a brilliant smile. "I always get to the succubus card and want to try out the powers myself."

Hugh should have been used to it by then. He watched them saunter off, arms around each others' waists, and experienced a second of chronological vertigo.

It wasn't the frank sexuality of the modern era that unsteadied him, but the lack of shame that accompanied it. How different it was from the rigid moralizing he'd known as a boy; and later, from what he'd observed on Earth through the centuries. But now he saw everywhere what he'd only regularly seen in Caelum . . . and Lilith, who had been shameless in all things.

It had always been one of her most admirable—and frustrating—traits.

One of her more distinctive ones, as well; when she'd operated in her typical servant's disguise, it had often been her unapologetic mien that had led him to suspect her true identity. Over the past sixteen years, the instinct to search every face for Lilith underneath had faded, and it was only when a certain expression, a mischievous laugh, or the tilt of a woman's head reminded him that he was struck by these instants of recognition.

There were worse things, he decided, than having unexpected flashbacks to his centuries as a Guardian or nightmares that left him sleepless for months at a time. He wasn't certain if he should bemoan or rejoice that his life had become so uneventful that the most exciting episode that week had been a forecast without rain—but it was better than an existence permeated by a lack of faith in his role.

And his memories of that time were not completely unwelcome.

A light breeze picked up as he walked across the quad. A pair of students—engineering, Hugh judged by the spill of books on the grass—began an impromptu game of Frisbee, and he had to duck as the plastic disc whizzed by his head. They shouted an apology; he grinned to himself, and mentally adjusted that week's tally. Exciting moments: two.

He might not have a Guardian's reflexes anymore, he mused, but as long as he came out of a Frisbee incident unscathed, his life wasn't so terrible.

As he drew closer to the Humanities Building, however, the heavy sensation that had grown so familiar of late returned to his stomach. Not dread, but something akin to it. Unable to define it precisely, he'd suppressed the feeling.

Given that Savi had noticed it, he'd not suppressed it well enough.

He took the stairs two at a time to the fourth floor, where he shared an office with Sue Fletcher, another adjunct professor. At least he could be certain that it wasn't his occupation; he enjoyed teaching, and as he paid little attention to the politics of academia, the bureaucracy did not engender the same negativity in him that he witnessed in many of the other faculty.

But if he could not ascertain the root of the problem, no matter—whatever the feeling was, it would eventually pass. Given enough time, everything did. Perhaps he just needed to meet with Colin, engage him as a fencing partner. The vampire would be safe acting as a target for his restlessness, and Hugh would be hard-pressed to find a more experienced opponent.

Or one who would remind him of everything he wanted to leave behind.

No; it was better to forget Colin's offer. Better not to get involved with problems that, as a human, he couldn't solve.

Not that he'd been particularly successful solving them when he'd been a Guardian.

By the time Hugh reached his office he was brooding, though he was careful to keep his dark mood from his expression. He hadn't scheduled any appointments, but it didn't surprise him to find two people waiting outside the office door: a tall, barrel-round man, pushing fifty; and a woman—the male's younger, vibrant opposite—her short auburn hair and tailored navy suit neat and efficient. Judging by the man's bearing and gray suit, probably law enforcement, though not quite clean-cut enough for FBI.

If they'd come to question him about Savi, they'd have been

federal; a visit from local officers was unusual, but it wasn't alarming.

He supposed if he turned around and ran, it would cause another exciting moment—but it would hardly do to act in such a manner just to ease his ennui.

He shook himself, frowned. Where had *that* bit of nonsense come from?

Better to get this over, before another ridiculous notion could occur to him.

CHAPTER II

"Professor Hugh Castleford?" Her inflection made his name a question, but Hugh didn't doubt they knew exactly who he was. She smiled; her eyes remained flat and cool. "We're Detectives Taylor and Preston of the SFPD." She indicated herself first, then her partner.

"Detectives." Hugh nodded his acknowledgment as he slid his key into the knob. "What can I do for you?"

They came in and took in everything with a single glance. Hugh scrutinized them as quickly as he put down his bag and seated himself behind his desk. They moved in tandem, the familiarity of a long partnership. Taylor sat in the chair facing his desk, her feet placed neatly in front of her. Preston dragged the visitor's chair from Sue's side of the office, whirled it around and straddled it. "We're looking into a missing person's case," he said. "Javier Sanchez. He's in one of your classes?"

Hugh easily pictured Javier: quiet, intense, bright. "He was in Composition last term." He studied the detective's solemn countenance and unease settled across his shoulders. Would they have come in person to question him about a *missing* college student? Or did they suspect worse?

"But not this semester?" Taylor flicked a glance at her partner.

Hunching his shoulders in his worn jacket, Preston asked, "Have you seen him since your Comp class?"

"Several times; the latest was a month ago Friday. At Auntie's, on Irving Avenue."

"Your aunt's?"

Taylor's demeanor warmed slightly. "It's a restaurant, Joe. Southern Indian," she said. The corners of her mouth tilted in amusement. "You'd be popping antacids like candy."

Preston grimaced; though the expression seemed to age him ten years, his sharp gaze never strayed from Hugh's face. "How would you characterize Mr. Sanchez's behavior?"

"Normal." Silence followed his succinct description. Hugh recognized the tactic, and obliged them by adding, "A few of my current and former students meet at Auntie's every Friday night to play DemonSlayer. It's a CCG—a collectible card game. Javier is one of the regular players. I didn't notice anything out of the ordinary when I spoke with him."

The detectives didn't look at each other, but he felt the undercurrent that passed between them.

Tight-lipped, Taylor flipped open her notebook. "Will you give us the names of the other attendees?"

Hugh recited the list without hesitation. When he finished, Detective Taylor nodded and tucked her notebook away. "Thank you, Dr. Castleford. You've been helpful."

He hoped that would prove true. "I'll be available should you have any more questions."

Taylor stood, then paused when her partner was slow to do the same. The hint of mirth Hugh had seen before appeared again. "Ask him, Joe."

With a sheepish grin, Preston reached into the inside pocket of his coat and withdrew a slim paperback. "I wondered if you would sign this for me."

Hugh automatically accepted the book, and stemmed the shout of laughter that always rose whenever he saw the red cover and embossed silver lettering that spelled his name. The black font used for the title seemed to drip blood, and the 'T' resembled a silver dagger.

Lilith.

It had never been intended for a public audience, but two years after he'd written it, Savi had found the file while rebuilding his computer and assumed Hugh had been a stereotypical English grad student cum frustrated author.

She'd been fifteen years old when she had used an Internet translator to transform the Latin text into English and had it printed at a vanity press as a gift. She'd also had access to a large bank account and contacts with online distributors. The print run had been two thousand copies; of those, Hugh had received twenty.

His narrative ability was mediocre at best, and the translation awful. The final, terrible product had become infamous among Hugh's colleagues when he'd been studying at Berkeley; and later, among his own students. Fortunately, when he'd applied for his position at San Francisco State, the department heads thought he'd intended it as an ironic statement about the corruption of language over time. He continued to let them think so.

The copy he held now had been well-worn: dog-eared, spine-creased and the pages splotched with coffee stains.

"It's my stakeout book," Preston explained.

His partner sighed heavily. "No offense. But . . . he reads it *aloud.*"

"None taken." Hugh opened to the title page, wrote a brief message and his signature. "I can obtain a new copy for you; this one is ready to fall apart," he said as he slid it back across the desk.

With a wry glance at Taylor, Preston said, "I'll keep that in mind." Without checking the dedication, he pushed the book into his pocket and gave it a protective pat, then rose to his feet. He rolled the chair over to Sue's half of the office, paused and looked at her political posters and haphazard stack of papers and books. "Professors today aren't nearly as stiff as I remember them."

Hugh glanced down at the shirtsleeves he'd folded back over his forearms and his khaki cargo pants, and silently agreed.

Preston continued, "Although from your accent, I suspect yours were. The U.K.?"

The detective was making a rather broad guess; Hugh's accent was almost imperceptible—certainly too slight to pinpoint an origin. His first language most closely resembled French, but they wouldn't have recognized it as such now. "My formative years were spent traveling throughout Europe. And my tutors were, indeed, very strict."

He felt Detective Taylor's penetrating gaze on his face before she turned away. "Let's get started on these names. Thank you again, Dr. Castleford."

"When you find him, I should be relieved to hear from you," Hugh said. His tone spoke for him: alive or not.

"I'll let you know." Preston touched his pocket. "Thanks again."

Hugh sat quietly long after their footsteps receded down the hallway. They were very good; they hadn't given away much between them, but Hugh was certain they thought he had been involved in Javier's disappearance. How deep their suspicion went, he couldn't guess, but it was enough to take his fingerprints by asking him to autograph the book.

He couldn't resent their surreptitious method of collection; if it eased their doubts about Hugh and led them in the proper direction toward Javier, then it was for the best.

The detectives would find little to act on. The few items in his past that skirted legality—the birth certificate and school records Michael had provided Hugh after he'd Fallen—had been tested seven years before by the FBI, when they'd been investigating the fake identification Savi had been creating for her underage friends.

No, the only real secrets Hugh possessed were laid bare in the book they'd used to collect his fingerprints.

An irony, he mused, that only he could appreciate; to every other human, his story would remain fiction. From the date of his Fall, he'd determined not to share the truth about his past. A strange decision from a Guardian whose gift had been Truth, perhaps, but honesty would serve no purpose.

Who could believe his tale? Even Savi, who considered him as close as an older brother, would look at him askance if he told her he'd been born during the reign of King John. Could Savi, for all her brilliance and trust, really understand the steps he'd taken from a castle in Britain to her side when she'd been a young girl?

No. Nor did he want to place the burden of *trying* to believe him upon her; he would continue to isolate his history from those closest to him.

And in the end, seeing the book in print had done what writing it had not: put his past into its proper perspective. The gaudy cover and horrible prose were silly; so had been his attempt to recreate Lilith.

He looked around his office, suddenly struck by the institutional paint, the economical furniture, the windows no wider than an arrow-slit. So different than Caelum—but had he simply traded one comfortable institution for another?

His stomach tightened, heavy beneath his chest.

He recognized *this* feeling: futility. It will pass, he reminded himself. But he picked up his keys, and walked out.

With the sun and physical exhaustion, it always passed more quickly.

❧

Lilith found the body near the edge of the southern lake.

When she'd followed the nosferatu's trail through the park, she'd caught the scent of human death and had expected to find a mutilated corpse. But this . . .

Death held few surprises anymore, but this one stunned her. For several minutes, she stared with frozen recognition at the arrangement of flesh and bone with her head bowed and her hands fisted in her pockets. She knew the ritual that had been performed here. God, how well she knew it.

Lucifer must be connected. What bargain had been struck, that the nosferatu also had knowledge of this ritual?

Dread knotted her stomach and rose like bile in her throat.

What had they done?

The crunch of bicycle tires along the recreation trail shook her out of her numb reverie, and she quickly dropped into a crouch to avoid being seen. The remains weren't far off the path, but had been hidden from easy sight by patch of willow scrub. Fewer than twenty-four hours old, they hadn't suffered significant decomposition or putrefaction, but it wouldn't be long before they were discovered. Though this portion of the park wasn't as heavily visited as others, it was typically used by joggers and bicyclists; she hadn't changed her clothing since leaving the federal building, and her suit would be memorable in these surroundings.

The sound of the bicycle faded, only to be replaced by the light, quick tread of a runner. Lilith breathed a sigh of frustration. Why couldn't these idiots be like normal humans: their asses on a sofa, eating potato chips and staring vacuously at a television?

Growling a little, she thought about jumping out of the bushes in full demon mode to see just how fast the jogger could run, but the idea didn't cheer her. She turned her attention back to the remains instead, and examined them with an objective eye.

The ground had been cleared, creating a circle of dirt almost three feet in diameter. The victim had been dismembered—not a surprise, as nosferatu often tore their prey apart—but the symbols carved into the skin across the torso were not as usual. And in the middle of his chest, a name was spelled out in a grisly, flowing script.

Moloch.

She frowned. That didn't make any sense. The victim's new, demonic name should have been written there, not that of a nosferatu—and instead of death, there should have been a transformation. Had the ritual failed?

On the trail, the runner's steps slowed and came to a halt on the other side of the scrub. She heard the catch and pause in his ragged breaths as he recognized the scent of death. Fuck. Nothing to do now but slip away before he saw her.

And then he sighed. It was a simple exhalation, full of resignation and disappointment, but its familiarity sent a shiver racing along her skin. Hardly daring to believe, she reached out with a psychic probe.

Hugh.

She closed her eyes against a creeping sense of inevitability, and Lucifer's voice rang in her ears: *His death will be yours to give, or your soul mine to keep.*

Could it be a coincidence that he should happen upon this scene? She knew it couldn't be; somehow, between the nosferatu and the ritual and Hugh, she was certain that Lucifer's long-held plans were finally coming together, and the pieces were falling into place.

Where would she fit?

She should flee, and keep Hugh unaware that she lived; her father depended on her to play a part. A demon worked under concealment, creating temptation by using the target's ignorance against him and manipulating with lies. Hugh was no longer the Guardian she'd known, but a human. He was nothing to someone like her.

She opened her eyes, saw the ruin that had once been a man. And waited.

CHAPTER 12

The sun shone low and warm at her back; it cast her shadow across the clearing and must have prevented Hugh from immediately recognizing her. He narrowed his eyes against the light, and she rose to her feet.

Age had roughened the soft perfection of his youth, broadened his slim form. His golden skin was bathed in perspiration from his run, the sheen catching the sun and highlighting strong cheekbones and dark, slashing brows. His mahogany hair was cut short, erasing any hint of curl. The line of his jaw had once been smoothly curved, as if an artist had tenderly formed him from alabaster; time had proved a less patient sculptor, but the straight, clean angles were in as beautiful proportion.

His clothing, she noted, was as atrocious as ever, but afforded a much nicer view than his brown robe. The thin blue T-shirt—sleeves torn away, a faded rainbow emblem on the front—clung damply to the muscular planes of his chest, and his loose navy sweatpants had small holes at the knees. Only his shoes were in decent condition.

No paunch, no thinning hair. He'd gained weight, but no fat.

His bare arms looked as taut and defined as the day she'd first seen him practicing swordplay in a castle courtyard.

Wanting to berate herself for caring, but unwilling to miss the moment of recognition, she searched his expression and waited . . . for any reaction. Surprise, hate, joy: she would take anything.

His firm, sensuous lips parted slightly. Surprised, then. She would have been satisfied with that, but there was more: doubt, in the minute wrinkling of his brow; violence, in the clenching of his right hand, as if he wanted to materialize a sword.

Of course he doubted, she thought. He'd killed her, and because all demons could shape-shift, he assumed that someone intended to deceive him. She considered pinning him to the ground and stealing a kiss as she had so many times before, but the gruesome scene between them kept her where she was.

"Hello, Hugh."

If he'd been trying to convince himself that she was just a human with an uncanny resemblance to a demon he'd once known, she'd shattered that by knowing his name.

A muscle in his jaw flexed. His breathing had eased into a deep, even rhythm, and his eyes were cold. "You aren't worthy of that face. Shift into another."

His voice had deepened over the years. Lower, with a rough timbre. Pleasure rushed through her, tinged with delicious irony. "I can't."

The human form that she'd hidden from him for years was now the only one Hugh would see. It wouldn't be long before he deduced that she wasn't everything she had once been.

She sobered quickly. "No demon would take on this appearance, Hugh. Mine is not a popular visage Below."

He remained silent, returning her comment with a flat stare. Finally he looked away from her, and turned toward the macabre arrangement on the ground.

"Two nosferatu," she said. "Last night."

"No blood," he murmured, then glanced at her sharply. "Two?"

She nodded, thinking about the blood. If the ritual she knew had been performed, it would have been everywhere: coating the remains, soaked into the ground, congealed into puddles. "Together, in the northern end of the park." A grin flashed over her lips. "I killed them both."

"Good," he said softly.

She shrugged. "It was fun." Hearing a pair of bicycles along the path, she eased into a crouch.

His gaze slid down to her neck, and she knew he wouldn't miss the faint pink of healing skin at the front of her throat. His fingers clenched again. "You were hurt."

The concern and anger in his tone that he tried to hide, but couldn't, sent a thrill down her spine. She grinned. "I *knew* you still cared."

Humor lit his eyes, but it quickly faded and he stood in silence, watching her. He used the hem of his shirt to wipe the sweat from his face, revealing a tight, rippling abdomen and smooth golden skin above the low-slung waistband of his sweats.

"I thought you'd be fat," Lilith said, her gaze fixed on his stomach.

The corners of his lips twitched. "I thought I had slain you."

"You did. My father brought me back."

He frowned, his brows drawing together. He swallowed before he said, "I cut through your heart."

And it would have killed any other demon—Lilith had thought it would kill her, too. "Imagine my surprise as well. Perhaps it is one of the benefits of being Lucifer's creation, rather than one of his brethren—you ought to have removed my head." No amount of blood would have revived her if she couldn't drink it.

"I should have," he agreed.

Had he not bothered, assuming that the injury through her heart had been enough—or had he not been able to mutilate her form in that way? But she had no time to ask.

"There are two bicyclists coming. Get down or they'll see you."

He turned toward the path. "I need to ask them if they have a cell phone, and call the police."

Growling low in her throat to capture his attention, she darkened her skin to crimson, and curving horns sprouted from her head. She licked her lips with a forked tongue. "Get down, or I'll let them see me."

He barely spared her a glance. "You told me the same thing in Paris, after the revolution. You were bluffing then, and you are now."

If her skin hadn't been red, he might have seen the blush spreading across her cheeks. She hated recycling her tricks; being caught doing it was worse. Not that it was exactly the same—her threat in Paris had been intended to blackmail him into bed—but it had been a ruse he'd easily foiled by calling her on it.

But circumstances were different.

She stood. The bicyclists were still out of sight, past a deep curve in the path.

Hugh eyed her with amusement. Apparently, he thought she would drop to the ground at the penultimate moment. "Your wings will add authenticity."

"My suit is real." She grimaced, thinking of the holes her wings would tear in the fabric. Her charcoal three-piece pantsuit had been tailored to hide the bulge of her gun, and lay immaculately over her lanky form. "And my salary is pathetic. I don't want to buy another."

"Your salary?" He shook his head, as if to clear sudden cobwebs. "You have a job?"

"Everything has changed since you've Fallen." She took a deep breath. "Give me five minutes, Hugh. Then you can call the police. There's more going on here than just two nosferatu killing a human."

His brows rose. "No attempt to bargain? My time for yours?"

"Bargains don't have the same allure as they used to," she said. Feeling him waver, she added, "Please."

❦

He'd become soft, Hugh thought as he sank down onto his heels. A murder had been committed, he'd found a demon hovering over the kill, and he was letting her convince him to wait because she'd said "please."

That word alone should have shaken him out of the madness taking hold of him—this *couldn't* be Lilith. However, despite his painfully vivid memory of her death and his certainty that she'd never deigned to say "please" before, his instincts said she was who she appeared to be.

Her laughter, the wicked tilt to her eyebrows as she perused his body, the fluidity of her movements, and her habit of positioning herself so that she was ready for combat in an instant—

they told him the truth, impossible as it seemed. This was Lilith. A subdued version, perhaps, of the demon he'd killed sixteen years before, but another demon couldn't have imitated her so well. Their egos prevented them from completely disappearing into another personality.

And those Below might have known Lilith and he had shared a singular rivalry and planned to use their history against him, but they couldn't have known to choose the form she currently wore, nor realized its significance. Only Michael had been present the night she'd called for the Guardian to save him. Only Michael had known that Hugh had thought her an angel when she'd bent over him.

Her skin paled and the horns slid back into her skull; he regarded her steadily, conscious of the odor of death in the air and the ache of sudden inactivity settling into his leg muscles. She'd pulled her midnight hair into a high, tight queue, and the severe hairstyle emphasized the arch of her eyebrows, her Mediterranean-olive skin, and angular cheekbones.

He resisted the urge to reach out, to trace the beautiful line of her features with his fingertips and ascertain they were real.

Hugh had only seen that face once again, in Seattle. He didn't know why she'd chosen a human form to die in instead of her demonic one. Perhaps she'd hoped to inspire pity and mercy in those last moments? Or, considering her acute sense of fatalism and her flair for drama, maybe she'd simply thought it appropriate, bringing them full circle from that first night.

He rested his elbows on his knees and laced his fingers together instead. "Two minutes," he said.

Expecting her to triumph over his capitulation, he was surprised when she said without humor, "You need to walk away, and pretend you never saw me, or this." She gestured toward the massacred body with her head, but her gaze never left his face. Her irises were dark brown, almost indistinguishable from her pupils, and her expression grave.

He sighed. "You know I can't."

She sucked in a breath between clenched teeth and continued as if he hadn't spoken. "I will erase any evidence that you've been here." She glanced down; the ground was soft from the weeks of rain, and his shoes left clear impressions in the soil. "You'll remain outside the investigation, and anything that follows. Just walk away. Now."

He shifted to ease the stiffness developing in his legs, and her face brightened. She thought he was going to go, he realized. Shaking his head, he said, "I won't leave him here; nosferatu and demon influence over him ends now."

"He's dead." Her voice shook with frustration, and he wondered at her vehemence. "It's a corpse, not a human."

"If it weren't for the nosferatu, he still would be human," he said quietly. "Why does it matter if I'm the one who finds him?"

His question seemed to puncture the intensity he had sensed building within her; she exhaled deeply, closed her eyes and pinched the bridge of her nose, as if warding off a headache.

Momentarily taken aback by the gesture, Hugh stared at her. She'd never seemed so human as in that second; demons couldn't develop headaches, and yet she'd performed the movement as if it was familiar, natural.

Guardians kept their habitual gestures long after they'd been transformed. He tried to remember if she'd done it before, and couldn't; but there had been thousands of other actions, small and large, that had seemed as human. He'd always attributed them to her acting skill, and the length of time she'd been living with mankind—nothing about it felt artificial now.

He pushed his uneasy thoughts aside when she lowered her hand and glanced up at him with a wry smile. "You've always been a stubborn ass, Hugh. I hate free will."

Meaning that if she could, she would force him to leave—by carrying him away, most likely. When he'd been a Guardian, she might have tried; now, she was hampered by rules against interfering with a human's will.

She stood before he could respond. "My two minutes have passed," she said.

Surprised that she'd adhered to his time limit, he absurdly wished he'd taken her offer of five minutes. He hadn't learned more about the occupation she'd mentioned, or any of the changes she'd said had occurred.

He shouldn't *want* to know—he'd deliberately left all that behind.

She turned to go and hesitated. That should have warned him, but it wasn't until she looked back over her shoulder and he saw the mischievous gleam in her eyes that he realized her intent.

He didn't have time to make a decision, or protest. A

Guardian could compensate for a demon's speed; Hugh could not. Between one moment and the next, she was across the clearing, bending down and covering his mouth with hers.

Anticipating a forceful kiss, he began to resist, but his tension drained away when he felt the difference in her touch. She'd done this before, but never so gently. Her hands remained at her sides; with light pressure, she ran her tongue across his bottom lip. She exhaled softly in pleasure, and her breath filled his mouth with heat.

And he was the one who reached up, clasping her nape to pull her more tightly against him. Who sought her tongue with his, suddenly starving for the taste of her. *Lilith.* How did she affect him so deeply, and after so long? Could not time have dimmed this, too? But no, it was as fierce as ever; need for her burned through him—and he had no defense against it now.

He pulled away and fought for control, forced himself to recall where they were.

She watched him with dark eyes and a small, knowing smile. "You never let go."

He laughed, and it sounded harsh and bitter. "I have."

"I remember."

Silence fell between them. Finally, Lilith straightened. "Go away, Hugh. I killed the two nosferatu, but the city is overrun with them. Lucifer is involved—with the nosferatu, with this death—but I don't know how. I do know that your being here isn't an accident."

He waited, sensing that she wanted to say more. When she didn't, he said, "My decision to take a run this afternoon was an impulsive one, Lilith."

"I won't be able to convince you it wasn't a coincidence then." She sighed. Pausing, she looked away from him. Her nostrils flared delicately. "When was the last time you spoke with Colin? With this many nosferatu in the city, he must be in danger."

He frowned, wondering at her familiarity with the vampire. "Last evening."

Her body was rigid, her eyes alert as she skimmed the area surrounding them, but she sounded almost grateful as she said, "You are protecting him then?"

"No."

She glanced back at him. "Why not?"

At her admonishing tone, defensive anger slipped into his reply. "And how should I protect him? I have neither Guardian strength nor speed."

"You must be pleased to have such a compelling reason to shirk your duties." She backed up a step.

Her retreat when they'd just begun to argue jolted him out of his anger. She never ran from a fight with him; she might delay it to gain an advantage, but never leave in the middle of it. She was deliberately provoking him, but not for his sake.

She wanted someone—probably not human—to think all connection between them was gone, that everything but antipathy had vanished.

By all rights, it should have.

"This is nothing," he said, watching her expression closely. "Only sixteen years. I managed to shirk my duties for eight centuries by not killing you, and I had far less compelling reasons."

The corners of her mouth turned up, but no trace of humor tinged her voice as she spoke. "And, observe: I still live. Your restraint was for naught, as was slaying me." She scented the air again, took another step back. "You know, Hugh—the outside looks better than ever, but inside you've become a worthless, self-pitying wimp. What a fucking waste."

She stalked away, throwing over her shoulder, "Don't worry your pretty head about Colin; I'll protect him tonight."

And she was gone.

Hugh stared at the space where she'd been standing, his stomach heaving as if he'd been sucker-punched. Attempting to fight off the nausea by taking deep, cleansing breaths only filled his lungs with death and rot.

That she'd said it to deceive another didn't make it any less true.

No wonder she'd managed to convince so many men to kill themselves; she saw right into them, stabbed deep, and twisted.

CHAPTER 13

Lilith ran. She didn't know if the Guardians she'd sensed pursued her or stayed behind with Hugh, but she wasn't going to give them a chance to kill her. Not now.

Michael and one other. Selah, perhaps; Lilith didn't know her scent well enough to be certain.

Rushing through traffic, glancing off bumpers and rebounding with a few choice curses, she made it across the city to Fisherman's Wharf within minutes. The area was lousy with tourists; she'd be safe among them.

It was the second time in twenty-four hours that she'd had to flee for her life; normally, she'd have been upset by the repeated humiliation. Instead, she strolled through Pier 39, grinning like an idiot.

Their reunion had gone well, until she'd had to call Hugh a spineless worm.

A stiff breeze skimmed across the pier, carrying voices and a mixture of aromas. She singled out an oily, musky thread, and followed it to the northwest end of the dock. A crowd always gathered near the sea lions that sunned themselves on the boat docks. If she mingled long enough, she could determine whether the Guardians had followed her; if they had, the strong odor of the sea lions might mask her scent, and provide enough confusion to enable another escape.

She couldn't feel Michael or Selah now, but she hadn't expected to; Michael was particularly adept at blocking psychic probes, and Hugh had been Selah's mentor. He'd have taught her well.

Too well, she thought with a touch of self-disgust. Lilith hadn't known the Guardians were near until she'd scented them the usual way: with her nose. Until that moment, she'd been stupidly unaware of everything except Hugh; she'd been swimming in his flavor, intoxicated by the brief taste she'd had of him.

Her lips held the tang of sea and fish now, but she rubbed her tongue against the roof of her mouth, savoring the memory of their kiss, trying to recapture the sensation. She'd never before noticed that humans smelled and tasted *alive* in a way immortals could not; when Hugh had been a Guardian his body had been sterile. Today, she'd perceived the routine of life on his lips: the bitterness of coffee, the warmth of cinnamon toothpaste, the bite of pepper and tomato.

She'd decided she would kiss him again and soon. But first, she'd had to pretend—for the Guardians' sake—that her interest in him had vanished. If they knew how he affected her, they'd be at an advantage, and expect her to approach him again. It did not fit her plans to show up at Hugh's house only to find Michael and Selah waiting for her.

Better to let them think she found him revolting. Michael could easily look into Hugh's mind and find the same fear she had, and verify the reason behind her apparent disgust.

The number of people watching the sea lions had dwindled, so Lilith joined a group of retirees on their way to a restaurant. Conscious of her dark and formal suit amongst the plethora of pastel knit shirts and khaki shorts, she smiled brightly at a grandmother and inwardly cursed Lucifer. Once, she could have looked as matronly as any of them and shifted into different clothing with barely a thought.

With a short laugh, she forced her shame and embarrassment away; neither emotion was useful, and limited her as much as her missing powers did.

Strange, that someone like Hugh harbored doubts about his worth, but the fear had been real and lurking at the edge of his thoughts like a sharp-toothed eel. He had probably been able to feel its presence, but it would have slipped away if he attempted to see or name it. Her experience had allowed her to simply catch hold of it and drag it to the surface—but she'd been surprised when she'd felt the shape and heft of it.

She couldn't determine if the fear was recent, or if he'd managed to hide it when he'd been a Guardian. If it was new, then what had Hugh become in the past sixteen years to give him such doubts? Was it just a fear—or an unconscious acknowledgment of truth?

Either way, if—*when*—Lucifer decided it was time for Lilith to fulfill her bargain, she could easily manipulate it, make it grow and fester like a cancer.

Her stomach was heavy and throat tight when she broke away from the retirees and darted through the restaurant kitchen. She found the exit, joined a small party of teenagers leaving the pier, and waited with them for the bus. Squeezed in among tourists and commuters, she determinedly forced thoughts of Hugh from her mind.

Bad enough that Guardians might sense her vulnerability—disastrous if another demon did.

By the time she entered the federal building and passed through the security check, her psychic defenses were tight, impenetrable. Even so, she was almost relieved when her query at the front desk received the same response as earlier: SAC Smith was unavailable.

Smith might have the answers she sought, but he would wonder why she asked them—and, given incentive, he had power to look deeply enough to find Hugh.

But he wasn't the only source of information.

She entered the stairwell and ran up one flight. The Bureau was housed on the thirteenth floor of the building; Congressman Thomas Stafford's offices on the fourteenth. The foyer welcomed her with soothing cream and aquamarine; the receptionist, in a conservative blue dress, narrowed her eyes and frowned. The perfectly coiffed redhead clutched her purse in one hand. Must be quitting time, Lilith mused. Not much daylight left.

"Is he in?" Lilith smiled her widest smile as she strode toward the desk.

"I'm sorry, but our offices have closed for the evening."

Lilith kept on walking. "Too bad."

The receptionist's mouth fell open, and her free hand fluttered in the air. "You can't go back there!"

"Silence, twit," Lilith said pleasantly. It wasn't difficult to find his office; she simply headed toward the corner of the building with the best view of the city. The double mahogany doors were closed, but unlocked. She shoved them open, pushed them shut behind her and engaged the lock. "Hey, Tommy."

Behind his desk, Thomas Stafford sighed and shifted from a demon to a middle-aged human. "Must you be so obnoxious with my staff, Lilith?"

"She's new," Lilith said.

The congressman vanished his swords and relaxed back into his chair. Handsome, tanned, with graying sandy hair and a perpetually honest expression, he was the image of the perfect West Coast politician. "Not really. She's been here almost two years." Peering at her through lowered lids, he added, "I assume you aren't here to kill me."

"Not today," she agreed.

The beep of the intercom was followed by the twit's urgent voice. "Should I call building security, sir?"

Lilith could see that he considered it for a moment before responding. "No. Thank you, Lynne. Agent Milton is an old friend of mine."

A lie, but then, not *all* of Belial's demons were idiots.

Lilith laughed softly at his compliance, and dropped into the chair facing his desk. Her gaze roamed over the room, taking in the expensive furnishings, the plush green carpet and dark wood, and the United States and California flags hanging in the corner. "Your constituency has been kind to you."

"I've been kind to them. What do you want, Lilith?"

She leaned forward and picked up a grizzly bear paperweight from his desk. "There are nosferatu in the city—a lot of them. I want to know why."

"Ask Lucifer or Beelzebub."

Looking up from the ceramic animal, she pinned him with a stare, let her eyes glow crimson. "I'm asking you," she said coldly.

He spread his hands, palms up, the consummate politician. "Ease down, halfling. They started coming in about a month ago; they travel in pairs, so every demon's attempt to hunt them has failed. Every one of *my* liege's demons' attempts, that is."

Lilith frowned. "They won't kill Lucifer's?"

"I don't think Lucifer's demons are hunting them."

That matched what she'd been able to parse from Mondiel's cryptic outburst. "What of the Guardians?"

It was no surprise that the demons had been killed off; they fought singly, never trusting their brethren to watch their back. But Guardians would work together to rid the city of nosferatu if they could.

Not that they'd been very successful ridding it of demons— but demons couldn't kill humans, only tempt them to murder or suicide. Anything more would interfere with human free will. The nosferatu followed no such rules, making them an immediate danger.

"I'm hardly privy to Guardian intelligence, halfling," he said.

She snapped her teeth together in frustration. Really, this should be easier. Hopping onto his desk, she perched on the edge closest to him. To his credit, he didn't flinch. "This *halfling* ripped two bloodsuckers apart with her bare hands this morning. Want proof?" She waved the fingers of her sword hand under his nose. Despite numerous washings, the stink of the nosferatu's blood lingered on them; she'd smelled its nauseating odor all day. "Just imagine what I can do to you with this little bear here, particularly as you've been riding a desk for twenty years." She hefted the paperweight and bared her fangs with a smile. "Come on, Tommy. Give the halfling a break."

"You're *Lucifer's* halfling." Disgust filled his voice.

"I'm not the one who followed him in his rebellion, then put him on the throne Below."

She felt him relent; he pushed back his chair and wandered over to the window. "Last week, a contingent of thirty Guardians located a nosferatu nest. Only one or two made it back to Caelum's Gate."

Unbelievable. They must have been heavily outnumbered— and surprised—to endure such a loss. Could so many nosferatu exist in one place without the Guardians being aware of it? Or had the nosferatu been assisted by Lucifer's demons?

"Since then, we've heard reports that Michael is scouting the city alone, preparing another advance."

Michael wasn't alone in the city; there had been another

Guardian with him. Stafford's information was incorrect—or he was lying.

He was probably lying; she would have. No sense in giving an enemy accurate data—not that the exact numbers mattered. Even if Stafford exaggerated, and in fact only ten Guardians had been defeated, then Michael's next strike would have to include at least four or five times that many. How could he hope to bring in such a large group and remain undetected by humans?

And how had the nosferatu managed to hide? They didn't *need* to feed, but how had they managed to live amongst humans and control the bloodlust?

"I've looked over the missing persons reports and murder dockets for the past three months," Lilith said. "I couldn't find any activity that might be related to nosferatu, and no spike in frequency."

She didn't mention the body she'd found that morning; Hugh was too closely connected to that memory, and she didn't trust this demon any more than she did Smith.

Hopefully, that human had been the first. And the last.

"Vampires," the congressman said flatly. "The nosferatu have been hunting down their offspring and feeding from them. I've had several vampires come to me for help, but"—he spread his hands in a helpless gesture—"as one of Belial's, I can offer little protection."

Even if he hadn't been powerless, Lilith doubted he'd have helped the vampires. She pushed her rising concern for Colin aside; she had good psychic blocks, but she didn't want the congressman to suspect she might be worried about a vampire's well-being, nor let him know that she'd become friends with one.

There were some things demons just did not do, whether they followed Belial or Lucifer.

Outside the office window, the sun descended slowly toward the horizon. Sensing that Stafford had nothing more to tell her, she slipped off the desk and landed silently on the carpet. "Thank you, Congressman. You've been helpful."

His deep chuckle made her look back over her shoulder. "If platitudes such as those fall so easily from your mouth, you've spent far too much time amongst the humans."

She gave him an assessing glance. His current form fit him comfortably. "As have you."

"Perhaps. Earth is preferable to your father's kingdom." His humor faded. "Join us, Lilith. You would be welcome on Belial's side. Once he takes the throne, he promises to restore us to His Grace."

She arched a brow, her cynicism obvious. If Belial won, did Stafford honestly believe the demon lord would relinquish the power he'd spent centuries securing? "Thanks for the offer," she said. "But I'll take my chances with the devil I know."

❧

The activity around the crime scene had settled into a slow, methodical rhythm. Uniformed officers milled around the perimeter, just outside the yellow tape that cordoned off a section of the path and a hundred foot circumference around the body. Floodlights had been set up to illuminate the area, and a team of officers walked in ever-widening circles, searching for evidence with flashlights in hand. Within the tape, Detectives Preston and Taylor consulted with the medical examiner, and a pale-faced photographer recorded the scene on film.

From his seat atop a picnic table thirty feet away, the strobe of the flash left afterimages on Hugh's vision. He couldn't see the body on the ground, but didn't need to; it was impossible to forget.

A uniformed officer had already taken his information and initial statement, along with the woman's whose phone he'd used. She had been sent home an hour earlier, but Detective Taylor had asked Hugh to wait until she or Preston could collect a full recounting of his discovery of the corpse.

How had she managed to fight *two* nosferatu? The few times they'd worked together in the past had been while hunting the creatures; even with their combined skills against one nosferatu, they'd rarely emerged unscathed.

She'd been lucky not to have been torn apart.

Lilith. He bent his head, ran his hands through his hair. Hard not to smile, knowing she was alive, but it was a pleasure dulled by dread: Lucifer did not give second chances. He did not *give* anything, but made his subjects pay for them with his favorite currency: pain.

What had Lilith's price been?

A shout from the team sweeping the outlying vegetation drew his attention. Preston ducked his round bulk under the tape and jogged heavily toward them; he'd taken off his jacket, and the dull glow of his white shirt allowed Hugh to track his progress outside the reach of the floodlights.

"The nosferatu placed his clothing and possessions beside a fallen log. The searchers just found them," Michael said from behind him.

Though the voice was familiar, Hugh froze and had to stifle his impulse to leap into a defensive posture. The day's exciting moments were becoming less and less welcome.

Michael walked around the side of the table and sat down, the wood creaking under his weight. He wore a crisp EMT uniform, but the short black hair and bronze skin were his own.

"You're cold," Michael observed.

Hugh glanced down at his bare arms, and fought the rage that began rising in his gut. Cold, hungry, tired—and alive. "Are there any nosferatu here?"

"No. Only their scent on the body and the surroundings." Michael watched him for a long moment. "The symbols allow the nosferatu to call for power, for a transformation."

Hugh nodded, but couldn't speak. A terrible pattern began to fall into place.

Why had he never seen it before?

Though Michael didn't appear to move, a woolen blanket settled on Hugh's shoulders.

Hugh pulled it securely around his chest, gathering the edges together in his fisted hand as if containing himself within the coarse fabric.

Michael's corroboration of the nosferatu's involvement should have relieved him. He'd been wondering for the past two hours if she'd been lying to him, and he hadn't been able to read the truth. He had been wondering if she'd tempted someone into performing that ritual. Had been wondering if he'd let his memories of her cloud his judgment.

Instead of relief, a new concern rose: if Lilith had been telling the truth about the nosferatu, then this probably wouldn't be the only death to result from their presence.

"If you aren't protecting them, then these men don't need your assistance." They needed Michael to slay the nosferatu left in the city, needed him to prevent further rituals.

"You do."

With a hollow laugh, Hugh drew the blanket tighter and nodded toward the clearing. "So did he."

"You are not in danger from the nosferatu."

"But I am from Lilith?" Hugh guessed and shook his head. Lilith was many things, but unlike the nosferatu she wasn't a murderer.

And he knew her tricks too well to fall prey to them.

"From Lucifer," Michael said, leaning forward to rest his forearms on his thighs. "Using this death and the humans' laws against you. He has more influence than ever. His demons have infiltrated the government and social systems in this and many other nations."

It was a different kind of power than Lucifer had previously wielded then. He'd always had indirect influence, using his demons to tempt humans to act in certain ways; putting his demons in positions of authority was a bold move and a cunning one.

"And Lilith?"

"FBI. Lucifer has her under Beelzebub's supervision."

Hugh gave a brief laugh. Trying to control Lilith would be a monumental task. "Why would Lucifer go to such lengths?"

"For you? I don't know. I can't see his entire plan yet." Michael raised his face to the heavens, and smiled grimly. "There was an Ascension."

Ascension—the opposite of a Fall for a Guardian. Instead of reversing the transformation and returning to Earth to live out the remainder of his life, a Guardian could choose to meet whatever fate the afterlife had to offer him. "How many?"

"All but seventy. And I lost half of them against the nosferatu."

Hugh stared at the ground, at the scatter of leaves and dirt. When he'd Fallen, there'd been thousands. That an Ascension had occurred didn't surprise him; immortality did not sit easily. Though an individual could make the choice at any time, occasionally a fervor would sweep through the corps, and many would go together. He'd witnessed two Ascensions during his time in Caelum, but each had only been a group of a few hundred.

"So many?"

Michael glanced at him. "You were an inspiration; they agreed that this is an age that does not need the influence of Above and Below."

A hard laugh escaped him. "Did they misunderstand me so badly? A fine teacher I was." Better for humans to make their own way—and better were there no demons to tempt them; but as long as there were demons, there *had* to be Guardians to check them. If one Fell after losing faith, or five hundred Ascended to show theirs—it mattered little. But to destroy the corps when Lucifer still held power?

"If it is any consolation, the majority of those who stayed were your students. And there were a few others who were on assignment on Earth." Michael shook his head. "It was inevitable; there were too many, and not enough were active. Lucifer's methods had changed, made him less visible—the danger was not so apparent or immediate." A wry smile pulled at his mouth. "I knew it was coming, though I'll admit I did not think it would be so many."

"What will you do?"

"Fight. There is little else to be done."

There was no blame in Michael's tone, nor disapproval, but Hugh felt the cold, heavy weight of his Fall settle in his stomach, banking the fury that had burned there.

But Michael was shaking his head. "It is better that you are human. If it ends, if they destroy the corps and slaughter the vampires, there will be no one who knows the truth—except for you."

A burden Hugh would rather not bear.

He rubbed his forehead with his free hand and thought of the other responsibilities he'd shunned. One, at least, he could make amends for immediately. Michael could offer protection that Hugh could not.

"The vampire Colin Ames-Beaumont could assist your cause."

The table trembled under the force of Michael's silent laughter. Hugh grinned a little as well, and added, "He is proficient with his sword."

After another bout of laughter, Michael managed to say, "Selah is on her way to his residence. When you spoke with her, Lilith indicated her intention to see him."

Hugh's humor vanished. He let the blanket fall from his shoulders, stood, and began pacing in long angry strides away from the table. Finally he turned and faced the Guardian. "You'll not kill her."

Michael regarded him carefully. "A strange command, given the source."

"Perhaps," Hugh said, his throat rough. "But you'll not kill her."

"No," Michael said, and gracefully rose from his seat. "I won't. If I didn't in the thousand years after her transformation and before yours, I see no reason to do so now."

Her transformation? Hugh frowned, but had no time to question the Guardian. Michael abruptly turned and walked toward one of the waiting ambulances and disappeared into the back of the vehicle.

"Dr. Castleford?"

Hugh turned. Detective Taylor had spoken his name, but her gaze slid past him. Toward the ambulance, Hugh realized. After a moment, her attention returned to him. "Did he speak to you?"

"He brought me a blanket," Hugh said.

He could see she wasn't satisfied, but she didn't pursue a more direct answer. Instead, she held out a small, clear evidence bag. "We found an identification card from San Francisco State. We cannot determine if it belongs to the body, of course, until forensics identifies the remains. Do you recognize this student?"

Hugh knew it was the victim's; Michael had told him. He looked blindly at the small rectangle of plastic, letting the picture and letters blur. Cowardly not to focus, but he didn't want to know.

"Dr. Castleford?"

He blinked, and drew in a ragged breath. "Ian is one of my students."

Taylor's mouth hardened into a thin line. "When was the last time you saw Mr. Rafferty?"

"A month ago," he said, and forced the next words out. "At Auntie's."

"Playing DemonSlayer," she said, her voice flat. "A game based on your book."

"Yes."

She lowered the evidence bag. "I'd like you to come to the station for an interview, Dr. Castleford. If it's convenient."

"It is," he lied, and knew it was the first of many.

CHAPTER 14

Night had fallen by the time Lilith got off the train in Richmond. Slipping into an alley, she stripped off her shirt and jacket and vanished them. The skin on her back rippled as her wings materialized; she sighed in pleasure and took to the sky.

A three-quarter moon rose behind her, slinging a dancing path of silver light across the bay. Each powerful beat of her wings made her feel strong, invincible. She gained altitude and speed, her hair tangling behind her. The wind stung tears from her eyes—the only kind of tears she'd shed in two thousand years.

How could Hugh have traded this kind of freedom for a life on the ground? He could have given hers without losing his own.

Using Alcatraz to orient her approach to the city, she flew into Golden Gate Park and found a secluded area in which to dress. If the Guardians had managed to follow her from the federal building, and during her underground trip around the Bay Area, they would attack her now.

Minutes passed without her sensing anything out of the ordinary. Torn between relief and disappointment—she didn't want to die, but a fight would have been enjoyable—she walked out of the park, and caught the first bus that would take her south. She'd run enough for the day.

The bus was almost empty. She chose a seat in the back and growled softly until the only nearby passenger, a teenager strung out on meth, freaked out. The driver kicked him off at the next stop, and Lilith was able to call Colin in relative privacy.

He answered on the first ring. The loud, jingly tones of a TV game show played in the background as he said, "Agent Milton, my dear, I'm going to murder you."

She grinned. He'd been a member of the British aristocracy as a human and hadn't let go of his accent; every threat of violence that rolled off his tongue sounded like an invitation to tea. "How's my puppy?"

"He . . . they . . . *it* is fantastic. Eating everything in sight. And last week, it killed and ate two nosferatu who were intent upon ruining my rather spectacular visage. Which, I confess, makes up for the outrageous expense of feeding it for the last six months." His voice lowered. "And I believe it is keeping my new visitors away as well."

Lilith sank back into her seat and closed her eyes in relief. She'd deliberately left the Guardians with the impression that she'd go to Colin's house that night. The vampire's cryptic response confirmed that at least one waited outside—combined with Sir Pup's protection, Colin would probably be safe. "The nosferatu won't risk coming after you with hellhound and Guardian stench everywhere. Especially if it's Michael's stench."

They fell silent, and she heard a car salesman screaming about finance charges. The high volume on the television wouldn't keep the Guardians from hearing his part of the conversation, but it might mask hers.

She waited until the game show resumed before speaking again. "Do you have your weapon?"

"Next to me."

"If anyone but me knocks at your door, use it." Pausing, she reconsidered. After their confrontation in the park, Hugh might seek out the vampire. "Unless it is He-Who-Shall-Not-Be-Named."

"Voldemort?"

She envisioned his smirk, and wondered how he'd managed to make it through two centuries on a steady diet of pop culture and little else. "The other one."

"Does this mean the ban is lifted, and I can finally talk about him?"

Oh, how she'd love smacking him around for the amusement in that question. "Yes."

"Why now?"

Lowering her voice to a whisper, she admitted, "I need you to tell me his name." She could use her computer to look up Hugh's address, but she didn't know his surname, or even if he still used "Hugh."

She had to yank the phone away from her ear when he shouted with laughter. What had ever possessed her to become friends with a vampire? Particularly this one. "I swear, Colin, the only reason I only tolerate you is because you're extremely handsome."

That quieted him. "Oh?"

Ah, Vanity. Thy name is Colin Ames-Beaumont. "That's all you're going to get until you give me what I want."

She easily imagined his grin as he said, "Christian name is the same. Family name is a stony demesne, often of the motte and bailey variety, and a dead automobile manufacturer with a first name not unlike an English king who liked to behead his wives."

Hugh Castleford. "Thank you, Colin."

"I'm glad you've returned."

She stared up at the bus's ceiling, trying not to feel uncomfortable. They'd been friends for a decade, but she still wasn't accustomed to someone caring about her. "I'll see you later this evening," she managed. "Don't die between now and then. Unless my dog is hurt or unhappy—then you'd better wish for death before I get there, because I'll kill you slowly and painfully."

"Don't ring off," he said quickly. "You promised more. Give me a *lot* more and I'll tell you the name of the woman not-Voldemort is living with."

Her gut twisted. "I could strangle it out of you."

"Through the cell phone?"

Rolling her eyes, she quoted, " 'The world is changed because you are made of ivory and gold. The curves of your lips rewrite history. . . .' "

And decided to strangle him later.

❧

The windshield wipers swished out a soothing rhythm, and unintelligible codes crackled from the police radio at regular intervals.

Hugh scrubbed his hand over his face as they neared his house, trying to fight the queasiness that riding in a moving vehicle always gave him. He didn't have a watch, but he thought it must have been nearing midnight—the interview had not been long, but the waiting had been. Taylor and Preston had not wanted to let him go, but had no reason to keep him—sending him home with the uniformed officers had not been an act of kindness, however. Hugh was certain that they'd be watching his house after they'd dropped him off.

A few minutes later, he stood at his front door and smiled grimly as the cruiser pulled out of his driveway and parked next to the curb. They were in for a long, boring night—but they were welcome to try to follow him when he went for his morning run.

Inside, he toed off his shoes and shrugged out of his damp T-shirt, balling it up and tossing it in the direction of the door to the garage and the laundry. The upstairs windows had been dark; Savi was either asleep or out. Considering the hours she and her friends kept, probably out. She was going to be upset that he hadn't called her from the station, but she would likely be involved soon enough, as the detectives verified the story he'd given them.

And Hugh hadn't wanted to give her news of Ian's death in those surroundings.

Anger and grief welled up again, but he tamped them down. They served no purpose; better that he channel them into action. And for once, the gym he kept had no appeal.

He'd thrown Colin's number and address into the garbage by his bed. He strode soundlessly through the darkened house, shaking off the last of his nausea. Once he'd met with Lilith, had seen the body, his decision to avoid the vampire had seemed ridiculous. If not for the trip to the police station, Hugh'd have met with him. And now, it did not seem so terrible to ally himself with someone who might know something about the nosferatu, and why they had begun ritualistically killing humans.

He sat on his bed, and reached down to pick up the slip of

paper from the bin. Lilith would have known more, but he
didn't trust himself around her. Not that he knew where to find
her. Michael had said FBI; perhaps Savi could—

His skin prickled. His hand stilled, and he looked up, into
the opposite corner of the room.

Clinging to the ceiling, Lilith stared back at him, her eyes
glowing in the darkness.

"Should I get my sword?" he asked softly and switched on
the lamp.

"That depends on what you plan to do with it. I prefer my
heart intact."

She dropped to the floor. Her human form had vanished beneath the crimson skin and black wings, claws and fangs. He
studied her, wondering how much of this was truly her, and how
much of her was the form she'd worn earlier.

She had clothes on—not the suit from earlier, but an updated
version of the tight leather breeches and corset she'd begun
wearing in the mid-eighteenth century. Black boots ended at her
knee. She did not wear the clothing out of modesty; they
molded to her curves so well they left little to the imagination.
Nor did she seem to intend them to titillate. Her heels were low,
and her shoulders squared in a strong, rather than seductive,
posture.

Perhaps she wore them as a defense? Suddenly aware of his
own half-dressed state, he had the urge to find a shirt, to put
even a flimsy barrier between them.

But she would take advantage of such a telling gesture, and
so he remained where he was.

His gaze lit on her bare arms, the upper slope of her breasts.
"Vanish your clothing."

Her eyes widened. He'd surprised her, but only for a moment. She quickly recovered and said, laughing, "Oh, I do like
you better when you are human." She leaned against his teak
dresser, and with an easy push from the heels of her hands,
lifted herself onto the dark surface. "I'm surprised they took
you down for questioning. It should have been a simple matter
of taking your information down and conducting a preliminary
interview, then calling on you later to follow up."

"I knew him."

Her smile faded at his quiet announcement. The red glow
left her eyes.

Standing, he said, "He was my student." Her fingers clenched on the dresser's edge, but she didn't move as he approached. "His name was Ian, and he was nineteen years old. I saw his best friend this morning; tomorrow, I'll be telling another group of his friends that he's dead. But I won't be able to tell them how or why. Do you know?"

She shook her head, her bottom lip pressed between her teeth.

Disappointment twisted in his stomach. Why had he thought she'd tell him the truth? "I'm not as adverse to lying as I once was, which is for the best. For I won't be able to tell my students or the detectives that I *have* seen something like what had been done to him before. Not the ritual, but the script that was used. But it wasn't in Caelum, where I might have expected to see it. The Scrolls there are in a human language. Latin," he added when curiosity flared across her expression.

Then she stiffened, as if in realization. "Where?"

"Here." With the pad of his thumb, he traced a curling pattern on her right shoulder. Her skin was red, without blemish, but he could easily recall how pale it had been, washed clean by the rain. His hands had left bloody prints; he'd wiped them away with his robe, but he hadn't been able to erase the markings that had patterned her torso like vermillion tattoos—they'd remained indelible on his memory, as well. "And here." A series of chevrons and dashes, from the hollow of her throat to the edge of the corset. He pressed his palm between her breasts, felt the heat of her body through the tight bodice. "And here, though different from Ian's, a design that—"

She caught his wrist. "Stop."

For a moment, he could scarcely breathe. There had been more—many more. Carved into Ian's body, and, sixteen years ago, echoed in her lifeless one.

"I should thank you for killing them," he said hoarsely. "But I'd rather have them alive to answer the questions I cannot."

Her eyes searched his. "And once they gave answers? What could you do then?"

"*Then* I'd kill them." He pulled away from her grip; she opened her mouth and then closed it, her lips curving slightly. Releasing a long breath, he walked to the window and pulled the drapes back. The cruiser still waited by the curb. "I didn't misunderstand you; I know what you meant. Even if I received answers, I'm the only one who could believe them. And giving the truth to the detectives would only increase their suspicions."

The pane was cool against his forehead. Foolish of him to turn his back on her, but he needed a moment to gather his thoughts, to push aside the emotions that threatened to overcome reason.

She didn't give him the opportunity.

"And this is why you want to get me out of my clothes? To see if you can find answers beneath the glamours? Will you parade me naked through the police station as your defense?"

"Perhaps." He smiled, and turned to find her standing beside him, her hip against the sill, arms crossed beneath her breasts. "Though I'm less concerned with defense than protecting those connected to me. You may have slain two, but there are more—and I want to know: Why Ian? Coincidence? I have difficulty believing that."

"That has always been one of your greatest faults: your difficulty believing anything," she replied evenly.

"Yours is accepting too readily, because it is easier to live with than the alternative."

Grinning, she said, "And will you destroy me for it this time?"

He couldn't bring himself to see humor in it. "No."

She tilted her head, studying his face. Could she read him? Psychic blocks took practice and concentration—and though it was uncommon for humans, who didn't recognize the need to have strong mental defenses, it wasn't impossible.

Her brows arched, her eyes glittered with amusement. "Ah, yes; it's no longer your job to kill me."

If she thought that was his reason, she could not read him at all.

Leaving her by the window, he gathered a shirt and jeans from the walk-in closet and used the relative privacy to strip off his sweats. Was Savi upstairs? If she heard them talking, she wouldn't interrupt; but if she thought he'd returned alone she might come down.

"How long have you been waiting here?" He'd fastened his jeans and was shrugging into the shirt when she swung the door wide. Her gaze roamed over the neat—if sparse—piles of clothing on the shelves, finally coming to rest on him.

"Almost two hours." She watched his fingers as they worked

their way up the buttons. "I spent most of it looking through your housemate's things. You aren't lovers?"

"I prefer not to seduce children." Not that, at twenty-five, Savi could be considered a child. She would have been furious had she known he often thought of her that way.

"I remember one young woman you wanted very badly. Granted, it wasn't so unusual then, but she was still a child."

He lifted a brow.

"Isabel?" she prompted.

"I was two years older than she was, not eight hundred." A slow grin spread over his lips. "And I haven't thought of her as anything other than 'the countess' or 'the lady' since my transformation. I didn't remember her Christian name," he said. "Interesting that you did."

For an infinitesimal moment, she seemed nonplussed. Then she returned with a lazy smile of her own: "Your sense of humor has obviously been restored now that you're human, for you surely jest; I don't believe for a second that you've forgotten my brilliant mimicry in the castle stairwell."

No. But he was not likely to tell her the only reason Isabel's face—if not her name—had remained so clearly in his memory was not because of his youthful infatuation with the lady, but because Lilith had once inhabited her form. Even his shame upon mistaking the countess for Lilith upon that wall walk had faded; but every moment with the demon, and every emotion she had aroused, remained all too clear.

"And whose form did you mimic this afternoon?" he asked. "Do you no longer fear Lucifer, or does he no longer forbid beauty?"

She shrugged lightly, but he saw the flicker of shame in her expression before she covered it with irony. "It is a punishment."

Uncertain how to interpret her statement and sensing she would not volunteer to clarify it, he murmured, "Aye. Mine." He cupped her chin in his palm, felt the heat of her throat, the beat of her pulse. Beneath the obsidian horns and crimson skin, he could see the same features she'd worn in her human form. The bone structure was the same, the line of her nose, the shape of her eyes. "I can only hope it is a short-lived tyranny."

She pulled in a sharp breath as he released her. Intent on putting space between them, he began to brush past her, but she stopped him with a hand on his forearm.

"I'm going to kiss you before I leave tonight," she said. Focusing on his lips, she moistened her own. "I'm feeling generous, so I thought I would warn you."

The wicked slant of her brows told him it was not generosity at all, but an attempt to unsettle him.

It worked. His muscles tightened in anticipation, and he was swamped by memories of other kisses, stolen and bargained. Of the hot press of her mouth. Of the sounds she made when playfulness became passion—and ultimately, frustration.

He'd held himself distant when he'd been a Guardian, but his indifference had been dishonest. And though a part of him wished to thwart her by initiating the kiss now, he did not trust himself to keep it a purely defensive maneuver.

Shaking off her hand, he strode to the nightstand, swept up Colin's number and headed for the living room. And tried not to acknowledge the part of him that wanted to kiss her—not to undermine her ploy, but for the pleasure of it.

CHAPTER 15

The world was a better place when Hugh bent over in those jeans. She stifled her disappointed sigh when he straightened and walked toward the door. "Running scared?"

He cast a rueful glance over his shoulder as he left the room. "Yes."

She grinned, following him. It wasn't fear in the rigid line of his shoulders, the slight stiffness in his tread.

He was aroused—and resisting it.

The narrowness of the hallway forced her to fold her wings tightly to her back or risk scraping the paint from the walls. She hadn't spent much time in this part of his home, preferring to investigate the girl's—Savitri's—apartment instead. It had been an explosion of metal and plastic; computers and electronics, many of them half-assembled, had littered every available surface. A geek's paradise.

Lilith hadn't cared for it, but the DemonSlayer paraphernalia she'd found in one room had fascinated her. Sketches, games, cards—she'd vaguely known about the video game, but had never paid attention to the details of its storyline. Wouldn't have this time, either, but the connection between Hugh and the girl led her to take a closer look. To her surprise—though much of it inaccurately represented demonkind—it contained just enough truth in the relationship between nosferatu, demons, and halflings to make Lilith wonder.

Had he told Savitri the truth? How deep did the trust between them run? And, given the girl's age, why? Theirs wasn't a lovers' bond.

The soft, rhythmic pad of his bare feet against the dark hardwood floors was muffled as he entered the living room and stepped onto the thick rug at its center. Unlike the mess upstairs, everything here was uncluttered, minimalist. She would have thought it sterile, if not for the colors. Bright jewel tones and dark woods warmed the room: a rich blue sofa, a supple leather ottoman in chocolate brown, gold paint on the walls. Behind her, the kitchen boasted more wood, stainless steel, and a deep, luxurious red.

Apparently, he abhorred white.

He picked up a remote control, and she snorted in surprise. Did he intend to sit down and watch football next? "You've become quite the domestic, haven't you?"

A smile played around his mouth. "I can even program a VCR."

She couldn't. Suddenly feeling out of place in her demonic guise, she turned toward the bookshelves and forced herself to ignore the heavy settling of her stomach. "At least you still read," she muttered. She glanced at a title and rolled her eyes. *"The American Ideal: Literary History as a Worldly Activity?"*

"Too domestic?" he asked, and she heard the amusement in his voice. He knew she was uncomfortable, and he was enjoying it.

She could return the favor. Running her hand along a row of books, she said, "I think it'll be a soft kiss, at first. I won't touch you anywhere but your mouth. Fangs or no fangs?"

He grinned. "No fangs, please."

She nodded solemnly. "I'll keep the horns, though. They make wonderful handholds. When you are overcome with desire, you can pull me closer with them."

The television illuminated his features with a soft blue light; his lips were pressed tightly together, and he shook with silent laughter.

"I'll be certain to remember that," he finally said.

"It wouldn't be gentle for long, would it?" she mused. "It never is with us. I'd have to touch you. I didn't force you when you were human before, but perhaps I would now. Do you remember the temple and Mandeville?" Her voice deepened, deliberately sensuous. "Would be simple to do the same to you—but I would not leave you waiting for more. I'd wrap my hands around you, stroke you until you begged. Taste you until you were weak. Ride you until you could no longer stand."

He drew in a ragged breath, as if the air around him had thickened. Only with effort could she keep herself from betraying a similar arousal; the images her words conjured gathered like liquid fire beneath her belly.

His throat worked, but she anticipated his response. "It would be free will, Hugh. You already want it." She slid the flat of her palm up a book spine, imagined the hardness and heat of his erection. The rigid shaft strained against its denim confines; the racing of his pulse matched hers.

Unable to resist, she approached him, ran her fingers down the front of his shirt. He stopped breathing. The flesh under his clothing was taut, hard. She wanted to rip it away, smooth her hands over the skin beneath. Run her tongue over the ridges of muscle in his chest and abdomen, licking and tasting. She settled for flattening her palm against his pectoral, relishing the tension she could feel coursing through him, the beating of his heart.

He caught her wrist as she began to slide down to his stomach, lower. Immediately releasing her, he pinched the bridge of his nose as if to steady himself, then let his hand drop to his side. He looked at her without expression. "I'll oblige you then. Vanish your clothing, lie down on the sofa and spread your legs."

Her mouth fell open. "What?"

"I'll admit, I want to fuck you. So we will fuck." His hands went to his waistband, and he began to unbutton his fly.

As if mesmerized, she stared at his fingers as they worked at the fastenings. The tails of his shirt covered him, but the movement of his hands allowed her glimpses of white cotton briefs stretched tight by his cock. She swallowed and glanced at the sofa.

Did he really mean for her to do as he'd commanded? The *way* he'd commanded it?

Despite the hardness etched across his features, his control, she could feel his heart pounding, smell the perspiration tinged by sexual arousal—but also by unease and determination.

He desired her, would fuck her if she complied with his demand . . . but he didn't want it now, not like that.

She didn't either.

"You win," she conceded wryly and held up her hands as if in surrender.

His expression did not immediately warm, as she'd expected it to. The intensity of his cold blue stare held her frozen. The he slowly blinked, releasing her. His hands trembled as he refastened his jeans.

"I'm sorry," he said. "That was . . . unfair."

Something in her chest squeezed painfully, but she shrugged and said, "I'll admit you surprised me: I've never heard you swear before. It was wonderfully vulgar."

A reluctant smile pulled at his mouth. "Compared to my students, I'm not very proficient."

She would have laughed but for the change that came over him: his shoulders slumped, and he ran his hands through his hair in helpless frustration. It had been the mention of his students, she realized; he grieved for one now. Wondered if he'd brought death to the boy just by knowing him.

"Are these the nosferatu you killed this morning?"

She turned to face the television and frowned. "What is this? When is this?"

"They burned Polidori's. Three nights ago." He glanced at her curiously. "You didn't know?"

"I've been out of town," she said, leaning in to examine the nosferatu on the television screen. He likely wanted to put faces to the creatures who had killed his student. "These are not the same."

"Damn," he said softly, and she smiled.

"I must be a terrible influence."

She felt his gaze on her. "You are." The words held no sting, though, as if he'd said them by rote, his mind occupied by weightier problems. "Lilith, the designs on your skin . . . did the nosferatu—"

"No." She couldn't look at him. "My father did."

"Why? What purpose have they?" He tilted her chin with his

fingers, brushed his thumb over her bottom lip. His eyes were troubled; for her sake or Ian Rafferty's, she didn't know. "As punishment?"

"For power." She smiled bitterly.

"Whose?"

She closed her eyes. "I don't know. Your student's were different. Not much, but enough to convert the ritual into something beyond my ken."

Tension suddenly radiated from his body. "Have you done this to a human?"

Wanting to laugh but unable, she shook her head. "No. I tried, once."

She saw the realization on his face, the memory. "To me, in the ruins of the temple. But you told Michael to take me instead." He swallowed thickly. "What would it have done?"

He knew; she saw it in his eyes. Her throat was tight. "Guardians and vampires are not the only halflings," she said, barely above a whisper.

"Nay," he breathed. A low moan sounded from his chest, a tortured denial. "Lilith—"

"Do *not* pity me," she said stonily. "I made a choice."

"To be this?" His voice was harsh as he wrapped his hands around her horns, forcing her to look at him.

"I didn't want to die." She ripped out of his grip; his strength was no match for hers. But she did not have the strength to turn away from him. "And this is what I am now, what I have been for two thousand years. This is my role," she said with finality.

A war seemed to rage within him for a few breathless moments. She knew he wanted to argue, to question—to convince her she was wrong. He'd always done so, and sixteen years couldn't erase the custom of eight hundred.

"Do you think Ian had to make a similar choice?"

She released the breath she'd been holding. It was not a permanent reprieve; he would consider her revelation, examine it in context of his memories before bringing it up again. "I can't say, Hugh. The involvement of the nosferatu . . ." She trailed off, knowing she wouldn't need to explain.

He hesitated, and then said, "Another of my students is missing. Javier Sanchez. If it's related to the nosferatu, the detectives are outclassed. *I* am outclassed."

Shaken, she stared at him. He trusted her to help protect the young man? And more unbelievable: "Do you intend to fight them?"

"I'll find a way," he said, his blue gaze level and determined. A half-smile creased the sides of his mouth when she continued to gape at him. "Do you think I'm going to descend upon their nest with sword in hand?"

Finally recovering her wits, she said, "You really must do something about your imbecilic martyr complex."

His deep laugh rumbled through her. As if drawn by the sound, a seal-tipped Siamese cat strolled in from the kitchen, glanced at Lilith and just as effortlessly dismissed her, rubbing her long feline body against Hugh's legs. With the ease of familiarity, he scooped up the cat, nestled her against his chest and began stroking beneath her chin. The tendons in his forearm flexed with the movement, drawing Lilith's gaze to the taut muscle.

"You may be in excellent shape for a human, but you're no match for the nosferatu."

His brows drew together. "Of course not."

"The Guardians—"

"Michael did not know Ian," he said quietly, but she felt the force of his anger and frustration. "I don't intend to rid the world of nosferatu, only try to help those who have been targeted because of *what I used to be*." He breathed deeply, as if to calm himself, then added with a wry smile, "I'll leave the slaughtering to those who are more able."

Like her. She absently rubbed the column of her neck, remembering how close her last encounter with the bloodsuckers had been. The next would probably not go any better. "Lucifer has told his demons to let the nosferatu be."

His hand stilled on the cat's fur. "You killed two this morning."

"I don't dare again," she said. "I've hunted enough rogues to learn I should avoid becoming one."

"I would not ask you to take that risk."

She could not read his expression, but she felt his withdrawal, his disappointment. He didn't attempt to convince her to help, to appeal to her humanity; in the past, he would have. His easy acceptance that she wouldn't—couldn't—destroy the nosferatu shouldn't have shamed her, but a dark ache bloomed in her chest.

She needed to go, before it could become something painful. She'd come in through an upstairs window—she'd leave the same way.

"Lilith."

Pausing, she turned.

"You didn't carry out your promise." His eyes searched hers. "I assumed that was your purpose for coming here, yet you've forgotten it."

She gave a short laugh, though her heart tripped unsteadily beneath her breast. "Are you *asking* me to kiss you?"

"I want to know why you are really here."

Sighing, she closed her eyes. "Lucifer hasn't included me in this alliance with the nosferatu. I'm certain he has other plans for me."

His sudden tension broke through his psychic blocks, filling the room. That some of it was tinged with worry for her nearly undid her. "What plans?"

She swallowed past the tightness in her throat, finally looked at him. "We made a bargain in Seattle. A life for a life."

Hugh flinched as if struck; the cat hissed and leapt from his arms. His face pale, he unclenched his hands and stated, "Mine for yours. He brought you back to life on the condition that you would take mine."

She nodded.

"A bargain made after I killed you." His voice was stiff. "It's fair."

Blinking, unsure she'd heard correctly, she echoed, "It's fair?" Rage built, made her voice shake. "What you did to me was . . . it was *right*. It fit, it was the way it should have ended between us. And he hasn't called in his part of the bargain yet, but he will soon. The next time I see you, it will be with the goal of tearing you down, tearing your soul apart until you can't live with yourself and you take your own life. And it's *fair*?"

"When did you become concerned with fairness?" She had been shouting, but his soft reply rang in her ears. Amusement crinkled the corners of his eyes.

Her mouth snapped closed. She shouldn't be. With anyone else, she wouldn't be.

He sighed, and his smile faded. "You won't be able to break me."

His certainty should have offended her, but it was despair

she felt instead. "Do you think I cannot find the darkest part of you and—"

"No, Lilith. I've no doubt of your skill, nor do I think you are too weak."

Her lips pressed together, and she blinked away the sudden sting in her eyes. *Now* he looked for goodness in her, the humanity, when there was little—if any—left. Because she couldn't do the ritual, and transform him into a demon, he thought she would not carry this through either.

She didn't know how she would, but she couldn't face another Punishment, or the consequences of breaking her bargain with Lucifer. She *was* weak. She was afraid.

Most demons were.

"I have to, Hugh."

He nodded slowly, his gaze intense upon her face. He'd tucked his thumbs into his pockets, hunching his shoulders defensively.

Standing in the middle of that near-empty room, he looked incredibly alone.

But not lost.

Lilith averted her eyes. "Goddamn it all," she whispered, and streaked up the stairs before she could do something foolish.

Like follow her heart.

❧

Colin Ames-Beaumont raised his glass, drank deeply of the crimson liquid. He tried not to grimace at the lack of taste—pig's blood. While satisfying on a basic level, it did not assuage that deeper thirst or slide like liquid lightning across his tongue.

He set the tumbler on a side table, briefly considering changing his glassware to stemware; drinking blood from wineglasses was much more dramatic, elegant.

Apparently Lilith thought so, too.

"You have no style, Colin," she announced from the French doors that opened to the balcony. She didn't bother to ask permission to enter, but crossed the room, throwing herself facedown onto a striped damask sofa.

He raked his gaze over her, his expression amused. "You have more than enough for the both of us, my dear," he said.

She turned her head toward him and smiled; no humor touched her eyes. "I was hoping you would notice."

He'd have to be blind not to notice. And, notwithstanding his long, platonic friendship with her, he couldn't help but appreciate the brief sight of her sweetly rounded bottom encased in the black leather before she settled her wings against her back, hiding the view.

"If it was up to you," Colin said, settling himself into an adjoining chair, "I'd skulk around the house wearing a tuxedo and cape."

"Well, you wouldn't have to skulk. Lurking would be accept—"

She broke off as a black form silently streaked past Colin's chair, almost knocking it over. He righted it just as the huge dog launched itself onto the sofa, whining and barking and wriggling. Colin couldn't see how she wasn't squashed beneath the hellhound's bulk, but Lilith laughed and kissed each of the dog's three noses, patting and rubbing the three enormous heads. She didn't seem to care that the thing was as big as a Bengal tiger, or that a flash of its teeth could make a nosferatu flee in terror. Its tail wagged with barely restrained joy, and its tongues slobbered over her neck and face in desperate welcome.

Colin shivered. Though he'd taken care of the hellhound for the past six months, and many times before that, it'd usually adopted the guise of a Labrador retriever. Its true form was . . . disturbing, even to a vampire as old as he was.

Still laughing, Lilith gently pushed the dog to the floor. "Lie still, now." It complied, and she turned back over, raising her head and resting her chin on one hand so she could see Colin, her other hand trailing over the side and resting on Sir Pup's shoulder. She shifted as she tried to find a comfortable position with the bulk of her left wing pressed tightly against the back of the sofa. After a moment, she gave up, simply making the wings disappear.

Colin would have made the attempt to view her bottom again, but with her torso elevated he had a glimpse of her cleavage which he was determined to enjoy.

He didn't leave the house often anymore—not when he could sense so many nosferatu in the city. They'd curtailed his nighttime activities to the extent that he was reduced to drinking animal blood.

They deserved to die for that alone.

"Did you see He-Who-Must-Not-Be-Named?"

Her eyes glowed red for a moment. She stood up, walking

over to the window and looking out. The hellhound stuck close to her heels, tongues lolling. Colin waited, knowing she'd speak when she was ready.

"Yes," she said finally. She rested her hand on the leaded glass pane, her nails tapping lightly.

"Did you reprise the sword fights of old?"

"No," she said, giving him a reproachful look. "He's just a human."

Colin quirked an eyebrow. "That only explains why you can't kill him. Those ridiculous 'thou-shall-not-kill-or-eat-or-maim-humans' rules that you demons follow for some reason. But just because you are stronger, faster, have the ability to fly and can shape-shift doesn't automatically suggest victory over a well-trained human. Surely you remember what my sister did to the nosferatu who transformed me, and Emily was 'just a human.' "

"She also had Michael's sword," she said with a slight scowl, and Colin bit back his laughter. Lilith had never liked Emily, thought of her as a spoiled aristocrat with her head in the clouds. She turned back to him. "You're envious of my power, admit it."

"You possess only two more abilities than I do; I've strength and speed, and I don't see the need for the rest." Then he had to admit, "Well, perhaps flying—but not shifting. I have no wish to take on the form of a bat." Or upset the perfect composition of his features.

She rolled her eyes. "You've been watching far too much television. We can't transform into animals. Although, it would be entertaining to see you flapping around outside a window."

"It would shrink important parts of my anatomy to the size of a pin," he said, shuddering.

Lilith smiled, resting her hip on the windowsill. "And when was the last time you used that part of your anatomy?" she taunted.

Almost twenty-five days—yet another reason to slaughter the nosferatu. Colin stood and moved to the sideboard, refilling his glass. "More recently than you have."

"I've never used *yours*." Her gaze narrowed on the tumbler in his hand as he took a sip. "Animal blood; how long have you been drinking it?"

"The better part of this month."

Her focus shifted; she studied his length, and a brief psychic touch flitted over his mind. Colin didn't argue; admiration un-doubtedly accompanied her exterior examination, and he rather liked it when she looked. When anyone looked.

It was unfortunate he could not.

"No tremors," she said finally. "And you've not yet de-scended into drooling stupidity. What is the other effect of pro-longed pig-sucking?" Her eyes widened in mock surprise. "Ah, yes . . . no sexual drive. Want to see if that vital part of your anatomy still works? Tonight, with me?"

He choked on a mouthful of blood; Lilith burst into laughter. When his coughing fit subsided, he gave her an admonishing stare. "Bloody hell. You did that on purpose," he said.

"Maybe," she said, her dark irises sparkling with amuse-ment. She tilted her head, resting it against the windowpane as she regarded him. "Did I scare you?"

"Good God, the very thought inspires fear enough to shrivel me permanently." He paused, realizing that she had neatly turned the conversation away from her encounter with Hugh. "And I suppose I would just be a substitute for him."

Colin knew it was a testament to the strength of their friend-ship that she didn't tear his head off for daring to suggest such a thing.

"I'm not an idiot," Lilith said flatly. She didn't move from her place at the window, but her fingers clenched into fists. "I paid for my weakness once before, and no human is worth two Punishments."

"But he was worth one?" He couldn't resist asking.

"Colin . . ." she began warningly, then paused. On the floor, Sir Pup growled low in his throat. Lilith cocked her head to the side, as if listening; standing slowly, she put a finger to her full lips, gesturing for Colin to remain silent. Mischief lit her face.

Whomever she'd heard probably had no idea of the trouble he was in.

"You vampires," she said loudly, "don't know the joy of de-stroying lives."

Playing along, he said, "I've ripped out a few throats in my time." He watched as she moved quietly toward the balcony doors, which had been left open after her entrance. A sword ap-peared in her left hand, a length of metal chain in her right. Wings sprouted between her shoulder blades.

He pursed his lips in silent envy.

"Throats?" Lilith forced a laugh, gazing intently outside. "You've got to go for the balls to really do some damage."

"It's not as easy to drink the blood . . . there . . ." He trailed off when she and the dog disappeared. The crash of the French doors swinging against the wall signaled the force with which she'd opened them. He winced, mentally tallying up the cost of glass replacement for each shattered pane.

A heavy thud against the roof rattled the chandelier. Colin eyed the swaying crystals, willing it not to fall. The house shook as something slammed into the side. A car alarm from across the street began blaring, followed by the crunch of metal. The alarm stopped.

Moments later, a grinning Lilith hauled an unconscious Guardian onto his balcony, dragging her through shards of glass as she pulled the mass of white feathers and golden flesh inside.

Colin rolled his eyes heavenward and sighed. Surely nothing good would come of this.

Lilith crouched next to the Guardian, reaching down and lifting the head by the tangle of blond hair to look at her face. "Selah. I thought so." She chuckled, and glanced up at Colin. Her tone was playful—and wicked. "So, Colin . . . do you want a pet?"

The Guardian's neck was long; the skin, smooth and unblemished. He touched his tongue to the tips of his fangs; the bloodlust was slow to respond. "Does Guardian taste better than pig?"

Lilith grimaced, wrapping the chain around the Guardian's wrists. "I'm not likely to ever try either. And you're a freak, even for a vampire; so for all I know, their blood will kill you." She glanced at Colin, raked her gaze up and down his body. "Only one way to find out."

CHAPTER 16

"Are you certain this will hold her?"

With a practiced eye, Lilith studied the chains and manacles, gauged the strength of the bedposts and the padlocks. "No."

Selah still hadn't regained consciousness. She lay on Colin's bed, arms stretched above her head. The puncture wounds in her neck had already healed over. Lilith hadn't watched Colin feed, but of course it hadn't hurt him. She'd known that very well, yet it had been entertaining to watch him waver between the desire for living blood and the uncertainty of its effect.

He must have realized she was lying, however; he wasn't inclined to risking himself. He might have guessed she wasn't inclined to risking him, either—but after his comment regarding her Punishment, she hadn't been above punishing him a little in turn.

His skin was flushed with Guardian blood—or anger. If it was anger, it wasn't very potent; he was shaking his head in exasperation, but a smile tugged at his mouth.

"You are a bitch, Lilith."

She patted his cheek as she passed him. "You adore me. And Sir Pup will watch her until daybreak. I need him for something else then." The hellhound gave an inquiring whine; Lilith glanced at him and shook her head. "You can't eat her. We may need her later. No. Not even one bite." She grinned at Colin, whose face had paled. "Obedience training. I don't want him to forget he can't eat human-shaped things while he's on Earth."

She heard the vampire choking as he followed her downstairs, and she wondered if he was upset over the thought of sharing a meal with a dog, or just squeamish.

Probably squeamish. He'd been a terrible fop when she'd first met him; that hadn't completely changed. He was also incredibly tightfisted. He wouldn't relish the idea of all that gore in his expensive and tastefully appointed bedroom.

As she had no intention of letting Selah die—not when the Guardian could be so useful—Colin needn't have worried.

Not that she would tell him that. She enjoyed unsettling him; it kept their friendship interesting.

"I must confess I'm pleased he remembered that while you were gone," Colin said as they entered his study. "As I happen to be a human-shaped thing."

"A very nicely human-shaped thing," she agreed.

He sighed, and it was more amused than harassed. "You want something."

"I do," she said, but needed to gather her thoughts before she could fully articulate it.

The fight with the Guardian had restored most of her good humor, but more importantly, cleared her mind. She couldn't think around Hugh, hadn't been able to feel anything past the ache and frustration rioting within her.

And she found it ridiculously hard to lie to him; for a demon, whose life was based on lies, it meant he brought out the worst in her. Her lips curved. She had to admit she liked the irony of the worst in her being what a normal human would consider *good*.

Lucifer, she was sure, would not be amused. Nor would he approve of what she was about to do—but he wouldn't have to know.

She strolled over to the fireplace, examining the painting hanging above the mantel. A life-sized self-portrait: Colin's gray eyes stared back at her, his blond hair in a slick, old-fashioned style. He'd painted himself in modern clothing this time—an elegant silk shirt and pants, much like his current attire.

"Your nose is slightly off; it's a bit longer."

Coming to stand beside her, the vampire looked up and self-consciously touched the tip of his nose. "What about the rest?"

"Your hair." Lilith tilted her head, studying the original. It was softer without the heavy pomade. "The color is right, though."

He nodded. "I cut off a piece to be certain."

She glanced back up. In that moment, the face on the canvas seemed harder, less vulnerable than the vampire beside her. Colin would not appreciate that observation, however. "You knew John Polidori."

His brows rose. "Yes."

"Do you still have any of his letters in your possession?"

"Yes." He watched her, his expression curious.

She took a deep breath. "How do you feel about forgery?"

"Artistic, carefully orchestrated forgery? Or just your run-of-the-mill check-cashing scheme?"

Snobbery, even in this. Lilith blinked, keeping a tight rein on her laughter. "Artistic. Of a sort."

"I wholeheartedly support it—out of necessity if nothing else," he said. "It's difficult to get through two hundred years without mastering the art of falsifying documents."

Frowning, she said, "I have."

"Difficult to *pass as a human* for two hundred years without mastering it," he amended with a smile. Then he said, slightly horrified, "What are you doing?"

She quickly unlaced her corset, let it drop to the floor. With barely a thought, she stripped off her glamours, stood before him naked from the waist up.

His gaze was riveted on her shoulders. "What are those?"

She didn't glance down at her arms, her chest. As plans went, it wasn't a very good one. A distraction, really, and an opportunity to use the little power she owned in this human world.

"A way to make life a bit more interesting for the SFPD," she said.

❧

At six, Hugh left Savi sleeping on the sofa, snoring into a pillow she'd brought from her room.

And ran.

An hour before, two officers had relieved the pair who'd sat through the night. If Hugh had been less tired, if the memory of

Lilith's stricken face and Savi's red-rimmed eyes had been less immediate, he might have taken pity on them.

It was petty and unsatisfying, but still he veered away from the roadway circling through the park, where the cruiser had followed him at a discreet distance. Smiled as he heard the car doors slam, and the pounding of stiff-soled shoes on the wet grass. The officers were young and athletic, but couldn't possibly keep up with him.

Rose and gold streaked the lightening sky, the chilled air was heavy with the odors of the lakes, birds filled the park with their chirping; Hugh kept his eyes on the ground in front of him and pushed himself hard. Twice he had to stop and run in place, waiting for the officers to draw close enough to stay within sight—no sense in taking his pettiness to a degree that seemed evasive—but it was several miles before he noticed the dog.

He loped along about fifteen yards to Hugh's left, keeping pace without effort. Though shaped like a domesticated breed, he was as large as the wolves that had once roamed the medieval forests. San Francisco had strict leash laws and he wore no collar, but he looked too healthy and well-fed to be a stray. Sleek black fur covered rippling muscles, and his eyes shone brightly in the pale morning light.

Perhaps too brightly. Uneasily, Hugh cast another glance to the side; the dog turned his head and seemed to grin.

Colin had said a dog was protecting him. Hugh had thought it a joke, but now he wasn't certain.

Hugh eased down to a jog, and the length of the dog's stride shifted. Then, as if his legs were too long for such a slow gait, he transformed until he was only a few inches taller than the average retriever.

Hugh stopped beside a tree and braced his hand against the trunk, then doubled over and laughed until his stomach ached.

Eventually, a quiet growl brought him to his senses. The short hairs on the back of the dog's neck were raised, and his gaze was fixed on the approaching officers.

"They're no threat," Hugh murmured, and he wasn't surprised when the dog relaxed, lying down with his muzzle on his front paws. "Are you Colin's?"

The dog shook his head, his ears flapping wildly.

"Lilith's."

Canine lips stretched back, as if in another grin.

"Everything all right, Castleford?"

Both men were flushed and winded, but neither showed any signs of temper. The younger one, Hugh judged, couldn't have been more than a year or two older than Savi.

"Everything's fine," he said. "Just a stitch. I'll take it easier on the way back."

The older one sighed with relief. "We'd be grateful."

"We'd also be grateful if you ran by a coffee shop on the way back," the other added with a grin. "We weren't expecting a morning run, and we'd like to refuel."

Hugh nodded absently and glanced at the ground where the dog had been. It was gone—or hidden.

A hellhound. He'd never seen one before, but what else could it be? They were rumored to be nearly uncontrollable, feared by demons and nosferatu.

Yet somehow Lilith had befriended this thing. And despite her declaration that she was determined to fulfill her bargain with Lucifer, she'd sent it to watch over him.

This time as he ran, he let himself remember their conversation from the night before instead of using the exercise to drive every thought from his head.

She'd been human once.

Why hadn't he seen it before? His gut burned, but he forced himself to keep a steady pace instead of trying to outrun the pain his ignorance—and now knowledge—brought. How easily he'd dismissed the humanity he'd seen within her, so certain that such a thing would be impossible. Yet it made sense of everything he knew of her: her difficulty in carrying out the more horrific demonic tasks, her father's constant disapproval, her low status in the demon strata, and the conflict he sensed within her—all the result of her human side fighting the demon within her. How Lucifer must relish Lilith's internal dilemma, even while hating the human cause of it. Guardians had been created because their humanity assisted them, creating a bridge between humans and Above. Lucifer must have found a way to do the same with the ritual, creating a demonic version Below. Only in those circumstances, the human side would have been a disadvantage: the human propensity for empathy, love and pity warring with Lucifer's demands that she should never feel those emotions.

Why had she accepted Lucifer's bargain two thousand years ago?

I didn't want to die. And yet she hadn't seemed to care that Hugh had slain her.

His steps faltered. He knew what destroying her had done to him. He'd wanted to save her, to give her freedom—but he had lost her, and much of his humanity, in the doing.

If she managed to kill him, what would it do to her? The only choice was to convince her not to make the same mistake he had. When she tried to tempt him, he would have to wage a counterattack to halt her self-destruction. He knew her weaknesses, had refrained from exploiting them for too long for fear of his own.

Demons damned humans through temptation—perhaps a human could save a demon the same way.

❦

Her flight to Los Angeles had taken more time than she'd anticipated, and her clothes still reeked of smog and copy-machine toner when she arrived back at her apartment.

Sir Pup waited for her; the odor of the park and Hugh lingered on his fur. He glared at her with four eyes, but refused to look at her at all from his middle head. She grinned.

"I *meant* police officers. You didn't really think he might be harassed by pigs?" She dumped a pile of dry dog food into the bathtub, promised she'd bring bacon to Colin's house for his dinner, changed into her suit and ran out the door.

An hour and a half later, she was sitting at a table centered in a small conference room, accepting a paper cup full of coffee from Detective Preston. He took a cup for himself; judging by the exhaustion lining his face, one he desperately needed.

But his pale blue eyes were alert, and though he gave nothing away in his expression, his psychic scent burned with curiosity. Strangely, it wasn't directed toward the manila envelope and disc that lay on the table between them, but at Lilith.

Uneasy, she tried to redirect his attention. "Should I—"

"She should be here in a few. Trying to light a fire under the ME's ass." He leaned back in his chair, grinned. "And Andy's the type to keep someone waiting when she thinks they might be butting in on her case."

But Preston didn't think so; she felt no animosity from him.

She rested her elbows on the table and smiled over the rim of her cup. "If that was my intention, Detective, then I wouldn't have told you I was coming in. I like to take over jurisdiction by surprise."

"I know." His grin faded. "I helped dig up Paula Roberson."

Lilith set her cup down. "You were in Seattle."

He nodded, scratching his whiskered jaw. "Transferred here about thirteen years ago. Couldn't take any more of Chief Bowman; he was a real dick, and he wasn't going anywhere, so I did."

Her lips twitched. "I thought it was just me."

"No." He looked her up and down. "Though he must have been pissed when you showed up, some gorgeous young thing fresh out of Quantico, waving that profile around. And then being right, down to the last detail. Even guessing where White hid the victim's bodies, based on some mumbo-jumbo psychology shit. No offense."

"None taken," she murmured.

As if struck by a memory, he chuckled and nodded to himself. "God, you nailed that bastard. I'll never forget his face when we walked into his accounting firm and put him under arrest. Pissed his thousand dollar suit, started babbling about angels." Preston paused, glanced back at her. "You weren't there. You deserved to be. He was under suspicion, but we had nothing substantial on him until you showed up. He'd certainly never have given us the location of those graves."

"My superiors decided I'd caused enough of a diplomatic problem with the locals," she said dryly.

His brows rose. "Oh, Bowman cursed your name for at least a year. Might still be cursing it, for all I know. If you hadn't been—what, seven years old?—when White killed the first one, he'd probably have tried to get you as an accessory, claiming that was the only way you could have known all that. If you don't mind me saying, you've aged well. You don't look a day over twenty-six or seven." He looked her over, then down at his own solidly fat stomach.

She smiled and said, "I made a deal with the devil."

"Heh. Anyway, between Thaddeus White pissing himself and seeing Bowman's glory taken by a bit-of-nothing fibbie—no offense—you made my year. So when you call me and my partner up and say you've got something that might point us in the right direction on a murder that makes White's slice-and-dice look pretty, I'm willing to listen."

"You may not like what I have to show you."

He shrugged, and every bit of humor left him. "I don't like any of this."

Neither did she. His compliments had taken the exhilaration out of the game; she felt no guilt in deceiving him and his partner, just as, sixteen years before, she had no compunction against writing the stack of lies that led them to Thaddeus White. It was unfortunate she couldn't dislike Preston; *then* it would have been fun.

But in the face of his respect, it became something she just had to do. At least it was of her own volition, not forced by Lucifer.

Caused by him, perhaps, but not forced.

She became hopeful again when Taylor finally came in. Lilith stood, and was subjected to a flat, searching stare followed by a cool handshake.

She could dislike this woman.

Then the detective ruined it by turning to Preston and commenting, "You're right: she *could* kick my ass."

The older man flushed slightly. "I told you; she has six inches and thirty pounds on you."

"Oh, at least forty," Lilith said, glancing down at the detective's wrist. It looked as fragile as a swan's neck.

Taylor sighed. "Dammit." She pulled her fingers through her hair, and every strand of her neat, auburn bob fell back into place. Though Lilith could feel the other woman's weariness, hear it in the hoarseness of her voice, none of it showed on her face or in her posture. "So, Agent Milton—what have you got for us?"

"Maybe nothing," Lilith said, and pulled a sheaf of paper from the manila envelope. "I received these in my inbox six months ago. Forensics looked over them: no prints, no DNA on the original envelope, and the paper was a brand and weight used by every major print-and-copy store in the region. I've been sitting on them, because though they were a curiosity, they didn't seem to relate to anything."

Taylor accepted the copies, unclipping them and passing half to Preston. "It looks like an old letter." She flipped through the pages. Lilith waited for a moment. Taylor paused, her breath hissing through her teeth.

Preston glanced over, his eyes widening. "What the hell?"

"When I heard the . . . nature of your victim's death, I thought of these. I see I'm not wrong in thinking they are similar."

"Where did you hear?" Preston glanced up. "The details weren't released." There was no accusation in his gaze, though Taylor's was suspicious.

"One of the agents in the Bureau has a brother who works for the ME," Lilith said truthfully, knowing that would be enough. Cops talked to one another, and the method of this murder was a remarkable one.

Taylor nodded, and squinted down at the page. "I can't even read this."

"There is a typewritten transcript at the bottom of the stack. A handwriting expert has verified the letter was written by John Polidori, who wrote a popular vampire tale nearly two hundred years ago. You can see his signature on the last page. We don't know who the 'L' in the salutation refers to. And we don't have the original letter, only copies."

"What does it say?"

"The text of the letter details a dream that he had, in which he witnessed the end of the world at the hands of huge men with fangs and pointed ears. He calls them 'nesuferit,' probably from a Latin word meaning 'not to suffer.' That drawing is his depiction of the torture they put him through in their attempt to transform him into a vampire, before they finally set him on fire."

"You've got to be kidding me," Preston said at the same time Taylor exclaimed, "January 4, 1822?"

Lilith nodded. "The year after Polidori died."

The detectives exchanged a look.

Taylor set the letter back on the table and folded her hands. "Is this some kind of sick joke, Agent Milton?"

"Yes. But it isn't mine."

Silence met her reply. Preston looked at the drawing Colin had made that morning, then at his partner, then back to Lilith. "Goddammit. Goddammit! What are we supposed to do with this?"

His outburst wasn't directed at Lilith, but the frustration of having a relatively straightforward investigation shot to hell.

But Taylor thoughtfully tapped the jewel case beside Lilith with her forefinger. "Why would they send this letter to you?"

"I've made a name for myself in some circles debunking paranormal phenomena, exposing leaders of Satanic cults for fakes, that kind of thing. It's possible whoever sent this to me did it as a challenge."

"So you've become Mulder," Preston said.

"Scully, actually," Taylor said. Preston's brows rose, and she added with a shrug, "She was the skeptic." She glanced back at Lilith. "There's more, isn't there?"

She nodded, relieved. If Taylor was listening now, too, it made this much easier. "A club downtown—Polidori's—burned to the ground last week. I went to KRON this morning and got footage from the newscast, including a few shots that had been edited out for the broadcast. It includes a scan of the crowd. There are men who match Polidori's description of the ne-suferit very nearly perfectly."

"Nosferatu?" Preston said, then hastily added when both Lilith and Taylor looked at him, "Or, guys dressed up like them?"

"I wonder if Ian Rafferty frequented that club. Or if our professor is also in that footage," Taylor mused.

If, through some coincidence, Hugh had been there, Lilith would never have given her the disc. And would probably have made the cameraman, reporter, and the news file database quietly disappear.

Preston let out a long sigh. "So you're saying that whoever did this has a copy of the original letter, and is thinking of using it in some delusional scheme to transform himself into a vampire instead of just playing at it? Or maybe more than one plan to, like members of a cult? And setting fire to the club bearing Polidori's name was some kind of symbolic thing?" he summed up, then groaned softly when Lilith nodded. She fought to hide her grin. It was always best when *they* said it; people were always more likely to believe what came out of their own mouths. "What a mess."

"At least these guys won't be too hard to find," Lilith said. "When you see the tape, you'll know what I mean."

"Joe," Taylor said suddenly. "Let me see the book. He never makes mention of any kind of script, but there's lots about the nosferatu and vampires. If the original letter is in his possession, or even a copy of it, and we can prove a similarity between that book and what's here in this letter, showing he had knowledge of it . . ."

What book? Lilith's stomach tightened. Why did she get the feeling she had just made a critical error, and that her attempt to divert their attention from Hugh had done the opposite?

Preston reached into his jacket and withdrew a paperback. "He'd have to be the ballsiest nut ever to have published clues to his insanity ten years before he goes on his killing spree."

Taylor opened the slim volume and began leafing through the pages.

Lilith stared at the title and author's name for a full minute before she croaked, "May I see that?"

CHAPTER 17

It came as no surprise to Hugh when, toward the end of his last class period, Detectives Taylor and Preston entered the room though the door at the back of the lecture hall and took two of the empty seats.

That Lilith was with them did surprise him, though it shouldn't have. When would he learn that he could never assume he knew what she would do?

The day's lecture consisted of a discussion of Donne, and he half-expected Lilith to raise her hand and say something scandalous. But she remained still, watching him silently through the last ten minutes of class.

That alone put his guard up.

He was determined to save her, but he didn't want to hang himself in the process.

They approached him as he began stacking his papers into his pack. The detectives' guarded expressions told him that despite his alibi, despite their questioning last night, their suspicions had deepened.

Was Lilith the cause? He glanced at her, trying not to show undue interest or familiarity, though any man in his right mind would have stared. She'd coiled her hair neatly behind her nape, emphasizing the fierce, lush beauty of her features. Her suit jacket hung slightly open; the crisp shirt, the vest buttoned snug over her flat belly and breasts, the fall of her pants doing little to hide the strong, lithe form beneath.

It would be more suspicious not to look, he decided, and searched her features for a hint of her emotional state. He did not have to look very long: a thin red line ringed her pupils, as if she barely held back their crimson glow.

She was angry.

That was . . . unusual.

"Detectives," he said, and gestured toward the students still remaining in the room, talking to one another or gathering their books. "Shall we take this to my office?"

Preston nodded. Hugh brushed past him without pausing to see that they followed. Outside the room, the two officers who'd been shadowing him all day long were gone. Sent home? Was he no longer under surveillance because he was no longer a suspect, or was it a temporary reprieve?

His lips twitched. Of course, the other option might be that the detectives were here to arrest him. But, as they hadn't immediately done so, he did not think that the case.

Michael had said Lucifer would come at him though the system, using mankind's justice against him. Was Lilith the face of that? If so, strange that she was angry. If the detectives had followed her plan to entrap him for these murders, she should be ecstatic, gloating.

Remembering how her hellhound had watched over him that morning, he shook his head. He couldn't make sense of it, and the short walk from the classroom to his small office was not long enough to determine Lilith's role.

Relieved to see that Sue wasn't in the room, he laid his pack on his desk and leaned against the front. He didn't want to sit behind it; too easy to seem as if he was hiding behind its bulk. They were here on the offense, and he had no intention of giving them an advantage, even if it was only of position. The room was not large, and four standing adults did not fit comfortably. The detectives made no move to sit in the chairs, or to shake his hand in greeting. Their gaze quickly moved around, as if to determine if he'd changed anything from their last visit, if he'd hidden anything.

Standing behind them, Lilith did not look away from him, and he held her gaze.

As if noticing his attention, Preston said, "This is Agent Milton, of the San Francisco FBI. She's agreed to assist us on this case."

Milton? Hugh quirked a brow, but his voice was flat as he said, "I'd like to see your identification, Agent Milton."

Taylor and Preston looked surprised and offended, respectively, but Lilith's expression never changed. She approached him, flipping a wallet from the inside of her jacket, and held it open.

"Closer, please," he said pleasantly. "I'm not wearing my spectacles."

Her mouth tightened, but with annoyance or laughter he could not determine. Reluctantly, he dropped his gaze from her face to the ID. "Lily," he murmured. He raised his eyes to hers again. "I like it very much."

He said the words like a caress, so softly Taylor and Preston couldn't have heard him. Lilith did. Her lips parted slightly, and the red faded from her eyes. Heat replaced it, was quickly banked.

She snapped the wallet closed. "Satisfied, Dr. Castleford?"

Hooking his thumbs in his pockets, he smiled. "Not yet." Her breath hitched, but he allowed his gaze to slide past her toward the detectives, pleased for the moment that he'd disconcerted her. His voice hardened. "But I will be when you discover who killed Ian."

"So will we, Dr. Castleford." Taylor's tone echoed his. "I hope you don't mind if we ask you a few more questions."

Hugh nodded. "I didn't think you were here for the poetry." Lilith backed away. She sat down at Sue's desk as if to participate only as an observer. He could feel her studying him, and though he did not look directly at her, he could sense the slight shift in her posture, in her mood when Taylor gestured to a manila envelope Preston carried.

"You studied literature, Dr. Castleford. Do you know of a John Polidori?"

Hugh fought the urge to look at Lilith for her response. "Of course. He wrote *The Vampyre*—a story that originated from a challenge Lord Byron gave to a group on holiday on Lake

Geneva in 1816. Mary Shelley conceived and wrote *Franken-stein* that same summer. Both are considered classic gothic tales; *The Vampyre*, in particular, was a strong influence on Stoker's *Dracula*. Nineteenth-century lit isn't my area of expertise, however. If you need information relating to Polidori, Byron, or the Shelleys you'd be better served asking one of my colleagues."

"What is your area of expertise?" This, from Preston.

"Sixteenth- and seventeenth-century drama, poetry." This time, he did allow himself to glance at Lilith. "I wrote my dissertation on Milton's use of the demonic female figure."

Her chin dipped, but from this distance he could not read her expression.

"And is it from Milton that you got your ideas for your book?"

"Which one? I have two books that include discussions of Milton's works that have gone to academic press."

"*Lilith*."

His stomach clenched, and he would have done anything for clear vision at that moment. He let his gaze rest on Lilith for a long second, felt no reaction from her. "In part." He turned, opened the side pocket of his bag and pulled out his glasses. "What has this to do with Ian?"

"Just gathering as wide a range of background as possible, Dr. Castleford," she said. "What of the nosferatu? They are in your book, but Milton makes no mention of such a thing in his work."

He paused, glad that he was partially turned away so that he could better hide his surprise. They'd made a connection between Ian and the nosferatu? Lilith must have had something to do with it, but why? He slid on his glasses and looked at her. She shifted in her seat, and once again he saw her tightly contained anger.

How to answer Taylor's question? He had the feeling anything he said would damn him in the detectives' eyes.

Did Lilith intend for that damnation to be literal?

He thought quickly. When did the word enter the human lexicon? "The nosferatu has been a traditional part of vampire literature since the late eighteen hundreds. I think Stoker was the first to use it in English."

"Seventy years later than Polidori?"

Hugh nodded. The truth was, Polidori might have known it through Colin. Guardians and demons had long called the creatures *nosferatu*, and a few vampires knew the truth behind their origins. Colin was one of them. "Yes, but again, this isn't really my area. I didn't research the book very carefully."

He didn't meet Lilith's eyes, afraid he would begin laughing if her expression was even slightly amused. Afraid he would see something other than amusement.

Had she read it? He fought the slightly sick, vulnerable sensation it left in his gut, forced himself to push that thought aside.

The detectives exchanged a look. "You're an educated guy," Preston said abruptly. "Do you know any other languages?"

"Yes. Quite a few." Several that were extinct.

The older man scratched his chin. "Any ancient languages? Can you read obscure writings, that kind of thing?"

Were they trying to determine the nature of the writing used in the ritual? Of course—they assumed it was a human language. "Latin and Greek," he said carefully. "But nothing older or nonphonetic, such as hieroglyphs or cuneiform."

"Why would you study them if your area of expertise is English lit?"

"In the sixteenth and seventeenth centuries, all of the English writers read and wrote Latin and Greek," Hugh said dryly. "It was a standard part of their education, so I made it part of mine." Not exactly true, but answer enough.

Taylor pulled a sheet of paper from the folder. "Have you ever seen writing like this?" Both she and Preston watched him carefully.

Symbols covered the page. The ink smelled fresh, as if they'd recently been copied by hand.

He recognized many of them from Lilith's skin, from Ian's corpse, but he shook his head. "No." He pretended to study it. "It looks a bit like Devanagari script, but I'm certain I've never come across a series of glyphs like this in my studies." Raising his head, he added, "Perhaps the linguistics depart—"

"Thank you, Dr. Castleford. We'll consider that." Taylor snatched the paper back, her impatience showing in the tightness around her mouth, the narrowing of her eyes. She knew he was giving her indirect, runaround answers—but did she want the truth?

He didn't think she would. And he didn't dare offer anything more without knowing what input Lilith had in their investigation.

She still sat, her gaze fixed on his face, her long legs stretched out in front of her, ankles crossed. But for the crimson glow around her pupils—did she not know she did that, or was she warning him of her anger?—her expression was unreadable.

God, but he needed to get her alone. Needed to question her and break through her defenses. To get to the truth, to bring her humanity to the fore before she destroyed both of them.

"Aside from the DemonSlayer games at Auntie's, do you know anything of Mr. Rafferty's activities?"

Hugh returned his attention to Detective Taylor. "He played football in the fall, I think. His papers often used analogies comparing the sport to devices in literature."

Preston gave a bark of laughter, which he quickly smothered.

Hugh allowed himself a smile. "It could be tedious reading at times."

"As tedious as your book?" Taylor said sweetly.

His smile faded. "No." Behind the detectives, Lilith's eyes shone furiously crimson. He frowned at her, and as if remembering herself, she visibly regained control. "I don't know much beyond the football. I imagine Courtney Eliot would."

"His girlfriend," Preston said, and Hugh nodded. "So during those game nights, he never talked about clubs they might have frequented? Any type of music he liked?"

"If he did, I don't recall mention of it."

"Do any of the other students who meet talk about a specific hangout, a place they got together?"

Hugh shook his head. "I don't recall any," he said truthfully. "I'm often at the restaurant, but I'm not active in the game itself, so I'm not privy to many of the conversations that take place while they play." He checked the clock over the door. "They'll be meeting tonight, at eight. If any attend, that is; I imagine most of them have heard about Ian by now."

Even as he said it, he knew that many of them would be there. It was human nature to gather and grieve, sharing their memories of the life they'd known.

And often dangerous to grieve in solitude. He knew that well.

He didn't dare look at Lilith for the ache in his chest. If she was trying to read him, she would feel it. Would she think it was for Ian?

"Are you familiar with a club called Polidori's? Have you ever heard any of your students mention it?"

Startled, his gaze locked with Lilith's, and he suddenly understood. She'd somehow pointed them in the direction of Polidori's, suggesting a link between it, the nosferatu, and Ian's murder. And, because of the book bearing her name and its contents, it made him the primary suspect, solidifying the detectives' suspicion that he'd been involved.

"No," he said flatly. Lilith looked away, her jaw flexing as if she wanted to speak but could not.

His hands clenched in his pockets. A moment alone. Then she was going to talk. If he did it well, didn't hold back, she was going to scream.

❧

"He's smart," Taylor said. She unlocked the sedan's door, then looked across the blue metal roof at her partner and Lilith. "And he knows it. I expected that his arrogance would lead him into a mistake, that he'd claim to have some knowledge and show off, but he gave us a neat runaround."

"Smug bastard," Preston agreed. "What was your impression, Agent Milton?"

Her lips tilted slightly. The look Hugh had given her as they'd left had created the most significant impression; she could still feel the arousal the heated glance had stirred within her.

She didn't know what he was thinking, and she didn't like how eager she was to find out.

But as she couldn't tell them that, she gave them an answer by rote. "I think he knows we're on to him; you should continue surveillance, see if he tries to cover any tracks he might have left. If nothing else, he'll be wondering what we didn't say, and he'll want to determine if he's left any evidence, or if someone connected to him has revealed more than they should have." She paused. "If he's our man."

"You don't think he knows something?" Preston raised a brow.

"Knowing is not the same as perpetrating," Lilith said.

Taylor smiled thinly. "But it might make him an accessory. He's our strongest lead, Agent Milton, but don't think we aren't investigating every possible avenue."

Lilith heard the territorial note in the other woman's voice and couldn't care less. She had her own territory to protect; it made no difference hers was not a case, but a man.

"She's not suggesting we aren't doing our job, Andy."

Knowing she was going to piss them both off, Lilith said with a shrug, "Maybe I am." She had to force away the regret that rose when Preston's expression cooled and Taylor's hardened. "That book you showed me was not written by a man congratulating himself on his mental prowess. '*The demon from Hell itself, burning and terrible, speaks with fearsome intonation, "No recourse will you find, no escape from my horrific clutching. All your souls are belong to us,"*' " she quoted, shaking her head. "It's ridiculous tripe, not an intellectual treatise designed to stroke his ego."

Preston raked his hand through his hair. "Then explain why an obviously educated man would write it so badly, except as a puzzle for others to decipher?"

"I can't," Lilith admitted. And she didn't care; there were other portions of it that concerned her more. They could talk of codes and hidden meanings; she just wanted to know why Hugh had written her story with the skill and care of a retard.

And why he'd lied to her for eight hundred years. The anger that had boiled in her belly for hours began to rise again.

"You looked through that book for the first time on the drive here," Taylor said. Her psychic scent radiated suspicion and disbelief. "But you quoted that passage verbatim."

"And so you think I'm not being honest about having read it before?" Lilith guessed, unwilling to mince words. She grinned, and despite the absence of fangs and horns there was more demon than human in the expression. Her fingers clenched on the rear door handle, denting the metal. "Just like Castleford, I'm really fucking smart."

Cerberus's balls, she was being incredibly stupid. Her stomach and chest ached, her head felt ready to explode. What was wrong with her? She needed to get out of here, to settle herself. Through her ignorance of the book, she had screwed up the letter as evidence that would help direct the investigation away from Hugh. Now she was alienating the two people who might hold Hugh's fate in their hands.

Better human detectives than Lucifer to own that fate? Or Lilith, once Lucifer called in her debt to him?

Before either detective could launch into the angry response Lilith could feel them getting ready to deliver, she held up her hand, took a deep breath. "I'm sorry. That was out of line, and I apologize." She smiled sickly, and she didn't have to fake it. "I don't think I'm feeling very well, and I'm taking it out on you."

Taylor stared at her for a moment before giving a short nod, getting into the car and slamming the door. Preston hesitated for just a moment. "Agent Milton—"

The words wanted to stick in her throat, but she forced them out. "I know. I wouldn't want to ride back with me, either. I won't have a problem making my way back." She sighed, leveled a look at him. "You have something on this guy, something you haven't shared with me. This book isn't reason enough for the certainty you two have that Castleford's your guy."

Preston opened his door. "I'll send a copy of the file to your office for you to look over. We can use your expertise, but"—he gave a humorless snort of laughter—"if this is how you work with others, I can see why the Bureau keeps you out of the locals' faces."

She deserved that, Lilith mused as they drove away. She opened her fist, and the mangled door handle dropped to the pavement with a clatter.

Petty pleasures. She'd existed on them for far too long.

She wanted deep, meaningful pleasure. The kind Hugh had promised with his eyes in his office, with his lips as he'd spoken her name. The kind she couldn't have.

The building in which Hugh was now, teaching kids who probably didn't know their ass from their balls, sat only yards away, at the other end of the parking lot. Easy enough to walk back there, see if he'd follow through on that promise.

She closed her eyes so that she couldn't be beckoned by the curving concrete and glass, and the man within. Was her desire to have him stronger than her desire to avoid Punishment?

She breathed out slowly. Yes.

But any emotion that forced her to choose between him and herself was a treacherous one, and she couldn't trust it. After all, it was the type of emotion she had spent her existence engendering in others. That choice would only be destructive for both of them.

It was reason enough to walk away—but she couldn't.

❧

She heard the clacking of his computer keyboard from the hall-way. Her ego bruised that he hadn't been sitting in silence, brooding, she opened the door.

"That took longer than I thought it would," he said. Lilith frowned, wondering if she'd been so predictable when her deci-sion to come had been one of the most foolhardy choices she'd ever made.

He was certainly predictable in his lack of reaction; he didn't look away from his computer. From her angle, the glare of the screen on his lenses made his eyes impossible to read.

"I know what you're doing; I read it in your book. You're try-ing to provoke me by ignoring me. It won't work."

"Only because you make it impossible to ignore you. And I daresay you would have been provoked even if I had given you notice."

Smiling, she rested her hip on the edge of his desk, thumbed through the papers and books spread across the surface. He con-tinued typing. A paperback selection of poems stood on edge next to his monitor; she picked it up. "Donne?"

Hugh only grunted an assent.

Lilith pursed her lips. "He was fun when he was young. Then he met me, and he only wrote sermons after." A glimmer of a smile around his mouth. Much better. "You, too, have be-come something of a monk in a man's clothing. You may have discarded your robe, but this . . ." She gestured to the Spartan office, the stack of student essays—and remembered the de-scription of Caelum in his book, its white sterility. "You've ex-changed one monastery for another," she realized.

An infinitesimal flinch, as if her comment had struck some-thing painful within him; but still, he did not turn to face her. "And what have you become?"

"Certainly more patient," she muttered.

"Yes." He paused, and finally looked at her. "I fear I am less."

"You could *only* be less patient than you were as a Guardian. Though imagine my surprise, when I discover that so much of it is false." With a sarcastic lift of her eyebrow, she quoted, " '*Demons remain a stranger to physical need; like a demon, deceptive and concealed, remained I.*' "

"This is why you were angry," he said slowly. "Because you learned I used my Guardian powers to hide my body's response to you."

"You lied." Even as she said it, color washed her face. They revealed too much, those two words. How she had depended on his unfailing honesty; how she had desired—needed—his attention.

Worse, she was a demon making an accusation of a lie; it would have been laughable, had it not been so humiliating.

And he seemed to understand, damn him. His gaze softened. "I didn't know. I *felt* it, Lilith. I just didn't allow it to show. Demons don't experience physical desire; I protected myself as best I could. If I'd known you weren't . . . if I had guessed . . ." He trailed off. "But I didn't know it could be anything other than a game for you."

She averted her eyes. It shouldn't have been. The sense of betrayal she felt was a result of her vanity, her certainty that had he desired her as strongly as she had him, he couldn't have held his glamours. Shrugging, she said, "It was nothing."

His mouth thinned. "Was it?"

"Yes," she said, and he relaxed into his chair as if she'd said the opposite, turning back to the computer screen. Suddenly, she didn't care if he intended to or not: she was provoked. She unclenched her teeth, her voice low and silky. "Though I'm pleased, knowing you have no defense against me now. That I could come over there and have you begging for me within moments."

"Let me finish this e-mail first." His tone was mild, disinterested.

Her breath hissed out. She launched herself over his desk, landed behind him, and caught a glimpse of her human name and a mention of swords before he hit Send.

Slowly, he swiveled his chair around, tilted it back to look up at her. "Will you materialize your horns?" he said, his expression unreadable. "If you are here to lead me to prison by my cock, I'd like something to grab onto in turn."

Prison? Her eyes narrowed, and she pushed away her disappointment that he hadn't seen the truth behind her ruse with the detectives. But how could he have? "That's what my tits are for, you imbecile." Planting her foot on the seat between his thighs, she gave his chair a shove.

Stupid, to unbalance herself like that. Quickly—he was faster than she'd thought he'd be, but when had she last fought a human?—he pulled on her knee and rose up and bent her back over his desk. Books and her gun jammed against her spine and shoulders, his hips wedged between her thighs.

How the hell had that happened? He'd planned it, that was certain. But she couldn't question him, didn't have any breath except to laugh when he grinned and said, "Good-bye, monk" and lowered his head to her breast, pushed aside her vest and began suckling her through her shirt.

Her arms rose of their own accord and she slipped her fingers into his thick hair, her nails against his scalp. She meant to shove him away, but her back arched and she pulled him closer.

His teeth caught her nipple. Oh, God, if the pain in Hell was anything like the torturous pleasure of that bite, humans would be lining up to jump into the Pit.

He reared up, unfastened her vest but didn't take the time with her shirt. Buttons flew.

She groaned, half-laughing. "I told you my salary—"

"I've been domesticated." He stared at her bare skin, her taut nipples. "I'll sew them back on." And then his tongue was hot and wet against her.

Her laughter was lost as he began thrusting his hips in time to the pull of his mouth. His arms, braced on either side of her head, trembled as if it took all his strength to keep it slow. The rhythmic friction against her sex was nearly unbearable. For Hugh, too—his shields fell, and she was slapped by a wave of desperate arousal that equaled hers, tinged by surprise and fear. *Too much, too fast, too good.*

He'd expected to be in control. Her eyes blazed.

His teeth scraped her breast as she tugged his head up. A growl of protest sounded from his throat, silenced when she said, "You still think to resist me? *'Temptation the demon was; an angelic face and false impotency my only defense.'*" Her voice mocked him, though she would have done as well to make fun of herself. "You no longer have that defense, yet you cling to it."

"I'm no longer impotent, either." He rocked forward, and smiled wryly when she bit her bottom lip to keep her moan from escaping.

She was so wet; the scent of her arousal should have embarrassed her. Her fingers still threaded through his dark hair. Why did she not let him go? It was a human response, a weakness—

"Lilith," he said hoarsely, and he was staring at her chest again. "Where are the others? There are but half the symbols here."

Oh, fuck.

CHAPTER 18

"Get off," she said tightly. "Now."

Her glamour had failed. How could his touch make her lose her control—her sense—so quickly? Re-forming it over her skin took barely a thought, but it was too late. His eyes found hers, and she shoved away the shame of his seeing the proof of her Punishment.

He nodded, began to ease away from her. "I didn't—"

A rasp of metal as the doorknob turned. Lilith's eyes widened, and Hugh barely had time to pull the edges of her shirt together before a woman—forty, plump, smiling—opened the door and shuffled in, carrying a tall cup of coffee and weighed down by several bags. Her mouth fell open when she saw them.

She recovered quickly. "New student?"

Hugh grinned. "A particularly slow one. Sue Fletcher, Lily Milton." He introduced them without a trace of embarrassment, though he was still between her legs and she was lying atop his desk. Despite herself, Lilith began shaking with laughter. "You don't have to go, Sue; we were just finishing."

"You look as if you've just begun," the other woman said,

cheeks pink. "I'll drop off this stuff and go grab something to eat. But I have an appointment here in half an hour," she added apologetically.

Hugh lifted his brows. "That's more than enough time."

Sue chuckled and turned toward her desk to unload her bags; Hugh pulled Lilith to her feet. The door closed again a few moments later, and Lilith tried to summon the shame and anger she'd felt before the woman's entrance, but couldn't. She glanced down at her shirt. "Can you really sew?"

His heated gaze lingered on the vertical slice of exposed skin. "No."

"Shit," she said, and busied herself tucking and buttoning. The vest would hold it all together—mostly. She didn't look at him. "You have friends."

"A few."

"Have you told them?"

"No."

She nodded, then slanted a glance at him. Not much space here behind his desk. Less than two feet away, he leaned against his bookcase, the heels of his hands resting on the shelf behind his hips. Despite his easy posture, she knew he was calculating, weighing, considering.

"It must be lonely," she said before he could draw any conclusions about the symbols. Distract him by delving into the personal. Once, she would have used sex; but, as touching him had unsettled her so much she had lost her glamours and been unaware of Sue's approach, she was too susceptible to it to try now.

His half-lidded stare never wavered. "Better than the alternative: did I tell them the truth, they would be forced to decide whether to believe me. It is a measure of trust that I'm not willing to ask from them."

"You fear rejection?" She snorted. Tried not to remember the regret she'd felt when she'd pushed Taylor and Preston too far. "Fine friends these."

"Don't, Lilith," he said softly. "Don't twist it."

And she saw the quiet pain in his expression then, felt the isolation that weighed on him. She should use it against him—would have to, eventually.

But not yet. Not until Lucifer demanded it.

She arched a brow and let her eyes glow. "I like twisted. And I well remember how you began to believe. If you like, you can invite a party of your friends to your home. I'll show up, attack you, transform and scare the hell out of them. I may not be Michael, but I can be very impressive." She flashed her fangs before retracting them again and grinned. "I'll even recite the terrible dialogue from your book. '*Away, foul fiend! Suck thy bloody heart of death!*' is my favorite—though I don't recall saying that when we fought the nosferatu in Lille. I was not that ridiculous until I came to America."

The corners of his mouth lifted into a smile, but his gaze was thoughtful. "You didn't know about the book when you left last night."

"Oh, I've known for years and years," she said, rolling her eyes.

Something tense within him seemed to ease. "You pointed them to the nosferatu and Polidori's somehow, but it was never with the intention of increasing their suspicions of me. You *were* angry about the book itself, but also because you failed to redirect the focus of their investigation." His eyes narrowed. "What did you do?"

Sex again, and quickly. "I didn't kiss you last night," she said, and stepped forward, crowding him into the bookcase.

"I won't forget to ask again when you are done. I'm not so easily distracted as that." He caught her waist, pulled her up against his lean, hard length. "It must have been something ridiculous for you to hide it with a kiss," he said against her lips. But he did not kiss her—no, he must be waiting for her to initiate it.

"Not very well thought out," she agreed. "Colin saw me naked."

His free hand buried in the coil of hair at her nape. "Many people have seen you naked." Then he stiffened. "He saw the symbols."

A flash of jealousy from him, and she triumphed in it. His shields were good, but they were not as strong when she was this near to him, touching him. She only had to keep herself under control. Her hands curved over his shoulders, his muscles warm and firm beneath her palms. "Why did you write the book?"

"Are we bargaining?"

"Not officially," she said. "Just . . . trading."

"And you'll kiss me if I do—or if I don't?" Humor and need in that deep-voiced question.

She slicked her tongue over his bottom lip, quick as a cat. "Come now, Sir Hugh. Don't disappoint me."

His eyes darkened, and he drew his moistened lip into his mouth for a moment, as if to savor her flavor. "I intended to give it to Michael. What did you give the detectives?"

"Blow jobs," she said, and he laughed. It rumbled from his chest, through hers; her nipples tightened, still appallingly sensitized by his tongue, his teeth. She willed herself not to feel them and concentrated on the shape of his eyeglasses. *Not* the gorgeous blue behind them. "Colin and I forged a letter. Why would you give it to Michael?"

"Because of Donne. And Shakespeare and Marlowe and Milton. What were the letter's contents?"

Her throat tightened, and she could barely answer his question. "We described a fake dream, in which Polidori saw the nosferatu and a person who'd undergone the ritual. You remembered what I'd told you during the fire in London—about my attempts to earn a second immortality?"

His fingers smoothed the hair at her temple. "Yes—though for other reasons, as well. And the letter also included the symbols? Colin copied them from your skin?"

"Yes. Why did you publish it?"

He shook his head, and his smiling lips brushed hers. "I never intended to. I had intended it for the library in Caelum, if Michael—"

She had to silence him; there was no control in the way she took his mouth, took the confession from his tongue. It was not gratitude that burned in her chest—could not be. The book would destroy her if Lucifer ever discovered its existence. Knowing Hugh had tried to give her what she'd never obtained on her own should not create such an upwelling of pleasure within her, except that it was another vulnerability of his to exploit.

And Lucifer would make certain that she collected his weaknesses like butterflies in a case, to pin and examine.

Eight hundred years—she should have known them. He should not have been able to surprise her. Even human, even in this modern age, the scent and taste of him should have been familiar. Yet there was a newness in his response, a newness in the impatience and the force of it. His lips moved over hers, heated and insistent, and laced with a hunger that matched her own.

She shouldn't have been matching anything—certainly not hunger.

And bringing the kiss to a halt shouldn't have been difficult, but she lingered over it before pulling away. She answered the question in his gaze with a mischievous grin, and twisted her hips, a teasing rub against his arousal. "*Not* kissing you would have been a repression of your free will."

"Stopping represses it," he said ruefully. "But I don't think half an hour would be enough, so it is best we stop now when we can."

Best that she withdrew from him, as well. She hid her reluctance as she unwound her arms from his neck and backed up to sit on his desk. His hair was mussed by her fingers, his lips reddened from her mouth. Had she hurt him? Her stomach dropped. It would have been so easy to do so without noticing, as lost as she'd been in that kiss. She looked down, stabbed her fingers into a container full of metal binder clips. Crushed one with a pinch. She knew her strength—she did not know him. Not anymore. "What were your other reasons?"

"You're cheating," he said. His gaze fell to her fingers, then back up to her face.

She reviewed their exchange, realized he was right. It was his turn to question. Dammit. "Then continue the quiz, Professor."

He smiled, and she would have given anything at that moment for the power to shift into a schoolgirl's uniform. To sway her plaid skirt-covered ass in front of him as she crawled across his desk. She sighed.

Lucifer had taken the fun out of everything.

She shook her head at his puzzled expression. "I was wondering how many students you've had on this desk."

There was something wicked in the way his eyes glinted with laughter, something sinful in his slow, "I thought of you as I had every single one."

Images flashed in front of her eyes—forbidden sex, bent over the desk, rough and slick. Young, nubile limbs and his masculine strength. She had to swallow her jealousy before she said, "Liar."

His smile widened. "If you want the truth, you'll have to ask in the trade." Obviously considering his own question, he brushed his thumb against his jaw, rasping the afternoon stubble. She tensed, expecting him to ask about the missing symbols on her skin.

It was senseless to be so ashamed of it; but, whether she liked her role or not, her identity had been tied to her demonic powers for two thousand years. For Hugh to have evidence of how easily Lucifer could strip her of her abilities, how she'd been degraded, how little she mattered to those Below—the thought was mortifying. Even demonkind would like to reject her; in that, she was no better than the nosferatu.

But it was almost as difficult to answer when he finally asked, "If the nosferatu and Lucifer are setting me up for Ian's murder, then why do you try to thwart it? Do you intend to betray your liege?"

She shrugged, and told him what she would have told Lucifer. "It will be difficult to fulfill my bargain and drive you to your death if you sit in jail. Keeping you free will allow me better access to you." Another clip flattened between her fingers. "What were your other reasons?"

"To be certain I didn't lie to myself about my past, and my reason for slaying you: to give you freedom, aye—but at what expense?" He drew a deep breath. "And to capture you, in whatever form I could. I have done nothing but search for you since that night. My work, this career is but an excuse to find you again."

She fought to keep her voice hard, emotionless. "Do you not know I'll use this against you?"

"I know." His hands clenched in his pockets, as if anchoring himself to the spot. "Do you not still wish for your freedom?"

"The bargain changes the price," she said quietly. "Before, fulfillment required my service. Now it requires your death. What is this girl to you? Was she worth your Fall?"

His brow furrowed. "Savi?" At her nod, he said, "I hardly knew her then. It was only after I had Fallen that I returned here to San Francisco to see how she fared. Her grandmother took me in; and, as soon as she recovered, Savi did, too. I did not Fall *for* her. She was the catalyst, but not the cause."

"Why does she live with you?"

He smiled slightly. "She is rebelling. And I had an empty room over my garage."

She heard more than he said: he'd wanted the company,

wanted to ease his isolation. Had it worked? Why had he never taken a wife, found companionship in another way?

"What was the cause?" Two questions now, without offering information of her own.

He flicked a glance at the clock above the door. "Our time has almost passed."

"We are uneven in our trade," she immediately protested.

His voice was low, entreating. "Spend the afternoon with me, Lilith. I'll give anything you ask for free."

Temptation ripped through her, but she shook her head. "I have to get back to work." The surveillance team had returned—she could hear them in the hall. She could pass off a brief visit as official, but not an extended meeting.

"Then spend the night with me."

It would leave her absolutely defenseless, when she needed to strengthen her resistance to him. "What was the cause? In the book, you only say that you saved a girl from a demon. I know that is not all of it; you told me that night you forced your Gift on a man." Her breath came hard and fast. "Tell me, and I will spend the night with you."

His eyes darkened, his jaw clenched. "I won't hide it from you—even if you try to use it against me in your bargain—but I don't want it to be the reason you come to me."

Her laugh held an edge of desperation. "Then tell me, and I will not."

"Lilith—" He broke off, laughing and shaking his head. "Nothing is owed in this. Come to me tonight, or do not—but it is not a condition of the telling." He waited until she nodded. "A demon was working on Savi's father, an innocent. Murray and his family were inside a restaurant. The demon had followed them, and I found him outside, killed him. I had to wait with the body, make certain it wasn't found until I could get it to a Gate without being seen." He paused, rubbed his forehead. "Savi was nine. She had a brother, a year older. It was late, but their home wasn't far from the restaurant, and they walked. Mother and father, both successful surgeons, and two children. Easy targets."

"Targeted by a human?" And nothing to do but watch. A Guardian couldn't prevent a human from exercising free will, even if that will meant death for others.

He nodded stiffly. "And even I'm not faster than a bullet. Was not. I ran as soon as I heard the first, but—"

"Faster than . . . you tried to stop him? You interfered with his will?"

"Yes. I arrived, too late for all but Savi. And she'd seen him, had seen his face when he'd shot them—he was going to kill her for that. I put myself in between, but the bullets went through, hit her anyway. I took her to the hospital, but it didn't look like she would . . ." He trailed off, and his face hardened. "So I went after him."

Lilith's gaze dropped to his waist, imagined the bullets tearing through him. She'd done worse to him, but the thought of anyone else . . . "Good," she said.

A tiny smile on his lips. "But it was not that, Lilith. Not *only* that. It was Vlad, and the boy in New Orleans, and a thousand others I hadn't been able to help because I had to deny my will for the Guardian code. I had to serve . . . but I could no longer. And I broke." His smile faded, and his tortured gaze held hers. "But I also knew there would be no one to free you after I Fell. So I found you. I made certain you did not believe in your role, that it was because you were bound to service as well, then . . ." Again he faltered, his throat working. "Though it must have been for naught, for you are bound again."

Her heart thundered beneath her breast. "You would have let me live if I had believed it?"

"Yes." His voice was hoarse. "I knew you feared the Punishment failing your bargain would bring. For centuries you told me what would free you without actually asking me to do it— and I knew that if you asked it would be tantamount to a betrayal of your service. But if you truly served him . . . if the only thing that held you to Lucifer was the fear of Punishment, I could not leave you in that."

"If you knew, why not earlier?"

"I was too greedy. Too weak. And for centuries, I had searched for another way to save you, yet never found one." He gave a half-laugh and scrubbed his hand over his face. "Allow me some defense, Lilith."

No. "Would you have slain me if you had known I was a halfling?"

He stilled. "I don't know. Could you have Fallen?"

"You mean Ascend?" Her mouth curved, but there was no

humor in it. "No. Lucifer has never reversed the transformation." And if she had asked for it, he would have called it a betrayal of their bargain, a renunciation of her service to him.
Hugh had been right in that.

He closed his eyes, and his chest rose and fell on a heavy
sigh. "Yes. I would have."

It was not the answer she'd expected. She felt him watch her
as she walked to the door. Her hand on the knob, she turned—
and gave him a little bit of what he'd given her. "It worked.
Those two hours, before Lucifer found me—I don't know if it
was Heaven, or Oblivion, or something else . . . but it was two
hours of freedom. Two hours without Hell clawing at my back."
And reason enough to risk Lucifer's anger now; she owed Hugh
freedom, even if it was only an earthly freedom that kept him
from being imprisoned on false charges.

His eyes glistened, and she had to look away.

"Is this why bargains no longer have any allure? Why you've
changed?"

"Have I?" A smile pulled at her mouth. "If I have, it might
just be when I'm around you. You are a corrupting influence, to
be certain. Soon I'll be *good*." She shuddered facetiously.

He gave a choked laugh. "Perhaps you should be with me
more often. Complete your bargain, Lilith—only spend a hundred years in the doing. Torment me for decades. After all that
time, old and decrepit, I will finally give in to you, and in the in-
terim you will discover how corrupting I can be."

"Don't tempt me, Hugh." Her eyes glowed in warning. "It
would take very little persuasion for me to do just that—and it
would be a torment."

"For me?" He shook his head.

Her smile was pure bravado. She opened the door and
paused. Looked at the desk. "How many?"

His cheeks colored slightly, and he ran his fingers through
his hair. "None." Her brows rose, and their gazes locked.
"Ever."

The air left her lungs in a rush, and she sagged against the
doorframe. "Why?" She stared at him; what was wrong with
women, that they hadn't taken him? Or had they tried and been
rebuffed?

His eyes were shadowed. "When I first Fell, I was too . . ."

"Fucked up?" she offered.

"Yes." His voice was grim. "An eight-hundred-year-old Guardian transformed back into a human teenager. And later, it seemed dishonest to be with a woman—truly be with her—when I couldn't divulge my history, and any developing love would be based on lies. I'm not designed for casual sex simply to relieve my frustration; I don't think there is any sin in it, I just cannot do it."

"And when you were a Guardian? I thought it was a love-fest in Caelum." So different from Hell, where lust and physical pleasure were forbidden to halflings—and impossible for demons to feel.

His mouth quirked into a smile. "For many. But I served, at first, with religious—and celibate—fervor. Later, many of the Guardians were those I'd mentored. They were students, and it was . . . awkward."

"But there were those you hadn't mentored, and after a while those you trained would be—" She broke off as she realized the truth. "And there was me."

"Aye." He didn't look away. "I spent so much time resisting you, I could not be certain that I would not think of you when I was with another. So I was not with any others."

Crazy chivalrous martyr. She ignored the melting warmth that stole through her. "Are you offering yourself up as a virgin sacrifice then? You think that will be enough, that you'll have the skill to tempt me? You don't have a prayer."

His gaze raked over her form, heated and intense. "I don't need prayer—I have eight hundred years of imagining what I would do to you."

"I will use that against you as well," she said, breathless.

He grinned suddenly. "And *that* is something worth praying for."

❧

Lilith heard ASAC Bradshaw coming, but had nowhere to hide. She'd claimed desk space in one of the empty cubicles in the guts of the department office, and she was hemmed in by a wall and the gaze of the rookie in the cube across the aisle who hadn't taken his eyes from her since she'd returned from San Francisco State. For a moment, she considered going through the rookie to make her escape; he'd been stuck with background checks for the past couple of days, droning away on the telephone. He was probably ready to put a gun to his head. A visit to the hospital and an exciting tale of a crazy demon would have been doing him a favor.

She looked up and sighed. No escape there, either. The ceiling panels would never hold her weight.

"Agent Milton." He held a package in his hands, his dark skin in sharp contrast to the thick white envelope.

The SFPD shield decorated the upper left corner. Preston had been quick; too bad Bradshaw had intercepted it. She hoped she wouldn't have to go through *him*.

"Sir."

"Since your return, I've asked that all your correspondence come through me first." He paused, as if expecting her to object. When she said nothing, he continued, "This arrived by courier not ten minutes ago. I don't remember a request for assistance from the Ingleside station, Agent Milton. And I'm certain I would have heard of it, as Captain Jorgenson is a particular friend of mine."

"I approached them, sir."

"What did you approach them with, Agent Milton?"

"Expertise, sir. They have a recent murder in which the ritualistic nature resembled one of my previous cases. I delivered files which I thought might help their investigation, and the detectives asked for my assistance in preparing a profile."

"This may come as a surprise to you, agent, but we do have standard procedures, particularly when dealing with other agencies. I expect you to follow them."

"Are you forbidding me from assisting the SFPD on this case?" Lilith asked, her voice cooling to match his. "Sir."

"No." With a flick of his wrist, he tossed the package onto her desk. It landed with a solid thump. "But as you represent this agency, I do expect you to act with a measure of decorum."

Her eyes widened. "When have I not, sir?"

A muscle in his cheek flexed. "I hear one thing about you ruffling feathers, and I pull you. One misstep, one bit of questionable evidence, and I pull you."

She barely held her wince in check. Hopefully, Taylor wouldn't complain about her earlier conduct. "Yes, sir," she said meekly.

If he was suspicious at her sudden compliance, he gave no indication of it. With a final, hard stare, he turned and left.

The rookie had his nose practically pressed to his desk, determinedly looking as if he hadn't heard or seen a thing. She waited until he glanced up, gave him a conspiratorial wink. "I slept with his girlfriend. He didn't take it very well."

He blushed to the roots of his prematurely-receding hair. Sweet boy. Hugh used to blush as easily. With a grin, she swiveled her chair around and ripped open the envelope.

She'd only read through half of the reports when the thick reek of nosferatu penetrated the air. *Several* nosferatu. Her psychic shield snapped up, but she rose to her feet unhurriedly, and looked over the tops of the cubes. Any nosferatu would be tall enough to be visible, but no bloodsuckers were in sight.

Uncertain if she'd be back to collect the reports, she vanished them into her cache. There were weapons there, too, swords and guns; she let her mental touch linger over each one in turn, but she fought the urge to arm herself. She could do so quickly enough, if she had to.

Though instinct demanded she protect her back, she walked boldly through the office, following the scent trail to the primary conference room. She picked up the physical odor of nosferatu there—along with a demon's, just as recent: SAC Smith.

Beelzebub.

She wavered, disinclined to face the other demon, but she needed to know if he was with the nosferatu.

Out, past the front desk, and they stood in the hallway near the elevators. Four nosferatu, hulking in black suits, bowler hats covering their pointed ears and bald heads. Smith glanced at her with a smile that seemed to fill her blood with ice crystals—even in his tall, bulky human form, he stood inches shorter than the nosferatu. And another human, whose scent was disturbingly familiar, almost like—

Her heart thudded sickly, as if unwilling to accept what she was seeing, feeling; her expression remained impassive, disinterested.

He smelled like a combination of Ian Rafferty and nosferatu.

And he was in the shape of a man.

"Lilith," Smith said. Like Congressman Stafford, he'd adopted a handsome blond visage; unlike Thomas, there was nothing friendly or open in his features, and his body was ridiculously muscle-bound, as if he couldn't bear the thought of being perceived as weak. "Let me introduce you to our guests."

The elevator dinged, opened. No one moved. The nosferatu stared at her with hooded, expressionless eyes, but she felt the malevolence that emanated from them. The thick carpet muffled the sound of her steps, and she fought to control the racing of her pulse that would give her away.

No fear, she told herself. But it was difficult, given the combined power before her, and the implication of the man-nosferatu.

She drew to a halt a respectable, but not cowardly, distance from the group. "Sir."

Chuckling, Smith held out his hand. She had to unclench her fist to place her palm against his. His skin burned hers, a thin trail of smoke rising from their clasped hands; she smiled, as if the stink of burning flesh were sweet.

Beelzebub had his petty pleasures, too.

"These gentlemen," he said as he pulled her toward the nosferatu, "were dismayed to learn that you had slain two of their brethren."

She looked at each one in turn, spoke deliberately. "And I was dismayed that I received notice regarding our new alliance *after* I killed them." Nodding at the creature that smelled like Rafferty, she added, "I'm pleased to see that Moloch's ritual was successful."

Surprise flared from the nosferatu, distrust. Apparently, she wasn't supposed to know either his name, or that the ritual had taken place. Smith's grip tightened on her hand, grinding bone.

"Leave us, Agent Milton," he said through clenched teeth. "Await me in my office."

She gladly began to turn away, but a rough voice stopped her.

"One moment, halfling." Moloch laid his hand on her arm, each of his teeth shifting to points, his tongue and the inside of his mouth turning black. "I require a taste, to test your trustworthiness."

Disgust spread from the surface of her skin, deep into her stomach, followed by a rising panic. He wanted her blood. And with a taste of her blood, her psychic blocks would be useless; nosferatu could open the strongest mind with a simple nick of a vein.

A secretive smile curved her lips. "Trustworthy? Lucifer would not be pleased if I were such."

Moloch's face contorted, but Smith snatched her hand from the nosferatu before he could bite. It had been a risk, but the demon warlord *was* uncertain of the extent of her knowledge, and her trustworthiness . . . or of Lucifer's. Probably all three.

"Leave us, Lilith." His anger was palpable.

She grinned, tossed her hair over her shoulder, and strode away on trembling legs.

CHAPTER 19

After the soundless cocoon of Beelzebub's office, the noises surrounding her cube seemed loud, frenetic. Or perhaps it was the pounding in her head. She'd expected a punishment from Beelzebub, but it had been something more frightening: an instruction to traverse the Gate by midnight.

Summoned by Lucifer.

She didn't glance at the rookie, but sat, holding her burning palm against the cool desktop. The phone was in front of her. So easy to lift the receiver, to call him and hear his voice. Would he still be at the university? Home?

She had an excuse: he'd want to know what she'd read in the files Preston had sent. He needed to know about the nosferatu and his student. But she couldn't risk being overheard. She'd be lucky if Lucifer didn't destroy her; she shouldn't give him additional reason.

The pain in her hand faded to a mild sting. Her laptop was in her cache; she called it in. Her mouth twisted in self-derision, but she still went to the university website, looked up his e-mail address. Was she so desperate for contact with him? Even in this cold, distant way—

She didn't have to send anything; it was waiting for her in her inbox. A simple message, with a document attached.

`Spend the night with me.`

The document was several hundred pages, all in Latin. She read through the first pages, her eyes blurring. *This* had been written with care, reverence. And her fingers shook as she typed out her reply:

`I can't.`

❧

Hugh hadn't walked more than two steps into Auntie's before she had his left cheek in a fond, if uncomfortably tight, pinch. She gave a half-indignant laugh as he swept her forward and hugged her tiny frame—partially to break that hold on his cheek, and partially because he needed to. Her bangles clicked and sang, and her bright turquoise sari held the thick, warm scent of garlic and onion that permeated the restaurant.

"You treat me very poorly," she said when he let her go, smoothing her hair as if to make certain every strand remained tight within the long black braid. "An old woman doesn't deserve your attention?" She harrumphed, though her eyes were bright with amusement. "No gratitude, no respect."

Even after forty years in San Francisco, her accent was heavy; but as she spoke in English he answered in kind. "I owe you everything, Auntie," he said, pressing a kiss to the back of her hand. "Where would I be today if you hadn't given me a job and a bed to sleep in?"

"A doctor." Her lips pursed, as if she were trying to be stern rather than smile. The red *bindi* she'd painted between her brows wrinkled. "You wasted your time serving here. If you had spent more time on study, you could have been a fine surgeon, married a physician."

The bell atop the door jingled. "Dr. C!"

Hugh lifted a brow. "*Doctor* C, Auntie," he emphasized, and grinned when she pursed her lips again in disapproval. Then he turned to greet the three who'd come in. All former students, they had been coming regularly on Fridays for almost two years. They'd heard about Ian—probably through Savi—and there was a lot of head shaking and disbelief before Auntie urged them to get something to eat.

Hugh and Auntie watched them as they walked toward the buffet. "It's a terrible business, what happened to that boy," she said. Then she looked him sharply up and down. "Come into the back."

Knowing he was in for the feeding of his life, Hugh followed her. According to Auntie, all things were made better with food. A lot of food.

The restaurant was small, and, as it was known better for its lunches and takeout, not very busy in the main dining area in the evening. The tables near the back, where the gaming group usually congregated, had already been pushed together in preparation. He had always loved the atmosphere, the bright silks on the walls, the worn but comfortable benches lining the walls, the cane chairs, the air redolent with spice. He nodded toward a silk painting of Kali on the far wall, the material a soft cream, allowing the blues and reds of the goddess's skin and tongue to stand out.

"Did Ranjit bring that back from his last trip?"

"He's a good boy, thinking of me." She slanted Hugh a look from under her lashes before pushing open the swinging door to the kitchen, and he laughed as he followed her through.

Heat and humidity hit him instantly, throwing him back to the years he used to wait tables, running back and forth between the kitchen and dining room. Keeping occupied, earning his way through college—cleaving to the grandmother and granddaughter. And it had been in these kitchens that he'd slowly, slowly healed.

But not completely.

A small office, not much larger than a closet, sat to the left of the kitchen entrance. Savi sat at the desk, entering in the day's receipts into the computer. He paused, and she looked up.

"Are you well?" he said.

She shrugged, dragged her fingers through her short hair. "Okay, I guess. Considering." Her gaze sharpened. "I brought the swords, as you requested in that e-mail."

She waved her hand toward a duffle bag on the floor. The canvas bag hadn't been long enough; the hilt of the katana protruded from between the zipper teeth. "Thank you. Brandon, Matt, and Zack are here."

"I'll go out to see them in a minute." She looked at him, unsmiling. "And this is the second time in a week you've asked me for an address—and the second time I had to break a few laws to get it. Are you going to tell me what's going on? You're in real trouble, aren't you?"

"Yes." He could give her the partial truth, at least. "And I will tell you, but I'm about to be stuffed."

The humor in her eyes eased the heaviness that had sat with him since receiving Lilith's reply. "She got me when I came in, too. I don't think I'll need to eat for two weeks." She tilted her head. "So, who's this Lily Milton, and why do you need her info?"

He felt the flush rise up his neck, and she stared at him, fascinated.

"You have a *thing* for her." She pursed her lips, and for a moment she looked exactly like her grandmother. "That's kind of weird. I know you don't date often—actually, never—but this isn't the way to woo a lady."

He leaned his shoulder against the doorjamb, laughing so hard that Auntie peered around the corner of the wall to look at him. Wiping his eyes, he gestured toward the swords and said, "Trust me, this is *exactly* the way to woo her." He took a deep, shuddering breath. "Savi, her real name is Lilith."

Her mouth fell open. "You're joking." Her eyes narrowed when he shook his head. "It explains a lot, though. What was it, in high school? She got to you so bad that you turned her into a demon in your book?"

"Not exactly," he choked.

"Well, in any case, you might be interested in what else I found out about her." With a mischievous grin, she added, "I poked around."

"Good," Hugh said, his own humor fleeing. "I need every advantage I can get." The headache that had been threatening since late afternoon began to throb in earnest. He rubbed his forehead, fighting his guilt at using Savi to gain any of those advantages. But he couldn't do this alone—not completely alone.

Auntie cleared her throat, and he looked up to find her glaring at him, a platter in her hand. "Come, *beta*. Eat."

❧

Colin waited in the alley beside the restaurant, the smell of food threatening to overwhelm him. His mouth watered, but it was a craving that had more to do with memory than actual hunger. "I may as well be one of Pavlov's dogs," he said with a touch of bitterness, and ignored the look Sir Pup gave him. He slipped on a pair of sunglasses. "Very well, then. Harness?"

The hellhound obliged by calling in a guide dog's apparatus, and allowed Colin to fasten it over his shoulders.

Across the street, a male and a female—one tall and fat, the other tiny—stopped next to the police cruiser parked at the curb. The man made a gesture with his hand, and Colin heard the passenger window slide down.

"Anything?"

"No, sir. He went home, ran in the park, then came here."

"And you say that Agent Milton left his office after you returned to your surveillance?"

"Yes, sir."

The female sighed, and tilted her head back to look at the sky as if exasperated. The pale skin of her neck seemed to glow under the streetlights, and Colin's fangs throbbed in response. If he hadn't glutted himself on the Guardian still lying unconscious and chained to his bed, he probably would have taken the opportunity and protection of the hellhound to hunt. As delicious as Selah's blood had been, he preferred them awake.

It was difficult for a woman to admire him when she was unconscious.

"This isn't good, Joe," she said as they crossed the street. "Something's way off."

"Yeah," her partner agreed. "We'll get Jorgenson to talk to . . . what's his name? Bradshaw?"

"Yeah." Resignation in her voice.

He moved deeper into the shadows, waited for them to go inside. A few minutes later, he followed them.

The hostess was older than she appeared; and though her eyes widened at the sight of the dog, she gave no indication of the displeasure he felt emanating from her. As Colin disliked the hair and other . . . things . . . the dog had trailed into his house, he couldn't blame this woman for a similar reaction.

"You'll be having the buffet? Or you would like a menu?"

He bit back a sigh as his gaze skimmed over the table surrounded by young males—hot, thick blood. The full-bodied taste of the matrons in the corner. The delicate, ripe flavor of the lady detective filling her plate at the buffet. And the wild, tangy essence of the woman—little more than a girl—who came through a swinging door at the back to greet the group of boys at the first table.

"A menu, please," he said with regret.

"Of course. If you'll allow me . . . ?" She held out her arm, her bangles sliding up her forearm, almost to her elbow.

Colin stared at the pulse beating beneath the golden brown skin of her wrist before he remembered that he was supposed to be blind. "You're very kind," he murmured finally, inwardly cursing Lilith for talking him into this, and himself for going along with it. *In my long life. I've never seen beauty such as yours, Colin!* He mimicked her voice internally, then glanced down at the dog, who seemed to be laughing up at him as if it could read his thoughts. "She's a liar."

The hostess turned. "I'm sorry? This table isn't to your liking?"

"It's fine, thank you." Perfect, actually. From the bench, he had a view of everyone in the restaurant and could clearly hear each conversation. "I was simply instructing my dog to lie down."

"Ah, very good." Again, that flicker of distaste as she looked at the dog. Sir Pup's tongue lolled, dripping saliva on the wooden floors. Colin was certain the hellhound did it deliberately. "You are familiar with our menu? My granddaughter will read the items, if you wish."

As if she'd heard 'granddaughter,' the wild-tangy girl-woman looked over at them. Her breath caught as her gaze ran over his face. Sweet torture, to have that delicious morsel so close.

He smiled, savoring the anticipation that shivered up his spine. "Yes, please."

❧

Hugh scraped up the last bit of dal with a piece of ghee-soaked naan, slipped it into his mouth, then pushed away from the counter before Auntie could return to the kitchen and ladle more onto his plate. He opened the swinging door with his shoulder, still wiping the ghee from his fingers onto a napkin, his stomach pleasantly full but happily not bursting. Auntie was as manipulative as a demon when she thought he hadn't eaten enough.

Not that it was a hardship; a man could fall prey to gluttony rather easily when a meal tasted as good as—

"Savi." A whisper, a warning. No mistaking the ecstasy on the vampire's face as he leaned toward her arched neck and inhaled deeply. She didn't hear Hugh, but Colin did. A cruel, predatory expression flashed over his features before it changed to a look almost comical in its surprise. His eyes were hidden behind dark glasses, but Hugh felt the quick survey the vampire took of him before murmuring something to Savi that made her dissolve into giggles.

His tension subsiding, he finally noticed the silence that had fallen over the gaming table.

Taylor and Preston sat with them. The group had tripled in size, and the greetings from the boys held a note of guilt and unease. Preston rose to his feet, extended his hand.

"Didn't think you'd mind if we talked with these guys, Castleford."

Hugh stepped forward, shook it, not bothering to keep the wry smile from his face. The detectives hadn't been so friendly that afternoon, but they likely didn't want to raise any protective instincts in the group that would make them less open to discussing Ian, Javier or their professor. "Of course not."

Taylor gave Hugh a cursory glance, then looked past him toward Colin and Savi. Had she seen the fleeting exchange between the two men when he'd opened the door?

If she had, she kept her curiosity well contained, nodding toward her plate. "Excellent selection here."

"I'll convey your compliments to Auntie," he said. "Agent Milton couldn't join you?"

"No," Taylor said, not quite hiding the dislike beneath the flat tones.

Hugh's lips twitched. Lilith had that effect.

Another burst of laughter from Savi, this time with a deeper, throaty edge to it. He clenched his fingers in the napkin. "I don't know if you've had an opportunity to speak with Savitri Murray," he said. She'd been interviewed by uniformed officers and confirmed Hugh's story about the night before he'd found Ian, but as far as Hugh knew, hadn't talked to the two detectives. "But she created DemonSlayer. Any questions you have about the game, she could answer them; and she knew both Javier and Ian."

Preston and Taylor looked from him to Savi. The question on Preston's face was clear. "*Just* housemates," Hugh clarified.

"We had hoped to interview her today, before—" Preston stopped, but Hugh imagined he knew what had happened. Before Lilith had shown up with the symbols and the story that had led them to his office. "We intended to speak with her tomorrow."

Hugh smiled thinly. "I'm glad to speed things up, then."

A burning frustration stalked with him to Colin's table. The vampire looked up at his approach, but with a studied lack of focus in his expression. Hugh frowned; then he saw the dog on the floor, the harness, and understood why Savi was reading aloud a description of bhindi masala.

The hellhound grinned up at him.

"Savi," he said, his gaze never straying from Colin's face. "I believe the detectives would like to speak with you."

"Oh, but—" As if his words finally registered, the dismay left her voice and her tone hardened. "What detectives?"

He glanced away from Colin, found her staring over his shoulder at Taylor and Preston. "They just want to ask a few questions."

She straightened. "What should I tell them?"

She sounded as if she wanted to tell them to go to Hell and quickly. He noted Colin's sudden grin and had to smile, too. "The truth."

"All right." A little deflated, she sucked her upper lip between her teeth, the lower pushed out into a pout. It was a gesture she often made when she was torn between doing the correct thing and doing the thing she considered more exciting.

"The truth," Hugh repeated. Seeing how Colin was suddenly entranced by her mouth, he gave her a push.

"Oh! Will you, uh—" She gestured to the menu, to Colin's sunglasses. Then she slapped the laminated menu into his hand. "Take over? I was on forty-two."

Colin watched her walk away with a heavy sigh.

"No," Hugh said and took the seat opposite the vampire. The hellhound scrabbled to his feet, pushing his cold nose into Hugh's lap. After a brief, frozen moment, Hugh began scratching its ears. "She's my sister."

"Oh, come now—" Cutting himself off mid-protest, the vampire exhaled sharply. "Very well. If you call her sister, I'll not pursue her."

"I do." That relationship wouldn't have mattered to the vampire—most women were sister to someone, after all—except that *Hugh* claimed it. Two hundred years before, Hugh and Lilith had helped protect Colin's sister from a nosferatu . . . and from the newly turned, starving Colin.

Colin had very few scruples, but in his appreciation for that he remained steadfast.

With a petulant curl of his lip, the vampire said, "You're looking very"—he waved his hand at the stubble on Hugh's jaw, the casual roll of his sleeves over his forearms—"disheveled. Scruffy, even."

Hugh blinked, and a reluctant smile pulled at his mouth. "Better than the friar's robe?"

Colin shuddered, as if something unpleasant had crawled over his skin.

"You aren't here to critique my appearance."

"No. She asked me to spy on them. The critique is an unexpected bonus."

Hugh's stomach tightened. "Why isn't she here?"

"I don't know." Colin slid off his dark glasses. "Her message was rather cryptic. I'm supposed to watch the pigs in the muggle's kitchen, which I understand well enough. Though I might have gone to your house had the dog not led me here instead. And, afterward, I'm supposed to stop by her apartment and collect something to give to you."

Hugh nodded slowly, unsurprised that the vampire and demon had a system of code to speak in public. The hellhound whimpered and licked his hand, diverting him from his contemplation of it. "Are they speaking with Savi?"

"They're asking about the game and the nosferatu." Colin looked over Hugh's shoulder, an assessing expression in his eyes. "Did you tell her the truth?"

"Not yet."

He said no more, as Auntie appeared next to the table and her quick gaze moved between them. "You're a friend to Dr. Castleford?" She emphasized the title proudly. "You should have said."

Colin gave Hugh a brief, quizzical look before turning to Auntie with a smile designed to charm. The vampire maintained the pretense of blindness; his gaze rested just above her shoulder instead of on her face. "My apologies, madam."

The placement of Colin's lips, perfectly concealing the sharp points of his fangs without appearing to hold the smile in an unnatural position, was the most accomplished Hugh had seen; an untrained human would never be able to determine the difference. "Mrs. Jayakar," Hugh supplied. "This is Mr. Ames-Beaumont."

"Call me Auntie." A blush darkened her cheekbones to a rich cinnamon. She fussed with her sari, slipping her fingers along the sash as if to make certain it still covered the bare skin at her waist. "Are you from Great Britain, Mr. Ames-Beaumont?"

"Colin, please," the vampire said. "Yes, originally from north of London. But I emigrated some time ago."

"For your profession?"

Colin's eyes crinkled at the corners. "Yes."

Hugh opened his mouth, but Auntie lifted a single finger toward his face. He snapped his teeth together.

"And what is it you do?"

"I'm an artist," Colin said. "I paint."

She gave a startled glance at his unfocused eyes. Taken aback, she looked from the vampire to Hugh again, and Hugh said, "He's interested in the Raja Special."

She inclined her head, her expression brightening as she took in Colin's slim frame. Given a chance, she would feed him herself. Colin watched her walk toward the kitchen, but without the hunger with which he'd looked at Savi. His brows drew together, and he returned his attention to Hugh. "You've made a family for yourself."

"Yes." He looked across the table at the vampire, felt the hellhound's heavy head against his leg. "So has Lilith."

"Yes. She has spent many a night with me." Leaning back, he curled his lips into a mocking smile.

Hugh shook his head, grinning. "There is truth in that, but not what you suggest. She's your reflection, not your lover."

"My reflection?" The vampire laughed, as if startled by the idea. "Yes: vain, selfish, greedy." Despite his words, his gaze had warmed.

"Exceptionally loyal to those few she cares about," Hugh said, and rubbed the hellhound's ears when it gave a quiet bark of agreement. Difficult to keep the roughness from his voice. Before he'd Fallen, there had been no one else she'd cared for—but she hadn't been alone these past sixteen years. "She trusted you enough to show you the symbols."

"Yes, but she did not expose herself for my sake." Colin pierced him with a hard stare. "I don't know what was done to her; perhaps we should exchange information. She said it was not from the Punishment she received, but I don't know if I can believe her."

A low growl rumbled from the hellhound's chest. Hugh had to force the words out through the tightness in his throat. "What Punishment?"

The vampire blinked, and then his eyes narrowed. "She never used it against you," he said, a disbelieving laugh slipping from him. "She cannot speak to me without manipulation."

Hugh's fingers clenched. "Explain yourself."

"Tell me about the symbols first."

"She was human once." His chest ached, as it had whenever he thought of her revelation. He saw the surprise on Colin's face, then the confusion. "The symbols are a part of a ritual that transformed her into a demon."

"But—"

"Guardians. Vampires. It follows demonkind would have their own version." Hugh shook his head, anticipating Colin's question. His bitterness was self-directed. "I didn't know, either. I suspect only Michael did."

"Why the need to mislead the police?"

"One of my students was killed by the nosferatu, and the symbols were carved into his body."

Colin was nodding, as if in sudden understanding. "Hence the forgery of Polidori's letter."

"Yes," he said. "Do you have a copy?"

"She took the originals. They might be at her apartment, too. You may as well go in my place; being a courier has never appealed to me." He nudged the dog with his foot. "Sir Pup, do you have a key you could give Castleford?"

"Sir Pup?" Bemused, Hugh looked down at the hellhound, who was flopping his ears from side to side as if in answer to the vampire. A sweet pain sliced though him, left him open and vulnerable. "She named you *Sir Pup*?"

"The detectives are leaving," Colin said softly. "The woman just received a phone call; they're both getting up to go."

Hugh turned. Taylor and Preston's faces were hard, bleak. Taylor slashed Hugh a look, but they left without speaking to him. "Could you hear the voice on the other end?"

"No."

Auntie reappeared, her arms laden with trays, and Hugh stood up to help her. Savi slipped in between them, arranged the chutneys to her satisfaction, and transferred the platters to the table.

Colin stared at the volume of food, swallowed hard. Auntie waited with her hands folded at her waist, but as Colin continued staring without moving to fill his plate, she began scooping and explaining the location and taste of each dish, stopping just short of spooning bites into Colin's mouth.

Savi stood by Hugh, her head at the level of his shoulder. "He's very handsome," she murmured in Hindi. Colin glanced up, but the rapacious pleasure in his gaze turned to something painfully beleaguered when she added, "It's too bad he's gay."

Hugh looked down at Savi, then back at the vampire. Some lies were definitely useful. "Yes," he said, as the vampire choked on a mouthful of rice. "I suppose it is."

CHAPTER 20

The misting rain formed a halo around a light illuminating the front of a run-down apartment building. Though Savi had lifted Lilith's address from a law enforcement database, he doubted she actually lived there.

He frowned. Despite eight hundred years spent fighting them, he didn't know what demons did when they weren't convincing humans to create chaos. Like Guardians, they didn't need to sleep or eat, so it was possible there was no downtime; and unlike Guardians, demons were not social creatures—particularly not with their own kind. Lilith's friendship with Colin was an anomaly; any other demon would have considered it a weakness.

Rain beaded on plastic surrounding the bus stop, and steam slowly crept up the inside of the glass. Hugh shifted on the bench; his nausea from the bus ride across town had passed. He could either get out and check on the apartment—or sit here and do nothing.

He reached down and picked up the duffel. No matter how unlikely her presence at the apartment was, it would be foolish to go in unarmed. But he kept it covered—if someone else lived in the apartment, he didn't want to brandish a two-foot blade in her face.

The front security door was broken; inside, the row of dilapidated mailboxes confirmed her apartment number: Milton, 4D. Shaking his head over her choice of last name, he took the stairs two at a time, trying to ignore the smell of cat litter, dirty diapers, and frying meat that permeated the air. The stairs creaked under his weight; if she was in the apartment and listening, she'd hear his approach—and he knew she could probably distinguish his footsteps from the other tenants'.

Not that he intended to surprise her—he just wanted answers.

The fourth-floor landing carpet was well worn; ground-in dirt darkened what had probably been blue to a dingy brown. Lilith's door was the last on the right; a single bare bulb lit the hallway.

Hugh frowned, almost certain now that the address was fake. Why would she choose this as a dwelling? He could afford better, even if his only income had been his adjunct professor's salary—and she had access to whatever monies and connections had pulled the strings to create her current persona.

Deciding to follow through, now that he'd come that far, he knocked twice on the door marked 4D.

No answer.

He knocked again, then listened for sounds from inside. Water pipes groaned, but he couldn't be certain if they were from 4D or the rooms on the floors below. He tried the doorknob, and it turned in his hand.

He didn't hesitate to swing the door open, reaching into the duffel to grasp the handle of his sword. The room was dark, but the source of the noise became clear; within the bathroom, a shower was running.

His eyes quickly adjusted. A studio apartment, bare of furniture except for a twin-sized bed pushed into one corner, and a metal folding chair tucked under a cheap card table. Slung across the back of the chair was a suit—the same suit that Lilith had worn earlier. He could see the dull shine of photographs and manila folders spread across the tabletop.

Books were piled and stacked on every other available surface, stuffed into cases lining the walls, filling the open-faced cupboards in the kitchen.

Relaxing slightly, he flipped on the light and grimaced. Although clean, the studio was as shabby as the rest of the building. Evidence of water damage streaked the ceiling, and the linoleum in the tiny kitchen cracked and buckled. On the bed, a lumpy striped mattress looked as if it could have come from a jail cell; it had probably been included with the apartment, since Lilith didn't need to sleep.

She certainly hadn't bothered to decorate.

The shower shrieked as the she turned the water off. Mildly surprised she hadn't already charged out of the bathroom, weapon in hand, skin red and eyes blazing, Hugh pulled his own sword from its sheath, dropped the duffel onto the floor, and stepped across the room to stand next to the bathroom door.

The distinctive slide of shower curtain rings across metal followed by the squeak of old floorboards allowed him to track her movements within the room. A faucet turned, water splashed in a sink. Then the slow, steady brush of terry cloth over skin.

Blood rushed to his groin as the image immediately formed in his mind—Lilith, one foot propped on the edge of the tub, running the cloth down her long length of leg. Would her skin be crimson again, he wondered—or the pale silk she'd assumed that afternoon?

He'd find out soon; the floorboards creaked again, and he lifted his sword, holding it across the width of the doorway at neck height.

A rush of steam escaped as Lilith opened the door, stepping through—then belatedly noticing the sword aimed at her throat.

Crimson skin, he noted as her eyes widened, darting from the blade to him. But otherwise human in appearance. Her surprise was quickly replaced by indifference.

"If you are going to break in and point something at me, Hugh," she said, raising one hand and pushing the blade out of her path, "at least point something *interesting* at me."

Her gaze dropped to the front of his jeans, and then she turned away from him with a languid roll of her hips. "Did you not receive my e-mail? Or are you so eager to lose your virginity that you ignored it?"

He allowed her to pass, watching her as she walked across the room to a small closet door. She'd wrapped herself in a bright yellow towel that covered her from chest to mid-thigh; droplets fell from her length of dark hair with each step, creating tiny circles in the threadbare carpet. She moved with a lanky, casual grace that belied her agility and strength.

Sheathing his sword, he said, "No. Colin said you'd been Punished."

Her back still to him, she pulled several items from their hangers. Her voice was disinterested as she asked, "Did he?"

She pulled a black T-shirt over her head, then reached down, stepping into a whisper of blue satin. Hugh didn't look away as she skimmed the panties over her legs, catching a glimpse of the curve of her bottom as she lifted the towel to slide them into place. She let the towel drop to the floor.

The methodical cleansing, the lack of emotion: impossible not to recognize it. There was no need for a demon to bathe. She was going through a ritual, purging herself. For what purpose?

"Why are you dressing like that?"

She froze, then glanced at him from under her lashes. "You prefer me unclothed?"

"I wonder why I haven't yet seen you in any form other than Lily and the demon. I wonder why you wear real clothing, when you can create it with a thought. I wonder how it is that I surprised you in your home, and why you sent Colin to the restaurant instead of going yourself—in any guise. You enjoy those powers, revel in them."

He nearly took back his words as she glanced down at herself, and shame flickered across her features, erasing her amusement and leaving a blank, remote expression.

"Lucifer claims it is an effect of the blood loss and the subsequent resurrection," she said without emotion. "But I know a Punishment when I'm subjected to one."

"He has taken your ability to shift?"

"Except for my full demon form, and those in between. And to send dreams. A few other minor abilities, too."

Lucifer had that kind of power? "This is why the symbols are missing," he realized. "Why give you the form you use now?"

"To remind me that I subjected my will to his when he transformed me." Turning toward him, she swept back the wet curls that had fallen onto her forehead. "And to punish me for my long-ago vanity, I imagine. One of his promises was that I would never age, that my beauty would never succumb to time."

"Then he denied it," Hugh realized, following her to the table and laying his sword down. And when Lucifer allowed

Lilith her own face, it was not a reward, but a constant reminder of the choice she'd made. There had been many times Hugh had taken on the face of another, but he'd always been able to return to his true form.

"I often work undercover. More difficult to remain unnoticed with this face, with the *same* face each day. He relishes that difficulty," she said, but with that awful, uncharacteristic detachment.

Hugh studied her, looking for any emotion, and found none.

"Lilith," he hesitated, then lifted his hand to her jaw. "Are you well? What has happened?"

A shudder wracked her body. She pressed her cheek into his palm, then wrapped her fingers around his wrist and dragged his hand from her face. "Do not be kind to me," she said from between clenched teeth, her eyes glowing brightly. "You will destroy me with it."

Though her statement felt like a blow to his chest, he said, "If it brings you pleasure, I shall do my worst."

Her grip tightened, but the pain of it was nothing to the smile that tilted the corners of her lips. With a sigh, she released him. "I heard you come in; I was surprised by the sword. I did not think your babysitters would allow you to carry one around the city."

"They don't know," he said. "I left through the back of the restaurant." He'd taken the opportunity the detectives' precipitate leaving had given him; their surveillance team had not yet arrived when Hugh had slipped out. Savi and Auntie would likely be upset with him, but it seemed the only time to search Lilith's apartment.

An unexpected boon, that she was still here.

"At night?" She shook her head; the smile had not yet faded. "You couldn't have waited until the nosferatu . . ." Trailing off, she regarded him with narrowed eyes. "Have you ever heard of a nosferatu resistant to the daysleep? Or day*light*?"

"No. And the only vampire is—"

"Colin, I know. I don't know why or how he is, though. And no matter how I threaten him, he won't tell me."

Hugh knew, and he had no reason not to tell her now. "Michael's sword tainted Colin's blood when he was human. You remarked once on his sister's resistance to your suggestions; she came by it the same way: the sword."

"The spoiled little slut," Lilith said absently, as if her mind was working through something else. Hugh suppressed his grin.

"You saw a nosferatu during the day?"

She nodded, and her mouth thinned into a grim line. "Perhaps they used the underground parking structure to escape the sunlight, but they were awake."

He searched her face, caught the lingering fear that crossed her features. "How many?"

She held his gaze. "Five. And one was in a human's form. He had your student's scent."

"Ian?" His breath stilled, and his hands trembled as rage tore through him. Though she must have felt it, he kept his voice even. He would not make her a target for his anger. "The ritual gave the nosferatu that power? To shift, to resist daylight?"

"I think so," she said slowly, watching him. Then her gaze lowered to the table, and she pulled a report from a stack of files. "There was very little blood at the scene."

"Not surprising, given they are nosferatu," he said. It was a coroner's report, and he only gave it a cursory glance.

"No, but it is a change from the ritual I knew." Laying her hand on his, she opened to the second page. "Stomach contents."

He forced himself to read through the haze that clouded his vision. "Just milk and cereal."

"No blood. The blood is the key for the transformation—the power is derived by ingesting the blood that flows after the symbols have been carved. It's collected, and then the person must drink it before they fall unconscious from the blood loss. My guess is that instead of your student ingesting it, the nosferatu did—and they took in the properties of the transformation that way. Perhaps the one I saw took more than the others, or the full benefit of the transformation can only go to one. But nosferatu don't trust one another, so they would demand at least a share of the power, even if it is very small. And it does not take a great amount of blood, only the endurance to remain alive until the end of the carving. That is how I was made. And at the end Lucifer asked me if I wanted to drink and live, or die. And we made a bargain that I would serve him for as long as I had my demon powers." A bitter smile curved her mouth. "I assume that is not how Michael does it."

"Nay." He had to put the report down, clenched the edge of the table to control his hands' shaking.

She gestured toward his sword. "Do you want to stab me?"

As she no doubt intended, the offer startled him out of his

anger; but the energy coiled within his muscles did not fade as easily as the rage. He raked his hand through his hair, stalked across the room. It wasn't enough. He turned back. The detachment had settled over her again; she stood, looking at him without expression, her arms folded beneath her breasts, her demonic skin like a violent gash against the black shirt.

A few long strides and he was beside her again. She took a deep, sudden breath, as if something in his appearance unnerved her. A human response, despite her apparent intention to show none.

"This is not kindness," he said. He slid his hand over her jaw, behind her neck to thread his fingers in the damp curls at her nape. Her skin burned beneath his palm, sent warmth spreading through him.

Her gaze dropped to his mouth. "What is it?" Her chest rose and fell in a quick rhythm.

"Envy." He envied her control, desired it for himself. And when he touched her, his restlessness fell away. Left a new purpose in its place, a direction for the energy within him.

He closed the distance between them, grazed her upper lip with his tongue. And immediately wanted more. "Avarice."

"Wrath?" The word shook, with laughter and fear and—

He smiled against her mouth. "Lust," he corrected, and his voice was rough with it. He drew her lower lip between his teeth. Why fear? He couldn't hurt her. His wrist still throbbed from her grip earlier, but she . . . "Why is kindness more destructive than a sword?"

She closed her eyes, began to pull away, but he followed. "Gluttony." He whispered it against her mouth before kissing her, coaxing her open with the gentle insistence of his lips and tongue. Despite his claim, he drank from her with delicate sips; he had less control over his hands, and they gathered and pressed her full-length against him. Slid up her ribcage, over her peaked breasts.

Arching into his touch, she moaned low in her throat, yet amidst the desire he could still hear the fear. She responded, but held back. His chest tightened with an unbearable pain.

The last time he had kissed her thus, he had killed her.

❧

Hugh dropped his hands, staggered back. Lilith's stance mirrored his, her hands fisted at her sides as she stared at him. In her attempt to resist touching him, her nails had cut into her skin.

Of course, her resistance indicated that, for all her preparation, the emotions she'd tried to hide were not far from the surface. Lucifer would easily sense these, and physically smell Hugh on her. She'd have to cleanse herself again when he left. But for now, she was finished with suppression.

She licked her lips, slowly uncurled her fingers. "You've never been a proficient sinner. That," she said with a grin, "was not gluttony."

"If it had been, it would be the least of the sins I have committed against you."

Her eyes widened, and a laugh broke from her. "You're overcome by guilt . . . because of Seattle?"

His mouth compressed. "You are not free; and you are still afraid. I should have found another way."

"Hugh, I couldn't tolerate the idea of your Fall. I would have slain *you* had you not me first. Like this."

Quick as thought, she was back in his arms, her lips raised to his. His body was taut and hard, and he drew in a sharp breath.

She shivered, resisted the urge to rub against him like a cat. "Your sword, here." She called the broadsword in, placed it in his hand.

He looked down at the weapon, and his gaze flew back to hers. "Lilith," he said softly. "How did—"

"And mine."

He stiffened as the cold length of her blade pressed against his back. She drew the point up his spine, slicing his shirt but careful not to cut his flesh. With her free hand, she circled around his chest, smoothed her palm over the plane of his shoulder blade. "Your wings were here," she said. Her fingertips found the edge of the tear, and she pulled. The shirt ripped as easily as tissue. Bare, warm skin beneath. She slid her forefinger across his back, felt the shape of the bones under the sheet of muscle. "And this would have been the entry point for my sword. Between your ribs, through your heart."

She pressed on the spot, then raked her nails gently over it. The swords vanished, and he shuddered as if she'd released him from an invisible hold. "That does not absolve my—"

"I would not have regretted it." The words fell between them like drops of ice. "You have nightmares, do you not?" She knew he did, even without the confirmation in his tight nod. Impossible to have that level of guilt without it manifesting in some way. "I don't."

A wry smile touched his lips. "You don't sleep."

"I wouldn't have them even if I did. By that time, you were not worth the regret. There was nothing left of the man who'd once fascinated me, who'd ruled emotions I'd rather not have acknowledged. Yet you were still my tyrant."

His face whitened. His throat worked, and she dropped her gaze to the buttons at his collar. The top two were undone, and she began unfastening the rest.

"Will be easier for you to fulfill your bargain."

His voice was hoarse, thick. It took a moment for her to realize what he meant. She looked up from the smooth expanse of his chest. "No. That was then. Now, I would regret. Why else would Lucifer have waited so long? No reason, but for you to shed the skin of frost you wore as a Guardian, and to become Hugh again."

She pressed her hand over his heart, and he captured her wrist, held it still. "What do you need from me?" He searched her face, and she wondered what he saw there. "Do you need me to be as I was when I was a Guardian?"

She shook her head, laughing. "You cannot save me." Pushing the shirt from his shoulders, she vanished it before it hit the floor. Oh, but he was beautiful. Golden flesh, sculpted by his inner demons, and more perfect than any illusion he'd been able to create as a Guardian.

He lifted her chin. "I can try."

"I hate martyrs," she said, smiling. Her hands moved to the waistband of his jeans. Her fingers dipped in, stroked the hot, silken tip of him.

A broken, unraveling breath escaped from between his teeth, and the muscles of his abdomen stood out in sharp relief. "What is this?"

"Pride." She cupped her hand, slid down his thick length. She could have eased her way by unzipping, unbuttoning—eased the tight fit of her fist and his cock within the clothing. His groan made her glad she didn't.

"Mine?"

"No, it is mine," she said, and squeezed. Heat gathered low

in her belly as he shuddered again. "Though you have reason enough to be proud."

He laughed, but it held a desperate edge, and she could feel his need to move within her grip. "Vanity." He choked on the word as she pulled upward, pumped her hand at the crown.

"Aye, vanity."

He closed his eyes, and his hips jerked once, as if he had to thrust or expire. "The book."

"Mmm, the book," she agreed, her tone teasing. She spread a bead of moisture over the head of his shaft with her thumb. Her nipples were tight, and the slow heat had become a burning ache.

She ignored it.

"You don't like the translation?" he said, and his head bowed as she circled the crown again.

Her lips pursed. "Couldn't you have reprinted it? It's humiliating. But the original is very good."

"You wish another version? A new translation?" He was shaking, with laughter and frustration.

Her eyes narrowed. "You're *allowing* me to punish you this way, so that you feel less guilty for it."

"I hardly think"—he broke off on a gasp, clenched his teeth as she stroked down his length with pressure that bordered on the painful—"this is punishment."

"No." She released him, stepped back. If her grin was strained, she doubted he would notice. "This is."

She was disappointed, however, when he only stood stiffly, staring at her with amusement. As if his cock didn't strain and pulse, as if he weren't moments from release—she knew he was.

"I think I finally understand why Mandeville allowed himself to be tied to that wall. You make a man nearly desperate enough to drill a hole into a stone and rut."

"You aren't." He didn't even touch himself.

"I'm well-versed in this kind of frustration." He tilted his head. "My hand has been my only companion these eight hundred years. I'm glad this time it is yours."

He smiled as he approached her, lifted her palm to place a kiss in the center. Her breath caught, strangling her laughter.

"Mine are rough," he said, his voice low. "When I served d'Aulnoy, I always had a sword in my hand, practicing so that I'd be ready if he needed my weapon. And I carried the calluses with me into death, though I had not arms nor armor to take."

He smoothed his thumb across the heel of her hand, and she shivered. He still had a warrior's calluses, though he'd not lifted a weapon in years. As if divining her thoughts, he shook his head.

"These are not the same. Falling leaves its mark, but this is not one of them. This is the result of trying to forget—trying to understand—what I've done to you. And I have done naught but think of it these sixteen years. So, yes, I'm glad of your touch. Not only because it is soft, but because it *is*. I should never have rejected it."

Her gaze traced the line of his fingers, studied the contrast of tanned skin against red. He'd not been the only one who'd needed protection. She had, too—from his touch, from his kindness. There'd been safety in his rejection of her; and though she'd not known the truth behind his ability to resist her, she knew her weakness: she'd craved his touch as much as she had feared it would be her undoing. As a Guardian, he'd been safe.

But now he did not hide from her, could not hide—and the humanity that denied his protection denied hers as well. And this kindness would destroy her.

She pulled back her hand and looked away. Methodically, she began calling in weapons from her cache, placing them on the table. A sword, crossbow, rifle. She nodded toward the files. "Those are all related to the investigation." Daggers, a pair of semiautomatic pistols. Another sword. "There isn't much you don't know—except that Sanchez's mother told Preston and Taylor that she saw him leaving with you the night before she reported him missing. At least, with someone who matched your description and had a slight accent of indeterminate origin. Probably a demon. But it was reason enough for them to focus on you." She unloaded more weapons. "Take the reports with you."

"I will." He stood behind her, but she could hear the frustration in his voice. "Quite the arsenal."

"Yes." She paused, let her mind run over the remaining weapons. Took out a few more, then located her badge and ID. Her suit was on the back of the chair; she slid them inside the pocket and hung it in the closet.

When she returned to the table, Hugh was studying the pile of weapons on its surface. He reached down, slid his finger along the barrel of a pistol. "You don't need this many guns for work."

"No. I like them. And I've found they are effective against the nosferatu, as well."

"Slows them down?"

"Not much, but enough to help." She met his eyes, had to bite back a smile. "When I was allowed, that is."

"May I?" He picked up the pistol at her nod. "Michael and I used to practice with a flintlock revolver, but found it was too unreliable, and the damage too minimal to be of use." He blinked. "That was two hundred years ago."

"You should have tried them again."

He chuckled, set it back down. "The corps does not readily accept change."

"They should. Take it." She called in an extra clip. "But if you have to use it, make certain there isn't any evidence. It's registered to a man I arrested seven years ago."

Laughing softly, he shook his head. "And if I'm caught with it on my way home?"

Her lips quirked. "Run very fast," she said, but didn't argue when he left it on the table.

Next the books, and she set those on the already leaning tower beside the kitchen counter.

He squatted next to them, looked at the spines. The broad line of his naked back drew her gaze. After a moment's hesitation, she called in his robe and sword. Held them, waiting.

"These are from various public libraries," he said. Looking around the room, he realized, "All of them." He opened one of the covers, glanced back at her with a lift of his brows. "They must be overdue by now."

"I didn't check them out."

"Planning the downfall of mankind by stealing books from the library?" There was no censure in his tone, only curiosity. Then he froze, his gaze fixed on the items in her hands.

"There are no books Below. And if I take any with me in my cache, Lucifer will confiscate them. I can get away with it here because I can make the theft seem a petty pleasure. But if he realized that it was the books I enjoyed, and not the theft . . ." She shrugged. "He'd take my ability to read, and it is one of the few true pleasures left to me."

Hugh rose to his feet, his expression stark.

"I've seen him do something similar to a musician—took away the music he'd been creating in his head as an escape from the torment." She looked down at the robe, at the pile of weapons. "Everything that I need, everything that means anything to me, I leave here. I wash to rid myself of the scent that clings to me after living on Earth for a while. And then I strip away all that is human, because he hates it." She vanished her clothing, felt the instantaneous shift as she transformed.

He'd never seen the cloven feet or the scales that gleamed over her skin, but he did not flinch or look away. He stepped forward, lifted the bundle from her grasp, and dropped it to the floor beside them. The wool muffled the clank of metal against the carpet. "Lilith—"

"Do *not* be angry on my behalf," she growled. "Do not pity me. And do not be kind to me."

"Why? Should I think you less human because of what I see now?" His gaze traveled down her length, and she fought the urge to transform back, to hide.

"Because he hates self-pity above all other things, considers it an insult to his rule. And because I must go Below, and he will decide whether to make me fulfill the terms of our bargain, and destroy you, or to Punish me for stepping into—perhaps undermining—whatever bargain he has made with the nosferatu. I must present a face that is entirely inhumane, entirely without self-pity and completely in line with his goals, or he will destroy me. I must convince him he will be better served by our bargain than by my Punishment." She looked down at her hands—claws. Twisted, with obsidian talons. "There are no other halflings like me because, at some point, they have all wished for something human, a return to what they were, and he has destroyed them all."

No, not destroyed—what he'd done to them had been worse than destruction. It was that fate Hugh had saved her from when he'd killed her. He couldn't save her from it now.

She lifted her head. His shoulders were hunched, as if in anticipation of a wound. "And when you are kind to me, when you touch me, I desire what I cannot have."

And she watched the indifference enter his eyes, his withdrawal, knowing he would make no other choice. There were few things she could depend on, but the actions of this knight she would never doubt. He would subjugate his desires for the life of another. He would slay dragons when they threatened— and when a lady asked him to let her be, he would leave.

And if his leaving was like another death, it was only because she *must* be a dragon.

❧

He did not feel his legs as he went down the stairs; even the weight of his duffel, increased by the files—and the sword and robe she'd stuffed in at the last moment—was nothing. There was naught to do but leave, though he would have stayed, would have . . .

What? Earlier, he'd thought to use her susceptibility to him to prove her humanity, but if Lucifer would destroy her for it, he could not. Would not.

Cold rain pelted his bare skin—he paused on the sidewalk, abruptly aware of his half-naked state. She hadn't returned his shirt. A short, hard laugh escaped him as he dropped the bag. On one knee, uncaring that the wet concrete soaked his pant leg, he pulled out the robe, felt the familiar wool beneath his fingers.

The rain beaded on the material, the drops glistening beneath the streetlamp.

She'd kept it sixteen years. Unease filled him at the realization, though he couldn't pinpoint why. Suddenly still, he examined the rough weave for stains. It had been cleaned, and he would have been glad for it had he not the sinking certainty where the blood had gone.

He let it fall back onto the canvas, wiped away the water from his face. He could not wear it again. Foolish to have worn ever worn it, when it stood for a humility he had not truly felt. An illusion, as false as her demon skin—a denial of his will to a greater purpose, a denial he'd resented, but not resisted.

And when he'd finally resisted it, he'd destroyed the one person he'd most wanted to save. Had destroyed himself.

It would have made more sense for Lucifer to have forced her into the bargain earlier, when his soul had been hard but for the cracks Savi and Auntie had—

He rose slowly to his feet, his heart thundering.

Sixteen years.

Had Lucifer been interested in obtaining Hugh's soul, he would have acted earlier. But it was not Hugh's damnation the demon lord truly sought.

It was Lilith's pain.

Lilith knew that. The Morningstar spoke with doubled tongue; he forced Lilith to purge any humanity out of hate for its source, but wanted the pain it brought her when she could not. He'd waited sixteen years to call in the bargain as a Punishment.

But if she could convince Lucifer the bargain was not a Punishment, that she was eager to destroy Hugh, wouldn't Lucifer choose that which gave her greater pain? Would he not choose the real Punishment?

Instinct—sharp, predatory—led him back inside. She had expected him to leave, and he had; but sixteen years had not turned him into the boy he'd been before, the knight who lived for the chivalric code. Nor was he the Guardian who'd lost faith.

He was a man who needed to make certain she could not hide what she felt for him from Lucifer. When she returned from Below, he'd deal with the consequences then.

But she had to return first.

He moved with slow deliberation up the stairs, preparing. Giving himself completely over, losing himself in the memories of her—teasing, arousing—so that she would not feel the intent behind the action. He knew how to approach her, how to start, but to fully convince her . . . he had to feel his way through, find a vulnerability and exploit it.

She would hear him; and, indeed, she opened the door before he could reach for the knob—no longer in the shape she would use Below, but the form in between. The form she'd been so many nights: in the castle tower, his bedroom the night previous . . . Seattle. The black corset hugged her torso, the leather pants her legs to just below her knees. She was barefoot, and it would have made her seem vulnerable but for the sword in her hand.

He leaned against the door frame, hooked his thumb in his pocket and smiled lazily. "Shall we bargain?"

CHAPTER 21

No. The answer hovered on Lilith's tongue, but she couldn't force it past her lips. A demon had no choice but to consider a bargain, to hear the terms before rejecting it as unsatisfactory. He knew that. She eyed him warily, distrusting his stance, his smile, the impenetrable psychic block around his thoughts. And she distrusted herself, for the skip of her heart when she'd heard him returning. Would that she'd had more time, to banish the pain of his leaving, the lingering arousal.

As if he felt her probe, his blocks disappeared, leaving her mind awash with images of heat and raw sexual congress.

Her breath sped from her lungs, and the heavy, liquid melting she had suppressed weakened her knees, leeched the strength from the limbs she'd determined would be as steel.

"You have nothing to interest me," she said, but her eyes made her a liar. She couldn't look away from him, from the dark hair wet and tousled, as if he'd run his hand through it to shake off the rain. The drops that clung to his cheeks, ran in rivulets down his shoulders and chest, beside the bronze nipples puckered by the cold; she wanted to follow that trail with her fingers, her lips, her tongue.

Vanishing her sword, she turned away. And immediately re-alized it was a mistake when he stepped into the room, set his bag down, and shut the door. Locked it.

He had not taken her response as acquiescence, but had taken advantage of her reluctance to fight, to argue. She had retreated from a defensible position, and he'd claimed it for his own.

"Coward," he said softly.

Gathering herself, she looked over her shoulder and slanted him a wry smile. "Self-preservation is not completely divorced from cowardice, as you well know."

"Aye."

The guttural assent sent a tremor through her stomach. He'd discarded his accent, the language of his birth hundreds of years before, but it bled through when he was deeply affected or harassed.

Or aroused.

The memory of the feel of him, his hard length, lingered on her palm; she flexed her fingers against it. She refused to glance down, to see the physical evidence of that assent. Did not need to see it: he projected it as clearly as a child.

She stood still, silent as he approached and stopped a breath away.

"It was the first name you called me: coward." A gentle smile curved his mouth as he touched a curl above her ear, but the softness of his expression, his action, did not deceive her: she could feel the heat within him. "For not making sport of Mandeville. For caring more of a comfortable situation than obtaining power over him."

"Yes, and look what it got you: a freezing post on the allure and a sword through the heart." Her tone mocked him, but he only raised his gaze to hers, a hint of triumph rolling through his psychic scent.

"You offered me a bargain that night on the wall walk, my lady—a bargain I was a fool to have rejected. I will accept it now."

She shook her head. "It is not still—"

He halted her denial by placing her hand against his skin, drawn tight by cold and rain. "You can burn me with hellfire. What has changed that you would withdraw the offer? Are you so different you cannot sit on a man's lap without it being a kindness?"

It was a challenge—a trap, though she couldn't see his purpose. She withdrew her hand. "I am as I always have been," she said, and it took all of her control to keep the trembling inside her from manifesting outwardly. He would kill her with this; did he not see that?

He lowered his head. "I see your lie," he whispered against her lips. No part of him touched her, yet she felt enveloped by him, surrounded. Under siege.

Did he seek her surrender or her resistance?

"You cannot. You're no longer Gifted—" She wasn't making sense, couldn't think as his mouth skimmed down the side of her neck, still not touching her but for the warmth of his breath.

He straightened. His gaze was cold, hard. "I see your lie," he repeated.

He pivoted and strode toward her table; shaken, she stared as he sifted through the items there. Perhaps he could still see Truth, perhaps eight hundred years as a Guardian had left its mark on him in ways not entirely human—

A pair of handcuffs dangled from his fingers as he turned back. She laughed. "What do you think to do with those?"

"I think to obtain the power I once denied myself," he said, and though the reply sent prickles of unease down her spine, she let him slip them over her wrists, click them tight. She could break them if she desired. "Surely even your father would approve of it, for I intend to help you along in your bargain with him."

Was he mad? But, no, the purpose emanating from him wasn't tinged by insanity, only arousal. Curiosity and excitement—worse, anticipation—made her question breathlessly, "How?"

He scanned the apartment; his gaze lit on something behind her, and he began pushing her in that direction. A devilish grin creased his cheeks, flashed white teeth. "I get to play the demon. To tempt someone who has strayed from the path."

Her back hit the open closet door, the hinges squealing as her weight forced it as wide as it could go. He raised her hands, snagged the handcuff chain over the coat hook screwed to the top of the door.

"You jest," she laughed again. "And will you torture me now? Perhaps if you do so, I will be able to hate you and won't need to *pretend* to look forward to fulfilling Lucifer's bargain."

Her laughter faded as she caught sight of his face. He closed his eyes, as if against terrible pain—but when he opened them they were filled with determination.

The wild tousle of his hair should have softened his appearance, but his features were stark, edged with desperation. His gaze pierced her like blue steel: steady, resolute. He traced the line of her jaw with his forefinger. "Now we bargain, Lilith."

Too late, she realized his humor a moment ago had been a ruse, designed to lower her guard, to allow him to position her just so. "What are the terms?" she said, her voice hoarse.

"You will resist me as I torment you, as I prove your lie and your humanity," he said. "And forcing it from you will take mine."

"It is more like a wager than a bargain." Dependent not on an action, but an outcome.

"A wager binds as closely, does it not?"

He knew it did. "You'll hurt me?" She swallowed. Though she had been joking before, it might be a way . . .

"Yes," he said, his face carefully blank, and her stomach twisted.

She jingled the cuffs. "These will not hold me."

"The wager will." His lids lowered, his psychic blocks snapped back into place. The sudden absence of his emotions left her floundering to make sense of her own. "I have seen you do this to a human; but if you haven't changed, if you are demon, it will be nothing to you."

She searched his face, could read nothing in his expression. "You know it isn't."

"Then you best fake it—as I did for centuries. If you cannot hide your response from me, how will you from the Morningstar?"

Was he trying to *save* her? Would he never learn?

"He does not touch me." No one's touch, no one's kindness had ever affected her as Hugh's did.

"He does not have to."

She squeezed her eyes closed. He was right. "You'll destroy us both."

"It is equal consequence, then." He hesitated, and she looked up at him. "I will not hide from you, Lilith."

A reversal of their past. "And yet I must from you."

He nodded. She laughed bitterly, but could not deny the temptation of having him open to her. Finally.

And it was that temptation which decided her. "You are an imbecile to use a demon's methods."

He tipped her chin up. "I know." Pressing his lips to hers, he inhaled, as if taking her into himself. "Shift. Full demon."

It was a gentle command, one that didn't immediately register over the pleasure of that soft kiss. When it did, she smiled, shook her head. "You don't want that one; it will make this impossible for you." How could he desire the thing she became? It made her uneasy, ashamed, to think of him touching that form.

But perhaps it would be easier for him to be cruel.

"Your shape has never mattered; I have seen you in too many," he said, his eyes searching hers. "But it might be the mental defense you need. Shift."

A defense . . . she did not know that she had any against him.

But the wager had been made, so she transformed. And though he had seen her naked in this state less than fifteen minutes before, she was relieved when he told her not to vanish her clothing.

Her brows arched. "Mandeville I left with his hose around his ankles. Will you do the same to me?"

"Nay," he said, his voice rough. His hands trembled slightly as he brushed her hair back over her shoulders. "I won't leave you."

There was more meaning in his response than in her question, but she had no time to ponder what lay beneath the statement. His fingers skimmed the crimson scales on the arch of her neck, his thumbs meeting at the hollow of her throat, then running the length of her collarbone. "They are like newly blown glass." At the point of her shoulder, he traced the rounded edge of a scale with his fingertip, then circled behind, back up under her arm. "But softer here." His head dipped, and he pressed his lips to the vulnerable skin.

She clenched her jaw, her claws curling into fists over her head. So simple to break away, yet she could not. How long would he be gentle? When had he learned the torment was deeper when it followed pleasure? Had she been the one to teach him?

"Perhaps you would perform a reenactment in other ways," she said and pulled in the long, slender branch from her mental cache, let it fall to the floor. No decay in that space; it was as supple as it had been in the thirteenth century. "I striped his ass with this."

Hugh glanced down. "Perhaps you would have been better put to use preserving England's forests than whipping men with them." He cupped her bottom, lifted her against him. She gripped the hook with her hands, thought it might snap off—but, no, he easily supported her weight, her thighs alongside his hips, her wings pressed to the door.

Ridiculous, to be thrilled at his strength when hers was exponentially greater. She could kill him with a squeeze of her legs, and yet it was pleasure she wanted when she pulled him closer, hooking her ankles behind the small of his back and forcing his erection hard against her. Exquisite pressure. She grinned as he drew in a sharp breath.

He thought to play the demon? He should have chosen less capable prey.

"This is not resistance," he said.

With a lift of her hips, she stroked up and down his length. "I'll resist when you hurt me."

"I've no intention of hurting you physically." In her moment of surprise, he pushed her legs to the floor and spun her around. His weight forced her against the door, her cheek pressed tight to the wood. "I only intend to torment you, to prove your humanity." His breath was hot in her ear. "My idea of torment happens to differ from yours."

"You knew I thought—"

"That because you could not deny your human nature and save yourself, I would deny mine and be damned for it?" Gently, he bit her earlobe, then flicked his tongue across the scales behind it. She shivered, and she felt his smile against her neck. "How readily you accepted that your solution must require your pain."

"So speaks the martyr," she said bitterly.

Cool air against her nape as he lifted her hair. "Your tyrant." His fingers tugged at the lacings of her corset. The leather slowly loosened, and he eased back to slide it over her hips. Then his chest was warm against her back, wings crushed between them, his arms circling around.

She tensed her stomach muscles as he flattened his palms against her abdomen. The scales were softer there, rectangular instead of rounded. Though he couldn't see them, he would recognize their shape. They must remind him of a snake's belly, remind him of what she was.

Perhaps he was right—perhaps this body would be her best defense, despite his claim that it did not matter. It did not matter how she'd begun life; she'd been a demon for two thousand years. And demons did not feel physical arousal, took no pleasure from it.

She clung to that thought as he explored the curve of her ribs, where the scales hardened again. As his fingers traveled along the crease beneath her breasts. She did not breathe, would not expose herself. Waited for him to go further, to discover just how different this form was.

He cupped her breasts, ran his thumbs over her nipples. Pleasure shot through her, but his hiss of surprise and pain dampened it. She closed her eyes. Though she intended to laugh, her reply seemed carried on a sob. "A fine joke, is it not?"

Slight tang of blood in the air, and she felt his wariness. But he managed to express his humor, forced or not, better than she did. "Should I avoid any other portions of your anatomy?"

"All of them," she said into the door, her chest aching.

"Your teeth," he mused, as if she hadn't spoken. "Though it would be hard to kiss you with your face turned away from me, I should have liked to finally use your horns as handholds. Would almost be worth it to risk your fangs for that."

Damn him. She shook with laughter.

He laid his cheek against hers, his unshaven skin scraping, tickling. Her waistband parted as he untied the fastening. "I have missed your laugh, Lily."

Forcing away the bittersweet pleasure of that confession, she said, "You shouldn't have killed me, then." She meant it to be hard, cruel, but it escaped on a gasp as his hand slipped between black leather and blue satin.

"This is your resistance? This is your control?" His fingers stroked the moist fabric. "'Tis a weak showing." Then his bare skin was against hers, where she was wet and soft and hot, sliding against her clit, his calluses rough on the sensitive flesh.

"There are teeth inside," she said, panting. "Sharp as razors. They slobber in anticipation, that you'll be foolish enough to—"

He parted her, pushed two fingers deep. She moaned, her head falling back onto his shoulder. Thrusting his hips forward, he captured his hand against the door, his erection hot and hard against her bottom. The action shoved his fingers further inside, ground the heel of his hand against her clit. "Grab on to the door," he growled.

She could feel him shaking behind her, the tension that held him rigid. Without a word, she flexed her claws, ripping through the hollow-core door and clinging to the holes she made.

He rocked his hips, pushed his thigh between hers to widen her stance. "I've missed your heat."

Shutting herself away from the pleasure of his thrusting hand, the slippery, rhythmic pressure against her clit became impossible. "I only pretend to enjoy this."

"I've even missed your lies," he said, laughing breathlessly against her ear. "A demon would not come."

"As I will not," she said, though the liquid ache coiled through her, wound tighter. "It's only the power of this that excites me."

He slid in a third finger, stretching, pushing. "Whose power?"

"Mine." But she could not stop herself from pressing down, to take him deeper again. "You think that if I show any human tendencies, undeniable human response, it will"—he twisted his hand gently, and she had to grit her teeth to keep the moan inside—"mean that I am good. But humans are as capable of evil—ah, fuck—"

He pulled his hand away, fell to his knees. Yanked her pants down with him, pulled them all the way off. Cheap wood shredded beneath her talons as he turned her again.

He draped her thigh over his shoulder. "Go on," he said, his voice thick with arousal. Perspiration glistened over his cheekbones, his eyes were like glittering blue stones, but he was grinning. "Persuade me that you are in control. That you have power."

She forced herself to speak evenly. To ignore how near his mouth was to her. To pretend that as he rubbed his chin against her inner thigh, it didn't send shivers over her skin. "Demonic influence does not account for the evil done by humans—most of it is of their free will. Proving that a portion of my humanity still exists will not mean I am good. That *you* think it does gives me the advantage, the power in this."

His brows drew together. "You think I want you to be a paragon of innocence, like the countess?" A laugh rumbled from him, and he shook his head. "That is one thing I did not miss, for I don't believe I ever saw it in you. Nor did I ever want it."

"What do you want, then?" She told herself she asked so that she could deny it, to exercise that power over him. Not because his answer had shaken her, and she needed to center herself, to find something to hold to.

His lips parted, and he took a deep breath that rocked her against him, reminded her how exposed she was, wet and slick. Her legs quivered as his exhalation skimmed over her sex.

Despite that terrible vulnerability, she was dismayed when he slipped her thigh from his shoulder and stood. She tilted her head back, watched the play of emotions on his features, suddenly uncertain that she wanted an answer.

Softly, with his fingertips, he touched her chin, her lips, traced the arch of her brows. "I want you brimming with humanity, with feeling, so that Lucifer will choose to punish you for it by returning you to Earth to fulfill your bargain. I want to stop missing you. I want to wake up without nightmares and know that you are alive. You may not be good, Lilith, but you are the best thing in my life, and when you were not in it . . ." His throat worked, his gaze lowered before meeting hers again. "Does not matter if this bargain destroys me, for I did it well enough when I killed you."

There was too much in his intense blue stare to process, too much emanating from his psychic scent—except that he spoke the truth, and that it resonated within a hollow, unbearable place within her.

"You would manipulate me in this way?" Cerberus's balls, but she sounded so weak. Looked weak. Ripping the cuffs apart, she lowered her hands to his shoulders, clenched on the muscle there—not enough to hurt, but enough to remind him of her strength. And still, her voice shook. "It's the worst kind of manipulation, one without lies. You play your role well, Hugh. A fine demon you make."

"Aye. You call me martyr and ascribe altruistic motives to me, but I confess I think only of myself. It's an honest manipulation, but it is a selfish one, made entirely from what I want." The corners of his mouth lifted. "Sixteen years ago, you would have been pleased."

"Sixteen years ago you said you became me, and I got a

sword through the heart," she shot back, grateful for an excuse to think of anything but how his "selfish" declaration had affected her. "I've learned since then it's best not to be around those who resemble me in any way."

His gaze softened. "There are none such as you, Lilith."

"Because Lucifer has killed them all." Her hands trembled, and she took them from his shoulders lest they betray her. "You must see that you risk too much with this plan. I can't bear another Punishment."

"He has only taken your ability to shift into various human forms with it, to change your clothing. Is it so terrible not to have that power?"

"No," she said slowly. "But that is not what I speak of."

He stiffened, then lowered his forehead to hers. "All the more reason to make certain you return."

She closed her eyes, sagged back against the door. "Release me from this wager, Hugh. Let me try to convince Lucifer."

"I cannot." His lips caressed the side of her mouth.

She tried to move away as he licked her lower lip, but had no retreat. "My fangs," she breathed.

"Then I will bleed." But he lifted his head, silent until she looked up at him. "You may convince him, but if he thinks you take pleasure in destroying me, what will keep him from choosing Punishment instead? You lie too well—and you are most adept at lying to yourself. You tell yourself that there is no light without darkness, you convince yourself your role is to be the darkness so that light will exist—yet moments ago you admitted humans are fully capable of it without help from Above or Below. Do you think I don't know what you'll tell yourself as you move through that Gate? That your reaction to me was a scheme to draw my feelings for you into the open, so that you may manipulate them later, destroy me with them? That you have been a demon for so many years, it was impossible that you truly felt desire? And you would force yourself to believe it, because Lucifer will see if you do not, if it is only an illusion. But I won't allow you that lie, not when it might destroy you."

She laughed without humor. "And this is how you save me? With sex?"

"With evidence that you cannot lie away. For no matter what you say to yourself, no demon feels physical desire, nor physical release. Even you cannot rationalize it into something else."

"Release me from this wager," she said, her voice flat. "It will fail."

"If you don't return, then I will traverse the Gates of Hell to retrieve you." It was said like a vow, and she did not doubt the truth of it.

She steeled herself against it, and said harshly, "You would die. Release me."

"Then I would die sacrificing myself for another." He smiled, but it did not touch his eyes. "Perhaps Michael would turn me back into a Guardian, and I would try again."

"Release me." The pleading note in her voice terrified her.

He lowered his gaze, but not before she saw the pain that flashed across his features. "I did not truly want it to be force," he said, and turned her to face the door.

"And I didn't want it to be kindness," she said bitterly, placing her palms flat against the wood on either side of her head, the broken handcuff chains dangling. The top of the door was almost completely destroyed from her earlier response, but this time, she determined, she would resist. Shut herself away from his touch.

"At least I have never been raped by a demon," she said, her eyes burning.

"Aye," he agreed thickly. "Men can be infinitely worse."

And his hesitation was almost a cruelty, drawing out a moment that she'd rather have gotten over with quickly. She wouldn't care that it was born of the inner conflict she could feel raging within him. Unnatural for a man of his character to touch her in this way: against her will, even if by her consent—and she should not feel betrayed by it. She had given up her will long ago; it should not matter who used it against her: Lucifer, Beelzebub. And now Hugh.

"I'm sorry," he whispered, and she flinched away from the words. She pressed her wings together to block his view, block access, but he slipped his arms between the membranous folds and smoothed his hands down the length of her spine.

His groin rested against her bottom. She could no longer feel his arousal, only the breath that shuddered from his chest, his palms as he moved them around to her stomach. They slid up, cupped her breasts.

He laid his cheek against the top of her head. "The first time

I saw you, I could not stop staring at these," he said softly. "I think you meant to distract me so you could make your bargain." His thumbs caressed the outer curves, moved in, strayed close to her nipples. "They are still beautiful, even tipped with these razor ruby scales. And just as dangerous."

She squeezed her eyes shut.

"I kissed you then, without love or promise," he continued. "I could not do so again."

"Stop," she said, but the tightness of her throat made it a wordless sigh.

He pressed a kiss into her hair. Against her temple, where obsidian horn met crimson scales. He lifted her breasts; her nipples rasped against the wood grain. She should have laughed, it seemed so absurd, but had to bite her lip as the vibration quivered through the sharp, crystalline flesh. He must have felt her response, for he did it again.

Even that defense, he found a way around. And as if her pleasure fed his, he rocked against her, his shaft slowly hardening again. "How many times have I kissed you since? But I have never touched you thus, though you would have bargained for it, or tricked me into it." His left hand trailed down the line of her belly, circled her navel. "And I would have, but for the bargains and tricks. In Paris, you stood before me with auburn hair and a courtesan's body, and I would have traded the secrecy of our kind for a night in your arms." His voice roughened. "But it was not secrets I wanted, and so I declined, and kept my desires hidden."

She did not breathe, held herself still as his fingers drifted further down, traced the crease between torso and thigh. If she could have stopped the tell-tale pounding of her heart, she would have.

"Open for me, Lily."

She did not, clenching her thighs so tightly she shook with the exertion. No need for that much effort, except that she did not trust herself, did not trust her body to respond to her will. And despite her resistance, he slid the tip of his finger into the part of her with no defense at all—just enough to reach the small, erect organ at its peak.

As if to distract her, he swept her hair to the side, bit the curve of her neck. Followed it with a lick of his tongue. Then he gently rubbed her clit.

Her knees buckled, but he caught her, held her up with his

arm around her waist. His erection was thick and hard behind her now, insistent, yet he did not remove that last article of clothing.

She should not want him, naked and hot against her. Should not desire him within her.

"Open for me, Lily."

He worked his hand deeper between her thighs, her arousal easing his way. Wet, slick—she should not be. Her body did not need its breath, and yet she was panting with each stroke of his fingers. His scent surrounded her, and she took him in with each inhalation; he was inside her, had been for centuries.

This body should not be soft, should not be yielding.

And yet she was.

❦

The constriction in Hugh's chest, the thick ache in his throat began to lessen as she slowly parted her legs, let him in. He tightened his arm around her waist, forcing himself to ignore the painful rise of his erection, the exquisite torture of feeling her against him, but knowing he could not have her. Not like this.

She made no sound but for her rapid breathing, did not move but for the shaking that had taken over her upon his first command to open.

This was gluttony, to move his fingers inside her, and take more. She was hot, her inner muscles welcoming him. He did not need to invade her like this, could bring her release just by stroking her clit, but still he marauded, claimed. And it must be vanity, to swell unbearably when the first mew of pleasure broke from between her clenched teeth, when she began to writhe back against him, as if the thrust of his hand was not enough. Theft, to take what was not his, and call it his own.

He set his jaw, leaned his forehead against her nape. God, but she was soft; he'd never imagined her so. Made his hardness doubly profane.

I will not, he swore—it was selfishness that had brought him to this, but he would not take his own pleasure now.

Yet he had to acknowledge it for a lie; there *was* pleasure in this, ecstasy in the slick glide of his fingers, her weight against his arm—even in the frustration of denying his own release. And he sought hers, more quickly now, because he felt himself weakening.

He had never been good at resisting temptation.

"Lily," he urged, "come for me now."

She made a sound, and he could have wept when he recognized the denial. *Please, please.* He did not voice it, but his thumb, strumming over her clitoris in quick firm strokes, took up the same refrain: *please, please*. His fingers, thrusting within her: *please, please*.

She reached back between them; it was an awkward angle, but she reached and her palm ran the length of his cock.

"No, Lilith—" He broke off, sweat beading over his forehead, dotting his lip with the effort it took to hold his hips still. She supported herself now, did not need his arm, but he kept it around her for fear that did he have an idle hand, he would unbutton and unzip and force himself inside her.

Her strong fingers tore the button free, ripped the zipper down. The sudden release of pressure against his shaft was both relief and torment. Cotton shredded beneath her sharp talons, and then there was bare skin, and wet slick heat.

"Please, Hugh." And that seemed torn from her as well, but he gritted his teeth and closed his eyes, focused on the feel of her beneath his hand instead of the delicious, tortuous rasp of smooth scales and burning softness against his cock. "Please," she moaned as he plucked at her clit, as the first tremors shuddered through her. "Please," as her back arched, as her inner muscles clenched around his fingers, as her wings stretched wide and fluttered, vibrated.

His chest heaved, his skin drawn tight and hot as she relaxed against his forearm. Then she moved, rising and arching with another shuddering gasp, and the movement lodged him between her thighs, the head of his shaft pressing against his fingers, still buried within her. He tensed, shaking. Just one more moment of selfishness, he wouldn't . . .

He wouldn't.

But he withdrew his hand, slid forward with a groan. Heat, hot, hellfire, and only around the very tip of him, but it clasped him, drew him in. Only an inch, now two, but it was the most exquisite burning. "Lilith," he said, his eyes closing, his voice pleading. "Deny me." *For I can not deny myself.*

She could; their wager was done, he had gained what he'd wanted—her release, and it had torn him apart, that façade of kindness, of *right*; no good man would do this. Yet she didn't push him away, held herself still as he worked slowly deeper, deeper.

He felt huge within that tight silken grip, powerful as she yielded and stretched around him. Bowing his head, he thrust all the way in, trembling. He'd used the devil's tools, and they'd worked on him in turn, made him this. Or he had always been this. Tears stung, and he opened his eyes, blinked them away. "Lily—"

"Again. Do it again." A sobbing breath. "If you are going to destroy me, then don't make me settle for half."

He hesitated, and she gripped the top of the door with both hands, lifted herself. The dragging slide of her withdrawal ripped a moan from his throat, and he pushed her back down; unbearable to be outside her. Another long stroke. And again—deep, hard. Her scales rippled, smooth pale skin fading in and out. She cried out her triumph, her pleasure, and he gave himself over to his own, whatever it meant he was.

Only certain that he was hers.

CHAPTER 22

He wore the robe.

There was nothing left of his clothing but shreds on her apartment floor; he left them behind—the wool was better suited for flying through rain, anyway.

She held him securely against her, cradling him as if he were an overgrown child. He'd carried her thus once, when a nosferatu had torn her throat out and left her too weak to fight or fly on her own. Panicked, he'd clutched her to his chest until he'd found a Healer—Colin's friend—one of the Guardians Hugh had been mentoring. If that Guardian had refused to heal her, Hugh might have killed him—but it had not come to that, and he'd never been tested in that way again. Perhaps he should have been; it had only taken two hundred years to forget that panic, to shove it deep inside himself, and forget how it had tortured him to see her hurt. "I should drop you."

"Aye," he agreed. He would have agreed to anything she said, so long as she spoke to him. After her last, shuddering cry, everything she'd said had been a threat. But they'd been without force or anger, as if her vulnerability was a surprise—as if she were as frightened by her loss of control as he was his.

It was a fear he welcomed.

Below, the streetlamps along Haight Street guided them through the city toward Colin's house; they had to fly below the cloud cover to see them—risky, though the chance of detection was slim. "It was a good tactic, the diversion you created at Beaumont Court to save Colin's sister."

"It wasn't to save her," she said. "I enjoyed skewering you. I should do it again."

He rubbed his chest, remembering. "The nosferatu didn't expect it."

"Nor did you."

"No." He smiled. "Your letter from Polidori was not so successful a diversion."

"I should drop you," she said again, but her arms tightened.

$

Colin looked at Hugh and grimaced. "Good God, the horror. I'm too ashamed to invite you in."

Lilith pushed past them both, striding through the door and into the foyer. "Be ashamed then. And find him something to wear; something warm, as he's probably freezing. He's always freezing," she said on a mutter. Hugh began laughing, and she hastily added, "That thing doesn't fit him anymore. It looks ridiculous." The sleeves too short, the hem above his ankles. Though still lean and strong, as he'd been when a Guardian, his shoulders were broader; she'd clutched at them as he'd driven within her. He was taller, only an inch or two, but it had given him the height to find exactly the right angle, thrusting so deep . . .

She took a breath, released it slowly. It was best, she decided, not to think about why he wasn't in his clothes. Best not to look at him at all; it was too strange, a mature Hugh, the one who had drawn more from her than she'd felt in two thousand years—ever—in that brown monk's robe.

A familiar scent hung in the air. She paused, glanced back at Colin, then gestured to the ceiling. "Oh. Is she still up there?"

His eyes wide, Colin nodded.

Grinning, Lilith looked at Hugh. "He tied Selah up in his bedroom and has been feeding from her for two days."

"Is that so?" His gaze lit on her, and she warmed to it before she could remind herself to be distant, to be cold. "I don't suppose he was the onc who caught her, though."

"She trespassed," Colin said with an arch of his brow, clearly thinking that he needed to defend Lilith's actions—not realizing she needed no defense with Hugh. Not in this, at least.

Hugh's lips twitched, but his eyes were quiet, solemn. "As we all do."

He did not have to apologize; she knew what it had done to him to take her that way. Her throat tightened.

Colin sniffed the air, grimaced. "You smell like a human. And I wish you'd let me know you'd been one; perhaps then I wouldn't have been so frightened of you."

She turned, her eyes glowing bright. "Did you know about that ridiculous book? And didn't tell me?"

"Yes." He grinned unrepentantly. "I didn't want you to steal it from me."

She bit back her laugh, turned away, and walked toward the stairs. In less than an hour, she had to be through the Gate, and she couldn't go like this; she needed to wash, though she could not erase him from her skin. She needed to find disdain, anger and hate. But she searched within herself and could not. Not for Hugh, anyway.

Sir Pup bounded toward her when she opened the bedroom door, and she lauded compliments upon him for his fine Guardian-watching. Selah was awake, and her face suffused with color when she saw Hugh.

"Well done," he said dryly, nodding. His gaze ran over the chains, the manacles holding her to the bed. "It is a fine thing, to see a student excel."

The Guardian's blush deepened, but her eyes were bright with anger and disbelief. "You would align yourself with this demon?"

Mentor and student stared at each other; Lilith buried her face in the hellhound's fur. There was an undercurrent, a knowledge between the two she could feel but not penetrate.

"With *this* one, aye," he finally said. He accepted the pile of clothes Colin brought from the dressing room. He began pulling on the pants beneath the robe, casually, as if unaware how his declaration tore through Lilith, sharper than a sword.

Sir Pup whimpered and licked her face with multiple

tongues. "Come on," she said, and stood. She could not look at Hugh, not at that moment—so she looked at Colin and saw his wonder; damn him, he studied faces, and he would see too much in hers. "I'll feed him now, but I'm leaving him with you again. Take care of him or I'll kill you."

She didn't wait for his nod or his argument, but left the room quickly, the hellhound at her heels. Colin's self-portraits lined the hallway, and she ignored his knowing stare, just as she had in the bedroom. Bare feet sounded behind her; she could have outrun him. Could have, but still turned at the sound of his voice.

"Lily." Hugh stood, pulling up his zipper, the robe hiked over his hip. The sweater Colin had given him trailed from his other hand. His hair was damp again, wild from the flight; his dark lashes spiked, intensifying the blue of his eyes.

She should not see Caelum in them. Not heaven.

"You look like an imbecile." He looked beautiful. She stalked toward him, and he did not flinch, even when Sir Pup growled and slavered beside her. As given to dramatics as she was, her hellhound. She gripped the neckline of the robe, ripped it down the center of his torso. "I hate this fucking thing."

"I do, too," he said, laughing. "Take it, throw it into the Lake of Fire." Catching her hand, he brought it to his mouth and pressed his lips to center of her palm. Still smiling, but his eyes were dark now. "And come back to me. I'll find a way to free you again, Lilith, I swear it. Just come back."

She yanked her hand away, and rose up, slanting her mouth over his before he could move. Delved deep, capturing the flavor of him. Holding it tight and pushing it down within herself; then, abruptly, she pulled away. "I do not promise," she said, breathing hard.

He touched his lips, where the moisture from their kiss lingered. "This is enough."

It is nothing. Her hand clenched, but she did not speak; he would know her denial for a lie. She walked away, her heart thudding painfully.

She could not love him. Would not love him.

Should not love him.

❦

She did not turn around, or look back. Of course she didn't. Hugh let out the breath he'd been holding, then shrugged out of the remains of his robe. Slipped into the sweater, smiling to himself.

"Lilith left a satchel for you in the room," Colin said from behind him, then strode past him toward the stairs. "Green canvas. Ugly."

Hugh's smile faded. Without a word, he returned to the bedroom and shut the door behind him.

He watched as Selah looked up at him and disappeared from the bed; the chains that had been holding her fell back against the coverlet. Hugh waited, and she reappeared a few moments later beside him.

Why? He gestured with one hand. A modified version of British Sign Language—one of the changes the Guardian Corps had been willing to incorporate over the years to allow silent communication amidst creatures with preternatural hearing.

The Doyen said to protect them, she signed back, her mouth twisting. *The vampire would have let me stay if I had flattered him, but you know Lilith would have soon as killed me as accept my help.* She shrugged, and pointed to her neck with a grin. "It hasn't been all bad, but his vanity knows no bounds."

He's neither as shallow nor as useless as he appears, Hugh warned. *Nor harmless. Where is Michael now? Why protection? Is there a specific threat against them?*

Looking for the nosferatu; he's been tracking them, trying to determine the demons' and nosferatu's movements, make some sense of them. And not a specific threat—just that they have tried to attack the vampire several times, only to be chased off or killed by the hellhound. Michael believes the nosferatu are aware of your relationship to the vampire, will use it against you or her in some way, or else there is no reason to focus on him. Her head tilted, as if she listened to a conversation Hugh couldn't hear. "Are they truly friends? They are squabbling like children over the cost of keeping the dog."

"Yes." Hugh rubbed the back of his neck and kneeled beside the bag. The files were in the white envelope at the bottom. He reached in past the swords, and his fingers brushed cold, thick metal. The gun she'd offered at her apartment, and he'd refused. "She shows her affection in unusual ways," he murmured.

He pulled it out, a smile tugging at the corners of his mouth, and stuck it into the back of his waistband. He'd have to give it to Colin before he went home; should the police ever decide to search his house, he didn't want it among his things.

Selah sat on the floor next to him, again in his line of sight. A frown marred her brow. *You didn't tell her I could have 'ported out of the chains at any time.*

Hugh paused with the envelope half-opened, raising both brows in an expression of disbelief. *Do you want a demon—on her way to Hell—to have fresh memories of you and your Gift? You and Michael are the only two to move between realms without the use of the Gates; Lucifer would not dare attack Michael to gain use of that power, but a young Guardian?*

Do you not trust her?

I think that Lilith will do whatever it takes to return to Earth. I trust her to act in her own interest, and perhaps in mine; I don't expect her to extend the same courtesy to you.

But you could have given it to her to use as a bargaining chip.

His smiled turned bleak. *If she is forced to resort to bargaining with Guardian powers, then it is too late to save her; it would buy her but little time.*

Selah sighed, cocked her head to the side again. "She is gone; the vampire is on the stairs, coming this way."

His chest tightened. Gone. And her position so precarious; had he made the right decision, to force her to respond to him? He felt Selah's searching stare, the question she did not ask. "No. I'm not the man you knew."

"In some ways, perhaps," she said dryly. "But your loyalties lie in the same place."

"Has it always been so apparent?" He held her gaze.

"Yes. Not any individual thing you said or did; but after hundreds of years of failing to kill her, it was clear there was more than simple rivalry between you. We knew saving her had become your obsession. None of us were surprised when you chose to Fall after finally slaying her."

His throat closed and he nodded. Blankly, he looked down at the envelope in his hands.

"You killed her because she's a demon and you no longer cared to make the effort to save her, but discovering she was once human has made her worth fighting for?" Colin said from the doorway, sarcasm lending an edge to his question. The hellhound padded past him, sniffed Hugh's bag as if searching for a treat.

I remembered that I was human, he thought. But he only glanced at the vampire with mild reproof. "Don't be an ass."

"She's going Below," Colin said. "And she reeks of you and of her emotions."

Hugh rocked back on his heels, rose to his feet. "Think like a demon instead of a man. What would you do if you wanted to hurt her?"

Colin stared at him, then crossed his arms, shaking his head. "You manipulative bastard," he said, with a touch of admiration.

But Selah's voice held disappointment. "I am glad I did not learn *this* from you."

"Perhaps I should have taught you," he said tightly. "Perhaps the corps would not be cowering before a horde of nosferatu and beaten down by demons had we not spent centuries upholding impossible ideals. We were men, not angels. It was why we were created, and yet we put ourselves above men anyway, put our code above their lives."

Selah's eyes glowed, brilliantly blue. "No. We were created because Michael failed to protect your demon from Lucifer."

Hugh stared at her.

She looked away, as if ashamed she'd revealed that much. "Don't try to go this alone, Hugh. You may think you have no use for us, or our ways, but a complete reversal from our *impossible ideals* is not going to save her, either."

His muscles like ice, Hugh took a step forward. "What—"

The hellhound growled softly, his heads swinging toward the window.

At the same moment, Selah frowned, turning to face the same direction. Her sword appeared in her hand.

"Bloody hell," Colin said. He streaked across the room, opened a cupboard. Weapons lined the interior. "The basement is most easily defended." He slung an automatic rifle over his shoulder, and reached in again, selecting two rapiers.

"Six or seven nosferatu. And a demon." Selah glanced at Colin, then Hugh. "You can't fight them. I'll get you out of here."

Colin snorted. "You'll leave me here to be killed—and after I treated you so well?"

"We'll go to the basement," Hugh said. Demons liked to talk, to brag; they might be able to find out part of their plan if they allowed them enough time. "Selah, take these." He tossed the files to her, and they vanished midair. He knelt, pulling his weapons from the duffelbag; the Japanese swords felt light in his hands, and he smiled grimly. Hopefully, the nosferatu would not get so close he had to use them. "And the rest."

His broadsword and bag disappeared. He glanced at the hell-hound. The dog shook his heads, and he had but a moment to see Sir Pup transform—terrifyingly huge, barbed spikes rip-ping from beneath his fur—before Selah lifted him and they sped downstairs. A crash of broken glass and splintering wood behind them. Colin groaned, but the sound was overwhelmed by the tortured screams of a nosferatu, and the eerie chorus of growls from the hellhound.

Concrete walls ringed the basement; Colin barred the steel door. It wouldn't hold the nosferatu or demon back for long, but it would allow time to set up a defense.

The basement was almost empty; only a few boxes and portrait-sized crates lay stacked on the cement floor. "There are more weapons in that trunk." Colin pointed to the far wall.

"We should have brought the hound down with us," Selah said.

"He chose not to come," Hugh said, and strode to the fur-nace. The floor was cold beneath his bare feet. "Lilith will have taught him to take out as many as possible before they can reach us. Is this gas?" If it was, it could be a useful weapon—

"Coal," the vampire said. At Hugh's look, he shrugged. "I don't need heat."

"And you're too cheap for updates," Hugh muttered, but he couldn't stop his grin. He met Colin's eyes as the door bent in-ward with an earsplitting screech. Another nosferatu screamed, and was cut short by a wet, tearing crunch. Sir Pup's triumphant howl reverberated through the house.

Colin returned his grin, his swords ready at his sides. "I adore that dog."

Hugh did, too.

But even a three-headed hellhound couldn't be everywhere, and it did not surprise him when the pounding at the door stopped, replaced by a pounding on the ceiling at the opposite side of the house.

"They're coming through the floor upstairs," Selah said, and all three moved back, toward the trunk Colin had indicated earlier. *Should we 'port?* she signed.

Hugh shook his head, tucked one of his swords under his arm to sign, *Not until we must; this may be our only opportunity to find out more information. Remember, I'm safe from the demon, and we have the advantage of your Gift. They think we are trapped.*

"What are you two doing?" Colin stared at Hugh's hand, his brows drawn together. "What are you saying?"

Hugh gripped the hilt of his sword again. "I said"—a taloned fist punched through the ceiling, raining down wood and insulation—"let them come."

CHAPTER 23

The bridge swayed as another gust of wind ripped through the bracings, howling across the diagonal ribwork of steel. Lilith clung to the girders with her feet, letting her body swing, her hair whip around her. Below, waves slapped against the center mooring, the froth and caps white against the nighttime water.

This was beauty, man-made and natural. The symmetry of the bridge, the glittering San Francisco skyline, the dark rise of Angel Island in the distance. Beauty that drew millions—but it was only a thousand or so who had helped create the Gate beneath. Thirty years before, the Gate hadn't been there. But she'd seen it happen before: a site of despair and death, combined with the anger and frustration of a city, and slowly the fabric of the location changed, began to resonate differently. The temple where she'd met Hugh all those years ago had been such a Gate, though rarely used, and the energy reeking of sacrifice rather than suicide.

But violent death, no matter its form, left its mark. Here, mid-span, the fall was over seventy yards from bridge to water. A quick death. And there had been over a thousand quick deaths in the past century. Though none of them had been provoked by demons, it still served them well.

She sighed, and the wind stole it away. A mental probe verified the Gate's location directly beneath her; she could sense it as easily as her cache, feel its shape and size—but still, she did not fall. There was no reason to wait, no reason to wonder if it was death or something else that had shaped Caelum's Gates. No reason to remember the many times she'd followed Hugh to one, watched him disappear through it—yet had been unable to sense or use it herself.

The memory did not bring her as much pain as it had once; and there was no reason to wrap her arms around herself, relive his touch, and recall how everything had faded against the pleasure of it.

But she was still upside down, clinging to the steel and feeling the vibration of wind and traffic through her, when she heard the distinctive clank of boots against metal, the squeal of brakes and shouts for help. She closed her eyes. If he waited long enough, there were people who were trained for this, who might be able to talk him down—

Someone screamed, and Lilith swung over, hard, stretching her wings and bracing against the impact. He slammed into her, and she fell with him, rolling over and over until her wings caught air and she lifted them up, up. Cerberus's balls, she was going to be seen. Around, the other side of the bridge, and she threw him onto the pavement between two stalled vehicles, barely remembering to take her human form before she straddled him, slapped him across the face.

He stared up at her, his eyes wide and stunned. Sixteen years old, maybe. She slapped him again, leaned in close to growl, "You stupid little shit! Are you dying, wasting away? Did you kill your mother or rape your baby sister? Have you torn your girlfriend's head off and smashed her body to pieces? Is it that fucking *bad*?"

"No," he choked, and began to cry. Horns blared, drivers pissed off that traffic had stopped for something as routine as a jumper. Small wonder a portal to Hell had opened beneath them.

"Come here again when you do, and I'll push you myself. There are things like me waiting for you down there, waiting to eat your flesh and suck the marrow from your bones." Her eyes were illuminating his face, glinting red off his tears. Her voice softened. "And get some help, for fuck's sake."

Sirens from the north; she stood and looked at the crowd that had circled them. A man crossed himself and backed away, and it was then she realized that though she'd taken her human form, she hadn't vanished her wings.

"A miracle," another woman breathed.

The boy sobbed on the road, his cheeks bright from the abuse she'd given him. Her eyes were glowing crimson and her wings were visible for everyone to see. Suddenly tired, Lilith shook her head. The man retreating in fear was closer to the truth. There was nothing good in this, in what she'd just done.

Was not a higher power that had kept her there, delaying until she saved the boy. It had been Hugh. She'd been thinking of him, which was exactly the opposite of what she should have been doing, if she wanted to save herself.

She backed up, leapt over the rail; there were no screams, only the pounding of feet as they rushed to the side, as if to see what she did.

She hit the icy water, and vanished through the Gate.

❧

The huge, handsome man who came through the ceiling smiled, but the two nosferatu behind him did not. Hugh preferred the honesty of the nosferatu.

From upstairs came another crash and howl; one of the nosferatu flinched. But the demon only shook his head, as if the hellhound was a mild annoyance. "Dr. Castleford, I presume?"

Colin choked on a laugh. He knelt beside and just in front of Hugh, the rifle raised to his shoulder. Selah held her swords ready on his other side.

"Beelzebub." Hugh nodded his acknowledgment, though he was just as tempted to mock the demon. They relied on clichés whenever in their human form; Lilith had not, except to twist them, but then she didn't need to simulate human expression.

He'd known that, but like many other times, had ignored the evidence in front of him.

Beelzebub's face changed, and Hugh quickly pushed all thoughts of Lilith away. Too late.

"Ah, sweet, delicious halfling," Beelzebub said. "She has betrayed you. I was most pleased when she told us your location.

It's too bad she has to pay homage to our liege, or she would have personally enjoyed your surrender and deaths."

Behind the demon, the nosferatu shifted impatiently. They did not want talk; they wanted to fight, to kill.

Hugh smiled. "You do not lie well."

As intended, the insult sparked the demon's temper. His eyes began to glow. "Do you think, human, that because she fucked your brains out that she loves you for it?"

Colin began shaking with laughter. Selah shot him a quelling glance.

"Do you know why she helps us? Because she is a worm, full of fear. Because I once cut her to pieces as Punishment, and she will do anything to avoid that pain again. She'll do what we ask, including helping us procure your loved ones for the ritual. She has already given us two more."

Truth and lies; difficult to separate them, when his blood pounded at the thought of Beelzebub torturing her—that had been truth. Who had been taken? Could he find them, stop it? "I think you had to Punish her because you cannot control her," Hugh said, his voice carefully contained. Shift the focus from Lilith, from any students who might be in danger. "Just as you barely control the nosferatu with you."

He did not need psychic sensitivity to feel the way the nosferatu bristled, nor the demon's sudden wariness.

"Not subservient," the one on the left said, his voice guttural.

"Ah," Colin nodded. "That is why you wait for his signal to attack us. Because you are not subservient."

Nothing worse for a nosferatu than to be mocked by a vampire, yet it did not move. Colin slanted a glance back at Hugh, the understanding between them clear. Beelzebub *did* control the nosferatu, either through a bargain or some other agreement . . . and the nosferatu hated it, but would agree to subject themselves to the demon to gain the power offered. What was worth that trade? The ability to transform into human shape? Daylight?

It did not seem enough—not when two nosferatu could stand outside a burning club and pass as human. And darkness was not so terrible when human advancement could make it bright as day.

Beelzebub spread his hands. "We three have equal opportunity; one of you for each of us. And each of us likes to play with our things."

"And those still upstairs?" There couldn't be many left.

"They will have to lick the remains," the demon said, smiling again. "And then perhaps we will travel to your house, and they will feast on the girl there."

Savi. Hugh tensed, but he kept his voice even. "Do I have anything to persuade you otherwise?" This must have been what the demon had been waiting for—Hugh had something he wanted. It was the only reason to threaten Savi; the demon would probably try to bargain for her life.

"Submit to the ritual." The demon smiled, and he indicated the two nosferatu with a sweep of his hands. "I have friends who desperately want to tear the girl apart, but they will settle for you."

A lie. No doubt they would enjoy killing Savi, but they *needed* Hugh. It would not be settling.

"Why?"

"Is always better when the sacrifice is willingly made. The power of free will," Beelzebub said.

That was truth. Selah gave him a warning glance, and he understood; they were running out of time, and the nosferatu out of patience.

Hugh shook his head. "No."

His denial snapped whatever had held the nosferatu back; Colin began firing. Selah held out her hand, ready to teleport them to safety. Hugh's fingers brushed hers, and then he was knocked back, slammed against the concrete wall. Not the demon, who couldn't have killed him—the nosferatu stared down at him with burning eyes. Just enough time for a quick slash; the nosferatu howled in surprise as his belly opened—he'd not expected a human to have Hugh's speed. The creature's hand shot out, connected. Dark spots swam before Hugh's eyes and he felt himself fall, the swords slipping from his grip.

Dimly, he heard the rifle fire cease, and the second nosferatu's angry cry as Colin went to work with his blades.

The nosferatu's teeth sank into his neck; unlike a vampire's bite, no pleasure in this, but a dark tearing through his mind. He heard the demon yell for the nosferatu not to kill him, wondered if the creature was going to listen.

His lower back ached, throbbed where he'd landed on Lilith's gun.

God, but he loved her.

The nosferatu eased back, grinning, his lips rimmed with Hugh's blood. "And we will have her, too."

Arrogant and proud creature—bragging in the midst of a fight, even when victory seemed assured, was a terrible habit. It did not give Hugh a lot of time, but enough to slip out the gun and pull the trigger.

The safety was on. Hugh fumbled with the unfamiliar weapon. Hard to say who was more surprised, Hugh thought, as the nosferatu's eyes widened before he trapped Hugh's hand to the floor, and began laughing.

Sir Pup cut his laughter short. The hellhound took the nosferatu's head in one mouth, and clamped down on each arm with the others. The nosferatu's body jerked. A sickening crunch, and Hugh rolled out of the way of the gush of fluid, swayed as he climbed to his feet. "Selah," he said, the sound barely escaping his damaged throat, and he had to lean against the hellhound for support.

Colin was retreating from the nosferatu, slowly wearing against the creature's superior strength. Selah glanced over at the vampire, ducked a slice from Beelzebub's sword, and dived for Hugh, her wings outstretched as if to block him from the demon's sight.

He needed to see that Savi was still safe. Selah grabbed his arm, and he rasped, "Savi," opening his mind to give her an anchor, though his blood would have been enough.

The world spun around him, and they crashed onto a table; it collapsed under their combined weight, sending metal and plastic skittering across the floor. Pain seared through his side, but he forced himself to remain conscious, look around.

From her small kitchen, Savi stared at him, a shattered teacup at her feet. Her mouth was drawn tight with fear and disbelief, and the remnants of grief.

Someone was sitting at breakfast bar, but he couldn't focus. Auburn hair. He knew—

"Hugh," Selah said urgently, "I need to get you to a Healer."

He shook his head, the movement an agony. "Colin first."

She nodded tightly, flicked a glance at Savi and the woman, and disappeared.

"Hugh? How the fu—ohmygod." Savi fell to her knees next to him, yanked up his sweater and pressed it to the wound at his throat. "What the hell is going on? What was that?" She glanced over her shoulder, and began whispering, frantic. "The cops are searching your place. They have a warrant—Javier . . . and Sue—they're both dead."

Other hands touched him. Taylor. Detective. Talking into a phone, a civilian down.

"Stay with the police," he said to Savi, not even sure she heard him. "Don't be alone."

She nodded, tears streaking her face. "Okay. Okay." And more voices now, but they were fading. No—

He was.

❧

Colin stumbled and it saved his head from being split in two, and the nosferatu's blade slashed his cheek open instead. It would heal, but only if Sir Pup stopped playing with that demon and killed the nosferatu, because it didn't look like Colin was going to last much longer—

But the nosferatu paused, and Colin realized that the demon had given the creature a command in some unrecognizable language.

"Your friends have abandoned you, vampire."

There was a sickening clench in his gut as Beelzebub spoke again, and the nosferatu laughed. The hellhound lay on his side, whimpering, the demon's sword through its belly. *Oh, no. No, no, no.*

But he forced himself to speak evenly, though the scent of Hugh's blood, the hellhound's blood, his own blood maddened him. "So they have." He smiled, his most charming expression, but could not hide his fangs. "Would you like to strike a bargain?"

Delaying, forcing the demon to wait to hear the terms; he could not believe he was going to end this way, in his basement, surrounded by ugliness and death. But why would the Guardian come back for him? Hugh was injured, badly, and Colin had spent two days sucking the lifeblood from her. "You have nothing we want; vampires are good for nothing but feeding their betters." The demon smiled. "It is another type of halfling that interests us."

What kind of halfling? he wondered, and said: "But I'm extraordinarily handsome." He used the demon's flummoxed pause to leap forward, avoiding the nosferatu as best he could.

Take out the demon first—the nosferatu was but a lackey, a valet, waiting for instructions from his master. No way to get out of this, might as well do as much damage as—

Selah appeared in front of him, and he slammed into her. He would have laughed and kissed her on the mouth as they teleported, as the world ripped away from around them, but something went wrong. Her eyes were wide and blue, and he could not see his reflection in them—but he saw the sudden horror and fear.

He recognized this place. "Don't look, don't listen," he said, his throat tightening. "Try again. Keep on trying." *Just please don't leave me here.*

The nosferatu and demon would have been preferable to this.

Lilith fell through the Gate with a rush of seawater, landing atop a stinking pile of—

It didn't bear thinking about.

No guards at this Gate, or in this territory. She glanced around, orienting herself. Barren, with red sand and crimson sky—it hadn't always been so. One thousand years ago, before the war between Belial and Lucifer, this had been one of the few *almost* pleasant territories Below.

But Lucifer had reshaped it after Belial had claimed the territory abutting this one, erasing temples and fountains, and setting loose packs of hellhounds to keep the rebellion from encroaching further into Lucifer's holdings.

Lilith quickly took to the sky; the hellhounds didn't differentiate between Lucifer's followers and Belial's, and it would be suicide to stay on the ground for long. Whatever she had landed in had probably fallen prey to them.

No, that wasn't right—hellhounds wouldn't have left any carrion. So it had been killed by something else; whatever it was, she didn't want to meet it. After the Second Battle, Lucifer had never managed to call forth another dragon from Chaos, and had slowly lost access to that realm and its creatures—including the wyrmwolves, from which he'd bred his hellhounds. But the things he continued to experiment upon and create from the remnants of Chaos were almost as frightening as a dragon, and usually uncontrollable.

She flew toward the throne. Even from this distance it was

easy to see, rising like a gargantuan spear from the center of Hell. If not for the demon's false corporeality, she would have thought it grossly phallic; but Lucifer had no masculinity to prove, and it was a symbol of military power in its simplest shape—and the most inescapable height. The ground Below had no curvature, and the column was visible from every corner.

Just as Belial's temples, newly built in the outlying territories, could be seen from the center though they stood not even an eighth as tall.

Perhaps men had existed as long as they had because the horizon and poor eyesight saved them from perpetual insult. Lilith grinned, trying to imagine Earth if all men, instead of a few in power, were constantly aware of their enemies' progress, and continually measured it against their own. Demons had not been blessed with such happy ignorance, and war had decimated the population on both sides. Unsurprising that many demons had gone rogue, or chose to live on Earth in whatever capacity they could, whether congressman or FBI lackey.

Much better than here, where the stink of death permeated everything. Lucifer's empyreal throne: built on rot, gilded by deceit. His cities had deteriorated since last she'd come Below. Though a simple thing for him to reconstruct them—little more than a thought—buildings lay in ruins, pitted by the sulphuric air. The lake had grown beyond its boundaries, and liquid fire ran in rivulets down the streets, melting away gold and dulling the black marble with smoke.

It had never been beautiful—too gaudy for beauty—but Lucifer's pride had disallowed him to rule over a kingdom in disrepair.

Strange, that it was now. She did not know what to make of it. But she did not know what to think of many things of late.

No. She took a deep breath, let the stinking air fill her. This was not the time for confusion, or for uncertainty. Not the time for sentiment.

She circled around the cities; though war had reduced their populations, the air above them was still busy with demons, like bees over a hive. And though a confrontation and fight might have steadied her nerves, she dared not risk it. Lucifer might approve of such squabbling—or he might not, depending upon his mood.

And it was the territories closer to the throne she needed to focus on, to get through, before she could think about fighting.

She flew through the barrier ringing the throne's territory—Lucifer's magic vanished her wings, and she plummeted. She'd known the barrier was there, could have prepared for it, but she'd seen halflings and demons try to avoid the fall and be punished for it. None could approach Lucifer without being reminded from whence they all came.

But she had no intention of crawling to Lucifer on broken limbs; it would inspire hatred, not pity. She controlled the descent, fast but not reckless, and rolled at the last moment. Breathed a prayer of thanks to the scales and hardened flesh.

A growl from beside her made her quickly amend, "Thanks to the Morningstar for giving me scales and flesh of stone," she said with an ironic smile, but Cerberus only cared that the words were correct, and thought nothing of the tone.

She did not stand half as tall as the hellhound's shoulder; a few more centuries and Sir Pup would be as large. "Your son is well; he begs for pettings and obeys my every command, just like a human's dog." Rage darkened the hellhound's eyes, and Lilith added, "I'd have a treat for you, but I fed the pup the last of the meat I had for being such a *good boy*."

Cerberus went still, as if deciding whether to kill her. But he would have only left the throne at Lucifer's behest and most likely to fetch her. Lucifer would not mourn her death, but he would punish Cerberus for disobeying him, and the hellhound weighed that decision now.

As Lilith had known he would, he let her live, pushing her forward with a violent shove. Through another barrier, from heat to ice. On Earth, the cold did not affect her; here, it bit and clawed, tore hungrily at her feet. Magic, most likely. Use of which Lucifer kept a closely guarded secret, as he did most knowledge.

She tripped as Cerberus pushed her again, and she sprawled flat—and squeezed her eyes shut too late. Only inches from hers: a face, frozen into the ground, frozen in an eternal scream of horror.

Darius. One of the demon halflings; once a murderer, Lucifer had transformed him—then later, destroyed him for taking pride in his human accomplishments. Impossible to serve Lucifer if one prided oneself in giving—or taking—life. When Darius had made that last trip to the throne, the halflings and demons had lined up, watched him walk though the frozen wasteland. He'd walked with his head down, placing each step carefully, though it was not so packed with those terrible visages and stepping room available. The demons had mocked him for his cowardice, for refusing to meet their eyes with pride as he marched to judgment. Such it was Below; to be destroyed for pride, and then mocked for lacking it.

But the halflings watching him had known Darius was thinking of how soon he'd be in that frozen stretch, and that he did unto others as he would have done unto him. They would not do the same—not until their own destruction came and they had nothing left to lose. Only a halfling already doomed would dare betray such a human sentiment.

Lilith rose to her feet; the ground was uneven, the faces mounded together with barely space between them. How many halflings were down there? How many had Lucifer determined had failed in their service to him? Once, the cities Below had swarmed with halflings; now, they populated this frozen stretch of Hell.

And though Lilith was the last of the halflings, she would not end like them.

As she always did, Lilith kept her gaze fixed on the Throne, stumbling across the field, refusing to look at those she stepped on. The silence in this realm was absolute; though her feet—taloned, softer than the cloven hooves, less likely to crunch and shatter frozen flesh—must have made noise as she walked, it didn't reach her ears. Nor could she hear Cerberus, though he walked next to her now.

Only the frozen, silent screams of the damned who had reneged on their bargains. Those who had been greedy or stupid enough to bargain with a demon, but not greedy or stupid enough to uphold their part in it. Not all halflings, but many were.

Lilith had been in the Pit, received Punishment there; the thought of that pain was less terrifying than an eternity trapped here, motionless. Particularly as the ice did not offer numbness or oblivion. Their eyes were not frozen. They wept and pleaded for release that never came.

His death will be yours to give, or your soul mine to keep.

Lucifer had chosen his bargain well; no matter her decision, it would bring torment.

But was one Punishment truly worse than the other?

Her eyes burned with cold; it must have been the cold. She looked down and took care where she placed her feet.

CHAPTER 24

Though the exterior of the throne and much of the interior did not lack for decoration—indeed, sculpted marble friezes and fretted gold adorned every inch—Lucifer's den was comfortable and understated.

As was Lucifer.

Lilith stifled her uneasy laughter as she took in his appearance: a human male, skin just beginning to wrinkle; soft brown eyes and a short brown beard, only a shade darker than the thinning, graying hair on his pate. A blue cardigan and gray slacks completed his look as a friendly, unassuming, middle-class retiree.

He waved aside her formal greeting, then sat in a wingback chair near a fireplace and invited her to take the matching seat. He gestured to a steaming pot on a small table, and said, "Would you like to take tea?"

Biting her lip to halt the bubbling, hysterical laughter that threatened to erupt, she simply nodded. Her hands were shaking, and she willed them to stop as he poured the tea into delicate cups, folding them together in her lap.

She had to sit perched at the edge of the seat to make room for her wings; she dared not vanish them, despite the human form *he'd* assumed. The wingtips lay on the floor on either side of the chair, the spread of their bulk leaving her unable to see behind her chair, even if she turned—she was vulnerable and exposed. Her cloven hooves looked ridiculous against the thick white carpeting; and when he gave her the tea, her claws were inadequate for holding the small porcelain cup.

Fear that she'd scratch the teacup made her tremble again, and he watched intently as the liquid sloshed near the rim. Suddenly certain that he would kill her simply for staining his carpet, she froze.

He smiled. Took a slow sip.

She didn't know if she should do the same. To leave it untouched would be an insult to him; to drink would be human.

Raising the cup to her lips, she held it there and spoke over the rim. "Thank you, Father."

Apparently, it was the correct response, as he didn't immediately destroy her.

"Ah, Lilith," he said, leaning back and crossing his legs at the knee. "You are such a disappointment to me."

"Stupid and weak," she agreed.

"Yes. I'm not certain what to do with you."

"In your infinite wisdom, I'm certain that whatever you choose will be the correct decision, Father."

"Of course." He set his cup on the table and steepled fingers that could tear apart mountains. "You told the human the truth of our bargain."

"Yes, Father. I find their terror is best prolonged and thereby better enjoyed when they know their damnation is imminent and inevitable."

"I prefer surprises."

She dipped her head. "I am but a lowly halfling, Father, and do not always make the best decisions, though I would try to emulate you."

"Do you think you could be as I am, Lilith?"

"I could never be half as magnificent, Father."

"You should lie to the human. You should lie always."

She lowered her eyes. "You are so very benevolent, Father, to share your wisdom with a worm such as I."

Perhaps she had gone too far with the last remark; he stared at her without expression, but the fire in the hearth leapt and crackled.

"I can smell his seed within you. It defiles my Realm."

"It was not my intention to defile, Father, only to offer proof of his weakening."

"And your own?"

"Is but a part of my design, Father. He thinks to save me, and I give him as much hope as possible toward that end: I plan to make him believe that my reaction and desire is genuine before I take that false hope away and destroy him, as per our bargain," she said, and her stomach clenched as she realized she'd done exactly as Hugh had predicted: attempted to lie to herself.

"Your pleasure was genuine."

She shrugged carelessly. "It was but a physical manifestation of the pleasure I took in deceiving him."

"You lie."

"As you wished, Father."

"You *care* for him."

She fell silent, not daring to hope that Hugh had been right about Lucifer's response as he had been of hers, that his plan might work after all.

"How delightful, then, that you must kill him." He sat forward, resting his elbows on the arms of the chair. "I have a surprise for you, Lilith. Two surprises, actually."

Tensing, she prepared to flee. "Yes?"

"The first is a visitor. We found him wandering the Pit."

She frowned, confused. But she recognized the long, confident strides of the Guardian who entered the den, his physical scent.

Michael.

Lucifer did not rise from his seat; nor did she, or turn to acknowledge him, though it left her blind to the Guardian's expressions and appearance.

"You are embarrassing me, daughter."

Anger in that statement; she leapt to her feet, forcing a smile. "I'm certain that the Doyen understands he is not worthy of notice when in the company of such as yourself, Father."

Michael nodded slowly, his obsidian gaze unreadable as it traveled between Lucifer and Lilith. With his black feathered wings, soot-stained toga and bronzed skin, the Doyen looked more the denizen Below than Lucifer, but she did not make the observation aloud.

"Would you take tea?" Lilith said.

"No. I have only come to look for someone I misplaced. I will be leaving shortly; I wished to pay my respects." Michael's tone made it clear he had little, if any, respect for the demon lord.

"Misplaced?" Lucifer echoed, and laughed. "Careless of you, I daresay. Be certain that if I find this lost soul, I shall find a place for him."

"Yes." Michael did not look away from Lilith. "I sense your halfling is eager to return to Earth."

"I have a bargain to fulfill," Lilith said quietly, wishing the Guardian would not speak of, or to, her at all. His attention would only put her in line of Lucifer's anger.

"Hugh. Do you truly believe you'll succeed where you failed before?" His lips quirked, and he turned to Lucifer. "You have indeed made her in your image; she fails too often to be anything but your daughter."

"She'll not fail in this," Lucifer murmured.

"All of those you transformed have been worthless, the result of a faulty ritual—else they would still populate this realm," Michael said. Lilith stood, absolutely still, and they spoke as if she did not exist. Vexing, but safer than notice. "And applying that false transformation to the nosferatu will not save you from inevitable ruin."

"It gave the halflings power; there was nothing faulty in the ritual, only the recipients."

"You could not make true demons from a human template."

"And that is why I shall succeed with the nosferatu," Lucifer said, smiling. "They are pure, of the original angelic orders, and their power will add to mine."

Michael started, as if in realization. Strange, Lilith thought; she had never seen him react with such obviousness. Would Lucifer know it was unusual?

"Their power to kill men," Michael said slowly. "That is what they trade; they would kill in service of you."

"Much more efficient than the halflings, don't you agree? And at little inconvenience to myself; they only wish for access to Hell, safety from my demons, and a territory in my realm in exchange. Belial's would be the perfect size, would it not?"

It would not. Though Lilith could readily believe the nosferatu desired a home—they had been hunted endlessly on Earth by demon and Guardian, and their rejection Above and Below had been their greatest Punishment, even greater than the curse upon them physically—Lilith could not imagine Lucifer allowing the nosferatu control of that much territory. A small slice of it, perhaps, but not all that Belial had claimed.

And why the transformation to daywalking and resistance to sunlight? It would not make a difference Below.

But it would in Caelum.

Michael glanced at her; shaken, she lowered her gaze. Her psychic blocks were in place; he probably couldn't read her. Lucifer might have been able, but his attention was focused on the Guardian.

"Belial is strong," Michael said. "I do not think he will fall easily."

Lucifer laughed, as if to convey how little the Guardian's opinion mattered. "I will succeed."

"Will it be as successful as your rebellion?" Michael said, his eyes glinting with mockery. "In your arrogance, you give too much away."

"Then Belial will have time to contemplate his imminent and inevitable destruction, and his extended torment will prolong my enjoyment."

Lilith bit her lip, but looked up in dismay when Michael said her name.

"Of course, Lilith plans her own rebellion."

"I am meek," she said quickly, flexing her talons. "Never rebellious."

"Hugh will not break; and, already, he manipulates you," Michael continued, still speaking to Lucifer as if she were not there. "Certainly you realize it was his intention that you should send her back to Earth, knowing you would choose to cause her the most pain by fulfilling the bargain? Truly, you do exactly what the human has desired."

Lilith sucked in a sharp breath.

She felt Lucifer's anger, quickly suppressed. Of course, he would never admit to being surprised or lacking knowledge. "Yes, I'm aware of his puerile attempts to manipulate me. But he *has* broken—has lost his humanity. My Lilith knows this well; it was that which led to her death." He rose to his feet, stood before Michael. "And what was it that broke him? That girl, and thinking that she had been killed. Easy enough to arrange like circumstances."

Wrong, Lucifer. Lilith smiled to herself, though she betrayed it by neither thought nor expression. It hadn't been that Savi had been shot; it had been the decision he'd made, that he'd no longer hold an ideal over human life. It had been reclaiming his will, his freedom—and his break had come from knowing that the only way to give Lilith hers was death. He'd nearly destroyed himself when he'd slain her.

"And your halfling will exacerbate his grief and bring about his death?" Michael shook his head. "He *will* find a way to save himself, do not doubt it. He has thwarted her before; he will again. Even human, he is stronger of mind than she. He is stubborn, and cannot tolerate failure in himself."

"A delightful flaw," Lucifer said.

Lilith clenched her fists, glaring at the Guardian. "One I shall happily use against him."

"Do you think so, daughter?" The demon's voice was soft. But though he probably would have liked nothing better than tossing her in the Pit, Lilith had already told Michael she was returning to Earth to fulfill her bargain. If Lucifer changed his mind now, it would appear he had not known of Hugh's manipulations.

Michael smiled, as if realizing Lucifer's difficulty. "She is your last halfling; therefore, I suppose she is the best of that failed experiment? I offer a wager. Your halfling's skills against my former pupil's resistance to them."

Lilith's lips parted in shock. Was he mad?

"What are the terms?" Lucifer asked, his eyes gleaming. "Do you wager your sword?"

"Should Lilith be the direct cause of his death, through whatever skills she employs *personally*—she cannot instruct a nosferatu to kill him, a more capable demon to torment him, nor manipulate another human into killing him—I will open Caelum's Gates to you and your kind for eternity. If she fails, you close Hell's Gates to Earth for five hundred years."

"It won't require skill," Lilith said dryly, though her heart pounded. "In sixty years I can jump out of a closet at his retirement home and induce a heart attack."

"And it must be done within the next fourteen days," Michael said. "Furthermore, you must discontinue the rituals until the end of the wager; his grief acts as an outside influence. The nosferatu must be dependent upon you for knowledge of how to perform the ritual; refuse to do it, and do not allow them to abduct more humans, until the end of the wager. I will not have you and the nosferatu kill all of his loved ones to assist Lilith, only to claim it was a separate action."

"Why would you enter into such an agreement?" Lucifer watched the Guardian carefully.

"I want him in the corps. As I'm certain you are aware, my ranks have been severely reduced of late. Hugh was my best warrior, the best mentor; and if he dies, it will likely be sacrificing himself to save *her*. He will accept the transformation again, and I will have him teach my new recruits, as I have neither the time nor inclination to do it myself, and no one else is as qualified as he is." Michael smiled coldly, and his gaze raked over Lilith's form. "And I believe I have little to lose, as I have the advantage here."

"Seven days, and you cannot speak of our wager with anyone else—human, demon, halfling, or nosferatu—except to instruct your Guardians that they may not attack my demons or the nosferatu, unless they are breaking the agreement and have begun the ritual on a human against the human's will," Lucifer countered, and Michael's brows rose.

"If you wish. Making Hugh aware of it won't change the outcome; he already has full knowledge of what Lilith is, and what she will try to do. And so long as your demons and the nosferatu are not instructed to perform any rituals nor abduct any humans, my Guardians will not engage them."

Lucifer did not try to hide his triumphant smile. "It is done, then."

"It is done," Michael agreed.

The Doyen spared her a final glance, then disappeared. Lilith stared at the empty space, trying to comprehend what had just taken place; beside her, Lucifer began laughing.

"He is surely not so desperate to have one man return to the Guardian corps," Lilith murmured.

"It is an act of desperation, but not for the human's sake," Lucifer said, returning to his seat. "His hold on Caelum is tenuous; he wagers what he will lose anyway."

"Why do you take the risk?"

"Do you think I make rash, thoughtless decisions?"

"No, Father," she said immediately.

He smiled, and a shiver ran over her skin. "It would be a risk, if not for the other surprise I spoke of. For it would be stupid to think that you could bring him to suicide within a week. Do you think me stupid, Lilith?"

Her eyes narrowed. "Only if it gives you pleasure."

"You dare too much," he said quietly, and leaned back into his chair. "Sit. I do not like you standing above me."

She complied, vanishing her wings. Whatever his next surprise was, she wanted to see it coming.

A book appeared in her lap. She looked down at the embossed lettering, the now-familiar cover, and saw her doom.

"I have overlooked the others for centuries; the poets and the playwrights whom you would have sought immortality with— is not the immortality I gave you enough?" When she did not answer, he said, "He only mentions my name three times, Lilith. Do you think you deserve such attention?"

Instinct demanded that she flee, but she couldn't move; his magic suddenly held her frozen, motionless. But she could speak, and the words tumbled from her mouth without heed. "Do you envy me, Father?"

His fingers clenched on the arms of the chair, and the fabric ripped under his nails. "When I made you, you swore to serve me for as long as you were a demon. You do *not* place yourself above me."

"I serve. I will serve until I'm dead of it," she said bitterly.

"Which will be sooner than you think should you fail in this new bargain." His eyes flashed. "Six days; you have six days to fulfill your bargain, to see him dead, and then I send the nosferatu to kill you."

One day less than he'd wagered with Michael; apparently, he did not trust her to fulfill her bargain. If she failed, Lucifer would likely lead an attack against the Doyen, and attempt to kill him before the wager ended.

"You do not destroy me yourself? Have you not the stomach for it, Father?"

He sat forward in his seat, smiling. "Will *you* have the stomach to kill *him*?"

"Even now, I am thinking of the best way to go about it." A lie. She could only think of escape.

He rested his elbows on his knees and whispering conspiratorially, "I've thought of one for you." Reaching across the space between them, he grasped her wrist, his skin slithering over hers. "But first, I have to take the demon out of you. No need for him to commit suicide if you can kill him with your sword. Six days, Lilith. You or him."

Her eyes widened, and she frantically tried to move—and could not.

His face transformed. Huge, terrible. Ice slipped through her, and the markings on her chest began to burn. Closing her eyes, she clenched her teeth and refused to scream, though it felt as if he tore her to shreds.

"Do you like your surprise?" he asked, laughing.

She looked up, though she could barely focus through the haze of pain. "I've had better."

And was grateful for the silence that followed.

CHAPTER 25

Hugh held his hand to his side as he shuffled across the hospital room, ignoring the tandem sighs of frustration from the detectives, just as he'd ignored the countless questions they'd asked since he'd woken.

Almost forty-eight hours since he'd last seen Lilith, and he had not yet heard from her. Those who might have known where she was, what might have happened to her, were equally silent: Michael, Selah, Colin—he'd have welcomed a visit from Beelzebub if it brought him news of her.

Thoughts of the demon made him close his eyes against a wave of doubt. He'd called the demon a liar when he'd said Lilith had procured another human for them, but had it simply been Hugh's arrogance that had blinded him to the truth? Sue had been killed, and Lilith had seen her alive the same afternoon. She'd been preparing herself, as if for a ritual—had he believed her explanation because he was accustomed to catching lies?

If they had threatened her with Punishment or death, would she lie to him, help with the ritual—and he'd been too desperate to believe her to see the truth?

He couldn't believe it . . . didn't want to believe it. But he couldn't force away the doubt.

"I don't think you understand, Castleford," Taylor said as he gathered the clothing Savi had left for him earlier. Every movement ripped at him with angry teeth. "The last thing you should do right now is leave here."

"You said I was not under arrest. You have no reason to keep me here." His voice was still hoarse—a bruised windpipe. The bandage around his throat and the sutures beneath itched, multiple contusions pulled and ached, but it was his ribs that bothered him most: two cracked, one broken. Each breath burned.

"Putting you back in that bed would suit me just fine right now," Preston said.

Taylor laid her hand on Preston's arm, then stood and walked over to Hugh. "Look, Castleford," she said, taking a shirt from him and unfolding it. He hesitated, then accepted her help, sliding his left arm through the sleeve. She moved around to his other side, easing it over his shoulders. "I don't understand what I saw in Miss Murray's house. Frankly, I'm a bit . . ." She paused, as if searching for the right word. ". . . freaked out by it."

"And the idea that the shit you talk about in your book might be true," Preston added.

"We've just told you we have two eyewitnesses who will testify they saw you dump the bodies of Sanchez and Fletcher in Harding Park. We have a fire at a location that matches a name and address written on a note found during our search of your house, and the owner of that house—whom we know you spoke with only hours before the fire—is missing. We have a missing FBI agent, with your torn clothing, traces of your blood and semen, and your fingerprints at her apartment."

"Along with almost half a million dollars in stolen books and an arsenal of stolen weaponry."

Taylor flicked a glance at Preston. "Our case against you seems solid—except that we were talking to you when you allegedly made the dump in the park. Except for reports of howling from several of Beaumont's neighbors, and another eyewitness in the area who told the police they saw someone matching the description of a nosferatu exit the house after the fire started, accompanied by a man she later identified as FBI Agent Smith—who, two hours ago, took over our jurisdiction in the investigation of the three murders, Milton's disappearance,

Beaumont's disappearance, and the fire. The three bodies have disappeared from the morgue, and though we are being told by the Bureau that they've taken possession of them, we have no records of transfer, nor any evidence that they've been picked up through official channels. We don't like what we're seeing, Castleford; and now his office is denying our requests to share information. It reeks of a cover-up, or a setup. And the few things my partner and I have to go on are an unbelievable story from me, and a letter whose authenticity is questionable, at best. And that you show up with an injury that looks like something out of a horror flick, and that the doctors tell us your rate of recovery has been . . . unusual. But we have no evidence to give to my superiors that might protect you—and I don't doubt Smith will be coming after you soon. We *can* help you," Taylor said. "But we need you to give us something, too."

He smiled for the first time since awakening. "That sounds very much like a bargain," he said. Pulling away from her, he slowly walked back to the bedside table and collected his eyeglasses. "But not one either of us can fulfill. I don't have any evidence to trade, and you certainly can't protect me."

"If you don't have physical evidence, we'll take information."

"What good will anything I have to say be? Even your partner doesn't believe you," Hugh said, glancing past her to Preston.

The older man stiffened. "I do."

"You only believe that *she* believes it."

"Perhaps that is true, but it doesn't change the fact that he is willing to listen," Taylor said. "And I couldn't blame him for not believing what he has not seen."

He'd once told Lilith almost exactly the same thing, but referring to a priest instead of a detective. His chest ached at the memory, more fiercely than his injuries.

Where was she?

Taylor's cell phone rang, saving him from an immediate response; she scowled at the display before answering. Her tone changed quickly, and she looked at Preston, wide-eyed.

"Tom's sending the images through now," she said, and handed her partner the phone. Tucking her hands into her blazer, she rocked back on her heels and waited, watching Preston with an expectant—almost triumphant—expression.

Hugh turned away, looking over the room to make sure he'd left nothing unpacked. It was white, sterile—exactly the type of room that made him most uncomfortable, and he'd heal no more quickly here than at home. And, when she returned, Lilith would know where to find him.

If she returned.

"They could be faked," Preston said suddenly, with a note of aggrieved disbelief.

"Dr. Castleford, is Agent Milton a demon?" Taylor asked.

Hugh's ribs protested as he jerked his head up, turning back to stare at the detectives. Preston held the phone in his hand, frowning down at it.

Taylor's eyes narrowed on Hugh's face. "She is. And you knew who she was when we visited your office with her on Friday." She made a disgusted sound. "And the setup congeals. She gave us the letter, which, because of your book, only made us more suspicious of you."

Hugh looked between the two of them, then at the phone; relenting, he offered, "She didn't know about the book. The letter was designed to lead you to Polidori's and the nosferatu, and to remove suspicion from me."

As if understanding the information meant that he was bargaining, Taylor countered, "You must realize telling us that only implicates you in a conspiracy to falsify evidence. Why is one agent from the FBI planting evidence against you, and another agent trying to do the opposite? Why would she use the letter, instead of bringing forth real evidence to clear your name?"

"There is none. And the semen and the blood at her apartment *are* mine." Hugh glanced at Preston. "She has to lie; she's a demon. She protects herself by lying. It allows her to excuse any good that comes from it."

"Why would she need the excuse?" Preston rose from the chair, gave the cell phone back to Taylor.

Hugh's expression hardened, and he shook his head. "No. It's your turn."

A smile played around Taylor's mouth, and she gave him the phone. Hugh had to squint to make out the picture on the display: black and white, slightly blurred—but the figure in the center was undeniably Lilith. In her human form, except for the dark outline of her wings. A small, dark figure lay at her feet.

"Press the back arrow," Taylor instructed.

With his thumb, he moved through two more pictures: a

close-up of Lilith's face, and the grainy image did little to conceal the resignation in her expression; and another, from a different angle, with her back to a small crowd—she was poised on the bridge railing, as if about to leap over. His throat closed; wordlessly, he handed it back to Taylor, and waited.

Preston said, "Accórding to witnesses, she caught a jumper, then jumped over the side herself."

The relief and joy that washed over him left his knees weak, and he slowly sat down onto the hospital bed. "She saved him?"

"Scared the shit out of him, too." Humor in the detective's gruff voice now. "Of course, he was so high on meth, a squirrel might have done the same."

Hugh's breath caught as realization struck: she'd interfered with his free will. Oh, God no.

"We've had a hell of a time keeping them out of the media," Taylor added. "I had one of our guys clean up these images from the traffic cams, but if they get out . . . er, Castleford, are you okay?"

She wasn't coming back.

He clenched his teeth, but still the harsh sob tore from him. No possibility that she was being forced to help the ritual out of fear of Punishment; she couldn't be, to then save a boy from suicide. Punishment, destruction, or transformation—Lucifer *had* to do one, and he'd never allowed a halfling to Fall. Had never reversed the transformation. Had she been so certain she would be Punished or destroyed that she'd forced Lucifer's hand? Had she so little faith that he'd find a way to save her?

Or had it been because he'd only talked of saving her? He'd opened himself up to her, but he'd never spoken of love. Had kept that part of him back.

His breath came raw, tears burned. And he could only be grateful that she'd never seen his doubt. That she hadn't seen how he had failed her again . . . had not believed in her until too late.

✦

Salt, stink, rot, fire.

Running through it, sniffing, her trail bright and crimson above his heads and he had to keep one gaze on the sky, the other two gazes watching the sides. Wary of those like him but not-him. The distant howls of those like him, calling.

Hunt.
Chase.
Kill.

Ignore those urges, pass the hives. The frigid faces, screaming, hurting his paws. The musk of the father, growls but lets him pass when he widens his own jaws and roars. The strange, golden odor of the one who had healed him while the oil-paint vampire's den burned around him, and the yellow scaly one—distant, relief. And her, her. The voices speaking to her: *Kill him, you or him, must save yourself, fulfill your bargain, halfling, nothing.*

Cries of the guards, those who talk in hisses and lies, their delicious fear. *Hunt, chase, kill.* Tear through them, then into the dark, where she crouches, cold.

Different, but her arm curling around his shoulders, her voice, the same. Desperate, amused, tired.

"I'll hold on. Just run." Her weight on his back.

Run, run, run.

❧

"So, have you been laughing at Ganesh all this time?"

He felt Savi's concerned gaze, and forced a smile for her sake. Difficult, when he seemed empty, hollow. "No."

She shouldered his bag before he could reach for it. "Are you just saying that?"

"No. There are other realms."

"Have you seen them?"

"No."

"Then how—" She broke off and sighed. "Sorry. I'll save my questions for later. You've probably had enough of them. They're waiting out there to give us a ride home. I think you scared them. They didn't expect you to break down—oh, holy shit."

She stumbled back, and Hugh turned to look behind him.

"Michael." Hugh's voice was flat. "Should you feel inclined, I believe the two detectives outside could benefit from one of your displays."

Savi's eyes widened, and she slid her hand into Hugh's.

Michael's gaze flicked down to their linked hands. *I need to take the girl to Caelum. She'll be safe there*, he signed.

"From whom?"

The nosferatu. The Guardian's jaw clenched, muscles tightening beneath the bronze skin. *Lilith. She's coming back.*

Hugh's eyes closed, not daring to believe. "How?"

"I cannot speak of it."

His heart thudded. "Auntie, too," he finally said.

Michael nodded shortly, and Hugh turned to Savi. "You'll have to go with him of your free will; you have to choose to go, he can't simply take you."

Though there was fear in her gaze, excitement quickly began to replace it. "Where?"

"Heaven." Hugh smiled, but he couldn't keep the sardonic edge from it.

Savi placed her hand in Michael's without hesitation. *Too trusting, too accepting,* Hugh thought, but he could not fault her now for what had helped heal him sixteen years before.

Michael's eyes narrowed on the bandage at his neck. A pulse of power flowed from him; Savi staggered, but the Guardian slipped his arm around her waist to steady her.

"What was that?" No fear in her eyes now, only that wide curiosity.

"A display," Michael said with rare humor, and they disappeared.

Taylor and Preston burst through the door, their weapons drawn. They stared at Hugh, standing alone. He looked back at them without expression, taking a deep, pain-free breath.

"You have a camera in your phone, too?" he asked. Taylor's brows drew together, but she nodded and holstered her gun.

In the hallway, he heard two nurses chatting easily as they exited another room; Michael's power must have been closely contained, only felt by those in a very small radius. Though a hospital-wide healing might have been a more spectacular display, a Guardian's healing power only worked on injuries sustained from inhuman causes: a nosferatu's bite, a wound from a demon's sword, or a bad landing made during transportation.

"It's not much," Hugh said, peeling away the bandage at his neck.

"It's enough for now," Taylor breathed as he exposed perfectly healed skin. "It's *something*."

"Perhaps he has a twin," Preston said, but Hugh could hear the uncertainty in his voice.

"Those pictures from the bridge," Hugh said. "Has anyone else seen them?"

"No. And except for a few people, it would be taken as seriously as a grilled cheese sandwich," Preston said, shaking his head. "But there were witnesses, and we don't know what lengths these things would go to keep their presence a secret."

Hugh suddenly felt like laughing. "Not very far; they'd love the results of such a revelation. Imagine, if it became known that evil creatures, who could take any human form, walked among us." At their blank looks, he said with a wry smile, "You would never get another conviction, to start. A shape-shifting demon is the best defense."

Taylor nodded slowly. "Then why don't they?"

"Lucifer," Hugh said simply. "No demon wants to be singled out, or star in a world-wide broadcast."

"You singled out Lilith with your book," Preston said.

"She was dead."

"But no longer."

"No." He held Taylor's gaze with his own, saw the knowledge in her eyes. "But she's not behind the murders. Don't waste your time looking at her."

Preston's brows raised. "Who should we look at?"

There was a threat in that question, and the offended tone of one who didn't like being told what to investigate, but Hugh didn't respond to it. "The nosferatu. Beelzebub." He recalled the demon's appearance in Colin's basement, the witness who'd seen Smith leaving the house. "Who must be Agent Smith. Was the house completely destroyed?"

"No. Neighbors saw that one side of the house had imploded, and thought there'd been an explosion, so the fire trucks were already on their way. Were you there?"

"Yes," Hugh said. "There will be traces of my blood in the basement. There might be ash remains of several nosferatu."

"Within two hours you were at Auntie's; Milton's apartment in Hunter's Point; the Beaumont place in The Haight; and back to your place?" Taylor frowned. "You got around the city rather quickly."

Realizing what she was thinking, that he had also managed to be in two places almost at once, Hugh said softly, "I didn't murder those kids, or Sue. Some things are exactly as they appear, and some appearances are deceiving."

"We just have to trust you?"

Hugh ignored the mockery in Preston's tone. "No. You just have to look for the truth. Trust takes much longer." Eight hundred years, at times.

CHAPTER 26

Waiting had been easy for Hugh, once. Easy to let things happen around him, without doing anything himself. Now, when it was forced upon him, it ate at him with sharp teeth. He pounded the weights until he shook with fatigue, but the exertion was routine, leaving his mind busy and his thoughts drawing out endlessly—as time seemed to.

Javier, Ian, and Sue, dead. Colin and Selah, missing. Savi and Auntie, swept away to Caelum for their protection though no human had ever been taken to that realm before.

Had he failed them all?

Curled atop his desk, Emilia watched him, blinking lazily each time the bar clanged into its cradle. The minutes crawled by. It was near midnight when the cat rocketed across the room, screeching, her fur standing on end. His heart pounding, Hugh let the weights fall to the floor, and ran after the cat. He detoured to the living room when he saw it disappear under his bed. If the cat was afraid, then either a nosferatu had come to finish him—or a hellhound.

A scratching at the back door, then an urgent chorus of barks.

Sir Pup broke the latch just as Hugh skidded into the room, and he caught her as she tumbled from the hellhound's back. She was shivering—her clothing soaked through, her lips blue, her skin pale and bloodless.

Only one symbol remained on her chest.

"Lilith," he said, gathering her close against him. He pressed his lips to hers; they tasted of sea water. Her eyes opened.

"I'm really . . . fucking . . . cold." Her teeth chattered together, and realization and panic struck him at the same time. He lifted her; her head lolled back against his shoulder.

Human.

His eyes burned as he carried her down the hall toward the bathroom, as he set her down on the toilet seat, holding her up with one hand as he turned on the taps to fill the bath with the other. Working quickly, he unlaced the corset, stripped it off. The wet pants clung to her legs; weakly, she tried to help him, and with a final yank he ended sprawled against the opposite wall.

"Stupid . . . leather," she said, and whether she shook with laughter or cold he couldn't tell.

"I like them," he said simply, and slid her shivering form into the lukewarm bath.

Her breath hissed from between her teeth, her eyes squeezed shut. "I hate this. I can't *be* this."

His heart seemed to tear from his chest. Kneeling beside the tub, he pushed tendrils of hair from her forehead. "I know."

❧

She slept. Eventually dreams felt like madness, and she clawed her way out of them. Two thousand years without sleep, and she had forgotten how to tell dream from reality, forgotten how easily they fell away on waking.

She was still tired—exhausted—but it was a pleasure to open her eyes. A pleasure to see the wash of midmorning light across the room. A pleasure to see Hugh, leaning against the door frame, his arms crossed over his chest, his long body absolutely still. It was a protective stance, yet unguarded in its focus: as if he'd been content to watch her for an eternity, and had settled into the watching with his entire being.

Strange, that a man could do nothing but *be*, and it was a pleasure.

She grinned suddenly, rolling over onto her side and propping her head on her hand. One day as a human, and she'd descended into maudlin sentimentality.

Her movement seemed to spur his, and he sat down on the bed next to her, laying his hand across her forehead. The mattress was soft beneath her, the blankets a comfortable weight. At some point, he'd put a sweatshirt on her, and she felt loose fleece sweatpants against her legs.

"I have to kill you." Her voice was light, but she regarded him intently, searching for his reaction. "If a fever takes me first, Lucifer will be furious—though it would be his fault. Even a demon should know that a human body cannot easily withstand the frigid water in the bay."

His brows rose, and a smile seemed to flirt with his lips. His gaze touched everywhere his hands had not, as if looking for signs of sickness or injury. "Are you well?"

Weak, tired, with aches that she couldn't remember if they were normal or not. But she nodded. "I'm fortunate that Sir Pup swims very quickly."

He looked at her for a moment more, then said, "Very fortunate. I fed him a few small children as reward."

A few moments later, she held her belly and groaned, "Don't make me laugh. It hurts."

That smile that had appeared with her laughter immediately failed. His throat worked before he said, "Why are you not angry?" At her sigh, he continued, "Have you resigned yourself to this so easily then?"

She stiffened, then saw the brief flash of humor in his eyes and realized he was trying to provoke a heated response. Unwilling to give in, she relaxed back into the pillows, and pulled the comforter up to her chin. "I'm building up to it; within ten minutes, I'll be myself again."

He stretched out on his side next to her, crooking his elbow and looking down at her face. "Who are you now?"

According to the symbol over her heart, still Lilith. But she did not want to think of that at this moment; beneath the blanket, she ran her hand down her torso. "Do you want to come in and find out?"

His gaze fell to her mouth, but he shook his head.

She hid her smile, rounding her lips in an O of surprise. "What is this I've found? Round and"—she gasped exaggeratedly, and tented the blanket over her chest—"no longer sharp? There are two!"

"Not that large, certainly," he said, pushing the blanket back down. His brows drew together, and he studied her as if he'd seen something new in her features. "And so you delve into absurdities when you wish to avoid a truth, whereas I brood and overanalyze myself into permanent inaction."

"I hate that you know me so well," she said mildly, and then narrowed her eyes. "How are you resisting me? Is this your inaction?"

He grinned. "I would love to give in to temptation this time, but we don't have protection."

"Sir Pup—"

"Condoms." His hand found hers through the comforter and tightened when she looked at him, stunned. "Assuming that we live through the next year, I'm too old for children and far too—as you once put it so eloquently—fucked up."

She was, too. Bile rose in her throat; her body still too vulnerable, though in entirely different ways.

"I believe they call it 'having issues,'" he continued. His voice was rough, but his lips quirked into a smile.

His attempt at humor renewed hers. "Baggage," she said, grinning. "Though I'm certain such a thing didn't exist when I was born. Everyone was perfectly adjusted." Now she had two thousand years' worth, and the heaviest was her bargain with Lucifer. Her smile faded, and she sat up.

A moment later, she had him flat against the bed, and she straddled his hips. His gray T-shirt was warmed by his body heat; curling her fingers into the soft, worn cotton, she tugged and said, "Let's do this quickly. No drawing it out." When he nodded his agreement, she placed her hand on his chest as if to hold him down—but it was more for her support than fear he would try to escape.

He ran his palms up the length of her thighs, let them rest at the top. Holding her down, in turn. "There have been two more murdered."

"Your missing student? Who else?"

"Sue Fletcher."

Lilith hardened herself against the grief in his voice and delivered the next blow. "I have to fulfill my bargain in . . . what is today?"

"Monday morning."

"Four days. Michael made a wager with Lucifer; if you are not dead by the fifth day, Caelum's Gates will be opened to those Below. My father stipulated that the Doyen may not speak of it to the other Guardians; I don't know that they'll be able to help." But there was no reason Lilith could not speak of it; she was bound by her bargain to kill Hugh, but Michael's wager only included her in a peripheral sense. It depended upon the result of her actions, but she was not a participant in the wager itself.

"And if you don't kill me?"

"The nosferatu come for me on the fourth day. They will kill me if the bargain is incomplete; my soul will be frozen in Punishment, and Hell's Gates closed for five hundred years."

His hands tightened. "Colin and Selah are missing. Beelzebub—Smith?" At her nod, he continued, "—attacked us at Colin's house after you left. Selah managed to transport me out, but I don't know that they are alive."

She had to look away for a moment, her breathing ragged. Swallowing, she focused again and said, "Lucifer planned to transform me back into human even before Michael offered his wager. The nosferatu intend to take Caelum for their own and will act as Lucifer's assassins in payment."

"A nosferatu at Colin's could have killed me, but he did not pierce the jugular; I don't think it a mistake." His thumbs smoothed over her inner thighs, not to arouse, but to soothe. "We are both halflings who have been returned to our human forms."

"They will use Savitri against you; they know you broke when she was shot."

Hugh was shaking his head. "Michael took her to Caelum."

"But how—?" She sucked in a deep breath when she saw his face, the regret lurking in the lines around his mouth. "You have more. Quickly."

"Beelzebub tried to bargain Savi's life for mine and wanted me to submit to the ritual. They set fire to Colin's house. I have no weapons; my swords and your gun were lost during the attack. Taylor and Preston know you are a demon; they have pictures of you saving a boy on the bridge. Smith has taken over each investigation associated with the rituals, and he has witnesses who saw me in the park with Javier's and Sue's bodies, which have been stolen from the morgue, along with Ian's. You are listed as missing, presumed dead; I'm the primary suspect and all of the weapons and books at your apartment were confiscated."

She collapsed against his chest when he finished, and his arms came up, his palms warm and strong as he gently began to massage her lower back. "Please tell me there's good news," she said into his neck.

"I was fired." His solemn announcement surprised a burst of laughter from her. "Though it was not put so harshly as that. The university has kindly given me as much time off as I need during the investigation, but they don't think I will be needed in the fall or beyond that term."

"That cannot be legal," Lilith protested. "One of Lucifer's demons must be president of the university."

He grinned. "I actually think it was the result of the media attention. There are several news vans parked outside."

"You put this in the 'good' category?"

"Yes. It will be difficult for the nosferatu to attack us if we are under constant public surveillance—and if anything happens to one of my students, we'll likely know right away. And without my presence at the university, there will be less danger of my students there being targeted, though there is still a core group of DemonSlayer players."

"DemonSlayer—Lucifer focuses on them not just because of your relationship to the players, but because he finds the game offensive," she realized. "Its source bears my name instead of his." Lifting her head, she moved forward slightly and nipped at his earlobe. "Now: *real* good news. I want it."

He shifted beneath her, ran his hands up the length of her spine. She heard the smile in his voice. "Taylor and Preston are aware Smith and the nosferatu are corrupting the investigations in some way and may even be responsible for the murders."

"But they have little evidence," Lilith guessed.

"Very little."

She waited, then planted her elbows on either side of his head and rose up to look at him. Her hair fell forward like a curtain in front of her eyes, and she impatiently pushed it away. "That's it?"

"I was waiting for your contribution," he said. Gathering her hair at her nape, he traced his fingertips over the bare skin beneath.

She desperately tried to think of something. His lips were so close to hers. "I still have my job."

"With Beelzebub as your superior, that is indeed an advantage," he said dryly.

"This is what we have?" She lowered her forehead to his and smiled when she felt his breath quicken. "We are lost."

"And neither of us has ever proved a successful guide for the other," he said with self-deprecating humor. She brushed her lips against the corner of his mouth; his body tightened beneath hers, and his hands moved to her shoulders. "Shall we simply try to hack our way through the nest?"

"We lack swords, and I'm no martyr."

"We could throw books; I have plenty."

"Now who's delving into absurdities?" She licked his jaw; his unshaven skin was rough beneath her tongue.

"I've never thought clearly with you sitting atop me." In a smooth movement, he rolled and pinned her beneath him, his hips wedged between her thighs.

Laughing, she hooked her ankle behind his knee, pulled with her leg and twisted her torso. She straddled him again, but her laughter died. His eyes were arrested on her face, and the wealth of emotion in his expression made her chest ache.

"You are still strong, Lilith." She looked away, but he captured her chin, brought her gaze back to his. "Not as you once were, perhaps, but still strong. Not as fast, but quick enough. You have not lost the skills behind the demon's powers. And your psychic abilities are gone, but you have two millennia's experience reading faces, body language."

She dipped her head, but couldn't contain her sad smile. Though his Fall had been voluntary, he must know exactly how she felt. "And my cache?"

His mouth twisted with wry humor. "Pockets are a wonderful invention." His knee rose, nudged her back as if to draw attention to his olive cargo pants.

"Which are appallingly empty; I would kill for a rubber," she said, and meant it. Smoothing her hands against his chest, she absorbed his deep rumbling laugh through her skin, and felt an echoing rumble in her stomach. "I'm hungry," she realized, with a touch of wonder.

His gaze dropped to the spread of her thighs over his abdomen. "I am, too," he said gruffly, and heat shot through her.

"I'm more than willing to wait—" Her stomach growled again, loudly.

He gave a shout of laughter, and laced his fingers through hers. His muscles flexed beneath her legs as he sat up, the motion bringing his face close to hers, her bottom seated firmly over his erection. "You haven't eaten in two thousand years; I'll feed you first."

"Hugh—" she moaned softly as he scooted forward to the edge of the bed, her sex tight against the hardness of his cock, sliding over his thick length with each movement.

"I cannot think when you are on me," he repeated, his laughter strained now.

She caught his laugh in her mouth; it was a promise, this kiss, though it remained unspoken—all of her promises and bargains and wagers had been made with her tongue, but with tricks and lies attached to them. If only this time, it would be pure; and she lingered over it, tracing the contour of his lips with hers, feeling his response as he tasted and explored the shape of her. There was an answer on his lips and tongue, but she did not allow herself to hear it; she had little worth giving but a promise, and would not take more than she offered. She pulled away—and already, the mischievous smile on her lips was a lie, and her words had different meaning below the surface of them. "Then you should not carry me."

Should she be sorry that he read the truth? It was impossible, when he echoed what she'd just promised him in silence. "Then I must be fated to remain an imbecile, for I will not let you go."

CHAPTER 27

Over the years, he'd used Truth in an attempt to tear down Lilith's defenses; never had he thought he'd use it to rebuild them. Hugh prowled the length of the living room, debating the wisdom of forcing honesty upon her when she clearly wanted to hide behind lies. Her vulnerability had torn at him, and perhaps he should have allowed her that false defense—yet he could not. Had they the luxury of time, he could have waited until she recovered from the transformation. Waited for her to erect emotional shields to replace those she had depended on her demon physiology to provide.

But he knew—as she did—the nosferatu would come for them in four days, no matter the outcome of the bargain. If her shields were brittle and false, they could be easily penetrated. If they found a way to fight the nosferatu, to defeat Lucifer's bargain, she needed to be confident—not just in herself, but know he would support her, wouldn't fail her. And so he had forced her to acknowledge the emotional intimacy between them, as surely as he had forced the physical intimacy two nights before.

Manipulation, yet again. He'd become a master of it.

Books lay scattered from the police search, but he made no

effort to set them to rights. He paced instead, listening to the sounds she made as she showered and dressed, wanting to help her, but knowing that, did he offer too much now, she would not shed the certainty that she had become a burden to him. Ridiculous, that—how could she not recognize how much he *needed* her; not just to fight the nosferatu, but in every way possible? His body still ached from the frustration of wanting her, having her so close—but she was far too vulnerable to press that physical advantage. She would have used sex to forget what Lucifer had done, used it to conceal her emotions in yet another way. Another false defense she'd been trying to build, but that he couldn't allow. Despite her declaration that she was herself again . . . she hadn't been.

And he needed Lilith; needed the woman who'd survived as a demon, when no other human had. The woman who made him laugh without trying. The woman who was devious, and mischievous, and relentless. Whose vulnerabilities stemmed from her capacity for softer emotions, not her fear of them—

He tensed as he heard her on the stairs from Savi's apartment. Though the hellhound had been stretched out lazily in the pool of sunlight that streamed in over the kitchen sink, Sir Pup perked his ears at her approach, his tongue lolling in anticipation. With a wry grin, Hugh realized his expression must be a human reflection of the hellhound's.

Lilith wasn't the only one who'd exposed her vulnerabilities.

She strode into the room with the long, loose-hipped gait of a warrior, strength in the set of her shoulders. Her dark eyes were intense as she surveyed him, and his body hardened in response to the piercing, claiming expression within them.

No shyness in that gaze, nothing coy or hidden. He stared at her in return, letting his gaze drift down the length of her. She'd raided Savi's closet, and the small black T-shirt with SIN CITY emblazoned across her chest made his lips quirk into a smile, even as the cling of material to her firm breasts, the outline of her taut nipples sent heat spiraling to his cock. His khakis— with pockets lining the pant legs—hung low on her hips, and the bare skin between the hem of the shirt and the waistband almost brought him to his knees, so that he could kiss that pale strip, bury his face against her abdomen and worship her as she deserved.

There was a wicked tilt to her lips as she finally turned to glance at the hellhound. "Don't eat his pussy." She sauntered into the kitchen; Hugh followed her, unable to tear his eyes from the dip of her spine, the sway of her hips. The ends of her midnight hair brushed against the small of her back with each step, and the rhythm seemed to echo the heavy pulse of his blood.

He swallowed, and gestured to the cat, lounging on the top shelf of the empty bookcase. "I believe he and Emilia have called a truce; she will take the upper regions of the house, and he will reign over the lower."

The condoms had been an excuse; no reason he couldn't withdraw before spilling his seed. He had that much control, didn't he? A medieval method of contraception, certainly, but—

"We need weapons." She slipped into the stool at the breakfast bar, brought one knee up against her chest, her heel at the edge of the seat. Not a perch, but close.

"I don't think we will be able to access your apartment or Colin's house without drawing attention to ourselves." Grateful that the granite counter concealed his erection—now *he* was hiding, he realized with chagrin—he began unloading plastic takeout containers from a paper bag. "Unless attention is what we want."

She shook her head. "Beelzebub must know I am here, but—" Breaking off, she looked at Sir Pup. "Are there any near to hear us?" When the hound flapped his ears, she continued, "I prefer they think I'm going to kill you. What is this?"

A bit of eagerness in her voice that she couldn't hide; Hugh smiled and began loading dolmathes on a plate. "Greek. I ordered when you were in the shower." He raised a brow. "You were in there quite some time."

"Masturbating," she said, her tone matter-of-fact, and the container he'd been holding skidded across the counter. It was a lie, but the image the words conjured—Lilith, dripping with warm water, her hand between her thighs—was as powerful as if it'd been truth.

"Lilith," he said, and he couldn't contain his laughter, nor the harshness arousal lent to his words. "Have pity."

In a slow, deliberate movement, she unzipped one of the pockets at her thigh. Slapped a handful of square foil packages onto the granite. His breath stopped. "I have pity. Seven pities. I remember seeing them when I searched the upstairs apartment last time, and despite her rebellion, she has not used them since then. But you said food first."

"I am an idiot."

"I am hungry."

She bit her lip, as if to ward off the grin he could see pulling at the corners of her mouth. His cock ached. He made a mess of the lamb moussaka, in such a hurry was he to scoop it onto the plate.

Her gaze fell to the dish, and her smile faded. "I can't eat anything that has bled."

He froze and looked up. Seeing the fleeting shame, the horror, he took out a clean plate and began filling it with more dolmathes, horiatiki, and then poured lentil soup into a bowl. "Does it bother you if I do?"

She shook her head, but he set the first plate on the floor, along with the remaining moussaka. Sir Pup rose immediately, devoured it within moments. She pursed her lips, watching the hellhound. "I didn't lie."

"I don't eat meat with Savi or Auntie, either," he said with a shrug. He passed her the food and began piling his plate high. Deciding it would be easier to get through the meal without her pity staring him in the face, he slid the condoms off the breakfast bar, stuffed them into his pocket.

She watched him, laughing with her eyes. A flush rose over his neck, and he turned to the utensil drawer. "Fork?" When she answered him by scooping up feta cheese and olives with her fingers, he collected glasses from another cupboard and a bottle of wine from the icebox.

"I was right; you have been completely domesticated." But there was appreciation in her voice as he opened the bottle, filled her glass with the pale golden liquid. She took a bite of a dolma, closed her eyes. "Oh, these are good."

"Aye," he agreed, tearing his gaze from her mouth. His own food didn't appeal to him nearly as much, though he hadn't eaten since the previous evening.

She didn't notice his distraction; she was examining the grape leaf and its contents. "My favorite treat when I was a girl was something very similar to this."

Silence fell as she took another bite. Standing with the counter between them, he stared at her, unwilling to ask, though curiosity burned within him—he had forced enough from her.

Lifting her wineglass, she took a sip and looked over the rim at him, her eyes dark and amused. "I've been married twice."

His fingers clenched; aside from that small betrayal, he waited, motionless.

"The first when I was fifteen, to a general in my father's army. The second, six years later—a Roman senator, who was assassinated within three years of our union." She grinned when he raised a brow. "I didn't do it; though I would have, had I the opportunity."

His unreasonable jealousy faded. He choked on a laugh, gulped his wine to clear his throat. "Why?"

She shrugged. "The marriage was a political alliance, but despite his promises to smooth relations between Rome and Carthage, he helped implement the plan to destroy us without mercy."

"You were illegitimate?" he guessed.

"Yes," she said with an ironic smile. "But still useful as a pawn."

From her tone, he understood she was also speaking of Lucifer. "Is that why you were transformed? You were a pawn?"

She nodded, and she said without inflection, "Immediately after my husband was killed, I returned to Carthage. It was just before the siege began, and my father had been convinced that a sacrifice would be needed to save his city. Rome would descend upon us like a dragon, but with a human sacrifice—but not just any human, one of the ruler's progeny—to the right gods, we would be spared. And I was . . . expendable."

"Lucifer convinced him?" His voice was hoarse.

"Yes."

Her simple answer kindled fury within his chest. "Where were the Guardians?"

"There were none," she said. "And Michael arrived too late—delayed by a creature Lucifer had created and let loose near the city. And once the ritual was complete, Lucifer offered me power, beauty, and immortality, and I took them." A hard smile curved her mouth. "And he offered revenge; had I been a better daughter, I would've died willingly for my father and my kingdom in that ritual. But I wasn't, and I relished the chance to revenge myself upon him."

"Did you get that chance?"

She shook her head. "No. Not on my father; Rome destroyed him before I could."

He reached across the counter, cupped her cheek in his palm. She raised her eyes to his, and her expression was entirely without self-pity, without bitterness. How could it be?

"How can you not want to revenge yourself upon me?"

"You would let me?"

His eyes darkened. "Aye."

"Martyr," she muttered, but her smile warmed. "I was willing to die that night; that's the difference."

"Are you willing now?" He couldn't allow her to sacrifice herself; it would be his death, as well.

"No." She grinned. "I intend to wipe the Earth clean of nosferatu and demons, then salt the ground in Hell. Are *you* willing?"

To die for her, aye. But he only said, "We'll need more salt." Her grin widened, and she popped an olive into her mouth. Withdrawing his hand, he took another drink and calculated in his head. "You were twenty-four?"

"It's fitting, isn't it? Like Faustus." She grimaced. "Only my twenty-four years were free of demons."

He laughed. "Mephistopheles would have cowered before you. So you are almost two thousand one hundred eighty years old."

"With either four days remaining, or sixty years. Either way, I'm the oldest woman on Earth. Of my few accomplishments, it's one I can take pride in," she said, her eyes shining with amusement. She lifted the soup to her mouth.

"And I the oldest man." He rubbed his chin, felt the stubble there; he should have shaved. It would not do to scrape her skin. "It may be more than sixty years," he said absently.

She lowered her bowl, wiped her upper lip with her thumb and licked the tip. "Sixty-five? A significant difference, indeed," she said, rolling her eyes.

"Most likely twice that." He frowned slightly, realizing that if no demon halfling had been transformed back into human before, she would not know the consequences of it. "Lilith—" he paused, unsure how to explain it. He did not know the reason behind it, only that it was true of every Guardian who had Fallen. "You'll age relatively slowly. Look at me—really look. I am, in human years, thirty-three."

Her gaze traveled over his face. "You do look younger than that, but modern nutrition and medic—"

"You are simply too accustomed to me at seventeen," he said, smiling. "And without eyeglasses. I am changed, but only by seven years' worth, at most. Do you not notice your strength?" He thought how she had easily tossed him over on the bed. "Perhaps because you were a demon much longer than I was a Guardian—but you almost equal a vampire. I have only half that."

Her mouth was hanging open.

"It leaves its mark," he said, pleased that he could be the one to tell her. "You are probably the strongest, fastest human woman on Earth."

She smiled, but dipped her head as if to hide her surprise. "I *like* that. A lot," she added thickly, and he laughed.

"How do you think you survived a trip through the bay? And you recovered from it within hours. Did you think I was speaking metaphorically of your strength? Of your quickness?"

She lifted her shoulders, and said with a note of embarrassment, "I thought it was your idea of a pep talk, your supportive teacher role. 'Believe in yourself,' or some other twenty-first century self-esteem shit."

"No." He laughed softly, trying to imagine himself saying that to Lilith—or to anyone else. "And your strength is not anything near what you had before; it isn't enough to defeat a nosferatu should you have to wrestle one," he said. "But you won't be helpless."

Her eyes narrowed. "What did you refer to earlier—the nosferatu not biting into your jugular? Don't tell me you fought one."

It was his turn for embarrassment. "I did not intend to fight it; I misjudged the control Beelzebub exerted over them." Her brows lifted in a mocking gesture, and she gestured with her wineglass for him to continue. Hugh quickly recounted the flight to the basement, focusing on the hellhound's victories to direct her attention from his own idiocy; she grinned and tossed Sir Pup cheese from her plate. "He killed the nosferatu who attacked me, and finally Selah was able to teleport us out," he finished.

"She can 'port?" Surprise in her voice, then realization. "That's how she got the kid out of the tomb in New Orleans—

and why Michael allowed her to return with him. She can get to safety without a Gate."

"Yes. She went back for Colin," he added, his eyes troubled. "They could have made it out, but I don't want to raise false hope."

"Was Sir Pup there?" She turned when he nodded, and threw another piece of cheese. "Did they make it out? The vampire and the Guardian?" The hellhound whined and barked, wagging his tail. Lilith's mouth relaxed into a smile. "Yes. More difficult to tell without feeling his emotions, but I'm certain that was 'yes.' And Michael had said he was looking for someone in the Pit. It might have been Selah and Colin—though, if they were there, he did not find them. Perhaps Colin made her teleport to Paris for a shopping expedition," she said dryly.

Hugh knew she didn't believe it, but made no comment. He briefly described Beelzebub's attempt to bargain Savi's life for his, and her expression became pensive.

"I agree with your assessment; he needs you for the ritual," she said, shaking her head. "But what use could you be?"

His lips quirked at her blunt phrasing. "Moreover, why would Lucifer strike the bargain with Michael? If you kill me, Beelzebub and the nosferatu would not be able to use me. Which leaves three possibilities: Beelzebub is betraying Lucifer in some way; Lucifer thought you would be persuaded to perform the ritual when you killed me; or, the ritual and the bargain with Michael have the same end."

"Caelum," Lilith said, and Hugh nodded. "But I don't see how including you in the ritual would secure Caelum for them. Nor do I think Beelzebub would betray Lucifer."

"Does he think you would perform the ritual on me?" His eyes locked with hers.

"Perhaps," she said slowly, and looked down at her plate. "I tried once and failed; it's possible he thought that with the proper incentive, I would try again. Before Sir Pup came for me, his demons were conditioning me."

"Conditioning?" Hugh stiffened. "Torture?"

"Of a sort—they couldn't physically hurt me, of course; the Rules prevent it. But I was in a dark chamber, and they continually spoke of how you don't care for me, but only for your own success in saving me; that it was your life or mine—" She must have seen his expression, for she paused. "I wasn't hurt."

He could barely speak past the rage clogging his throat. "It was something Vlad might have done. In a few more days, you would have been starving, dehydrated—hallucinating. You might have done anything at that point, out of your mind and hardly aware of it."

"Yes. I'm certain that's what they planned."

Unable to have it separating them any longer, Hugh pushed away from the counter, circled it. He tamped down his anger—and in truth, should he not direct it at himself as well? Had he not manipulated her, forced her to face Lucifer without defense?

And so he hesitated when he reached her chair; she swiveled the stool to face him. "Is this kindness as well?"

"Nay." He would have given anything to feel her skin against his; still, he did not reach out. "I do hate my failures, but it is not the reason I fight to save you."

"I know." She looked down at her hands, resting atop her bent knee. "I rarely trust a demon's words; lies are compulsory. Lucifer was upset that I had chosen to tell you the truth about our bargain. I don't think he realizes you would not be fooled by them, and so they are useless." A half-smile tilted her lips. "That could work to our advantage. I shall only speak lies, you shall divine the truth—and if we are heard, the demons and nosferatu will assume I'm fulfilling my bargain."

He shook his head, and his eyes searched hers. "We have both tried to solve our difficulties by going around them, and have only made of mess of it: you forged Polidori's letter, and it has created more problems for us than it has solved. I tried to subvert your Punishment by forcing pleasure from you, and he took your powers. Now the bargain's resolution is imminent, and the consequences no longer affect just the two of us."

"And you would have us confront the nosferatu directly?" she asked.

She began laughing, as if she'd imagined them fighting the nosferatu and found the thought hilarious. Mesmerized by the sound, he forgot his earlier reticence and tucked a strand of hair behind her ear. It was still damp from her shower, and he could smell his shampoo, his soap on her skin.

"Only that we should approach it differently than we have in the past," he said when she paused for breath. Her eyes shone with amusement, and her skin gently flushed with laughter and wine.

Sliding down in the seat, she raised her leg and rested the ball of her foot against his chest. "So you think I shouldn't lie?" She gave him a light push.

Automatically, he caught her ankle and used it to anchor himself, shifting his balance; when he had his feet well-braced, he smoothed his palm under the cuff of her khakis. The pants were too long; her foot, half-covered by the material, looked dainty, fragile—the opposite of what she truly was. Appearances were deceiving, even in this.

"No, I think it will be useful," he said finally. "But in this instance, it would not serve us. A demon would not believe you were following through on the bargain if you only spoke in lies."

Her brows drew together as if she'd taken offense, and he laughed. Never would it be said Lilith did not pride herself on her ability to lie, to succeed in any purpose with deception.

"Go on," he challenged. "Lie to me."

CHAPTER 28

She only debated for a moment. It was ridiculous; if he could read her lies, was it an assessment of her skill to hide them? But for what purpose?

"Your décor is atrocious," she said, testing.

His eyes widened in mock horror. "I shall kill myself immediately."

So that was the game. Lies that would lead anyone listening to believe her aims were to kill him. Lies that would serve a demon. "Colin would have," she muttered.

"I"—he lifted her foot, nipped sharply at her big toe—"am not Colin."

Her breath caught, and she struggled to keep the arousal that kindled warm and tight in her belly from spreading. Her toe, for fuck's sake. Ridiculous to respond to it. Or to the expression in his eyes: even with humor brightening azure to sapphire, even behind the shields of his lenses, his focus was so intense it felt like a touch.

He let go her foot. "You can do better," he said.

No, she could do worse. She drained her face of emotion. "You're a coward."

He smiled, studying her. A fascinating thing, how he translated the cues of her eyes and tone as easily as her words. "That does not fit the criteria: you must only speak lies. There might be truth in that. I *have* been a coward where you are concerned, else I would have pursued you as we both wanted, long ago. Perhaps we would not be in this position now if not for my cowardice."

Now, simply his voice—and a hot, spiraling ache began to coil through her. "This is *all* the fault of your cowardice," she said dryly.

"Much better, though absolutes make for rather easy lies."

"I think you are a coward." She grinned, and slid off the chair. His hands settled on her hips, as if she were a lady dismounting from a horse and he would support her until she found her footing. He did not remove them.

"Now you flatter me," he said, and then his smile faded. Standing, her gaze was on level with his mouth, and it was no effort to imagine flattering its beauty, the firm curve of his lips, the simple power they seemed to have over her. "It would be the type of lie you would need if you wanted to break me. But you are here to kill me. Given that you did not immediately pull out a sword and stab me through the chest, would you not try to convince me to lower my guard? To make me love and desire you, so that the betrayal is more sweet? Is that not what a demon would do?"

Her heart contracted, and for a moment she could not meet his eyes. She already wanted those things, but they were not lies, nor designed to destroy him. She was not a demon, and no longer served Lucifer—that agreement had been terminated when he transformed her into a human—but they probably still expected her to act like one. Funny, that demons would be deceived by truth, and only because they did not recognize it as Hugh did.

"So lie to me, if it pleases *you*," he said quietly, and slid his palms up the sides of her waist, beneath her shirt. "But do not do it for *them*."

She rose up on her toes. Lifted her mouth, not to kiss—not yet—but so that he couldn't mistake her teasing. "I wonder that you accept me so easily, knowing what I have been—what I *am*. You must have a terrible flaw, your soul irrevocably corrupted by temptation." Winding her arms around his shoulders, she leaned against him. Had she once thought him vulnerable in this human form? Difficult to remember why, with the broad strength of him so close.

"Easily? It has taken eight centuries, a multitude of kisses bargained and stolen, both of us dead and brought back to life, one terribly translated manuscript and thousands of lies for me to accept you." His voice was light, amused; but she felt the tension in his hands, saw the self-derision in his eyes. "I only wonder that it took me so long."

She did not. It would have been nothing like the emotional torrent she felt now: beautiful, brilliant. She would have turned it into something ugly, something safe—never realizing that there was another kind of safety in this, despite the threat of the bargain and the nosferatu. Never allowing it to just be.

Impossible to tell him that; it was easier to lie.

"I'm still hungry," she said.

He went rigid against her, and she dipped her head to taste the strong column of his throat. A reverberation against her tongue as a groan escaped him, but the sound was muffled as if he'd clenched his teeth. Did he resist her then?

Remembering his earlier hesitation, she bit him on the muscled arch between his neck and shoulder. He shuddered, but still did not do more than hold her, his hands firm at her waist.

Guilt, she guessed. That wouldn't do.

"I didn't like being taken against the closet door," she whispered silkily. Her tongue swirled over the stretch of skin below his ear. His erection rose taut and hard between them. Desire licked at her, then pulsed deep. "I don't remember how good it felt when you were inside me."

His breathing was ragged now, his fingers sliding around her back. "It shouldn't have been like that."

She laughed, forgetting to lie. "How should it have been? Gentle, with marriage vows between us? A lord and his lady, quiet in their bed, thinking of duty and England?"

"Not a betrayal," he said.

"Of what? Of whom? Not of me." She pulled back to look at him. His features were drawn tight, his eyes bright with self-directed anger. "I won't lie to please them, only if you do not judge yourself by a morality that has nothing to do with *us*. If I'd been any other woman, yes, what you did might have been unforgivable. But do you think I didn't feel your struggle? That

I didn't rejoice when you failed to resist? I want everything from you; I won't settle for half. I'm selfish and greedy. If I were a better woman, I wouldn't relish the knowledge that you risked your soul to save me; nor, after you'd fulfilled your wager, that you took me despite your honor, your sense, and your character, because you couldn't deny yourself. And I could have escaped you then, saved you in turn, but I chose to stay because I couldn't deny you, either. We are not human, nor Guardian, nor demon; we have made choices that have set us apart, but they were the only choices available to us. What was the alternative to that night? *Any* night—Essex, Seattle, last week? Every other choice ends in disaster or death. And we are on the cusp of disaster again, but I prefer four days with you than another thousand years as a demon." Her voice broke; she hadn't meant to say it, but now that it had been spoken she would not retract it. "That is the choice I make now. And to fight; there is little else to do."

She stopped, suddenly embarrassed by the vehemence of her speech. Though she knew he would not accept all she had said, some of the tension faded from him. He lowered his head, rested his forehead against hers. "Michael said the same thing: that there is naught to do but fight," he said, and laughed when she made a sound of dismay.

She closed her eyes, grateful he'd let her escape into humor. "Shit. The next time I sound like him, stab me."

"I will," he said, and brushed his lips over hers. "I love you."

She'd known—she'd known and yet had no idea that hearing the words would burst within her as it did, a release, a freedom. She trailed kisses quick and hard over his lips, missing his mouth more often that not. He was a fool to love her—she'd not known anything of love but to twist and ruin it. And it was only fair that she warned him.

"Imbecile," she said between his jaw and his neck, and he laughed again and lifted her against him, half-dragging her out of the kitchen. The bedroom—he was headed to the bedroom. Too far. Impatient, she twisted and tripped him, fell atop him on the corner of the living room rug, a tangle of legs and tongues. His hands were on her breasts, plucking at her nipples through thin cotton.

"Take it off," he commanded, but didn't wait for her and began pulling up her shirt. He paused for an infinitesimal moment, as if drinking in the sight of her—then his mouth was on her, suckling and licking before the T-shirt cleared her head, and she was caught in darkness, the black material trapping her arms and covering her face. Wordlessly, he reached up, fisted his hand in the shirt and hair, held her immobile.

And there was only his lips and tongue on the aching peaks. The scrape of his whiskered jaw on her skin. The thick ridge of his cock beneath her. Her spine arched, and she gasped as he captured her nipple between his teeth, not enough to hurt but to make her fall silent, still.

Blind, she waited breathlessly as he unfastened her pants and slid his hand inside. As he cupped her sex. Then moaned as he let go of her nipple and slowly, slowly swirled his tongue around the taut flesh.

She heard the smile in his voice, felt it against her breast. "Do you want kindness, Lily?" He pushed a finger inside her, and she pressed her bottom lip between her teeth to stay her cry of need. *More, more.* As if he heard that silent plea, he drew her nipple deeply into his mouth. Her blood seemed to carry fire through her veins. She panted, the small confines of the shirt hot and humid.

Another finger, stretching and thrusting, and she grunted with frustration and rocked against him, trying to spread her thighs wider, grind herself closer to him, needing more.

"What would be kindness now? Do you want to look?" He pumped his fingers, his palm slick with her arousal, gliding over her clit. "Do you want to see that I'm inside you? But not enough." His voice was hoarse. "I'd have to let go your shirt, free my hand to unzip. And you would see. Would that be a kindness? You wouldn't see what I do."

"What would I see?" she whispered, the words ragged.

His tongue began to trace a pattern on her skin. Realization struck, and she shivered, tried to pull away from his mouth. Didn't want him touching what Lucifer had put on her.

"No!" His harsh denial surprised her, the desperation and anger behind it. "Don't hide from me now, Lilith. I see it, but it's not all that I see. I'm not a fool in this. I can take it all. There's nothing you have been—or could do—that would make me reject you." His grip loosened on the shirt. Quickly, she ripped it the rest of the way off. And caught her breath at the stark beauty of him, the emotion that filled his eyes.

Unwilling to have anything between that expression and her, she leaned forward and removed his glasses. Tossed them on the sofa cushion. "What do you see?"

"Look."

And she rose up, looked down between them. He was fully dressed, she half-dressed—it should have been a wanton and sinful display. Perhaps it was. She couldn't care. She only saw her dark-tipped breasts, the nipples drawn tight. The whisker-reddened skin. The spread of her thighs over him, his fingers buried in her glistening sex. His marks.

"My angel, above. The firmament between." He touched her face, her breasts and belly. Moved his other hand, still between her thighs, where she was hot and wet. "Flood and furnace. It has left its mark, but there is no part of you that is Hell for me—and the only torment would be losing you again." He drew her back down against him.

"Good," she said fiercely against his mouth. "Because I'm too greedy to let you take your love back, and too selfish to push you away."

"Good," he echoed, and traced the seam of her lips with his tongue. Dipped inside to taste before pulling back. "Let me be kind to you, Lily."

But it was not kindness when the delicious torture of his fingers halted, and he withdrew his hand. She snarled in protest, but he only laughed, the sound roughened by his arousal. "Up," he said, pushing her up over the length of his torso, tugging down her waistband at the same time.

"Oh, yes," she said as she realized his intent, and scrambled forward on her knees, kicking at the pants until they came off. "God, yes, be kind. Be very, very—" The heat of his mouth seared through her, and she fell, her elbows hitting the rug, bracing her only by virtue of their construction, because every other bone in her body seemed suddenly weak and useless.

She gasped as his tongue brushed her clit, when it returned to stroke more firmly. Then she couldn't breathe, couldn't speak. His hands curled around her thighs, held her against him—but she wasn't going anywhere. Not with his tongue licking, darting, suckling. Trembling, she looked again, and he tilted his head back to watch her watching him, canted her hips to keep her against his mouth.

Leisurely now, he licked through the soft folds. Used his lips to tease at her clit. Her jaw clenched against the whimpering moans of pleasure that built inside her with each luscious slide of his tongue, and she only heard the wet slick sounds, the low encouraging noises that came from his throat. Until he said, "Open for me, Lily," and she laughed, shuddering with need, wondering how she could open any more for him.

He licked. "I won't settle for half." She thought he was throwing her words back at her, and she shook her head. He needn't worry—this wasn't half, he was giving her everything. But he growled with frustration and rolled her over. Pinned her wrists to the floor. "You don't have to hide from me. Lie, if you must, if you can't tell me with truth. But don't hide. Not when I'm touching you, not when I'm inside you."

And she realized she had been holding back, refusing him her response except for those she could not control. She'd been conditioned for too long; denying herself any pleasure, denying the acknowledgment of it.

She pulled her hands free. She didn't have to use her strength; he let her go, but didn't move from between her legs. His muscles were rigid with tension. His eyes searched her face, as if waiting for her to come to a decision.

And a part of her rebelled—*he'd hidden from her*—but the need in his expression quelled that vengeful little voice. She would do unto him in this, if only this—if only Hugh.

"I don't want you to touch me," she said.

His lips parted, his head bowed in relief. "Lie to me again," he said.

She grinned, and smoothed her hands over the muscular planes of his chest. "I don't want you inside me. I don't want you to be kind to me." She tugged, and his shirt joined his glasses on the sofa. Threaded her fingers through his dark hair, pulled him down and kissed him long and deep. His fingers worked between them, and then his skin was bare against hers.

He filled her palm, his length hot and hard. Each stroke of her hand pulled a harsh breath from him.

"I don't want to fuck you until you can't walk."

He groaned, thrust into her tight grip. The protuberant head was slick, and she swirled her thumb over it.

Laughing softly, she said, "I think you have a word fetish. Fuck." She whispered it into his ear, and he jerked against her.

"Why, my virtuous Norman knight likes a dirty Anglo-Saxon word. And lies."

"Only when you say them." His laugh was tortured.

She licked his mouth. "I don't want you to fuck my—"

"Lilith, for god's sake!" He fumbled with his pants, lying discarded beside them. "I need pity."

She did, too. He rose up on his knees, and he was beautiful, his erection ruddy with need, arching toward his navel. Her breath hitched, and the slow, throbbing ache centered in her core twisted, speared through her. His eyes were dark as he unrolled the sheath over his cock.

And then he bent, lifted her easily and set her on the edge of the large ottoman, hooked her legs over his arms. The leather was buttery soft beneath her.

"Do you want to watch?"

"No," she said and couldn't look away as he pressed against her, slid the thick head of his cock up and down, teasing.

He pushed forward. Sank into her.

It burned and stretched. Pain, just a little, but it was good— she hadn't felt it when she'd been a demon. She panted and writhed against her seat as he went deeper, feeding his shaft into her inch by slow inch.

He paused, his breathing harsh. "Am I hurting you?"

Yes and no were both lies, both truth. In answer, she pushed toward him. Full penetration, and she cried out, unable to contain it.

"Aye, Lily—like that. Let me hear it again." He withdrew, then stroked thickly back inside. Braced his forearms on either side of her. Another thrust, slowly, and he groaned in triumph, in pleasure as another cry tore from her. "I'm greedy, too," he said.

Her laugh ended on a scream as he began to drive into her, hard and fast, but even that sound was cut short as his mouth took hers and his tongue and breath pulled and pushed in rhythm with his cock. Unable to keep still, she arched up against him. Dropped her feet to the floor and lifted. And almost sobbed as the new angle allowed him even deeper, hitting just right with every sharp thrust, an overwhelming, terrible pleasure.

He slid his hand beneath her, to support her or to hold her still for him, she didn't know, didn't care. Short lunges now, each one quick and unbearably perfect. And her orgasm ripped through her, an unexpected release that left her shaken, falling, clinging to him inside and out.

Gradually, she became aware of his skin, slick with perspiration. The muscles in his back flexing under her hands. He slowed, waited as if to give her time to come back to herself.

Had it always been like this: laughing one moment, intense and earth-shattering the next? Full of need, then certain she'd never want for anything else? She could never be restless with him, never bored—never had been. Even stillness with him was a constant revelation.

She pressed her lips to his throat, blinked away the burning behind her eyes. "Four days is enough."

And then she pivoted, knocking him back, sprawling atop him. Rode him as she'd promised once, threatened hundreds of times. His fingers tightened; she didn't remember threading hers through his, but their palms were locked together.

"I can't love you," she said, and the thrust of his lean hips became erratic, a staccato beat.

"Lie." He panted the word.

She clenched her teeth, bore down, grinding against him. "I shouldn't love you." He tensed beneath her, and her name was a plea on his lips. But *shouldn't* was Lucifer's lie, not hers.

"I don't love you," she lied instead, and he arched beneath her, shuddering. The pulse of his release sent tremors through her again, and she didn't resist the simple human pleasure of it.

She lay on his chest, felt the racing of his heart, his ragged breathing. They eased, and he finally managed to say, "I should have given in the night on the wall walk."

Laughing, she turned her head and bit his shoulder. Licked, tasted salt and warm, satisfied male. His hand smoothed down the length of her spine. She glanced up at him, but he was staring at the ceiling, his gaze unfocused.

"I'll find a way, Lilith," he said quietly, and unease shivered over her skin.

But she didn't object when he mistook it for cold and was kind to her again.

CHAPTER 29

"Oh, Liiiiil-LITH!" Her father's singsongy call became a roar, demanding obedience. She tasted dirt and blood, and her stomach heaved in revulsion.

"If you puke, you're going to die." He sounded pleased by the idea.

Lilith forced her eyes open. Lucifer perched weightlessly on her stomach like a vulture. He'd adopted the form of a tow-headed young boy, eight or nine years of age; his jeans and T-shirt were pristine and dry despite the misting rain.

She tried to speak, but her tongue lay stiff and cold in her mouth. Lucifer tilted his head and smiled.

"You've got just enough left in you," he said. Plunging two fingers into the wound in her chest, he wriggled them around. "If he'd taken your head off, I wouldn't be bothering with this now." He wrapped his free hand around her jaw; withdrawing his blood-slicked fingers, he slipped them into her mouth.

" 'The blood is the life,' " he crooned, and then giggled.

A scream built in her throat but she dared not release it. She kept her mind and expression carefully blank. He could do much worse than this—*would* do worse if he knew the extent of her fear.

"I'm extremely displeased, Lilith," he said conversationally. "Are you a succubus? No. And yet you stood there: a whore with your mouth and legs open, begging for his sword. 'Kill me, kill me!'" He imitated her voice, his expression disgusted. "Where was the woman who, only two thousand years ago, sobbed so pathetically? 'I don't want to die!' You accepted my Gift—and let a Guardian take it without a fight?"

His voice had been rising, each word a thundering shout. A second mouth opened above his eyebrows, its voice terrifyingly calm.

"The same Guardian for whom you betrayed me before!"

From his forehead, he said, *"I try to imagine your reason for allowing him to Fall."*

"This is the second time you've proved your worthlessness and ruined my plans."

"You did not kill him, but perhaps your redemption lies in his humanity."

"But you won't again, Lilith; there is no more room for your errors."

"He would not have belonged to me, but as a human he will be fragile, susceptible—and he has shown his weakness: you."

"You no longer believe there is no light without darkness?"

"My plans for him are ripe, but all the pieces are not yet in place."

"I'll enjoy reminding you."

"Until that time, I have another project in mind for you."

Both pairs of lips smiled, and the mouths spoke together. "We will wait, Lilith. When the time comes, you will succeed where you failed before; his death will be yours to give, or your soul mine to keep. Have we a bargain?"

No, no, please, no. But she couldn't respond; he sighed, grabbed her hair and rocked her head back and forth in a disjointed nod.

"Wonderful!" he crowed. Reaching over her shoulder, he unfolded something from the ground and brought it to his lower mouth. The scent of it was both sickening and achingly familiar: Hugh's robe, soaked in her blood.

Lucifer began sucking on the coarse fabric, and the mouth

on his forehead said, *"He buried you, did you realize that? Shedding tears all the while. Quite touching. He wrapped you in this thing and stuck you in the ground."* His cheeks puffed out as his mouth filled. *"Did he think to give you peace? Foolish Guardian. There is enough blood here to reanimate you a thousand times over. And I don't even have to do the rest. You remember last time—"* He made a slashing motion with his left hand, and Lilith whimpered.

He grinned. "That's my girl. You've been a very good girl, haven't you? But that has to change: it's time to be bad again." Dropping the robe onto her chest, he leaned forward. Blood dribbled from his mouths. "Give Daddy a kiss."

❧

"Better now?"

Even before she nodded and said she was, Hugh knew she would lie. Sighing, he helped her to her feet, then closed the toilet lid and flushed. There'd been nothing left in her stomach at the last, but she'd still heaved as if her body could purge whatever the nightmare had left in her.

He knew the feeling well. Had recognized the terror and sickness when she'd bolted from the bed, her hand over her mouth. And though he'd known she'd hate him witnessing it—would consider it a weakness in herself—he'd remained with her, leaving only for a moment to collect pajama bottoms for himself and a covering for her. They'd been in the cramped, cold bathroom for almost an hour, silence between them but for his soothing murmurs when each bout of retching had taken her.

She swayed. He steadied her, his hands on her waist. The thin flannel robe he'd placed over her shoulders slipped, and he tucked her arms through the sleeves, tied the sash.

"Bulimia . . ." Her face was still pale, but as if to signify that she had finished vomiting, she reached up and pulled apart the messy braid Hugh had made to keep the hair from her face. ". . . is a necessary evil; I am too vain to gain an ounce."

He smiled and wordlessly handed her his toothbrush.

She met his gaze in the mirror as she scrubbed her teeth. Her eyes were dark and haunted, and his chest ached when she looked away. She spat and rinsed before carefully replacing the toothbrush in its container. Each movement was deliberate and precise, overly studied in its attempt at normalcy.

His throat tightened; she seemed brittle, overwhelmed. Yet he couldn't leave her alone. Searching for something trivial, something to make her smile, he glanced down at the uncluttered shelf beside the sink. "Throwing up will keep you thin, but if you are to completely indulge your vanity, we'll need lady-things: lotions, perfumes." Her profile was to him; her lashes were lowered, a thick sweep against her cheek. Her black hair tumbled the length of her back. "Cosmetics, though you don't need them. Brushes and jeweled combs. Spices and silks." He would gladly give her anything.

"Another razor," she said, turning toward him. Self-consciously, he touched his jaw, remembered the whisker burn on her skin. But she only pulled aside the bottom of the plaid robe, exposing the tops of her thighs, the length of her legs. "I dulled yours shaving."

His gaze skimmed from thighs to feet, and he sighed. "So you truly weren't pleasuring yourself in the shower earlier."

"My vanity could hardly bear you seeing stubble." Her hand slipped between her thighs, and she arched a brow. "But I couldn't finish the rest." She lifted the edge of the robe higher.

"There are refills in the cabinet," he said, his mouth dry.

She traced her fingers through the dark curls. "Shall I shape it like a heart?" Her eyes glittered with wicked laughter. "An arrow, pointing you in the right direction?"

He choked, torn between amusement and arousal. Though his erection was suddenly painful in its intensity, straining against the front of his pajamas, he remained where he was and watched her play.

How many times had he had her? He'd essentially spent the entire day within her, but it still wasn't enough—and the moonlight spilling through the room reminded him he had only three days left.

He forced that sorrow away as she leaned back against the wall, raised her knee and braced it against the sink. She shrugged, and flannel whispered to the floor. "Look"—she exposed pink flesh, swollen with desire; her slim fingers slid down, then inside, and his entire body clenched with need—"at how wet I am."

"Lilith—"

Her back arched, and she licked her lips. "Am I a bad girl, Professor?"

A change came over her, as if she'd said it in jest but it had struck a different note within her. Her mouth twisted, her eyes hardened. Hate and anger in that look—but not directed at him.

Before she could twist it back at herself, he crossed his arms over his bare chest. "I haven't seen any evidence that you are, Lilith." Challenge in his voice. "Nothing that earns the reputation you've cultivated, anyway."

She blinked, and her gaze refocused on him. Her foot dropped to the floor. Her smile was slow and dangerous. "You're going to pay for that."

§

An hour later, his throat was raw, his voice all but gone. Two hours later, she finally let him come, and he went over soundlessly, certain his jaw would never unclench and his body would never have enough of her lips and tongue. Never enough of the scratch of her fingernails and grip of her hand. The bite of her teeth and the rasp of her voice. Or the slick, heated clasp of her sex.

They had no more condoms; she'd taken him without barriers, and then used it against him, riding him to her climax several times though he could not take his own. And again, using her hands and lips and tongue until he was on the verge of orgasm, then sheathing him inside her body, forcing him to hold back. A sweet torment, to have what he most desired, but unable to have it in full. Exquisite agony to choose between the pleasure of being inside her, or release—and then to be denied choice. He had begged, but did not know what he begged for: both choices were torture, both mercy. Now she wiped the seed from his abdomen with a soft washcloth, and each stroke quivered through his sensitized flesh. He laughed silently; he'd thought his muscles were all but water, but they still responded to her touch.

"This was stupid," she said, but her tone was smug. He would have argued—provoking her had been the smartest decision he'd ever made—but his voice didn't work.

She tossed the cloth to the floor and untied his wrists. The bindings hadn't been tight, but it was a relief to lower his arms, to touch her as she lay down on her side next to him and propped her chin on her fist.

She looked down at him and laid her other hand on his chest. "I don't know that I can have children, anyway. I didn't when I was alive before." She leaned over, kissed his eyelids. "And despite immortality leaving its mark, not everything is healed, or made better, or stronger. You're still practically blind; I may still be barren."

He nodded, unable to do more.

She grinned. "But we'll buy more anyway." Scooting down, she laid her head on his chest. Her fingers circled his flat bronze nipple, and they both watched as the nub puckered. "I *am* good," she said. With a self-satisfied laugh, she relaxed against him and let her palm rest on his abdomen.

They lay in silence in the darkened room, until she finally said, "The nightmare—it was Seattle." A harsh breath ripped from him; though she didn't raise her head to look at him, she shook it in denial of his assumption. "Not you slaying me. My father. The bargain."

He waited; eventually, she turned her chin against his breastbone and met his eyes. He slid his arm around her, pulled her closer to him so he could read every nuance of her expression. Her breasts were a soft pressure against his chest, the bulk of her weight supported by her forearms, denting the pillow on either side of his head.

"The man who shot Savitri—do you regret his death?"

The man who'd killed Savi's parents without reason or guilt? Had murdered others as well? Would have killed Savi, simply for being able to identify him? "No," he said hoarsely, forcing it out. "The method. Using my Gift in that way. He shot himself of his own will, but I could have made certain he was caught, convicted—tried under human law—yet I did not." Each word scraped his throat like broken glass. "And we should not be executioners. Of demons, nosferatu, even vampires: aye, for there is little alternative to contain them but death. But Guardians should not execute humans, lest we become tyrants and think ourselves above them."

She touched his neck, he felt a tug as she slid her fingers up to toy with the short curls against the pillow. "You can sign with your hands. It's not as secret as you Guardians think." Her smile was wry, her gaze steady—and tinged with fear. "Are you certain you can take me?"

It wasn't sexual, that question—he'd claimed there was

nothing that could make her reject him, but she apparently thought whatever she was going to tell him would change his mind. Or perhaps it was what she'd just done.

His arms tightened around her. "I'm certain," he said, unwilling to let go to sign. Pain was preferable to that.

"I enjoyed it." She focused on her fingers, gently twisting a short lock of hair behind his ear. "When I first began, I enjoyed it. The first one was in Greece: a husband who had killed his wife for bearing yet another daughter. The second, a woman who'd tortured and killed her male slaves. A father who'd raped his daughter, then killed her when she became pregnant. On and on. And I tormented them until they took their own lives. I thought of myself as one of the Furies, a servant of the gods—not answerable even to the gods—and I enjoyed it for over a thousand years. Not because it served Lucifer, but because I thought they deserved it." She took a deep breath, met his eyes again. "I still do."

"Enjoy tormenting them?"

She shook her head. "That wore thin before I met you. And though it was still deserved, I no longer had a taste for it. In that you are right; we have no place in this modern age to be executioners. To assist, perhaps, but not to judge." Almost absently, she began rubbing her toes up and down the length of his calf as she spoke. "But I still enjoy the . . . the *game* of it. The challenge of trying to make the impossible seem an everyday occurrence, the extraordinary seem normal. That's what I did with them; I took their fears, paranoia and guilt, and used my powers and deception to draw them out—without ever letting them realize it was something outside of themselves. And that is the only part of my job that I enjoy now: coming up with explanations that, while sometimes absurd, at least were believable to someone who'd never seen a demon, a vampire, or a Guardian. Explanations that made sense within the context of the modern world."

He fought to hide his smile. Did she think he hadn't known this? That he would ask her to be something she wasn't—had never been? "So you are saying you could never be a suburban housewife." The words came out as a rough whisper.

"Yes," she said quietly. "There is truth in the mark Lucifer left on me: I will always be Lilith."

And she thought he would turn away from her because of

that? That he wouldn't stay with her? He briefly wrestled with the bitterness within him—she hadn't believed him, didn't think very highly of his declaration of love—and found it was easy to push away in the face of her fear. Far more important to erase it than to wallow in his own pain. He lifted his head and pressed his lips to hers, then flipped her over onto her back.

Only the barest light shone in from the windows, but it was enough to see the design between her breasts, the hesitation in her eyes. "Is that what this is? Your name?"

She nodded.

His mouth hovered over the mark. "What was it before?" He kissed the upper curve of the design, tracing it to the upper swell of her right breast.

"I don't know." Her chest rose and fell with her quick breaths. "He took it from me; he stripped all halflings of the memory of their human names. Michael would know, I suppose"—he closed his lips over her nipple, unable to resist the taut bud so close—"but it hardly matters."

He returned to the mark, his lips and tongue painting glistening strokes. *It doesn't matter,* he signed over his head, his mouth too busy for speech. *Did you choose Lily Milton?*

"Not Milton—" He heard the smile in her voice. "Lucifer wanted to remind me that 'They also serve who only stand and wait' as I spent my years in the Bureau, anticipating the onset of the bargain."

Hugh lifted his head and stared at her. "You're joking." It was the last line of a poem John Milton had written after he'd lost his eyesight; it questioned whether he was as valuable to God if he could not perform any great and heroic deeds that served Him.

She shook with laughter. "No. Lucifer is quite willing to twist anything that refers to Him to suit his own needs."

"And Lily?" He lowered his head again to tug lightly at her other nipple.

"I chose it," she gasped. "It is near to Lilith in sound, and I was tired of remembering which name I was supposed to respond to. You've called me Lily."

He slid lower, and his lips caressed the dip of her navel. *Only when I want to be inside you.* He had to use his hand to push her knee over his shoulder, then cupped her bottom in both palms and lifted her to his mouth. "Lily," he said aloud against the silky skin of her inner thigh. Beautiful, wild, fragrant. He inhaled, and her scent filled him. That it was laced with his own masculine odor sent possessive lust surging through him, and he barely held it in check. If he hadn't just spent two hours hard and begging for release, he'd have already been inside her again. "But only if you want it."

"The name?" She laughed, and tugged on his hair. "Or do I want your tongue on me, right *now*!"

"The name. Hold yourself open for me." He blew lightly through her curls.

"I love how you say it: Lily," she said the name languorously, her voice deepening; and he smiled against her skin. It echoed how he felt with her; he'd no idea it had been so obvious. Her hands left his head, then her fingers slipped between her thighs. "In that moment, I am soft and yielding." Her legs trembled as she bared herself, and he drank in the sight of her, wet and plump with arousal. "But not always, and only with you."

"Only with me," he echoed hoarsely. "Lily."

She shivered, and he bent his head. Her moisture flooded his mouth, exquisitely sweet, exquisitely Lilith. He'd meant to tease her, to draw it out, but as he laved lightly at her clit she begged, "Not soft now, Hugh," and he was lost. A growl of hunger escaped him, and he took from her mercilessly, lapped up her cries with each stroke of his tongue, each thrust of his fingers into her slick heat. She lifted, grinding her clit against his tongue, rubbing and rubbing, and he had to pump his hips against the bed to keep from slamming into her. Her back arched, her body drew tight beneath him.

"Harder, harder." It became her chant; he used his teeth. She came with a guttural scream, and still he licked and sucked at her, until the clenching of the smooth muscles around his fingers became flutterings, until she fell back to the bed and her hands dropped from between her thighs.

"Holy fuck," she said, her voice awed.

He chuckled against her belly, then rose up to lie next to her. Rolled her so that her back was against his chest.

"Lily," he said, his voice deliberately low and sensuous, and he laughed when she shivered again.

He waited for her to sleep, but she seemed just as content to lie in his arms as he was to hold her. It wasn't until the first rays of the sun settled in stripes across the bed that he spoke again.

"Lilith?"

She made a soft, drowsy reply.

"If waiting serves him, then we'll not wait." He already knew what would save Lilith, knew what he'd have to do. But first he had to make certain she—along with everyone else around him—would be safe from the nosferatu.

She tensed, then turned to face him. "I have a few ideas." Her smile was wide, wicked.

God, but he loved her. His heart ached, but he didn't have to force his laughter. "Are they absurd?"

Her eyes danced. "Oh, yes."

CHAPTER 30

What was truly absurd, Lilith decided as she scanned Hugh's closet for anything to put on her feet, was attempting to get around San Francisco without shoes. Or a car.

Once they got to her apartment, she'd have clothes—they wouldn't have confiscated all of them—but *getting* there was the problem. Sighing, she pulled out a huge pair of battered tennis shoes and slipped them on.

Hugh grinned when he saw her, but it was easy for him to laugh when he had jeans and boots that fit, and his shirt looked as if it clung to him out of sheer desperation, afraid of losing contact with his skin. She envied that shirt, hated it.

She clomped out of the bedroom. "They won't let us on the bus without shoes, and your precious Savi's feet are the size of a fairy's."

Was he still grinning as he followed her? She would have turned, except that she was afraid she'd leap on him and they'd be waiting for another hour. Or two.

"We aren't riding the bus," he said.

"Oh?" She paused to scratch Sir Pup's neck as he skidded up to them, his claws sliding on the wood floor. "You have a car?"

"No. I don't like enclosed moving vehicles: planes, cars, trains."

He *was* grinning.

She closed her eyes, trying not to laugh. "Your bike? Will you pedal me around on that trusty steed?"

"Aye, my lady. My bike. It will add to the absurdity." He grabbed her hand and pulled her to the garage; on the way, he opened a closet and thrust a leather jacket at her. "How can you wear leather but not eat meat?"

She slanted him an exasperated look as she shrugged on the jacket. It was too big, but a fine quality. "I don't eat leather. Why do you ride a bike?"

He looked over his shoulder at her. "It's too far to walk to the university, and I get time to think. *This* is for when I don't want to think anymore."

He opened the garage door, and her heart filled with lust and pleasure. A black BMW motorcycle stood in the corner, sleek and compact. Built for speed.

"Oh," she said. "Oh. I want one."

He tossed her a visored helmet, and she caught it by reflex. "That's Savi's, but luckily her head is bigger than a fairy's. If you tuck up your hair, anyone watching the news won't be able to see who you are."

She quickly wound her hair into a coil. "Can I drive?"

"Not a chance." He slung his leg over the back of the bike, patted the seat behind him. "I've seen you fly."

❧

The ride was too short. She rested her head against his broad back and clenched her thighs alongside his as they arrived in her neighborhood; he pulled to the curb a block away from her building. Her hair caught as she took off the helmet, then cascaded down her back as it fell out of its twist. She'd left her visor up; the wind had whipped tears from her eyes, and she hastily wiped them away.

Sir Pup sat on the sidewalk. He was too big to be mistaken for a normal dog, but he'd taken on a form with only one head. His tongue lolled, his tail waved happily; Lilith guessed that he'd enjoyed the run almost as much as she'd enjoyed the ride.

"We send him in first?" Hugh braced his feet on the ground and ran his fingers through his hair. Unshaven, slightly rumpled—but with a glint in his eyes that made him look dangerous. Sexy. He'd put in contact lenses that morning, and she realized now they were more practical when riding the motorcycle than glasses—but she almost missed the professorial air they had given him.

It was a safe look: safe and comfortable for *her*. This Hugh was new—another surprise.

He caught her studying him, and his gaze heated. "Lily?"

"We send him in," she confirmed, her voice thick. He hadn't argued when she'd outlined her plan to gather information, though it put him at considerable risk.

Sir Pup disappeared after a quick command to check the apartment for anyone inside. Lilith slid off the bike, watched as Hugh lowered the kickstand.

"When he comes back, we'll have him look after it. No one will steal it then," she said.

Hugh nodded. She knew he couldn't have missed the dilapidated housing around them, but he hadn't commented on it.

Of course he wouldn't. "They won't deign to come to this area," she explained, and slid her hands into her pockets. "Beelzebub, other demons. They prefer luxury, and I found the poorer my surroundings, the less likely I would be bothered by them, or have them show up unannounced." She smiled wryly. "And it takes almost all of my salary to feed Sir Pup."

He arched a brow. "You didn't just vanish it from a pet store? Like the books?"

"I have *some* morals; I won't feed my dog stolen food. And I didn't like meat in my cache. It makes me feel . . . bloody." She shuddered. "And I couldn't, even if I'd wanted—books were in the public sphere, but the meat was under private possession. I could have fought the butcher for it, I suppose, defeated him in battle and then vanished it . . ." She glanced at his expression and sighed. "I won't do it anymore. I *can't* do it anymore."

"Is it so terrible?" His voice was low.

"No," she admitted.

Though he looked relaxed, half-sitting on the bike and his hands tucked into his pockets, his intense regard sent shivers over her skin. "I'll give you all the books you want," he said.

She leaned down, and his lips were warm and firm under hers, full of love and promise.

And it was easy to let go her petty pleasures.

A ribald shout from a passing car broke them apart. Sir Pup lay at her feet, grinning up at them.

"Pervert," she told the hellhound, laughing. "All clear?"

He chuffed softly.

"Let's do this quickly then," Hugh said.

The hellhound had already broken through the locks and the police tape at her door. Though very little of it had been hers, her throat tightened when she saw the state of the room: stripped of books, the weapons gone . . . even the threadbare carpet ripped up, as if they'd searched for items beneath the floorboards.

Hugh's hand found hers, and he gave it a gentle squeeze. When he gestured toward the closet, she burst into laughter. They'd taken the door. She imagined a forensics lab trying to make sense of the ragged holes from her claws, the scrapings from her nipples.

She quickly stifled her amusement; very likely, the neighbors had been asked to contact the Bureau if she came home. A quick glance in the closet confirmed that it still held most of her clothes. She grabbed several items at random, breathed out a sigh of relief when she saw her suit hanging in its place near the back. Her heart lightened even further when a quick search of the jacket yielded her badge and identification.

"Got it," she said and began changing.

Hugh appeared at her side, a plastic bag in his hand, and piled her extra clothes inside. "Taylor and Preston don't seem the type to have missed your ID in a search."

Lilith frowned. "They aren't. It's evidence of an abrupt departure, perhaps under coercion—no agent would leave without his ID. This is probably Smith's work. The Bureau took over the investigation, yes?" At his nod, she said, "Then this is a result of their search, not the SFPD. They just got rid of the weapons and books, then left a mess to make it look good." There were enough demon agents in the Bay Area that the search could have been handled solely through them; no one would question poor investigation techniques.

"Did your saving the boy on the bridge force Lucifer's hand?"

Her zipper rasped as she yanked it up. Her holster and gun had been in the pile of weapons; she would have killed for them now. She hated to go anywhere empty-handed. "What do you mean?"

"You interfered with his free will when you caught him."
Hugh's gaze was dark with remembered pain; she sucked in a
breath, realizing how her action must have seemed deliberately
self-destructive.

"I didn't even think of that when I caught him," she said. "I
was just pissed that he was being so fucking stupid, and inter-
rupting my brooding time."

Hugh's lips twitched, but his gaze was serious. "But Lucifer
had to either destroy you or Punish you—or, since you were a
halfling, revert you back to human. He would have had to make
that decision even if I hadn't forced your physical response. So
had he already decided to *condition* you"—his mouth twisted
with quick anger—"or did he have to make the decision after
you caught the boy?"

"I don't know." She finished buttoning her vest, and met his
eyes—and suddenly saw what he was getting at. "You think that
even if I was brainwashed and went through with it, he never intended for me live much longer than it took to kill you."

"You had no shortage of time, no need to be conditioned before Michael made his wager. But if Lucifer had another dead-
line to meet and another bargain to fulfill—with the
nosferatu—he might have already planned your Fall and your
death."

She looked around the room and results of the half-assed
search. Smith was likely compiling and forging evidence in his
case against Hugh before he went for the arrest in Lilith's disappearance. A lot of work, when he could have easily spun a story
about an assignment to explain it, could even have covered up
the books and weapons . . . but had chosen to pursue a murder
investigation instead—without her body and little evidence of
violence. Had he planned on providing that body and violence
later?

Why bother, when there was enough evidence to take Hugh
into custody—even of short duration—for the other three
murders?

"I don't know," she said again, and slid on her boots. "All
I'm certain of is that Beelzebub's going to be pissed when I
show up with you at the Bureau and blow his murder case. *If* he
has time to be pissed when I'm pumping him full of hellhound
venom." She glanced up at Hugh and grinned. "Either way, it's
a good day to be alive."

❧

She wrapped her arms around his waist as they sped north to Tiburon. The smooth rumble from the engine was a constant presence between her thighs, through her body—pleasant, but not half as thrilling as the firm muscle of Hugh's back, his taut abdomen beneath her hands. Now and then she glimpsed Sir Pup running alongside them, ears flopping.

At first she thought the strange reverberation in the back of her mind was a result of the engine, but as they neared the bay it became insistent—and familiar. Overwhelming as they crossed the bridge, then fading again on the northern end.

Suddenly sick, she tugged on Hugh's shirt, signed for him to stop. A scenic viewpoint for tourists was off to the side; he pulled over. She tore off the helmet and walked to the low wall at the edge of the cliffs. Took deep, cleansing breaths. The hum faded, though it seemed an effect of her will rather than a lessening of its presence.

Hugh touched her cheek, smoothed back her hair. "What is it?"

"I can still feel the Gate." She pointed over the side, where the bridge spanned the mouth of the bay.

A thoughtful look slid over Hugh's features. "When in close proximity to them, I can still sense Caelum's Gates. Another mark left behind."

"This is normal?" She should have been relieved, but his expression made her wary. He wouldn't meet her eyes.

He nodded. "We can't go through them, but they still resonate." Abruptly, he turned and remounted the bike. "Come on. We have a visit to pay to our congressman."

Dread knotted her stomach, but she got on behind him. She felt the new tension in the line of his shoulders, feared she knew its source. It was one thing for her demonic name to be scrawled across her chest; another to have an invisible, irreversible link to Hell.

No. She squeezed her eyes shut, forced that evil little voice away. That wasn't it; those were her doubts, not his. The gentleness in his hands, the hot touch of his mouth—his words—had spoken for him endlessly the previous night and day.

But what had forced this withdrawal? She knew he didn't

want to hurt her, so why withdraw unless he thought he'd cause her pain? What would—

No. Oh, God, no.

If she'd had her gun, she would have shot him, injured him so badly he couldn't get out of bed, much less jump off a bridge. She dug her nails into his waist, and she might have thrown him from the motorcycle had he not turned into a driveway. She barely saw the manicured lawn, the landscaped borders of the drive.

She was off the bike instantly, shaking with rage. "You selfish fucking martyr."

Her throat closed when she saw his eyes, dark with defensive anger, as if her assault had hurt him. He spoke from between clenched teeth. "I don't want to, Lilith. That's why we're here: to find another way. But if there is no—" He bit off the rest. "This isn't the time."

A voice spoke from behind her. "But I'm enjoying it immensely."

Her hands flexed as she automatically tried to call in her swords—but there was no need. Stafford couldn't attack either of them; if he could, Lilith would never have risked coming here.

She turned, but Stafford's gaze was on Hugh, his blond eyebrows drawn low over his eyes. He stood in front of the entrance to his house, arms crossed over his chest as if guarding it. "I know you."

Hugh smiled coldly. "And I, you. Rael."

Lilith blinked, looking between them uneasily. She had not known Stafford's demon name; there were many of Belial's she did not know.

"You have slain hundreds of my brethren."

"Thousands," Hugh corrected softly. "As you have mine."

"Not as many," Stafford said, and opened his front door. "We are not equal. Do you still regard the Guardians as brethren?"

"Yes."

Stafford's eyes narrowed. "And yet you are Fallen."

"As are you," Hugh said. "Only I have not fallen as far."

With a quirk of his lips, Stafford gestured for them to come inside. "It is a pity that you dragged Lilith down with you."

Hugh shook his head at the same time Lilith began laughing.

"Oh, Thomas," she chuckled as she passed into the foyer. "Don't even attempt it. You can't break him, can't make him bend. Believe me—I've tried for centuries, and you aren't half the demon I was."

CHAPTER 31

How had Michael let it come to this? Demons in positions of power in a human government? Hugh took in the expensive furnishings, the tasteful décor. Oddly feminine touches throughout—flowers, patterns—were probably the influence of a designer who'd been instructed to make the room appeal to all his constituents; manipulation, down to the last detail.

Outside the windows stretched a multi-million dollar panorama.

Money was also power, and Rael apparently had a lot of it. Was it only Belial's demons who had managed to gain such a gilded foothold in human society—or Lucifer's as well?

Hugh's fists balled in his pockets, and he welcomed the cold that settled in him. It made it easier to think, to examine the pieces falling into place around him.

He knew feudal systems; from all Lilith had told him, Lucifer's reign resembled one. Protection—of a sort—and power traded for service and payment. But Rael did not have the same obsequious air as Beelzebub, or any of Lucifer's demons.

Any of Lucifer's demons, except for Lilith. She'd always resisted and hated her service, whereas Beelzebub seemed to find honor in it.

Rael was a mystery, but his willingness to cooperate was not. He hadn't taken his eyes from Sir Pup since he'd scratched at the door and Lilith had let him into the room. The hellhound hadn't transformed—appeared only as a large dog—and lay at Lilith's feet, staring up at her adoringly. Hardly a scene to inspire terror, and yet the demon looked almost sick with it.

"We need weapons, Thomas," Lilith said. Her hair caught the light streaming through the window, the deep black strands glinting blue even under the golden sunlight, as if they refused to be gilded with false color. He'd not often seen her in the daylight, no matter the form she'd taken—it suited her as well as the darkness did.

As if she'd felt his gaze, Lilith turned. She flashed a quick, mischievous grin, and something inside him warmed and softened. She was still angry with him, and he had no doubt he'd pay for it—and not as pleasurably as he'd paid before. Had no doubt they would argue again. But for now, he simply allowed it to be—and took pleasure in watching her work. Though it would be more difficult for her now. Hugh had made the demon uneasy; although he thought Rael rather enjoyed Lilith's presence, he did not appreciate Hugh's.

Rael stared at her, as if trying to probe her thoughts. He'd done the same to Hugh when they'd been outside and failed. Hugh doubted he'd be any more successful with Lilith—particularly not with the hellhound as a constant distraction.

"Why?"

Lilith shrugged, and reached down to scratch Sir Pup's ears. Hugh had to fight his grin; she'd never let the demon forget the hellhound's presence. An unspoken threat lay beneath that fond caress. "What if I said I plan to kill Lucifer?"

"I wouldn't believe you."

"And if you did believe me?"

"I still wouldn't give you weapons to do it; killing Lucifer is an honor that belongs to my liege."

Hugh's eyes narrowed. Rael actually believed that. "Because it would secure Belial's power Below?"

Rael nodded slowly, his gaze traveling between Hugh, Lilith and the hellhound. "Perhaps we can bargain."

Hugh's stomach turned to ice, and Lilith's gaze hardened.

"No bargains," she said, and Hugh relaxed slightly. "What if I said we'd kill the nosferatu with them?"

"I'd laugh," Rael replied, although laughter seemed the farthest thing from him at that moment. "You two? Even with your hellhound and an arsenal of weapons, you'd fail. And I don't think you play to fail, Lilith—so I wouldn't believe you."

"I don't. Thomas, be reasonable. You know I won't kill you, because then I wouldn't get any weapons. But what if I ask my puppy to eat your limbs one by one? Sure, they'll grow back, but—and you can believe me on this, because I speak from experience"—her lashes lowered, and she smiled down at the hellhound—"it really, really hurts."

Sir Pup woofed, as if in agreement.

Carefully maintaining his psychic blocks, Hugh turned away, and wandered over to a large fireplace. Pretended to study the pictures atop the mantel, though he didn't see them. She'd spoken the truth about her experience. Beelzebub had also mentioned a similar torture, but it had been so wrapped up in his manipulation and lies that Hugh hadn't been able to separate them perfectly.

He closed his eyes. Not now. He couldn't think of Beelzebub now. Lilith was carefully dancing around every reason but the real one; though the truth might be reason enough for Rael to offer his help, to tell the demon of their intent would also carry the risk that he'd betray them. One phone call would ruin the only real weapon they possessed: surprise.

And neither Hugh nor Lilith trusted the demon not to give them away.

Exhaling deeply, Hugh faced them again—and caught the flicker of unease in Rael's expression when the demon glanced at him.

"You could rob a gun shop," he said.

Lilith's brows rose. "That's completely inane. They don't have the kind of weapons we need, Thomas." Then her eyes narrowed, as if she too noticed something *off*.

Slowly, Hugh turned. Saw the wedding picture. Without a word, he picked it up and tossed it to Lilith. Rael groaned.

"Fuck me," she breathed, and peered closely at the photo. "Is she a demon? She looks bitchy enough to be one. Do you love her?"

"Yes," Rael said quickly.

"Lie," Hugh said and glanced with new eyes around the room. "Human, and you don't love her. And I'd wager she's an heiress."

Lilith grinned. "You kept this quiet, Tommy."

"You don't pay attention," Rael said, exasperated. "You never have. It was the Wedding of the Year in 2004."

"And it will be the Divorce of the Year in 2007 if I tell her about your lovers. I imagine she'll believe it readily enough; you aren't a sexual creature, can only simulate it, so you're probably cold in bed. Do you think it'd be hard to convince her you're getting it elsewhere? Do you think her daddy would like to receive a letter, complete with photos? Or the local news?" Lilith tilted her head. "Voters are unpredictable when it comes to these things. How far do you think you'll get with that kind of scandal? I don't believe for a moment you are aiming for anything less than president."

Rael was unimpressed. "In ten years, it will have been forgotten. Infidelity won't damage my political career—and my wife is as ambitious as I am. She'll accept that I might have other women, and eventually we'll spin it to our advantage: the couple who persevered through adversity."

Hugh stifled his laughter; Rael didn't think Lilith was done, did he?

Her eyes gleamed with amusement. "Have you seen what happens if pure hellhound venom gets into a demon? It paralyzes them. Think how easy it would be to pose you for photos then. I'll probably keep a few for my own enjoyment; you're both so handsome."

"I want to be on top," Hugh said.

Startled, Rael glanced at him, then turned to stare at Lilith. "This is San Francisco," he said weakly.

"True. But you don't plan to stay in California, do you? And we could always put Sir Pup on the bottom, make him a poodle; then there wouldn't be a conservative or a liberal in the country who would support you." She sighed. "I suppose you could remake yourself in another identity, but that takes so much *work*. Would that be worth it for a couple of weapons?"

Rael held up his hands, a smile twisting his mouth. "Very well." His eyes glowed. "But I can't just *give* them, Lilith. You'll owe me a favor."

She agreed before Hugh could object. "I can live with that."

❦

They found a motel in the Tenderloin to wait out the afternoon. It was cheap and ugly, but it wasn't any worse than her apartment had been. As long as it had a sink so she could wash away the blood later, Lilith was fine with it.

Sir Pup lay stretched out on the bed, and she practiced with him, asking for specific weapons and rewarding him with bits of cheeseburger when he called in the correct one.

Hugh sat at the table, cleaning a crossbow and inspecting the bolts for flaws. He'd worked over each weapon in that careful, precise manner—not just to ascertain the demon hadn't given them faulty weaponry, she knew, but to avoid discussing his plan to sacrifice himself for her.

But as she couldn't think of it without her throat tightening and her eyes burning, she avoided it as well.

Grabbing another burger from the stack on the side table, she unwrapped it and tossed it to Sir Pup. He caught it midair in a movement so quick she couldn't follow it and settled back down on the bed.

"Axe," she said and held out her hand. The hellhound was only a little bit off; the handle was at her fingertips instead of squarely in her palm, but she could compensate for it with a flick of her wrist.

The danger was not in his placement of the weapon, but in how slow she was compared to Beelzebub. She sighed, and glanced up to find Hugh watching her with his steady blue gaze.

"Two axes, three swords, a crossbow, a mace, and it's still not enough," he said.

She rubbed the back of her neck to ease the tension there, and nodded. "I was hoping I wouldn't, but I need a gun." Stafford hadn't had one, and Hugh had confirmed it wasn't a lie. What kind of asshole had unlimited storage for weapons and didn't pick up a gun? It was pathetic; everyone Above and Below, stuck in the Dark Ages. Frustrated, she kicked the corner of the bed, and it lurched across the room. Sir Pup woofed and grinned at the impromptu ride, but she didn't get as much pleasure out of it.

Until a pistol fell at her feet.

She recognized it; it was the same one she'd put in Hugh's bag on Friday night. She looked at Hugh, startled, then back at the hellhound. And remembered Hugh's story of how he'd lost it.

"You picked this up from Colin's basement? When did you plan on letting us know, you ungrateful cur?" Sir Pup opened his mouth, flopped his ears. The ungrateful cur was laughing at her. She fought to keep the smile from her lips and failed. "Was it the pig thing in the park? You're still punishing me for that?"

"Do you have my swords?" Hugh said from beside her. She hadn't heard him move.

Two slim blades landed on the mattress. Hugh picked them up and nodded his appreciation to the hellhound. "If we are looking for speed, these will be better than the heavy swords Rael gave us." Turning back to Lilith, he said, "So we didn't gain anything, but you are indebted to a demon again."

"It's not the same kind of debt. If I don't fulfill it, I don't spend eternity frozen in Hell," she said and strode past him to pick up the quarrels from the table. "And we gained these."

She returned to the bed, laid each bolt out on the mattress. Picked up the gun, pulled out the clip, and pushed out the bullets into a neat pile. She slipped out of her clothes and stood silently for a few moments, clad only in her underwear.

"Do you need help?" Hugh said quietly, removing his own shirt.

She shook her head, but she had to swallow several times to push down the sickness that began roiling within her. "The venom sacs are under his tongues. Only two incisions each, but they'll be deep and long," she said hoarsely. "Just hold the ice bucket underneath to catch the fluid."

"He'll heal quickly."

"Yes," she said and laughed without humor. "But it will hurt him. All these years he avoided Punishment, and now *I'm* the one to hurt him."

Sir Pup looked at her mournfully and shifted into his three-headed form, growing until he filled most of the queen-sized bed. Her vision blurred, and she spent a few minutes rubbing his noses, letting him slobber kisses across her cheeks. "You shouldn't let me do this," she told him, but he only licked her face again.

Dammit. She was drawing it out. "Can I have your short sword?" Her hands trembled.

Wordlessly, Hugh gave her the blade, and his palm lingered against hers, solid and warm. It was the sharpest of the swords, would cause the least damage and pain—but if she hesitated or shook, it would hurt him more.

Hugh withdrew his hand from hers, then brushed his thumb over her cheek. "He allows you to do it because he loves you," he said.

The knowledge didn't help steady her, but that simple touch did. She steeled herself and began to cut.

CHAPTER 32

"Sword," Hugh said as she exited the bathroom, and that was the only warning she received before he swung the blade at her head. Instinctively, she ducked and threw herself at his legs to knock him off balance. He staggered back into the TV stand; Lilith rolled to the side and leapt up onto the bed next to Sir Pup.

Probably a mistake; though it offered height, her feet sank into the soft mattress. It would slow her down. "Crossbow," she said, and the stock immediately landed on her palm—perfect placement. She closed her fingers around it; the skin around her knuckles felt uncomfortably tight, raw from the harsh soap and endless scrubbing.

Hugh lifted a brow as she raised the weapon to her shoulder and took aim at his throat. "The bolts are still drying on the table."

A quick downward glance confirmed the truth of it. The weapon wasn't loaded. They would ready it and the gun—bullet in the chamber, safety off—before they left, but she *should* have been aware of the crossbow's state before calling it in. Beelzebub couldn't hurt them, but if he managed to get past them they'd lose their chance to get the information they needed. There couldn't be any mistakes. "Shit," she said, sinking to her knees beside the hellhound. "That would have been very, very bad."

He nodded and dragged his fingers through his hair. "The venom didn't coat the bullets well."

"We just need enough to slow him down. A trace amount will do that." She ran her hand under Sir Pup's jaws; no swelling or abnormal heat. The incisions had closed and healed within the first half hour, but it had taken her twice that time to let him move from the bed, to let herself be certain he was no longer hurting.

Hugh watched her. "How did you manage to befriend a hellhound?"

It wasn't a casual query; he was leading up to something. Though she feared she knew what it was, she stroked the length of the hellhound's back and tried not to lie. "Eight years ago, I went through the Gate and there was a pack of hounds waiting. I was bit, once—halflings and humans are immune to the venom, so I wasn't paralyzed—but still injured badly enough that I'd probably have been killed. Except he was in the pack and managed to fight through and hold the others off. So I took him back through the Gate with me."

Sir Pup licked her hand, and she waited for the next inevitable question, dreaded it. She stole a glance at Hugh; yes, he was weighing her response, listening to what she had left unsaid.

"He must have known you before to have protected you," he said finally. "You spoke of a Punishment that he'd managed to avoid; did you help him in that?"

Dammit. "Yes."

A muscle in his cheek clenched before he asked, "What kind of Punishment did you suffer?"

"The normal kind," she said flatly and slid off the bed. Her suit lay folded atop the dresser, but she only picked up her shirt, shrugging it on before turning to face him. His unreadable expression made her chest ache; he'd closed himself off from her. He hadn't hidden anything since the night at her apartment, and she hadn't realized how dependent she'd become on the transparency of his emotions.

In the past, he'd hidden from her to protect himself. Had she hurt him so badly now, or did he hide to protect her?

"No," he said, shaking his head. For a moment she thought she'd been completely unguarded, had said it aloud, until he continued, "I don't know what 'the normal kind' is, Lilith—and Beelzebub will use it against me if he can. He mentioned it before, and I could not separate truth from lie; I was not prepared for it. It will be like charging in with faulty weapons if he can twist my emotions, yet you could prepare me for whatever he might say."

He shoved his hands into his pockets, and she could read that easily enough: he was angry, on the edge of violence. He wanted to move, but he forced himself to stay in place.

She turned away, laid the crossbow on the table. He was right, of course; she had to tell him. Beelzebub *would* use it. "Dismemberment. Burns. Eyes and organs taken," she recited. "They heal, or grow back, so it doesn't matter much. The worst is the contraption they make to keep the blood circulating." She couldn't look at him, so she busied herself refilling the clip with ammunition. "If the blood is gone, you die—and their fun is over. So it's collected and pumped up to a cistern. It has a hole in the bottom, and if they put your neck in the hole with your head inside, it plugs the hole and the cistern fills and they don't have to worry about it, because you drink or drown in it . . . either way, you ingest it and you stay alive, because *not* to ingest is a form of suicide, and that would be a failure in service to Lucifer, and you'd end up frozen in the field anyway."

His footsteps were soft; that she heard them at all must mean he'd wanted her to. He wasn't trying to take her unawares. He was giving her the choice to acknowledge his approach—or not.

She did. And his mouth was warm and sure on hers; no heat in this kiss, only tenderness and an offer of strength, did she need it. She would have preferred heat—she could distract him with that, avoid telling the rest of it.

He didn't give her the opportunity. His palms cupped her face when he pulled back, his gentleness its own vise, holding her still for his relentless, searching gaze. "As terrible as your Punishment was, that is not reason enough to have hidden it. Colin was surprised you hadn't manipulated me with it—and initially I thought he meant the loss of your shifting ability these past sixteen years. But it was this Punishment he spoke of. Was I the cause of it?"

Her eyes narrowed. "You take it upon yourself too easily. *I* was the cause; the decision was mine to make. I knew the consequences of it."

"Of giving me to Michael," he realized.

"That and interfering with your execution. Had Mandeville lopped off your head you would be neither Guardian nor demon. I interfered with his will and had to be punished for it."

His lips thinned, and his hands fell to his sides, releasing her. But he did not move away, and she couldn't mistake the tension in his long body. "Did you think I'd lament you'd ever saved me and sacrifice myself on a rack of overwhelming guilt?"

"I'll admit it had occurred to me." Arching her eyebrows, she said, "You were Catholic once."

He stared at her for a frozen moment, then turned away. Almost immediately he glanced back at her, the corners of his mouth tilted into a reluctant smile, unraveling the hard little knot that had formed in her chest. "You disarm me without effort; you always have—and for *that* I once felt guilt. I thought myself far too susceptible to your humor, to sin and temptation."

"And to my tits."

"Yes." His smile widened, and he gave her chest a cursory glance before meeting her eyes again. "And you do it again. You leave me defenseless, Lilith."

"If I can manipulate you with laughter and bend you to my will with sex, be certain that I'll keep you permanently disarmed," she said. "Because your defense is to fall down upon your sword."

His smile faded. "You think it is easy for me, that it is my first choice."

"I have seen you do it before," she reminded him.

The frustration in his voice echoed hers. "Aye, but if I were in the same position as I was then, I would not do it again." Her surprise must have shown on her face, for he gave a hard, short laugh. "What were my reasons? Guilt, for encouraging you, challenging you, and not knowing a way to stop you? Piety? Duty? Those are the reasons of an idealistic fool, a youth who imagines himself a hero. There was no gain in the lie I told; not for the baron nor the countess, nor for you. You think that by telling me of your Punishment, I will feel obligated—because of guilt, because of duty—to die for you. Yet none of these reasons are mine now: not piety, not guilt, and certainly not obligation."

She bowed her head, her breaths coming in sharp pulls. "You

are a fool to love me," she said tightly. "I did not ask this of you—don't want this from you."

"And yet you have it. You accepted me, knowing the type of man I am. Do you reject me now?"

She should; for his sake, she should. But his carefully even tone—after anger, laughter, and frustration—alerted her to the pain and fear beneath the question better than a shout could have. She glanced up, and though his gaze was calm and steady, his shoulders slumped as if in defeat, his body braced for a blow. And even did she say yes, she realized, he would not stop his efforts to save her; he would just do it alone.

Wordlessly, she shook her head. His eyes closed, and he released the breath he'd been holding. A quick step forward, and he swept her up and spun her around in a circle, his laughter a deep rumble in his chest. "You will be the death of me, Lilith," he said as he set her back down.

She bit back her grin. "That's not funny."

"Yes, it is," he said, and caught her fist before she could hit him. He pressed a kiss to the back of her hand, then to her lips.

"Promise," she said. "If I can't stop you, then promise that it'll be the last option, not the first."

"It will be the *last*, I promise you that."

This time she connected, and he laughed though it must have hurt him. She shook the stinging from her hand, and her heart clenched as she looked at him. His eyes bright blue with amusement; his beautiful, sculpted mouth; the strong, masculine line of his jaw and throat. And the rest of him: a warrior contained within that body, though little used for battle since his Fall. He'd not been able to deny his physicality, channeled it into different activities; he'd not been waiting to fight, but he'd been unable to resist what he was.

What he always would be.

Despite the mirth lingering at the corners of his eyes, the curve of his lips, his voice was solemn as he finally said, "I am here, Lilith." He gestured to the table and the venom-soaked bolts, to Sir Pup. "If I thought my death was the only way to save you, I would have you tied to the bed at home and spend my last hours lost within you. Four days are not enough to make up for the eight hundred I was too foolish to take for my own, yet I would try."

She nodded slowly; she could be content with that, for now.

After a glance at the clock, she said, "I saw a condom dispenser near the soda machine. We can make up for time now."

His gaze darkened, but he shook his head. "We need to practice; I haven't used a sword in sixteen years, and you are still unaccustomed to your new levels of speed and strength."

She rolled her eyes, though he was right. The room was smaller than Smith's office, but it would serve them well to test their skills within the tight confines, using the furniture as obstacles. "Sword," she said, and grinned when he did the same. "And when you are satisfied, Professor—may I screw you after that?"

"If we haven't been tossed out for making noise, certainly." He was quick; his blade flashed, and rang against hers. His smile was slow. "But as all of my students will tell you: I'm rarely satisfied."

Though she recognized his gambit—he intended to distract her—she could not stop the heat gathering within her, the moisture pooling low. She saved her breath for combat, or else she would have laughed: little did he know she was accustomed to fighting him with her body afire. Still, it took her longer than she'd anticipated. Cerberus's balls, but he was clever with his weapon, even disadvantaged by his lesser strength and speed, even taking care not to hurt her.

It seemed an eternity before she finally pinned him against the wall, her body pressed into his, her sword at his throat.

Perspiration slid down the side of his neck, and she suddenly felt parched, desperate to sip from his golden skin. Her chest heaved against his, her nipples tight and aching beneath the thin cotton. His denim jeans were rough against her bare thighs, his arousal hard and hot against her lower abdomen. "Satisfied?"

His hand fisted in her hair, and for a breathless moment she thought he would continue; he had several escape maneuvers from that angle: from his legs, from the leverage in that grip.

And when his sword dropped to the floor, it was hardly surrender, but a challenge.

"Not yet," he said, lowering his lips to hers. And his mouth was a much more effective weapon; she held onto her sword, but within seconds she was disarmed. Defenseless.

❧

The screams had stopped—or he and Selah had clawed so far into the cave the sound no longer penetrated the thick walls.

Too dark to see, but he could feel Selah's terror. His had faded days before, replaced by resignation, numbness.

"Try again," he said.

He hadn't taken blood from her since they'd teleported here; he barely had the strength to lift his hand, to search her out. Her fingers touched his.

And he knew she'd failed when she gave a shuddering sigh, let go his hand.

She'd promised not to leave him and had kept it. He'd brought her to this place, where giant scaled creatures tore and ripped and clawed. Where bodies dangled from a ceiling of frozen flesh, all but their faces exposed to the dragons' hungry jaws—but even without faces, they screamed. And screamed as their bodies regenerated and were eaten again.

He could feel more creatures—smaller but just as deadly, just as hungry—moving in the darkness; it would not be long before he and Selah were found, and had to flee again. But he had no strength to flee this time. And he was tired—so tired.

"Try without me," Colin said.

And when he reached out, she was gone.

❧

The security at the federal building was thorough, but they got through as easily as Lilith had predicted. A uniformed guard ran a metal detector over Hugh's shoes, then turned and performed the same scan on Sir Pup's harness. Hugh fumbled over the basket that held his keys and sunglasses, listening to the banter between Lilith and the guards as she went through the same routine. It was a short conversation, but revealing: she deliberately shoved many people away, such as Taylor and Preston—but for everyday, casual acquaintances, she allowed a friendly relationship instead of playing the bitch. He slipped on the sunglasses and studied her behind the cover of the dark-ened lenses.

She spent most of her time away from San Francisco on as-signments, away from Colin; had she cultivated any other friendships that weren't false? Or had her existence been as solitary as his?

They crossed the lobby together, just before five o'clock. The descending elevators were full, and most of the people headed out. She'd timed it well: late enough that the offices would be emptying, but before Beelzebub's assistant would have gone for the day.

"It's unfortunate you can't just kiss Smith and have the same effect on him as you do on me," Lilith said as she punched the button for the thirteenth floor. Her shoulders were rigid, her form tense—too tense.

Hugh slanted an amused glance down at Sir Pup. "Why is it that she's so determined to put me in a sexual situation with another man?" He caught her look and raised a brow. "I'll do it, if it makes you happy."

She pursed her lips. "Maybe when Colin returns."

"I wonder if *his* fangs—"

She growled low in her throat. "You'll touch no one's fangs but mine," she said, baring her teeth and returning her attention to the floor indicator.

He laughed softly and saw an answering shake of her shoulders. Then the elevator stopped with a quiet ring of a bell, and calm settled over him. Always, that calm before a battle; it was familiar and welcome, as was the thrum of his blood, the subtle tightening of his muscles.

Easy to fall into sync with her; he had fought her often and he knew her patterns. He made the rhythm of her stride his own, was as attentive to the cues of her body as he was the sights and sounds around them. The advantage of familiarity with the terrain and the people was hers; she took point, just slightly ahead of him. It must be strange for her to trust him at her back—to trust anyone—but she didn't hesitate or glance over her shoulder to confirm he'd taken his position.

She'd outlined the Bureau's layout before they'd come; Beelzebub's office was in the southwest corner of the building. Hugh quickly adjusted to the low-level noise of the office—telephones, chatter—and it faded into the background. Silence followed in her wake. Agents, casually leaning against desks, talking on phones, paused and watched her progress. More than once, Hugh saw someone begin to call to her, to express surprise or disbelief—or perhaps even to begin an inquiry—but stopping before making a sound.

It was not just the forbidding expression on her face, he realized, but the result of years of distancing herself from them. She'd established no camaraderie—and they felt no real concern for her beyond the loyalty of brotherhood. She'd cultivated that distance, and now she used it to move undisturbed. A high price to pay for a smooth journey, and he could see her regret that it had cost so much. Had she ever regretted it before? Or only now, when she was on the verge of making the distance irreparable?

Then she focused, and the regret dropped from her. The assistant's area lay outside the main office; an enclosed room, a waiting area with chairs, but no door—and the desk manned by a demon. It shouldn't have surprised him the assistant had taken the form of an elderly woman; Beelzebub would want his subordinate's appearance to be weak. She wore a headset over her gray curls, and was speaking into a microphone and staring at a computer monitor as they entered. Hugh smiled. Starched and efficient, but too arrogant to give them more than a cursory glance. Her psychic probe told her they were human; they couldn't be a threat. He wondered if she even bothered to scan the dog—probably not.

Lilith stopped in front of the desk, and slipped her hands into her pockets. "Keep your hands on the desk and your weapons in your cache, or my hellhound will tear you apart," she said quietly. "Is he alone?"

The demon's eyes widened with shock and confusion. Obviously, Beelzebub hadn't told her about Lilith's transformation. Her gaze slid past Lilith to Hugh and Sir Pup, and fear flashed over her features.

"No," she said.

Hugh gave a tiny shake of his head. Lilith's smile was cold and dangerous. "Run," she said. "If you stop before the Gate, he'll eat you." The demon hesitated, and Lilith sighed. "Or he can do it here; I have nothing to lose."

Whether Lilith opened her mind to the demon to convince her, or if it was simply a lack of loyalty toward Beelzebub, Hugh didn't know—but in the next instant the chair was empty.

Lilith grinned and turned to Sir Pup. "She is gone?" When the hellhound gave his affirmative headshake, she signed, *Demons only care for their own asses. But it won't take her long to realize he isn't on her heels.*

Hugh gestured to the open doorway of the waiting area. They'd hoped to arm themselves in advance, but there'd been too many agents walking past the room to risk it. Apparently, word of Lilith's return was spreading, and a few of the more curious wanted to catch a glimpse of her themselves. *We can't call in the weapons out here.*

"Shit." She took a deep breath. *Shut the door as quickly as possible.*

They'd practiced this, too. The door had to be closed for the soundproofing to cover the noise of the gunfire; it wouldn't completely muffle it, but outside the assistant's room it could be mistaken for a dropped file, the snap of a laptop closed too hard.

"I'll be right behind you," he said.

CHAPTER 33

She measured it in breaths. The first just before she opened the door, and it was used calling for the gun. Her hand was already in front of her, she only had to wrap her finger around the trigger. Beelzebub looked up. A blur as he leapt atop his desk, and Sir Pup streaked past her leg. *Don't engage him*, she thought— it wasn't part of the plan. A demon could kill a hellhound, but not a human, so she wanted Sir Pup as far away from him as possible. *Only surprise him, make him hesitate.*

She exhaled, fell to her knee, and waited for the click of the latch. The hellhound stopped in the middle of the room, bracing his paws and shifting. Two swords in Beelzebub's hands now. Just far enough into the room that Hugh wouldn't have to maneuver space for himself as he closed the door.

Not aiming for the eyes this time; easier to track their red glow than his body as he sped toward her. And Hugh would need them to—

Click.

She pulled the trigger. Less than four yards away, a crimson flower bloomed from Beelzebub's chest. Another from his gut.

His momentum helped carry him forward, but he was

slower. Vampire speed. Good enough. Two yards now. Her ears rang; she hadn't heard Hugh call for his weapon over the report of the gun. Had Sir Pup?

She saw the bolt embed in his stomach before she heard the twang from the crossbow's string, the thunk of its impact into flesh.

Beelzebub dropped.

A single breath, and it was one of the sweetest she'd ever taken.

❧

"Do I enjoy this too much?"

Hugh turned the lock, then glanced back at Lilith. She stood with her boot pressed to Beelzebub's throat, and cheerfully placed the point of the crossbow to his left shoulder. The demon roared as she shot a bolt through, pinning him to the floor. The feathered butts stuck up from his right shoulder and his wrists—necessary after he'd managed to rip the shaft of the first from his abdomen.

"No," Hugh replied. "What about his legs?" If the demon got his feet under him, it would give him too much leverage.

Beelzebub shifted, his clothes disappearing, hard scales covering his large form.

Lilith grinned. "A little late. Bet that took just about all of your energy, didn't it? But a tougher hide won't save you, and your belly's still nice and soft." She covered his eyes with her foot, then looked over at Hugh. *Any more venom, and he might not be able to talk.*

Sir Pup lay in front of the door; Hugh debated for just a moment before signing, *We need him as our defense there. Will more blood make you sick? I can remove his legs.*

Her lips twisted, and she tried to look affronted but failed. *Probably. And he's weak as it is: we can't take the risk he'll lose more.*

Hugh moved to stand next to the demon, examining him closely. The bullet wounds had healed, the scales closed up around the shafts of the bolts. Only the venom held him still, but they had to ride a fine line between weakness and full paralysis, and they didn't know how long the effects would last. "Axe," he said finally, and then lowered the edge against the demon's throat. More venom on the blade, but if Hugh used the weapon it wouldn't be to slow him down. "If you move anything but your mouth, I'll take off your head."

Lilith lifted her foot, stepped onto Beelzebub's stomach and crouched. She held the crossbow between her knees, tipped down so the bolt was aimed at his heart. "We need information," she said. "And it's going to be very simple—you answer our questions, or you die."

His burning red gaze moved between them. "Kill me. You will anyway."

"It's true I have not forgotten what you've done to me," Lilith said. "I'll slay you if I can . . . unless we strike a bargain. I don't kill you, and you answer our questions truthfully."

Hugh ground his teeth together, but remained silent.

"It is not equal."

She smiled. "You aren't in a position to bargain for equality. You have ten seconds to decide, or I kill you anyway. Starting . . . now."

At three seconds, Hugh signed, *He is too afraid of Lucifer, or that we will be able to stop the nosferatu with what we learn. There is no point in this.*

You have no stomach, Guardian, she signed back with a scowl. "Eight," she sang out, "nine . . ."

"You do not kill me," Beelzebub growled, "and I answer your questions."

"Done," Lilith said, and she glanced at Hugh, her eyes bright with gratitude. They hadn't planned on pricking his vanity with that short exchange, but it had worked. "Why do you need Hugh to be a part of the ritual?"

"Let me up first. I have agreed to answer."

"But you did not agree to stay in this room, and letting you up was not part of the bargain." Lilith smiled. "You don't do this very often, do you?"

Beelzebub's eyes flared at the insult. "The book is an offense to the Morningstar."

"Yes, but that is not why you need him for the ritual. You must answer the question asked."

"But *I* did not say truthfully."

Lilith's jaw worked, and though she hid her frustration well, Hugh knew she was berating herself for her carelessness in the bargain. A result of the quickness with which she'd had to make it, and an easy mistake, but not one she would take lightly. Hugh could read truth—and there had been truth in the response about the book—but Beelzebub had twisted the bargain so that the question had to be asked perfectly. And without knowing Lucifer's plan, Lilith did not know the questions to ask.

Hugh did. "Is it because my blood resonates with Caelum's Gate?"

"No."

"Lie." He glanced up at Lilith, saw her surprise and the subtle tightening of her mouth. He shouldn't have kept it from her, had hoped it wouldn't be true—hadn't even thought of it before she'd recalled him to the resonance with the Gates. "The ritual couldn't grant access through the Gates, because it requires self-sacrifice in the process of saving the life of another," he said aloud, thinking it through. "So Javier, Ian, and Sue . . . have any others been taken?"

"No."

Hugh nodded—that was truth and in keeping with the wager. "Yet you fought Guardians, must have had their blood. Is it necessary to take it from a human?"

"Yes."

"Truth," Hugh said. "Do I have to submit to the ritual willingly?"

Beelzebub's hand clenched. "No."

"Lie." He felt Lilith's gaze on him. "Another bolt through his left arm; he can move his fingers. Do they need Lilith's blood to get through Hell's Gate?"

"No." He smiled tightly as she aimed and fired, his fangs gleaming. "I will enjoy tearing you both apart."

Hugh glanced at Lilith as she reloaded the crossbow. "That was truth. Only ask questions he has to answer yes or no; be as specific as possible."

A long process, but Lilith was able to tease out the details of the ritual; she'd been correct in most of it. The nosferatu drank simultaneously, so that there would be no betrayal or inequality among them. One was chosen randomly to receive the full transformation; the others took sips to increase their resistance to sunlight and the daysleep. The bodies had been used to fuel the investigation against Hugh, but the nosferatu had reclaimed them for their cache, so there would be no decay in the symbols. There was no evidence that the body's decay would weaken the transformation, but they did not completely trust Lucifer's ritual.

Impossible to narrow down the location of the nest, however, except that it was in the Inner Sunset district. No use asking street by street; they couldn't attack the nest anyway.

Lilith tried another thread. "Does Lucifer plan to use Hugh's affection for me to convince him to submit to the ritual?"

"Yes."

Hugh nodded. She looked at him thoughtfully, then asked, "Does Lucifer plan to let the nosferatu kill me?"

"Yes," he hissed. "And I will enjoy watching it."

Hugh gave a slight nod, and she said, "Am I to be subjected to the same ritual?"

"Yes."

"Lie." A mocking smile curved Hugh's mouth. "Are you humiliated, knowing that two humans have gotten the best of you?" This was taking too much time, but much more humiliation, and he did not think Beelzebub would bother with one-word replies. The demon was enraged; Hugh doubted he could keep his control much longer.

"No."

Lilith laughed aloud. "I don't need his truth-telling to know that for a lie." She shifted her weight, her heels digging into his stomach. "I'm a gesture of Lucifer's trustworthiness, aren't I? Because I killed the nosferatu, and knew too much about Moloch, the nosferatu demanded he prove himself by delivering his 'daughter' to them."

"You are an abomination, a corruption of our kind," Beelzebub said. "You are no loss to us."

Truth, but Hugh did not confirm it. "Then why have they not come for you? If you are not to be subjected to the ritual, an attack on you does not break the terms of the wager," Hugh said instead, looking at Lilith.

She bit her lip, then asked, "But they are waiting because of the wager, aren't they? If there is a chance I can open Caelum, and Lucifer will triumph over Michael, he would take it. Is that correct?"

"Yes."

When Hugh nodded, she grinned. "I guess the golden boy isn't such an asshole. He tried to give us a week." Her grin quickly faded as Beelzebub growled again. Her eyes were dark and haunted when she asked, "Do you know of anything that could persuade Lucifer to release me from my bargain?"

Beelzebub's anger quickly changed to laughter. "Did I know anything that had that much sway over him, halfling, I would have used it to secure the throne. He has never released anyone from a bargain, and I know of nothing that could persuade him. It is simple: you kill your human, or you spend eternity frozen in the field—and I will spend eternity shattering your face to pieces and waiting for it to reform so that I may do it again."

Hugh's breath stilled. Lilith's face was pale, but she lifted her gaze to his and waited. "He speaks true," he said, forcing it past the tightness in his throat.

Her eyes closed in defeat.

"Do you have anything more to ask him?"

She shook her head. "You?"

"No. Step away from him." Cold descended over him as she stood, backed away.

"Don't let him up," she said. "The bargain doesn't require that we release him. Better to get away while he's still weak." Then she realized his intent, and she drew a sharp breath.

Beelzebub's eyes went wide. "The bargain—"

"Was that *Lilith* wouldn't kill you." Hugh stared down at the demon, his veins like ice. "You made the bargain too quickly and foolishly. The only choice you have is between the mercy of the axe or the hellhound."

"Coward! You will slay me when I am defenseless!"

"Not a slaying, but an execution. Lilith's Punishment. Ian. Javier. Sue. And countless other offenses which human law can never redress."

"You dare!" he roared. "You are nothing, a worm, and you dare execute me? For the lives of equally worthless worms? Do you know that they cursed your name, human? That I took your form when Moloch cut into the first, and the worm begged for mercy as I laughed. That Moloch wore your face as he took the woman, and the second boy, and that they screamed when the nosferatu fed from them. And I laughed and enjoyed every moment of their pain. That they cursed you, and begged, and pleaded. But *she* never begged, though for a hundred years I tore pieces from her. Did you know that she dreamed of you, of Caelum? That she waited for you to save her and take her to that place but you never came—"

Hugh's foot cut off the rest of the tirade. "Do you have any unfulfilled bargains?"

"Yes." An angry hiss.

Truth. "Then this will not be freedom." And he did not feel sorry for it, but he was cold . . . numb. He hardly felt the vibration as the axe dug into the floorboards.

But her hands were warm on his shoulders, even through his clothes; his skin burned where she touched him when she pulled him to his feet. "Thank you. I would have done it were it not for the bargain," she said quietly. "But I would have let Sir Pup eat a few pieces first."

He buried his face in her hair, held her tight against him. "You don't have to make me laugh. I do not like how it was done, but it *had* to be done."

And letting her go was difficult, but it also had to be done. He leaned over, picked up the axe. Wiped it off on the carpet and tossed it to Sir Pup. "Do you want his swords?"

She glanced over at the two swords Beelzebub had dropped and shook her head. "We could vanish the body. Carry it out and dump it over the bridge."

He wrapped his hand around the bolt in Beelzebub's right shoulder, pulled it out. "Why change our course at this point?"

"We knew we might have to kill him," she said. "But we did not know it would be this; we assumed it would be fighting, that he would have shifted into his demon form, and that it would clearly be self-defense." She gestured to the body, and he looked at the form beneath his hands. Except for the scales and fangs, Beelzebub looked human—and no one could mistake the wounds nor the precise decapitation as the result of a battle. "We understand this—but I don't know that they can."

He quietly removed the rest of the quarrels, let Sir Pup vanish them. There was nothing to wipe his hands on, so he let the hellhound lick them clean. "There is blood on the carpet," he said finally. "We were seen entering the office. Even if we remove the body, there will be no doubt we did something to him. With the body we have some explanation; without it we have none."

"We don't need an explanation, we need a fucking miracle." With a growl of frustration, she kicked a chair, then turned and glared at the demon's head as if she'd like to punt that next. He bowed his head to hide his laughter, and after a moment she smiled and sighed. "All right. What's the worst that can happen? You are thrown in jail and someone makes you his bitch, and I go to Hell. You call Taylor and Preston, I'll go get Bradshaw. I should warn you, though: I'm not his favorite person in the world."

Why wasn't he surprised? "This was your idea," he reminded her, smiling. The telephone was on the floor beside the desk; Beelzebub had knocked it down when he'd charged them. Hugh replaced the receiver in its cradle, sat on the edge of the desk, and dug in his pocket for the number.

"Well, the next time I have such an absurd one, stab me."

"I will," he said, and she threw a grin over her shoulder as she opened the door.

A man stood there, fist poised to knock. Her eyes rounded in surprise. Swearing, she quickly grabbed his tie and hauled him into the room, slamming the door.

Hugh slowly rose to his feet. The agent's eyes widened as he saw Beelzebub, then narrowed when they focused on Hugh. Recognition filled his expression.

"Fuck. Fuck." She pushed him up against the wall, his feet dangling ten inches off the floor. Though he outweighed her by at least seventy pounds, she lifted him as easily as Hugh would his cat. "Dammit, I was supposed to have time to explain, to get you ready for this."

Bradshaw. Hugh studied the agent's shaved head, the lean, dark face. The other man's hands hung relaxed at his sides; no fear in him, despite Lilith's display of strength and the demon on the floor. "I don't think he needs to be prepared," he said.

Her head whipped around, and she stared at him. "What do you—" Realization flared in her eyes. A long stream of curses flowed. She finally finished, out of breath: "A *Guardian!*"

"You asked for a miracle," Hugh said dryly. In spite of his tone, relief flooded him; it was more than he could have hoped for, wished for. They weren't completely alone in this.

She clenched her jaw, then dropped Bradshaw to the floor. "Someone up there hates me."

"It was someone Below," Bradshaw said, and straightened his tie. "Smith's assistant called from a pay phone, because she'd 'forgotten' to tell me that he'd wanted to see me before I left for the evening." He looked past Lilith to Beelzebub's decapitated form. "I guess she lied."

CHAPTER 34

Lilith knew she was extraordinarily lucky—but it was still humiliating. How could she not have sensed the truth? If she and Bradshaw had only a brief meeting, she could have excused herself . . . but ten years' acquaintance? And Hugh had been able to tell within seconds.

She glanced over at them; the two men stood near Beelzebub's body as Hugh recounted everything the demon had revealed about the ritual.

Sir Pup nudged her knee, and she leaned down to scratch his ears, frowning. The hellhound hadn't known, either—he was supposed to have given warning if anyone came to the door, but he hadn't sensed Bradshaw's approach.

"It's your Gift," she realized aloud. "A perfect psychic mask, so that you can pass as human." And like Selah's teleporting, the Guardians had hidden knowledge of the ability from demons, the better to use it to their advantage—and safety. Michael wouldn't place one of his Guardians in such a dangerous position unless Bradshaw had some protection. If he hadn't been able to pass as human, Beelzebub would have had him killed.

Bradshaw gave a short nod.

"And the others with the same Gift? All in subordinate positions to Lucifer's demons?" Though humiliating for her, it cheered her to think others remained unaware of the Guardians in their midst.

"There are very few others," Hugh said quietly. "It's a rare Gift."

An edge of resignation in his voice; he was pleased that Michael had managed to counteract the demons' foray into human society, but frustrated by the limitations of it.

Bradshaw frowned slightly. "How did you know? I never took this form in Caelum, and you weren't my mentor."

Hugh's brows drew together, and his gaze unfocused, as if he were remembering and thinking about it. "You didn't have any involuntary reactions when Lilith lifted you: no breathing change, no pupil dilation, no muscle reflex. You were prepared for Beelzebub—and prepared *not* to react. It was the response of someone who'd trained himself to stifle human impulse, but it takes decades of practice to reach that level of mastery over your body."

Lilith snorted with laughter. "As you well know."

He smiled, and his gaze heated as it skimmed her length. "I do." Then he shrugged, and glanced at Bradshaw again. "You overcompensate for your Guardian reflexes; fortunately, most demons are arrogant and self-absorbed, so they probably won't notice."

Lilith scowled. Arrogant and self-absorbed? She wasn't the one showing off and conducting an impromptu fool-the-demon lesson. "Thank you, Professor," she said, and his lips pressed together as if he were holding back his laughter. "Where are the nosferatu hiding?"

Bradshaw ran his palm over his bald head, as if uncomfortable. He shot a glance at Hugh. "You've found out more from Beelzebub in half an hour than I've been able to glean in years. We've concentrated our efforts since the nosferatu came into the city, but even Michael didn't know most of this."

Lilith's eyes narrowed. "Does Michael know where the nest is?" When Bradshaw nodded, she flashed a broad smile. "He's keeping it secret; he's concerned that if Hugh finds out, he will do something absurd." As well he should; if Bradshaw had known and refused to tell them, he'd likely be stretched out next to Beelzebub.

Bradshaw nodded again.

Hugh arched a brow, looked pointedly to the floor. "More absurd than ambushing a demon in a building filled with armed federal agents?"

His blue eyes were filled with amusement, and it was difficult to maintain her own sobriety. Difficult to keep her heart from her throat, from launching herself into his arms. Did he know how it affected her, his ability to shed insult, to laugh at himself so easily? "Rushing into a nosferatu nest is much more absurd than this," Lilith said. "The nosferatu can kill you."

"So could anyone outside this office, if he'd managed to escape us and raise the hue and cry."

Lilith grinned. "The hue and cry?"

"I would have shot you," Bradshaw offered. Every trace of mirth fled from Hugh's features, and Lilith placed her hand on his forearm. His muscles were like steel beneath her fingers. Bradshaw noted the exchange with a widening of his eyes, then added with a grimace, "On second thought, I couldn't have. Why are you human?"

"So that I can kill Hugh," Lilith said, waiting until Hugh met her eyes. Animosity between Guardians and demons—even a Fallen demon—was to be expected; it wouldn't disappear simply because he loved her. When she felt the tension ease from him, she turned to Bradshaw. "There's more Michael isn't telling you." Michael *couldn't* tell him; the stipulations of the wager forbade it—but they didn't forbid Lilith.

It didn't take long to outline the terms of the wager, and though it was obvious Bradshaw thought Lilith's soul wasn't worth the loss of Caelum and Hugh's life, he didn't say it aloud. Smart man, Lilith mused—he may not understand Hugh's protectiveness toward her, but he'd wisely decided not to test it.

"Where's Michael now?" Hugh said when Lilith had finished.

Bradshaw's brows drew together. "Your house." When they looked at him blankly, he said, "Selah came back, and Michael managed to go get the vampire."

Startled, Lilith met Hugh's gaze, saw the same relief and surprise reflected there. "Let's go."

Bradshaw's sigh caught them halfway to the door. "What am I to do with this?"

Lilith turned. "Spin it. You have the case files." She did a poor job of concealing her enjoyment when his jaw clenched.

After ten years of trying to expose her lies, he needed her to create more. This was difficult for him; she wasn't going to make it any easier.

"Lilith," Hugh said quietly. She arched a brow at him, and relented when he said, "Take pity."

It was only fair, she supposed; they had created the mess. She glanced at Beelzebub, slid pieces together, rearranged them. Bradshaw's abilities were going to make this much simpler than if she and Hugh had only themselves to rely on. "I suppose you don't want anyone to know you are a Guardian?"

"No."

Of course not, Lilith thought; the fewer who knew the better. A psychic mask was useless if a demon could pick the truth from another Guardian's—or human's—mind. "First, you are going to shift into Smith's form and walk us to the elevator. Then, as Smith, you'll put in for emergency family leave, transferring his cases to yourself, particularly the investigations involving the nosferatu." She nodded to herself, thinking it over. They had intended to use Beelzebub as the evidence Taylor and Preston had been looking for, knowing it wouldn't completely exonerate Hugh, but it would at least give more credence to his story—and though they'd have to keep it quiet it would allow the two detectives more maneuvering ability. Lilith didn't like the idea of all of the responsibility falling on the Guardians, via Bradshaw, just as it would have been the demons' when Beelzebub had taken over the case. "You're friends with Captain Jorgenson, Ingleside? Get his two detectives working with you; call them tomorrow morning, when you've got the files on your desk. They're going to come in with two nosferatu. Dead, of course."

"From the lake?" Hugh said.

Lilith nodded. "I'll give them an anonymous tip tonight. When I dumped them, I hadn't realized they wouldn't disintegrate in the sun. But it was after the first ritual, so they'd have resistance; they're likely still there." She saw the doubt on Bradshaw's face and frowned. "They already know a lot of it, and they aren't going to run around screaming about demons and vampires. It'll stay quiet if you make certain it stays that way. Run with the cult angle as in the letter. Keep your team busy tracking down phantom leads: hardcore Goth clubs, the missing bodies, linguists to explain the symbols and whatever shows up after the autopsy of the nosferatu, like body modification. Let the detectives go after us; we won't hide much from them, except your part in it, but I doubt they'll even mention to you the possibility that any of this is nonhuman; they'll be content, for the moment, just having access to the case again. But if they do, pretend to be skeptical until you get irrefutable evidence."

Bradshaw nodded slowly. "What will that be?"

Lilith shrugged, her heart suddenly heavy. "In about two days, you'll know. Keep Beelzebub's body in your cache until then. The blood, too." Sir Pup didn't have the precision to vanish something as amorphous as blood without destroying the carpet or leaving trace evidence behind, but a Guardian would.

"And what about you?"

She blinked, and an ironic smile curved her lips. "You finally get to suspend me, pending investigation of the stolen books and weapons found in my apartment." She slid her badge from inside her jacket, tossed it to him.

He reverently smoothed his thumb over the gleaming shield. "No spin on this?"

She shook her head. *It was all I had* was not a defense, and it wasn't worth the effort to create one. More important to concentrate on the last thing she had, the only thing that mattered.

She slid her hand into Hugh's. "Let's go," she said.

❧

Darkness had fallen by the time they made it through the rush-hour traffic. As they turned from Sunset Boulevard and neared Hugh's neighborhood, Sir Pup began running close to the motorcycle; she could hear his uneasy growls over the smooth rumble of the engine. She tightened her thigh muscles, felt an answering tension in Hugh's.

With a twist of the throttle, the bike rocketed forward. She let go of his waist and called for the crossbow. Though venom laced all of their weapons, the gun was too loud, the sword's range too limited. Sir Pup missed on the first attempt, and it smashed into the back of her hand before vanishing again.

Too much to ask, they were all moving too quickly; the hellhound sprinting, and they had to lean into the turns so deeply their knees skimmed millimeters above the rough pavement, the constant motion denying him a stable target.

She flipped up her visor and glanced back, up—there, the

pale figures against the night sky . . . two of them. Nosferatu. Were they just watching, or planning to attack?

Either way, she didn't want to be defenseless. "It's all right," she said quietly, "Try again."

Three streets away from Hugh's house now; hopefully the news crews had given up, or they were going to get one hell of a story. The crossbow landed in her palm, and she carefully turned—dangerous to throw off their balance, particularly as they decelerated.

The two nosferatu hovered as if uncertain, then turned and fled. Her triumphant laughter faded as she tilted her head farther, saw another figure flying directly above them. He held a blazing sword, and as she watched, it dimmed and vanished.

Michael.

About fucking time. She readjusted her aim as they rounded the last corner and pulled the trigger. The Doyen teleported an instant before the quarrel pinned his balls to his ass. Coward. Lilith burst into laughter, slapped her visor down and tossed the crossbow to Sir Pup.

The garage door rose when Hugh pressed a button on a device near the handlebars. Two media vans still sat in front of his house; a cameraman and a smartly dressed reporter scrambled out of the first van. Too late. Hugh pulled in, came to a smooth stop, cut the engine.

For a moment, the hum of the lowering door and her laughter were the only sounds in the garage. Then his helmet hit the concrete floor, and he reached behind with one arm and hauled her around astride him, her thighs atop his. Her laughter died on a wave of heat. God, but he was still so strong, so quick. He fumbled with her helmet, pushed it off. Half-lowered, his lashes were dark, thick, hiding the intense blue of his eyes as he glanced down her length, his hands everywhere, as if to be certain that she hadn't been injured.

"Lilith—God, Lily." His hands buried in her hair, pulled her down for a hard, searching kiss. His erection rose thick beneath his jeans and she arched back, finding an angle to stroke against him. Her panties were wet, soaking. He slid back along the seat, pulled her with him. *Hurry*. The tank dug into her spine. His hand moved between them. Something ripped.

Her trousers. She couldn't stop sucking, licking at his mouth long enough to protest. *Faster*. Rough denim against her skin;

he hadn't done more than unfasten them and his urgency made her wild, frantic. Dimly, she heard a voice at the door and Hugh's rough reply, and then he was inside her, his hot hard length thrusting deep. His mouth closed over her nipple and she came, her breath locked outside her and her inner muscles clenching in desperate, melting release. The motorcycle swayed and he hooked her knee over his arm and lifted, shoving into her again. A harsh moan tore from his throat as he withdrew, pausing with the thick head of his cock just inside before pulling all the way out.

She would have cried out at the loss, didn't care who might have heard her—but she was faster, stronger even than he was. A heartbeat's time, and she moved and her mouth surrounded him. A ragged, shuddering breath; his hands on her head; her name from his lips. She tasted herself, then he pulsed beneath her tongue; their flavors mingled, hot and raw. And it was not a rhythm, not routine—just life.

CHAPTER 35

"That was quick," Colin said from his reclining position on the sofa, and Hugh didn't need to see him to know a smirk accompanied the statement.

"You look like a wyrmrat," Lilith said, stripping away her trousers and tossing them toward the trash bin. She stalked into the living room, her long legs bare. "No, now that I'm closer: you look like a wyrmrat's ass."

A glimmer of a smile touched Hugh's lips, but when he took in the vampire's drawn, skeletal countenance, he had to agree with her assessment. Moving nearer the sofa, he noted the broken nails, the reddened fingertips. He was clean, freshly showered, and wrapped in Hugh's bathrobe, but the lingering odor of soot and burnt fibers hung in the air.

"This is your fault," Colin told Lilith as she examined his hands, but there was no accusation in his voice—only a deep, overwhelming relief.

"Many things are," she said mildly. "Are you lounging on the sofa because it shows your features to their best advantage, or are you unable to sit up?"

A brief flash of frustration and anger in his eyes before Colin looked heavenward. "The former, of course."

A lie. Hugh touched Lilith's shoulder. *He needs to eat*, he signed.

She glanced up as he began rolling his sleeve back over his forearm, then quickly back to Colin. "Where is Selah?"

"Caelum—Michael bade her to return, to tell your Savitri all is still well." His lips twisted with self-derision. "I believe she desired a few minutes alone as well."

Hugh frowned. Lilith wasn't concerned about Selah; that hadn't been the question she'd wanted to ask. Why would she be afraid of the answer? He crouched down next to her and offered his arm to Colin, turning his wrist up. Lilith swallowed hard. "I hear Sir Pup scratching at the back door," he said softly.

A wry expression chased across her features before she sighed and stood. "He probably wants to play fetch with that quarrel I shot at Michael."

Hugh watched her leave, then glanced back at the vampire. His lips were pulled back over his fangs, need burning in his eyes—but he waited.

"I don't think I can keep this from being painful," he said finally.

Hugh nodded; he'd known the vampire would have little control. Impossible, if he was as hungry as he looked. "It's for the best; if I'm pleasured by it, Lilith will likely force me to kiss you. And though you are rather comely for a man, I much prefer her lips to yours." Though his gaunt face lit with humor, still the vampire hesitated, and Hugh added, "I can stop you from draining me, do you lose all sense."

Despite those assurances, Colin must have taken care; the bite pained Hugh no worse than the slice of a sharp knife. He counted the draws, estimated the amount; when he heard Lilith's footsteps and the clatter of the hellhound's paws, he pulled back. Colin had taken little more than a pint, but already the hollows in his cheeks filled, his skin and hair regained some of its normal luster. Hugh clamped his hand over the wound as Lilith came into the room.

She arched a brow. "That was quick."

Hugh laughed and stood, but Colin was staring at the hellhound. "He made it out."

"Out?" She sat on the ottoman and tucked her legs beneath her. Hugh sighed as he went into the kitchen to grab a towel to wrap around his wrist; she'd delayed her return by changing her clothes, and his pants didn't look half as appealing as her bare skin had.

"Beelzebub put a sword through his gut."

Hugh froze mid-wrap, listening for her response. Would she blame herself for leaving the hellhound with them? Sir Pup had saved them, but had almost died in the process. Lilith was silent for a moment, and there was cold humor in her voice when she said, "Hugh put an axe through Beelzebub's neck."

His tension eased, and he walked back into the living room just as Michael teleported in. No use putting it off any longer then. He looked over at Colin. "Where were you?"

"Hell, I imagine," he said. "I have seen it before in mirrors—have heard the screams."

Lilith's face hardened. "The Pit?"

"No," Michael said. He stood rigidly in front of Hugh's bookcases, his black wings folded behind him, his arms crossed over his chest. A relaxed pose, for him. "Chaos."

❧

Lilith's breath stilled. Chaos. Lucifer had summoned the dragon from that realm. Sir Pup whined and lay his head on Colin's lap, and she was reminded that hellhounds were also descended from creatures of Chaos. Hybrids that Lucifer had made, hoping to control them better than the pure breeds. But Lucifer had not had access to the realm in millennia, slowly losing his power to call creatures from it. How had Colin and Selah found it?

"According to the Scrolls, even you are denied access to that realm. There are no Gates, and teleportation requires an anchor," Hugh said to Michael, his thoughts apparently echoing hers. He drew in a sharp breath as he realized, "Your sword. The dragon's blood imbued it with some of its power—and not only was Colin's blood tainted with it when he was human, we made him with the blood of a nosferatu slain by the sword. His blood was the anchor when Selah tried to teleport, and it took them to Chaos instead of my home."

Michael nodded. "Yes, but his anchor was too strong to allow her to transport them away." His gaze flicked down to

Hugh's wrist, and a tremor shook her as power flowed through the room. Sir Pup gave a sharp, happy bark. Hugh tossed the bloody towel aside, and moved to stand behind her; she realized he'd been staying away so she wouldn't see or smell the blood. Her heart swelled in her chest, left her full—too full.

She should thank the Doyen, but the words would not come to her lips. She glanced at Sir Pup, realized she had even more reason to be grateful. "You got him out of Colin's basement, healed him." Her voice was rough. The hellhound flapped his ears, grinning.

Michael's face did not soften. "I was almost too late."

"You always are," she said and took a deep breath. A Guardian had no obligation to save a hellhound. "I owe you."

"No," Hugh said. She tilted her head back. His eyes were cold, his mouth hard. "You don't." He waited for a moment, his gaze holding hers; then he looked up at Michael. "Take her to Caelum. Keep her safe there until the time for Lucifer's wager has passed."

Hugh did not include himself; he probably intended to stay and fight the nosferatu. She could—would—change his mind. At least he was trying to find options other than self-sacrifice. But the brief hope that filled her was destroyed by Michael's reply.

"I can't."

Hugh's body trembled behind her; she reached back, lay her hand on his hip. "You won't. Naught forbids you from taking humans but custom. You protect Savi there; you can protect Lilith."

"You know I speak the truth: I can't," Michael said softly, and then he was in front of her. A blade flashed, and her shirt parted down the front. "He left his mark. She cannot traverse the Gates, and I cannot take her to Caelum; her anchor is in Hell. And unlike Colin's, it is etched so deeply I cannot over-write it by force of my will." He stared down at the symbol between her breasts, his jaw set, his bronze skin drawn tight with anger.

Stricken, Lilith placed her hand over her name. Lucifer had left it deliberately then, to prevent her from escaping to Caelum. "Can you remove it?"

"Yes," he said. "But the price may be more than you are willing to pay."

◈

Sweat ran in rivers over his face. His arms and chest burned, but he couldn't stop lifting. From the living room, he heard occasional bursts of laughter from Colin and Lilith. A note of strain beneath it; neither the vampire nor she felt like laughing, yet they did. God, but he wanted to be with her, but his pain might force a decision from her that he prayed she would not make.

Did Michael remove the symbol, it would erase all that she'd gained since she'd become a demon. The lingering power and speed—but also the knowledge and memories from the past two thousand years. She would be a normal human woman, alive— lost in a modern world, but that would not signify if she lived in Caelum. And though Hugh had no doubt the woman she'd been had many of the same traits, same strengths . . . she would not be Lilith.

She would not know him, nor love him. The ache deep within his chest spread, burning into his gut.

He couldn't protect her from the nosferatu. Nor could Sir Pup or Michael—not every moment. And Lucifer would never let up; it would be too humiliating if a human got the better of him. Eventually, there would be a mistake made, and they would take her.

But she would be safe in Caelum. Her bargain with Lucifer would still be in effect, but without her having knowledge of it. And when Hugh eventually ended his life—it wouldn't matter when, tomorrow or in a hundred years—it would be for her. She would be the cause, and it would fulfill the terms. Her soul would be safe, and she would not be pained by losing him as she would now.

She would never know he'd existed. And he would stay away from her, to save her from ever knowing.

It was the best option for her. She would have Caelum, as she'd once dreamed—Beelzebub had not been lying in that. And when she eventually died—five decades, six?—she would not be frozen in Hell.

And perhaps, one day, did they destroy the nosferatu . . .

He forced away that thought. Even did the Guardians slay all, even did Michael allow him to visit Caelum, Hugh would still have to fulfill the bargain. If she loved him, it would hurt her when he finally did. And there was no guarantee that she would love him again; would it not be worse torment to see her, but not have her?

Nay. Her death would be the worst torment.

Michael appeared beside him, clamped his hand over the bar. *Destroying yourself in this way will not help her,* he signed with his other hand. The weights slammed into the cradle, and the bench shuddered beneath Hugh's back. No use fighting against the Doyen; the outcome would be laughable.

He sat up, bowed his head. Looked at his hands, his chest. "Where are ours?" Perhaps if he cut his out, it would not hurt as much. But, no, he *had* to remember. If he did not, he could not fulfill the bargain.

Michael eyed him silently for a moment. "The ritual is a false transformation. The effect is similar, but the method is different. The symbols are there, Hugh—but they are written on every cell, every particle of your being. And the longer they stand, the more they become your own. I can erase the depth of them when you Fall, but I cannot erase the whole without destroying you. I can leave a part of her, but there would be none left of you."

It did not matter; he could not be that boy again—he did not want to be him. He would carry Lilith with him, even did she exist nowhere else . . .

He rubbed his forehead with trembling fingers, then stood, and walked to his desk. In the bottom drawer was a thick sheaf of paper, and he picked it up. "Will you take the book, put it in the library?" A grim smile touched his mouth. Perhaps she would run across it, wonder at its author and subject. "It is not a Scroll and is missing much of her story, but I would be grateful."

Michael nodded, and it vanished from Hugh's hands. "Will you fill in the rest?"

"If I live long enough," he said, and ran his hand through his sweat-soaked hair. "I wanted to be angry at you for failing to tell me that she was a halfling—but I cannot. I should have seen; I knew how to look."

"You saw what was important." Michael hesitated, then said, "There are parts you don't know, and failings for which I'm culpable."

"Carthage? I know of it. Lilith said there were no other Guardians, and Selah mentioned that you created the corps after that failure."

Surprise flickered in Michael's eyes, and he shook his head, a reluctant smile pulling at his mouth. "Lilith was the last halfling made, but all those before had been . . . not worth saving. Each as inhuman as demons in their own way. And she was no innocent, but not a monster. Lucifer had become too bold, so I recreated the corps."

Hugh's brows drew together. Recreated? Had there been an Ascension, as widespread as the latest? "There is no mention of an earlier corps in the Scrolls, nor do any Scrolls predate the Latin." No surprise the Scrolls were in Latin if they'd been written after Lilith's transformation; it would have been the language most common to those in the corps after that time.

The Doyen's mouth flattened. "I destroyed them."

The former, older Scrolls or the Guardians? But Hugh knew him well enough to see that he would not speak of it anymore. Nor could he speak about the wager. "Savi?"

Michael gave a short nod. "Well. The nosferatu who followed you were searching for her. It won't be long before they realize she is out of their reach."

He did not need to say the rest. Nosferatu would not easily change their plans, but once it became apparent using Savi had become impossible, they would try to use others to force Hugh to submit to the ritual: Lilith, most likely—but if not her, his students.

How well could Lucifer control them? According to the wager, he could not instigate another kidnapping or ritual, but if the nosferatu became impatient and acted without Lucifer's consent . . .

Hugh shook his head and turned away.

❧

Steam filled the small room. Lilith quietly closed the door, began slipping out of her clothes. The outline of Hugh's body wavered behind the frosted glass; his hand was braced against the shower wall, his head bowed beneath the spray.

She stepped inside, and he turned toward her, gave a halfhearted smile. "Are you here to tempt me?"

"No." She ran her hands over his shoulders, and she kissed him. His lips were salty; she drew back, studied him. Not all of the moisture on his face was from the shower. "I'm keeping the symbol," she said.

His eyes searched hers; his muscles were rigid beneath her fingers. "Did you hear my conversation with Michael?"

"Colin did; he told me." And she knew he could have signed, kept it private—but he'd wanted her to hear, wanted to remind her that if she had decided to remove the mark, there would still be some version of Lilith in existence. Wanted her to hear that the woman she had been was reason enough for Michael to reestablish the Guardian corps.

"You would be safe. You would be free."

She shrugged. "Safety and freedom would mean nothing to the woman I was." She dipped her head, caught the stream of water sliding across the hollow of his throat with her tongue. "And I know it would not stop you from sacrificing yourself."

"Lilith—"

"I know," she whispered. "I know. But we have two more days; another option might present itself."

But there were not many left.

CHAPTER 36

Hugh woke just after dawn; she watched him leave the bed and gather his clothes from the closet. He murmured something to Sir Pup, and the hellhound gave a short bark of agreement. A run, then. She closed her eyes against the heaviness in her throat, her chest. An idea must have occurred to him, and he was working it through, teasing out the threads, examining the weave of it.

Unable to fall back asleep, she slipped into one of his shirts and padded barefoot down the hall. Colin sat on the sofa, watching spellbound as a woman chopped and sautéed on the television. Lilith rolled her eyes and continued through to the kitchen.

She poured a glass of orange juice and returned to the living room to look him over. "Did you hunt?"

"Why?" His fangs flashed when he grinned. "Are you afraid I'll eat you now that you're human?"

"Your clothes," she said, nodding toward the silk trousers, the tailored shirt. "Did you attack some unsuspecting fool and leave him naked?"

"I'd hoped you'd be afraid." He sighed dramatically. "As for the clothes, I'm a *most* beloved client at Wilkes Bashford. They delivered."

She stole a glance at the clock, and shook her head in disbelief. He complained about the price of dog food, and then paid unimaginable amounts for clothing. "Did you take a sip from the delivery boy?"

"And the housewife across the street." He paused. "Everyone in the neighborhood may be anemic by the time this is sorted out."

It might be sorted out sooner than Colin thought. The juice was tart and cold over her tongue, but she hardly tasted it. What was Hugh planning?

The silence stretched between them. Colin studied her features, and she wasn't certain what he saw there. Waiting became a physical ache; every passing moment seemed to unravel into an eternity. She searched for something to fill it.

"Are the reporters still outside?"

"No, unfortunately; I'd have liked a bite of the Channel Five correspondent. She's starred in my eleven o'clock news fantasies for years."

Hard to muster a smile, though she tried. "Did Selah return?"

The humor in Colin's eyes dimmed. "Yes. She's out with Hugh. Michael's still here, using the computer in the upstairs apartment."

Her brows rose, but he lifted his shoulders in an elegant shrug. "I can't make sense of it, either."

She nodded slowly. Michael must be in contact with someone—Bradshaw, perhaps. As difficult a time as she had imagining Michael typing, at least he wasn't using smoke signals or Morse code.

He must have heard them; moments later, he walked into the living room. No toga or giant black wings, simply a loose white tunic and cotton pants. No display of power in that appearance, and she wanted to curse at him for it. Perhaps if he had made a better showing of strength, Hugh would not take this all upon himself.

He met her gaze, his features without expression. "They are returning."

"You can stop him," she said without thought and was horrified when tears sprang into her eyes, as if the words had released a terrible pressure within her.

His visage blurred, but his words rang clear. "*I cannot.*"

Footsteps at the back door; she drew in great breaths, but though her chest filled and filled it seemed she could get no air. "Please," she whispered. "You know what I will do. You know what I am."

Michael shook his head. "So does he."

She turned. Hugh. God, but he was beautiful. And he did not look away from her, though he should have.

"I will submit to the ritual," he said quietly.

The glass slipped from her fingers, vanished before it hit the floor. She did not notice; her focus narrowed down to Hugh.

"No." A strong denial, but it would not be enough.

His jaw clenched, and he continued, "It is not just for you, Lilith. Eventually, they will use my students against me, Savi—even Colin. Or innocents that I don't know; it does not matter." He swallowed, and signed, *I can destroy the nosferatu.*

"Let the Guardians kill them; that is why they were created."

There aren't enough of them. There are very few left.

She shouldn't care; she shouldn't be startled. "You are not a Guardian."

They drink the blood in unison. If we replace my blood with Colin's, they won't discover it until it is too late. It will be an anchor; Michael and Selah can transport them to Chaos, though they think it will be Caelum. If Colin performs the ritual, he can change the symbols so that the resonance follows the blood, doubling the effect.

She squeezed her eyes shut. It was a good plan. "You could be healed."

Silence followed her statement, and she shook her head in denial.

"No, Lilith." His voice thickened. "It will use too much blood; I couldn't survive it. Michael can heal tissue, but he can't create blood that is not there." *And Caelum would be saved, for Lucifer would have lost the wager—you would not do it personally. The five hundred years can be used to rebuild the corps.*

"No," she said.

"It must be done anyway, Lilith. It fulfills your bargain—and the sooner it is done, the better. I would wait a hundred years, but even do we survive the nosferatu, there is no guarantee you would not have an accident. A car, the motorcycle. A stray bullet. If you died before me, your soul would be lost."

All would be saved but Hugh. She bowed her head.

"My name and my life are worthless," she said, and couldn't stop the tears from spilling. "But I would give them for you, do you not do this. I would give my soul for you to live."

She did not hear him move. He lifted her chin with gentle fingers, stared in wonder at her tears. "That is why I cannot let you. I would be worth nothing did I take a few days—a few years—in exchange for it."

Worth nothing. Only a week ago, she had stood across from him and reached into his mind, and found that fear lurking: worth nothing. A fear that did not have to be based in truth for it to be worked upon, for it to fester.

For it to break him.

The mark weighed heavy on her chest. She did not want to be this—but she could not let him die, and she did not know how else to save him.

"And so despite your claim that you are not a hero, you'll try to be one. Like the foolish boy you said you were." Mockery in her voice. A tone could lie, but more important her words did not—and she said them quickly, so that he had no time to consider nuances and words left unsaid. Made them painful, so that his emotional turmoil would cloud his reading. "You will try to do what is best for the most. Do you think you are a king, your sacrifice worth that much? You are not a king; you are not even a knight, stripped of your rank."

"I remember," he said harshly.

He was close; her hands were between them, beneath his line of sight. He would not see her fingers moving.

"What are you? You think to defeat those who once were angels? You are a man, a common man, saved by the lowest kind of demon. Never meant to walk among the angels." *They had run from Earth, and you never run from anything.* "You could never be compared to them." *Your worth is infinitely more.* "And you cannot save me this way." *It will destroy me.* "You are worth nothing." *To them, but not to me. You are everything to me.*

His features were absolutely still. "This is truth? You believe this?"

"Yes."

His eyes closed, and a sob rose in her throat when he opened them again; she'd seen this before. They glittered like blue ice. Not Caelum there, but the tormented faces Below—just as when he'd slain her, given her freedom.

She'd thought then it was a reflection of her Hell, but it was his.

His—and she was its cause.

"I will not be worth grieving then." His hand dropped from her face, and he turned away.

She stared after him; his broad shoulders were squared against her words. It was like being ripped in two, to cause him this much pain and know it had been for nothing. No, he did not break; but she would—

He stopped, thrust his hands in his pockets. He did not turn to look at her. "I can accept that you will always be Lilith, will always be the demon." A visible tremor shook him, and she pressed her fist to her teeth to hold in her explanation, her denial. *I don't know how to save you.* A demon knew nothing of saving, only lying and deception. "I do not understand why you still serve."

Roaring in her ears as he left the room. Blood in her mouth.

"Is this what you wanted, Lilith? Are you proud of what you've done?"

She did not know if Michael spoke, or if it was an echo of her last failure. But the answer—the true one—was the same.

No.

❧

He was not there to hold her this time.

The tile floor was cold beneath her legs; she couldn't stop shivering, though the window was open and the breeze warm. Her knuckles no longer bled, but she could still taste it.

No. She closed her eyes. Honesty with herself, at least—it was not the blood that had made her sick.

"You did well, daughter. Tore out his heart without lifting a knife. Smashing performance!"

Wearily, she looked up. Still the retired gentleman, Lucifer perched on the commode, patting his hands together. A golf clap. She shook her head, laughing at the absurdity; he had no claim over her, could not command her attention. "Did you climb up the tree?" She waved toward the window, wiped the tears from her cheeks. "It bears no fruit, and you have nothing with which to tempt me."

"Not even the lives of four boys?" Quickly, he shifted through four different forms before returning to the original.

Her back straightened. "You broke the terms—"

"No, no," he chuckled. "Your Guardian guessed correctly; the nosferatu grew impatient. *They* do not know how to stand and wait."

"They waited in caves for thousands of years," Lilith said dryly, climbing to her feet. "Perhaps they simply lose faith in you. Or they worry, because two humans managed to kill your lieutenant."

A flash of anger and heat before he was smiling again. "Regardless, it is a simple message I deliver today: you perform the ritual, kill the Fallen one—or the boys die."

So that he would have Caelum; her eternal Punishment paled in comparison to that gain. "You already lose control of the nosferatu; I can hardly accept your word that they won't kill them if I comply."

"You have little choice. But do you immediately tell them he will submit to the ritual, and make his students' continued living a condition of that submission, they will likely delay." He pursed his lips. "For a day or two."

Her jaw clenched. There was little choice if he did not lie about the boys being taken. And he was making certain the ritual would take place before the wager expired.

Hugh would sacrifice himself for a hypothetical danger to them, and for her soul; she would sacrifice him for the reality. Cut into him, kill him. Little wonder Lucifer was content for her to fulfill her bargain. Even if the act was brief, and her life not much long after . . . She could not imagine a worse torture.

As if he felt her acquiescence, he smiled. "I am pleased, daughter. Him, I expected—it is his nature to risk all for those he loves. But you cannot hurt them without making yourself sick. You tear him apart, only to puke from it." His lip curled. "Look at you. You embarrass me."

She tucked Hugh's shirt closer around her torso. "I'll be certain to wear this in front of your new subjects then, and call you 'Daddy.' "

A pile of clothes landed at her feet. "Appearances are everything. Do not disappoint me, Lilith." He leaned toward her, and she had to resist the urge to turn, flee. "And a little surprise."

A dagger appeared in his hand; she recognized the hilt.

Hugh's. The knife she had tried—and failed—to use on him in the temple. She raised her eyes to his. "Why?"

"I know you appreciate drama." He smiled coldly. "It adds a certain flair."

Carefully, she took the blade.

"Ah, Lilith," he said. "You're such a good girl."

She blinked; he was gone. The curtains fluttered at the window, and she hurried over to close it. Not that it would keep him out. He must have been using some kind of magic to prevent the others from hearing or sensing him. She touched the sill, and her eyes widened. The three symbols carved there: silence, surround, lock. A drop of blood in the center of each one. She destroyed them with a slash of the dagger.

"—LITH!" Hugh's frantic voice. He crashed through the door, Sir Pup on his heels; Michael teleported in, sword blazing. The hellhound leapt through the window, shifting to fit through the small space. After a quick glance around the room, Michael disappeared.

Hugh lowered his sword and was at her side in two long strides. His face was dotted with perspiration, his breathing rapid. How long had he been trying to get in? "Are you well?"

Was she? "I'm not injured," she said.

Truth, but the difference between question and answer was not subtle. His fingers shook as he brushed back a curl from her forehead—as if he had to touch her, but did not trust himself to touch her skin.

His throat worked, and he pulled his hand away. "Does he know?"

"That you will submit, yes. The nosferatu have taken some of your students so that you won't change your mind—we need to contact Taylor and Preston, have them make certain it wasn't a lie." It didn't matter if it was; they had little choice. Lucifer must love that. She rubbed her forehead, then signed, *But he doesn't know about Colin, nor the nosferatu. If he did know of a link to Chaos, he would care little for anything else until he had obtained it.* She frowned. *He must be concerned he will fail, to risk using his magic, and then leaving traces of it. He guards it closely, to keep his control over those who would take his throne.*

A short laugh escaped her; he well knew he did not have to fear such from her.

Hugh's gaze fell to the dagger in her fist, then met hers again.

"He must have taken it when he pulled me through the Gate in the temple." She set it on the counter, glad to be rid of it. "If he intended to increase my sense of fatalism, to remind me of the consequences of failure, it was the right thing to give me. I did not serve him that night," she said, her voice bitter.

He mistook the cause of it, and shook his head. "Lilith, I did not mean—"

Her heart suddenly thudded in her chest, and she did not hear what he said, could not hear anything but its racing beat. *She had not served.* It had been a rebellion, and it had given her Hugh—and it was the best thing, one of the few good things, she'd ever done.

She pushed past him, scooped up the leather breeches and corset, then went into the bedroom for her boots. Her pulse pounded in her ears, and she listened—did not even know if he said anything, though she could feel him watching her.

Michael returned. Sir Pup, Colin, and Selah stood at the bedroom door. In the living room, they had turned from her, their expressions showing disgust or rejection or pity. And she had deserved it.

"He is gone," Michael said.

She finished lacing her boots, stood. She didn't look at Hugh. "There is a dagger in the bathroom; I need you to check it for poisons."

The dagger appeared in his hand. Touching the blade to his tongue, he frowned and nodded.

Lucifer thought she might be able to begin, but he apparently hadn't trusted her to go through with killing him. She smiled wryly. "If you would clean it for me, I would be grateful," she said. "I'm going to perform the ritual with it."

Protests from Selah and Colin; one did not want to lose Caelum, the other was concerned for her. Nothing from Michael. He vanished the poison from the blade's surface and produced a sheath for it. Sir Pup lay on the floor, his three mouths opened wide in identical grins.

She did not look at Hugh.

She strapped the knife to her thigh, her focus on the buckles more intense than the act warranted. "Continue with what you're doing—Colin can procure the equipment from Ramsdell." She glanced up at him, and though his brow was creased with confusion, he nodded. Little that he did not know about blood or transfusions, but he had not been able to read the sign language Hugh had used to outline the plan. "Selah, you explain to him what we need—write it out." *Keep Hugh's,* she signed. *Colin will want to drink it, will need it after he gives his own, but don't let him.*

The blond Guardian's mouth was set in a mutinous line, but she gave a short gesture of assent.

Lilith looked at the Doyen. *Michael, store the blood in your cache.* "But first, go to the nest and let them know we're going to do the ritual tonight. A location of our choosing. If they touch Hugh's students, I'll kill him before he can submit to anything, and it won't matter if the wager is lost for they will have no access to Caelum." A lie, but only Hugh would know it. "The students are to be released after the bloodletting—but before the nosferatu drink—or else you will vanish it from the cups."

"Lilith," Hugh said softly.

"Don't ask me what I'm doing." She took a deep breath. The corset did nothing to hide the symbol between her breasts. "I need your bike."

"The keys are hanging by the garage door." Warmth in his voice. "Is this going to be absurd?"

She grinned. "Oh, yes."

And her attack wasn't as quick as she would have liked; he had time to lift his hands to hold her against him, met her kiss with open lips, and a laugh. She smiled against his mouth. Pulled back.

No ice in him now, but she was not done. "I have to do it alone," she said. His eyes searched hers; slowly, he nodded.

Relief filled her. She would do this regardless, but it was easier with his acceptance. She turned away, ignoring the looks from the others. Sir Pup trotted at her heels as she stalked toward the garage.

Time to be her father's daughter.

CHAPTER 37

The day wore on, but she didn't return. By the time the sun began to slide toward the horizon, Hugh felt scooped out, hollow. Preston and Taylor had arrived not long after Lilith had left; he had not needed to contact them. Four, taken that morning.

"Are the detectives still waiting in the living room?"

Colin nodded, checking the tube leading to Hugh's arm. He'd fed sometime in the last twenty minutes—already his color was renewed.

The last bag was almost empty; perhaps it was best she hadn't returned yet. She wouldn't want to see this, know the long process of the blood draw and transfusion. For all her wicked humor, the power in her when she'd decided to act instead of wait—instead of serving—he would still be her weakness.

He closed his eyes, recalled how she had looked when she'd pulled on the clothes she'd worn for hundreds of years—but had outshone them, as if they were only an accessory to the rest of her. A costume, put on for a play.

What had she done? He sighed, rubbed his forehead. And why had she to do it alone?

He looked up as he heard the click of Sir Pup's claws.

Then Lilith stood in front of him, her eyes dark, glistening. "I love you."

She had not said it without lies before. He'd always read the truth, but it was nothing to hearing it when it needed no translation.

And it filled him, left him unable to reply.

"I can leave the room," Colin said.

Her gaze sharpened on the vampire's flushed cheeks. "Did you drink from him?"

He shook his head. "Eleven o'clock news."

A ghost of a smile on her lips. She turned as Michael came into room. *Can you take him to Caelum—can your will override his anchor that much? We don't want him near when Lucifer realizes the truth about the blood.*

"Yes." The Doyen inhaled, and Lilith's eyes flashed with annoyance.

"Don't."

Apparently, she didn't want them to have knowledge of where she'd been, who she'd been with. Hugh slipped the small tube from beneath his skin, stood. Michael immediately healed the puncture, erasing physical evidence of the transfusion.

She glanced at him, then back to Michael. *I need to speak with you about the symbols, the ritual,* she signed. "But I need a couple of minutes with Hugh first. Alone."

Hugh frowned when he read the hesitation on Michael's face; the Doyen did not trust her. "Get out," he said, his voice harsh.

The Guardian's jaw hardened, but he disappeared. Colin left, and Sir Pup whimpered softly. Lilith smiled. "You, too, but sing for a while."

She closed the door behind the hellhound, and Hugh grinned when he began howling. With the point of the dagger, she quickly scratched out three marks on the wood beside the door, stabbed her thumb and placed a drop of blood over each.

Sudden silence.

Hugh saw the surprise in her eyes; she hadn't known it would work.

Surprise—but also uncertainty. "It's Lucifer's trick," she said quietly, and walked toward him. Her gaze flicked to the transfusion equipment. "Are you well?"

"Aside from a nigh uncontrollable urge to paint my self-portrait, yes." Better than he'd ever been; if these were to be the last hours of his life, they would be perfect hours, so long as she loved him, so long as she did not serve.

Her smile did not last. "I can't tell you what I've done," she said. "If you know, and they take your blood, they will know it, too. Once the nosferatu have drunk the blood, it is too late for them, but I can't have them warn Lucifer."

He slid his hand into her hair, laid his forehead against hers. Fear coiled in his gut. "Did you bargain?"

She did not answer, but said, "What I told you before, it wasn't truth. There was much left unspoken."

"I know." He felt her startle and smiled. "Not immediately, but upon reflection." And there had been nothing but time to think of it as he'd waited for her to return. To realize what his pain had not allowed him when she'd been saying it.

She drew back to look at him, her fingers tracing the line of his jaw, her thumb smoothing over the planes of his face. "You have never failed me, though I have failed you many times. I have always been waiting: for you to give me my freedom, for you to save me. And you gave me freedom in the only way you could, though it was Hell for you. You had no other options— but I might have, had I ever looked. The cowardice was mine. I was not strong enough, nor brave enough. Yet you always were."

His throat closed and he shook his head. Her fingers were warm against his lips, denying his protest.

"I have given you little reason to trust me, little evidence of my worth, but I need you to trust me in this. I will let you do what you must to save me—but you must let me save you in turn."

He studied her face, trying to read the mixture of emotions there. "What must I do?"

"Look away. When I am about to cut into your heart, look away."

It was the same thing Mandeville had asked of him—but Lilith did not need that kindness, would never ask it for herself.

But what difference could his seeing her make?

His lips parted as the truth struck him, and his laughter rang through the room. She was going to lie. And she did not want him to give her away; he would be weak from blood loss, his psychic blocks almost useless.

A demure smile curved her mouth. "I'm simply doing what my father wanted."

❦

She found Sir Pup at the threshold to the living room, his muzzles pointed toward the ceiling. A touch on his shoulder and the chorus ended.

On the sofa, Detective Taylor pulled her fingers from her ears and sighed with relief.

"You verified that they've been taken?"

"Yes," Preston said from the entrance to the kitchen, a soda in his hand. His face was haggard, drawn. The investigation had taken its toll on him—or perhaps it was just the past few hours.

"You know what to do?" Easier to include them than to fight them. Hopefully, Michael or Hugh had outlined their course very clearly.

Preston nodded. "Once they release the four, we take them and get them to safety." The nosferatu would be focused on the blood, and any demons wouldn't be able to interfere with the detectives' will to leave.

"Good," Lilith said and turned to find Michael.

"Agent Milton!" Taylor was on her feet now, her lips pressed tight. "It's *not* good. We know what you intend to do to Castleford, and we can't allow—"

"I'm allowing it," Hugh said, brushing past Lilith's shoulder. A small touch, but not accidental. Warmth spread over her skin.

"We don't care if it's murder or suicide," Taylor said. "If she tries to go through with it, we are obligated to stop her."

Hugh leaned against the doorjamb, smiled lazily. Heat raced up her spine. "You could come back after you've gotten the boys away. Risk the nosferatu and shoot her before she cuts out my heart." They likely didn't recognize the dangerous glint in his eyes; Lilith did, and a melting awareness pooled low in her belly. He glanced at her, and she realized he'd been trying to distract her with sex. That was her trick, dammit. "I think we've a problem; Michael showed them what he was, they've seen Selah and Colin, but they don't yet realize the danger from the nosferatu."

She frowned. Remembered that Taylor had already been convinced of their existence, but that her partner had doubted. Her gaze shifted to Preston. "You believed because you saw

Michael?" What was it with men, persuaded by that warrior-angel display?

The older man flushed. "Hard to refute."

Taylor shook her head. "And you may have once been a demon, but it doesn't change that you intend to kill a man. We don't understand a lot of the forces at work here, but I don't care whose law you think you are following. In this you'll follow ours."

Hugh began to speak, but Lilith said sharply, "Then arrest me afterward—no, I'll walk into the station and give myself up. We're the only access you have to those boys, and Hugh is the only way we have of saving them. This ritual is the only hold we have over the nosferatu now, the only reason they aren't slaughtering humans all over the city. You think these things are just serial killers, some creatures who get their kicks by slashing up a couple of humans? You think Selah and Michael are just pretty angels with wings and swords? You think my hellhound is just a freak three-headed dog? Show them your mean face, Sir Pup."

He shifted, taller than her shoulder. Spikes tore through his fur, scales rippled the length of his belly. Blood-flecked foam dripped from his mouths, his eyes burned with hellfire.

No mistaking the legacy of the dragon in him; no pretending he wasn't a creature from Hell.

Drama. Appearance—and it worked. Taylor paled; not from fright, Lilith realized, but with the understanding of what the nosferatu were, what might happen to the boys did Hugh not go through the ritual. Understood the choice he was making.

She couldn't resist an exit line. "You get those kids, and then you get the fuck out of there."

❧

Two more things to take care of—the most difficult first. No sense drawing it out.

He caught her hand before she could open the office door. He stared down at her, and he saw too much. *You don't have to make it irreparable.*

She sighed. *I like them both—respect them. And I like them the more for objecting to your death. But trying to explain to them that I'm doing this because I love you wouldn't have worked as well, nor as quickly.*

He ran his fingers through his hair in frustration. *I know,* he signed finally. *But you should have let me do it. If what you've planned doesn't work, I don't want you to be completely alone . . . after. I don't want you to drive everyone away.*

"After" wouldn't matter if this didn't work. "What time did Michael stipulate they meet us?"

The change of subject didn't faze him. "Midnight." Leaning in, he kissed her upper lip, then her lower. "We'll need to leave in four hours."

The expression in his eyes was a reflection of hers: not enough time.

"We'll split this, get it done faster," she said, her throat tight. "Sir Pup, the item." A small plastic bag filled her palm. "I have to talk to Michael. Make certain Colin goes to Caelum, and give this to Selah. Then we go to the bedroom and don't come out again until we have to leave."

He nodded, his gaze never leaving hers. His voice was low, rough. "I'm going to leave my mark, Lily."

Heat tore through her; her knees turned to water. She hurried through her silent explanation with hands that only wanted to touch him, to leave her own mark—then forced herself to wait.

Michael first.

§

Hugh found Selah and Colin in the kitchen. "Are you ready to go?"

Colin looked up, his anger still evident. "I can help you. My sword—"

"You can help us better in Caelum. And their supplies will have been used by now; they need to eat." Hugh gestured to the grocery sack intended for Savi and Auntie. No food in Caelum—Guardians didn't need it.

"So do I," Colin said, a silken threat.

"She's my sister," Hugh reminded him, then sighed. He understood the vampire's frustration—it echoed his own. Whatever Lilith planned had to be done in secrecy; it ate at him that he couldn't do more to help her. Colin likely felt as useless. "I need you to protect them afterward: Savi, Auntie—and Lilith. She'll be alone, just as your sister was before we came to help her."

A muscle in the vampire's cheek flexed. "Don't manipulate

me. You have humans assisting you, yet I cannot? Bloody ridiculous."

Another way, then. Impossible to say aloud the true reason—Colin was the anchor to Chaos. He probably wouldn't have accepted that, anyway; he was more concerned with helping them than worried about possible danger to himself. Hugh's voice hardened. "You're a liability to us. I'm sworn to protect you, Lilith loves you. Should you become endangered, you'll divide our attention and leave us vulnerable."

The vampire fell silent, his jaw set. Furious, but reluctantly accepting the truth.

Selah looked away from them, her gaze dropping to the granite counter. Hugh tossed the small plastic bag into her line of sight.

Her head jerked up. "What the hell—"

Hugh slashed through the air with his hand, a demand for silence. *After the boys have been taken, after the nosferatu have drunk the blood, use this as an anchor and return with whoever you find there, as quickly as possible. Don't open it before then; the scent might give her away.*

With her thumb and forefinger, Selah delicately lifted the bag by the corner. *Whose are they?*

I don't know, Hugh signed. Lilith couldn't tell him, and though he had his suspicions, he pushed them far back into his mind and refused to consider them further.

Colin stared at the bag, at the three severed fingers inside. Black nails, red skin—a demon's talons. "Did Lilith do that?"

Hugh nodded. Selah vanished the bag into her cache and shuddered.

A wry smiled pulled at the vampire's mouth. "Perhaps I should still be afraid of her, even human."

Laughing, Hugh said, "Then don't let her know you refused to go to Caelum. She'll send you in pieces, if she must."

He sobered suddenly, and slid his hands into his pockets. Caelum. One of the few things she'd dreamed of, forever denied her. Lilith should have been there, instead of risking all for a bargain she'd had little choice in making.

He met the vampire's gaze. "See it well, Colin. And bring it back to her."

❧

"You can't have the sword." Michael didn't glance up from the Scrolls spread out on the floor.

Lilith pursed her lips. "That's not why I came in here." The Doyen slanted her a glance, and she amended, "Not completely." *You have his blood?*

He sat back on his heels, studied her carefully. "Yes."

I need you to keep him alive with it.

You're human. If you are the one to cut him, I can't heal him.

She waved that off. *That is not what I ask. After the cups have been filled, I want you to keep him alive by returning his blood to him. I just need extra time.*

His eyes narrowed as he considered it, then he shook his head. *It cannot be done.*

It can be done. You are a Healer. Others are limited by their focus, their inability to take their perception down to that level. There is space within for you to place the blood.

Again he considered it; he wanted to save Hugh almost as badly as she did, despite the dangers to himself. Possession, will, and the integrity of the object—all necessary for calling items from a cache, or vanishing them. Demons, nosferatu, and most Guardians couldn't psychically move beyond the integrity of the whole body, or weapon; Healers could. But he would have to transfer the cells singly: tiny, precise transfusions into Hugh's continually flowing bloodstream.

His mouth firmed. *It would take the focus of a transformation. I couldn't protect you, nor defend myself.*

That was what she needed. Not just to keep Hugh alive, but to have Michael completely distracted by the process of it.

She took a deep breath. *Then you could give me the sword, so that I may protect us. I have the speed and strength necessary to respond to an attack, and I would not likely be challenged if I carried it.*

He stared down at the Scrolls for a moment, then looked up. *I will attempt the transfusion, but will not give you the sword.*

Her stomach tightened into a hard knot, but she nodded. Sinking down on her heels, she touched one of the Scrolls in front of her. "This is not the Latin."

"No." He slid a piece of notebook paper across the floor. *You must carve these into his skin.*

She traced the symbols with her finger, felt the sickness rising in her throat. "Follow the blood," she said in the Old Language. His eyebrows winged upward in surprise, and she shrugged. *They covered my skin for two millennia; when certain symbols disappeared, so did specific powers. And demons do not deign to speak in human languages when they are Below. I cannot read as fluently as I can speak, but I'm not as ignorant as Lucifer would like me to be.*

He did not try to take it from you?

I hid it well. And he never expects humans to have more than limited understanding. She glanced up, found him watching her. Quickly, she changed the subject. "Why aren't there many Guardians left?"

"An Ascension," he said quietly, still studying her.

Her brow furrowed. "Thousands at once? Like a cult?" Her mouth fell open when he nodded. *How could you lose control of them? Why didn't you stop the Ascension?*

His laugh startled her. "I don't control them, nor rule over them; I am not Lucifer."

That was undeniable. She shook her head, trying to understand the structure of power in Caelum, and finally said, "I don't think I could have been a Guardian."

She stood to the sound of his laughter and went in search of Hugh. She'd failed partially, but it was only in saving herself. Hugh might live now, and that would be worth the price she had to pay.

And the end, as always, would come too quickly.

❧

"Bloody hell."

Just like Michael to throw a vampire to the floor in the middle of a giant room and disappear. Colin rose to his knees, then thought better of standing before making certain—

There, the girl-woman. Savitri. She stared at him with those wide brown eyes, her fingers clenched on the back of a sofa. Her body was hidden from view, as if she were kneeling on the cushion—probably she had been taking a nap when she'd heard Michael dump him.

He must be in the Doyen's apartment; his brother-in-law had described it to him once: a single, enormous room—empty but for an armory, and a sitting area filled with mismatched furniture.

He grinned, flashing his fangs. "Are there any mirrors in here?"

She slowly shook her head. "You're not blind." No fear on her face, though she couldn't mistake what he was now.

He climbed to his feet, straightened his clothes. "I'm not gay, either."

"That's unfortunate," she said. Her eyes widened farther as he stalked toward her. "Because I think I'm half in love with Michael and I could use a friend to talk to about it."

He bit back his laugh. "You should run," he said. Still no fear. What was wrong with her?

"And leave Nani defenseless?"

He glanced past her, to the woman lying on the sofa adjacent to hers. A light snore came from the older woman's nose.

Savitri stared up at him. Licked her upper lip. "How strong are you?"

Did she appreciate his form? This was much better. If not fear, then admiration. He eyed the slender column of her throat.

"Are you strong enough to open the doors?"

Startled, he looked as she pointed toward the massive carved doors at the other end of the room.

"I have free will, but will alone can't force those doors open. I've spent four days trying."

He raised his brows, turned back at her. "Will you allow me a sip?"

"Yes. But I also haven't showered in four days, so it might be ripe."

Like a peach simmered in brandy and cinnamon. But he sighed and offered his arm. "Come along."

Her smile was blinding, and she darted around the sofa, tucked her hand into his elbow. "How is Hugh?" Something in his face must have told her; her smile faded, her chest rose and fell in a silent, sad breath. "Did Lilith return?"

"Yes." And when Colin had left, they'd been in the bedroom. Impossible not to hear their laughter, their soft declarations. Impossible not to recognize it as their farewells to each other.

His throat tightened, and they walked silently to the doors. They were heavy; he pulled, and dazzling sunshine poured through. Savitri stepped back, and he shook his head. "I won't burst into flames." If he didn't stay out too long.

She went through ahead of him, stopped suddenly. "Oh, my God. He gave this up to save me?"

Dumbstruck, he came to a halt beside her. Tried to take it all in at once: the pure white marble, the towering spires, the symmetry and beauty. "Don't be absurd," he finally managed. "He did it to save himself. And Lilith." And Colin was supposed to bring this back to her? How could he possibly—

"Where is everyone?" Savitri was turning in a circle, frowning.

He shook his head, and didn't know if he answered her or himself. "I don't know."

CHAPTER 38

He was embedded in her skin. His scent, his touch, his voice.

Even now, walking across the concrete floor of the warehouse Michael had chosen, she did not smell the stale air around them, did not feel the frigid temperature inside the building, did not hear the hollow echo of their footsteps. Dangerous, to be so lost in him, but she wanted to savor it for as long as she could.

It was not long.

A fluttering of wings surrounded them, but the figures dropping from the rafters were not what she'd expected. Guardians—about forty of them. A few landed awkwardly, and she glanced at Hugh to confirm her suspicion. His lips were thinned with anger.

She turned to Michael. *You brought fledglings?* She could understand bringing those in the latter half of their century of training. But a few here had no more than a year's skill. If there was a battle, they would be slaughtered.

His brows rose. *If I lose Caelum, should I leave them there to defend themselves against the nosferatu?*

Hugh's tension eased, and Lilith drew in a quick breath. A

lie was hidden in that question. If Caelum was lost, he would have time to transport them to safety. This was Michael's display, but one of uncertainty and weakness.

Definitely nothing like Lucifer. Even in frail human form, Lucifer never let it be forgotten how powerful he was.

Preston looked around uneasily. "Where are they?"

"Lucifer will want to make an entrance," Lilith said. Not just for them, but for the nosferatu.

Hugh met her gaze, a smile tilting the corners of his mouth. "Not the best place for it."

Lilith laughed softly in agreement. No, Lucifer would not appreciate the stark, empty warehouse, with its bare ugly floors and industrial metal siding.

Taylor glanced from Hugh to Lilith in disbelief. Hugh's smile widened.

His incredible mouth; she wanted to taste him, but she slid her fingers over his instead, locking his palm against hers. It was cool and dry; his calm fed hers. Sir Pup nudged her back and leaned one of his heavy heads over her shoulder. She reached up and scratched his chin with her other hand.

"They come," Michael said.

So easy to fall into position: the Doyen in front, Hugh by her side, Sir Pup just behind her. Taylor and Preston flanked the hellhound, and the Guardians formed a semicircle behind the small human group, their weapons drawn. As per the wager, they would not engage, only protect.

Hugh removed his shirt and threw it to Sir Pup. Lilith raised her brows, and he said, "Blood stains are difficult to remove, and I hate laundry."

Her lips twitched, but she understood this, too; it was an unmistakable signal of his intention to submit. And despite his lean, hard strength, the nosferatu and Lucifer would look upon him as frail, defenseless. As she had once.

"And we've ruined so many clothes this week. Very practical." She nodded sagely.

She heard Preston's snort of laughter behind them, but her own smile faded.

"You will be cold." Her voice was thick.

He touched her face. "I'll trust you to be kind."

She was holding his gaze with hers when they came, and she did not see Lucifer's display. She didn't miss it. It could never equal the intensity of emotion in Hugh's eyes, the beauty of the smile curving his lips.

This was strength, too—and it steadied her.

Perfectly composed, her psychic blocks as tempered steel, she faced the nosferatu. Ten yards away, they mirrored the Guardians' formation and were almost equal in number. In his demonic form, Lucifer stood with Moloch and two others who'd been transformed by the ritual. Behind them, the four boys stood wide-eyed with fear, silent.

Lucifer had not brought his demons, but that did not surprise her. His vanity would demand that he appear alone, declaring a lack of fear and no need for assistance—or to bring many, and show his power by demonstrating his reign over the demons. But no one would question his reign, so it was more important to him that no one questioned his fear.

And it would have been exactly as she'd wanted . . . had she the sword.

His dreadful crimson gaze settled on Hugh, then moved to Lilith. "You should know how to use this, daughter."

A machine appeared in front of Michael: an inclined bench lined with shackles and tubes, a cistern never at the top.

She shook her head, her eyes never leaving his. "Just the bench. He'll submit without restraints, and Michael will provide the method of collection. The blood is in the Guardian's possession until he releases it." This had already been stipulated, but apparently Lucifer had hoped to unsettle her with the device.

Lucifer stared at her for a moment; finally, all but the bench vanished.

Hugh immediately strode forward, and though her heart constricted, though she wanted to call him back, she walked with him. She knew he moved so quickly for her; no waiting, no drawing it out. She helped him settle onto the metal panel; half-standing, half-leaning, his weight supported by the jutting footrest. Her palms smoothed over his skin; he needed no assistance in this, but she needed to touch him.

Michael called in the table and cups. A long table, so that each nosferatu could lift and drink at the same time—but also serving as a barrier between the two sides. Not an effective barrier, should the nosferatu attack, but its own symbol: do not cross.

Lucifer approached the table and dropped a clay tablet onto its surface. "Cut these into him. Exactly like this."

Lilith glanced down at the multitude of glyphs and drew her dagger. "Just these." She turned the tablet over, carved out a small series: *Let the blood serve as the anchor, the Gate: follow the blood.* Impossible to tell if he was surprised. "Any more are for his pain, and your enjoyment; he will not be your entertainment."

"Michael gives too much away." A mocking smile twisted his lips. "Very well. It does not matter how many there are, so long as he bleeds. Then *your* pain shall be my entertainment."

She shrugged, turned back to Hugh. He regarded her steadily, his expression unreadable—not to hide his emotions from her, but to keep others out. How long could he hold his blocks? It had to be at least until the nosferatu drank; not only did he have to hide her lies from them, but his plan.

"Stay with me," she said quietly and lifted the knife. It trembled, and he reached out, covered her hand with his, and drew the point to his chest.

❧

Her face swam in and out of focus. He couldn't tell if he heard her now, or if it was an echo from before she'd begun. *Stay with me.*

It had not hurt much—she had been quick, the dagger had been sharp. But now the waiting, as she held the wide-mouthed glass ewer beneath his chest, watched it fill. A hungry chick, beak open for worms. He'd had to tip forward for it to drain better, and he was not certain how much she held him up, and what was done of his own power.

Three liters, that ewer. Even did Colin's blood strengthen him, he couldn't survive . . . Nay, nay—do not think of the vampire.

Stay with me.

"I will miss your laugh, Lily," he said. "I will miss your heat and your lies."

All his strength to lift his head; a moment ago, he thought he'd not had even that much left. She was staring at him, a fierce joy on her face. And a terrible sadness.

"I love you." Her voice was soft, but he heard it clearly. He leaned back, grateful for the support of the cold metal. She pressed the dagger into his hand, and he closed his fist around it.

She turned away. "It's done," she announced. The ewer was full; she began pouring it into equal portions under Lucifer's watchful eye.

Stirrings, odd murmurings among the nosferatu. He did not know the language, but their concern was palpable, the reason plain.

He should have been dead. He was weak, breathless, nauseated—but alive. He should have been dead.

An odd hum under his skin, in his blood. He'd felt it before, during his transformation to Guardian—and again when he'd Fallen. He turned his head.

Michael stared at him, his body rigid. His bronze skin glistened with sweat.

This would not fulfill her bargain. What had she done?

❧

"What have you done?" Moloch's voice. He approached the table, eyeing the blood suspiciously.

A cold smile touched her mouth, and she filled another cup.

The nosferatu turned to Lucifer, hissed the words in the Old Language. "Do you betray us, Morningstar?"

"You watched him bleed," he replied in the same tongue. She felt his gaze on her, trying to penetrate her thoughts. "Are you so foolish you cannot see? She loves him. She trades her soul for his life; she means to betray me by returning him to Guardian, preventing his death."

"And us? Does she betray us?"

The air around Lucifer began to heat with his anger. "Do you wish to know, taste her."

Cold fear twisted in her stomach, but she only lifted a brow and said, "Are you certain, Father? I'm hardly trustworthy. I may know more of your magic and symbols than you think; do you want him to know as well?" Filling her thoughts of symbols and blood on the windowsill, on a door, she opened her mind and showed him the truth of it. Hoped he would fear she knew more.

A weak gamble; he was not impressed. "A parlor trick, Lilith."

The last of the blood into the final cup; her hands were trembling.

Lucifer smiled. "Taste her. She is yours, anyway. Does not matter if I give her to you sooner than I anticipated."

She backed up a step. "Michael," she said hoarsely.

Moloch leapt over the table. "He cannot help you, halfling. The wager stipulated that there would be none killed for the rituals; we have no intention of using you. Does he attack me to help you, he loses."

She shot a glance at Lucifer; amusement gleamed from his eyes. And why not? He won either way: if Michael helped, Lucifer would take Caelum; if Michael did not, she was at Moloch's mercy.

Hugh's arm came around her waist. His still bleeding chest heaved against her back; he was too weak to help her, but he was trying.

Moloch laughed and shifted. Terrible, to see Hugh's face on that creature. "I must admit, I've taken a liking to this form. They trusted him, and screamed the louder for it being done by one they cared for. Will you?"

Shouts from Taylor and Preston—they could not understand what Moloch said, but no mistaking his intention.

"Michael," she said again. Her heart pounded. Her left hand gripped Hugh's forearm, she searched for the dagger with her other. "Please."

Too fast—his fangs were buried in her neck before her next breath. An explosion in her brain, a ripping, and he pulled back, his eyes wide.

"Michael!" Hugh's desperate shout.

A weapon in her hand—not the knife. The Doyen's sword. She did not know how to make it blaze, but she did not need fire. With this sword, even a human could kill a nosferatu; and she had more strength and speed than a human—not as much as she had as a demon, but enough. Moloch's torso thudded to the floor before his legs toppled over.

Her hand clapped to her torn throat; Michael's power knitted it together beneath her fingers. She shook her head, rasped, "Hugh." Forced away the sickness of feeling, seeing, smelling the blood everywhere.

Needed to keep it flowing into him. She stole a glance at the Guardian; he focused on Hugh again, and she breathed a relieved sigh. Behind him, Taylor and Preston lowered their weapons. She looked down. Two neat, round holes bloodied Moloch's temple.

It wouldn't have killed him, but it had probably helped slow him down.

Grinning, she turned back to the nosferatu, gave the sword a little spin. "The boys for the blood," she said.

CHAPTER 39

Hugh watched Lilith's face; he could understand nothing of what the nosferatu said as they argued amongst themselves, but she could—and it did not please her.

The fear of betrayal warring with the desire for a home. He filled his mind with images of Caelum, let them filter out. The nosferatu fell silent.

Until Lucifer spoke. "You saw him bleed. The symbols are true, the anchor will hold. You do not need these four to kill; once in my service, there will be much blood to spill." Arrogance, pride. He had not perceived a trick, except for Lilith's keeping Hugh alive instead of sacrificing him—and now the nosferatu's hesitation angered him, cast doubt upon the power of the ritual. Lucifer turned to Lilith. "Once they drink, they will be released."

Truth. But the moment the nosferatu drank the blood they would know the deception. Hugh's fingers moved by his leg, the signal hidden from the nosferatu and Lucifer.

"Agreed," he said quietly. Lilith's body quivered, but she gave no other sign of her dismay. He glanced over at his students; he had avoided looking at them until this moment—too much anger in him at the sight of their fear. "Are you guys ready to go? You want to go?"

Necessary to make it clear; this couldn't work without their willingness to go. And they'd have no time after to explain about free will.

Four pale, stricken faces nodded in reply.

The nosferatu moved forward as one, lifted the cups. Drank.

The hum in his blood ceased as Michael teleported. He and Selah, taking two boys each—they disappeared. The boys were safe then, but the screams of outrage from the nosferatu echoed through the warehouse. Weapons flashed as they came across the room on a wave of rage; the Guardians met them halfway.

Lilith scrambled back, pulling him with her. She pushed him as a nosferatu flew over their heads, and quick human hands caught him. Taylor and Preston.

"Sir Pup—get them out." The hellhound whined, but Lilith clenched her teeth and repeated the command, hauling Hugh to his feet.

Hugh could stand, had the strength. "Crossbow," he said, and Lilith let go of him again to swing at the nosferatu. She severed the creature's arm, but took a slice from its remaining weapon.

He aimed, fired. The nosferatu dropped, and she finished it with a blow through its neck.

"Get out." Blood streamed down her chest, splattered across her neck.

"They're going." He spared a single glance at the two detectives, struggling against Sir Pup as he sprinted for the door, carrying them by their jacket collars like a mother with kittens.

"You, too."

He only grinned and fired another bolt. It caught a nosferatu's shoulder, slowed him down. Gave time for the novice who'd fallen in front of him to rise up, strike a killing blow.

"Michael's back," Lilith said and began laughing.

The Doyen didn't have his sword, but he was more than effective picking off the nosferatu. Teleporting in front of them, touching them and taking them away. No need to respect a nosferatu's free will; no punishment for denying it—and now they had an anchor to somewhere other than Earth.

Fast, incredibly fast—ten, then fifteen. Twenty. The others tried to scatter, but the Guardians outnumbered them now, trapped them. Twenty-five.

"Sir Pup could have saved you," he said quietly. "Against Moloch—either given you the crossbow, or—" He broke off as he understood: she'd needed Michael's sword. Had risked her life for it.

"Yes." She met his eyes. "I want more than four days."

Hard to catch his breath suddenly. "You've always been greedy." But so was he.

Her gaze dropped to his chest, and her mouth tightened. "Where's Selah?"

He swayed, shook his head to rid himself of the dizziness. When he focused again, Lucifer stood in front of them. At the demon's cloven feet, Sir Pup's huge body lay stretched out, bloody stumps where two of his heads should have been. He held his sword to the last of the hellhound's throats. "Choose," he said.

Lilith went absolutely still, her features frozen in horror. "I'll kill you," she whispered.

"Choose. Save your soul and save your pet—or save the human." He flicked a glance at Hugh. "Much longer and it won't matter anyway."

It was true; Hugh's blood was still leaking out, and Michael couldn't replace it now. Before, it had been freshly drawn, then preserved in the Doyen's cache. The blood on his chest could not be recycled the same way. "Lilith . . ."

She turned to him suddenly, her face white. "Do you agree to give your will, your life to me? Will you let it be taken in any way I choose?"

Lucifer laughed. "You do not need his permission; why else would I have turned you into this?"

Hugh ignored him. "Aye."

She swallowed. "Then don't look."

Movement behind Lucifer's shoulder. Selah, finally. Michael. Rael, his left hand regenerating half its fingers.

And Belial. It must be: the demon looked a spirit of light, as if he intended to return to His Grace at any moment.

Hugh closed his eyes.

❧

Lilith watched as Hugh closed himself completely off, then turned to Lucifer. Forced away the image of Hugh's blood, of Sir Pup's prostrate, mutilated form.

A burst of power from Michael; she felt the injury from the nosferatu's weapon heal—but it could not help Hugh. She looked down, glanced quickly back up. Sir Pup still lay there; Lucifer must be using his magic to block it. Somewhere, on the hellhound's body, was a symbol that was preventing Michael from healing him.

Lucifer was smiling. "I created them."

She spoke to Michael. "Do you have any blood left?"

"Very little."

"Use it." Any extra time. Any.

The Doyen didn't answer, but the intense focus told her that he was transferring more to Hugh.

"Choose, Father."

Lucifer waited, smiling. He must have known Belial stood behind him, but he gave no indication of it.

Of course he wouldn't. But his rival's presence must be distracting; even Lucifer could not monitor Michael, Belial and Lilith at once . . . and she would be considered the least threatening, even though she held the Doyen's sword.

Belial came to them. He stopped beside her, and Lilith gestured to the sword in her hand.

"A weapon for a weapon," she said to him, her heart thudding. "Rael offered me one, and I promised to repay him. I offer this one to him and his liege—but I will not if Lucifer chooses to release me from my bargain."

Michael's face hardened, but he did not look away from Hugh.

"Choose, Father," she said. "Right now, Hugh is dying by my hand—but he has given over his will to me. And I *will* allow Belial to impale him. You'll lose the wager, because it was done at my behest, but not personally by me. And after his death Michael will make him a Guardian, so I lose nothing. You have only one choice: release me from my bargain."

Lucifer's eyes burned with hellfire. "You dare—"

"Choose, Father." Her voice commanded his silence, and she got it. "If you release me from my bargain, Michael has agreed to release you from his wager. You won't have Caelum, but you will not have to close the Gates to Hell. Is having my soul and Hugh's temporary death worth five hundred years without access to Earth?" Her brows rose mockingly. "Are we so important to you?"

Belial smiled. She couldn't look at him for long; his beauty seemed to incinerate her from within. "It appears you are," he said in the Old Language.

Lucifer did not move. Humiliation was already his, simply by being put in this position. Now he had to decide between the slight humiliation of releasing her from the bargain, or losing control of the Gates—and possibly his throne, if she gave Belial the sword.

"Choose, Father." She pursed her lips at his continued silence, then grinned. "There is little choice, isn't there?"

His mouth curled into a snarl. "I release you from your bargain. But you will always wear my mark, Lilith."

"Truth," Hugh said, the word no louder than an exhalation.

A smile touched her mouth. He had closed his eyes, but he had not left her—and he had feared that Lucifer would attempt the same as she. "I know," she said. "I will always be Lilith."

She turned and gave the sword to Belial. It flared to life in his grip.

Lucifer stumbled back.

She wrapped her arms around Hugh's waist. He blinked, looked down at her. His eyes were glassy, his breathing shallow. "Get him to a hospital, now," she said when Selah appeared beside them. Lilith could not go, could not teleport—her anchor was too strong. She would have to follow.

Selah touched Hugh's hand, and they disappeared.

The Doyen stared at Belial for a moment, then slowly nodded. He turned to Lucifer. "You will close the Gates upon your return; you have twenty-four hours."

Kneeling beside Sir Pup, she looked up and met her father's startled gaze. "I lied," she said. "You'd better run, Daddy."

CHAPTER 40

"Agent Milton!"

Lilith glanced up from Sir Pup's harness. Detective Preston walked quickly across the federal building's lobby, his hand raised as if hailing a cab. When he saw that he'd caught her attention, he lowered it and increased his pace.

Detective Taylor remained near the elevators.

"I don't know yet that I am still 'agent,'" she said. "But I imagine you are here to determine that."

Preston shrugged. "Just here for our debriefing with Jorgensen and Bradshaw." His gaze fell, and his tree trunk of a throat worked as he swallowed. "I thought Michael had been able to reattach his heads."

Lilith looked down. Sir Pup grinned at her, panting as furiously as any normal dog. It was easy to return the grin now; until Taylor and Bradshaw had returned to the warehouse, each laboring under the weight of the hellhound's massive heads—before Michael had located the symbol Lucifer had carved beneath his stomach that had prevented his healing—she hadn't been able.

"Michael did. This is the form he takes in public." Her teeth clenched, but it was not so difficult to add, "Thank you for your help that evening. And I'd appreciate it if you'd extend my gratitude to Taylor, as well."

"Yeah." He scratched his chin, studied her. "After Lucifer appeared in front of us and"—he made a chopping motion with his hands—"I've decided you aren't so bad. No offense, but she may take a little longer to come around."

"She may have the right idea."

"Maybe." His lips twitched before he turned his wrist, glanced at his watch. "We've got to get up there. Good luck, Agent Milton."

"Thank you," she said, and it fell effortlessly from her tongue.

Lilith waited until they disappeared into the elevator before urging Sir Pup forward to the next. *That* was not so easy; she'd have relished Taylor's discomfort. But as the next car stopped at the lobby and opened, a wicked grin spread across her mouth.

She'd been rewarded for waiting, after all.

"Good morning, gentleman. You look as ridiculous as always in that toga, Michael." She stepped inside, Sir Pup following at her heels. Rael moved uneasily to the side.

The doors closed. The hellhound shifted, filling up most of the elevator with his huge form. He turned his left head toward Rael, let his tongue loll.

The demon flattened his back against the wall, smoothed his hand over his tie. "We have something to discuss with you, Lilith."

"Do you?" She looked at Michael; a half-smile curved the Doyen's hard mouth. "Have you apologized to him about the fingers?"

"I did not cut them off," Michael said softly. His obsidian gaze held a slight warning—one Lilith willingly heeded.

She wasn't about to let any demon have knowledge of Colin's anchor to Chaos. The amputation had been extreme, perhaps, but after Selah had failed to bring the vampire back from the Chaos realm, Lilith had wanted the Guardian to have the strongest possible link to locate Rael and Belial in Hell.

Lilith simply hadn't known enough about teleporting; and she couldn't have asked if anything less than body parts would have sufficed without exposing her plan.

Hugh had told her afterward that a drop of blood would have

done—unlike teleporting to Chaos, Selah could go Below without an anchor. The blood only gave her a specific location.

"Any apology I give would be false," Lilith said. "I enjoyed it too much."

"It hardly matters," Rael said weakly, wiggling his fingers. Sir Pup pressed his flank against the demon's chest. "They healed."

"That's exactly what I wanted to hear," Lilith said. "I hope whatever it is you want to discuss is half as good."

❧

Not everything could heal.

The scars on Hugh's chest were still livid; like she, he would always wear the mark. But it was hard to accept that she'd been the one to put it there.

But she had not lost him—they had not lost one another. For that, she would have borne any mark, any burden.

He set the weight in the cradle—he was not finished, but it was the best opportunity for her attack.

Lilith straddled him before he could start another set.

He half-rose, but she pushed him back down. Kissed him until she felt the hard rise of his shaft beneath her. "I don't want you to think."

"You are in the best place to accomplish that." His hands settled on her hips, his thumbs began a lazy stroke of her inner thighs. And with that easy touch, she was disarmed. His eyes searched hers. "Did it not go as you'd planned?"

She dipped her head, smiled. Her fingers traced the powerful line of his chest, swooped in to circle the flat bronze nipples. "Bradshaw told them a story about my apartment being used as storage for a theft ring; that somehow the thieves had known it lay empty most of the time."

He grimaced. "That's awful."

"Terrible," she agreed, laughing. "He'll become more creative with practice." His abdomen rippled with muscle; she trailed her fingers over the defined ridges.

"An evil twin is not all that creative."

She pursed her lips, narrowed her eyes. "You couldn't have come up with better, given what I had to work with." And Moloch's transformation just before she'd killed him had been the most incredible luck—a miracle, if she'd been inclined to believe in them. "And the media started the 'evil twin' non-sense, not me."

Rising up, she slid her hand beneath his waistband, gripped him firmly. His breathing changed, deepened, and he watched her with a half-lidded stare. "The university called," he said. "They will renew my contract in the fall."

Her stomach clenched. Would he accept that offer? Or would he hers? Silk and steel and heat against her palm, and she began a long, slow stroke. "I am no longer with the Bureau."

And now his hands, deliciously rough against her skin. Sliding down, finding her hot and moist. "Tell me, Lily," he said.

She bit her lip, her head falling back as he pushed inside, his thumb working over her clit. "I don't want *you* to think," she gasped, laughing.

He sat up. Lifted her in an easy movement, his arms beneath her thighs, holding her open over his hips. The cool wall against her back. His mouth warm on hers. His cock slid through her wet folds, but he did not enter.

"Tell me, Lily," he said against her ear. Rocked against her.

How could she be so open, so vulnerable—so needy—yet still so strong? Safety in this.

He bent and his mouth closed over her nipple, pulling and biting at the taut peak.

"There are rogues—hundreds that fled before the Gates closed. And if Belial overthrows Lucifer, he won't be bound by the wager to keep them closed. Vampires. A few nosferatu that didn't join with Lucifer."

"And evil twins." She heard the smile in his voice as he moved to her other breast. "Shall we become demon slayers, traveling the country?"

"I want you to teach." And moaned as he nudged inside her.

Hugh paused, brought his face back up to hers. "That's unfortunate, because I told them I would not be returning." Her back arched as he sank into her; she writhed, trying to push down, take him all the way in, but he held her fast. "I've been offered another position."

She drew a breath. "Damn him—Michael!" The name came out as a scream as he suddenly thrust deep.

He shook with laughter.

"That is not what I expected to hear," he said.

Her hands gripped his shoulders; if he denied her legs movement, she would use him for leverage. "Don't stop," she panted.

"Oh, God, Lily." He buried his face in her neck, lifted her higher. Began pistoning into her with long, smooth strokes. "You know I can't."

"Can't teach them?" No, no—she needed him with her, needed—

"Stop."

"Good," she laughed breathlessly. Much better.

He flattened his palms against the wall, held her weight on his forearms. So strong. "You don't have to convince me," he said, working against her, into her with each thick slide.

That it was good? Her heartbeat thudded in her ears. "I can't think."

"Good," he said, and then she lost every thought. Only felt.

❧

"You cheated." She tried to glare at him over the top of her glass, but only succeeded in grinning. She sat a little deeper into the sofa, watched as Hugh pulled the cork out of the bottle with a slight pop. Sir Pup glanced up from beside the bookcase, then lazily lay his heads down again when he saw there was no food to be had.

Hugh laughed, topped off her wine, and propped his feet up on the ottoman. "Michael came to see me earlier today, but he apparently didn't tell you he'd already spoken to me when he made the same offer to you. Said that he'd managed to convince a few officials in Washington that they might need to fund a new division."

"Did he do the warrior-angel thing again?" Lilith rolled her eyes.

"I imagine so," he said. His eyes shone bright blue with humor. "Although he said Congressman Stafford also pushed for it."

She shook her head, still disbelieving that Rael had gone rogue, choosing to stay on Earth rather than fight with Belial. "Michael just wants you mentoring them, he doesn't care how it happens. And I think he wants to keep an eye on me." She laughed. "Exactly what I need, another father figure."

His gaze held hers. "What do you want?"

"I'll be directing operations: overseeing, then spinning the story." She shrugged. "It's the perfect job for me: I boss people and alienate them, I lie, and I kick ass. And I thought I'd pull some vampires in, if I can recruit them." Her bare feet slid over his. "You'd be training them, the fledglings and the human agents, and helping with operations. I'd need you there; I'd be an imbecile to waste you on rookies. But mostly I want to spend the next hundred years working beside you, and then come home with you every night."

He leaned forward, pressed a kiss to her lips. "I want that, too." He glanced up at the clock, and his eyes darkened. "I have something for you."

A thud and clatter behind them; she spun around on instinct. Michael stood for a moment, watching them with his obsidian gaze. His eyes lowered to her midsection, narrowed. His expression was grim when he raised his eyes to hers.

"You are barren. I cannot heal it."

She stared at him a moment, then shook her head and burst into laughter. "Good, because we are completely out of condoms." When he frowned, she said, "Idiot, just because we are settling down you think we want a kid? We already have Colin."

Hugh choked on his laugh. "Sir Pup. Savi."

"We are doomed," Michael said and disappeared.

"That's probably what he said in D.C.," she said, examining the huge paper-covered frame he'd left behind, leaning against the wall: ten feet wide, seven feet high. "Do you think he's still furious about the sword?"

"Probably." Hugh clasped her hand in his, pulled her around the sofa. "Colin painted this for you."

He reached up, tore part of the paper away.

"Oh," she said, and everything inside of her softened. The sky in Caelum *was* the same color. It blurred in front of her, and she turned away from it—found its original.

He slid his arms around her, enveloped her in his touch. A kiss, that was love and promise.

And it was kindness—more than kindness—to a woman such as her.

Turn the page for a sneak peek at
Meljean Brook's next paranormal romance,

DEMON
MOON

Now available from Berkley Sensation!

Colin rested his hand against the small of Savitri's back as he guided her past a long line of clubbers. As an act of courtesy, it proved a masochistic one; beneath his palm, the gentle curve of her spine moved in rhythm with her steps, with the beat of the music from inside. Matched the need throbbing within him.

He ground his teeth together, urged her forward a little more quickly. How could he be so desperate to feed? He'd taken enough for two days from the last blonde alone.

"It was popular before, but not like this," Savitri murmured.

Colin glanced at the queue; mostly human, but a few vampires waited as well. A growl rose unbidden in his throat. He didn't want her here; he didn't want to be here—yet he'd been unable to refuse her request.

And she hadn't even flattered him.

His gaze dropped to her neck; her short hair left it deliciously exposed. He should mark her as his. Protect her from the vampires here and the others inside. Inhale her, drink her, sink into her—

He swallowed thickly and forced the territorial hunger aside. What he wanted to do to her could not be considered protection.

"It's morbid fascination," he finally replied.

She sighed, and her lashes swept down against her cheeks. The investigators—and the press—had linked Polidori's to last year's ritual murders; burning it had been determined a cult's symbolic way of beginning its quest for immortality.

All lies, of course; Colin had helped fabricate them. But the story had entertained the public for months, and many of the people standing outside had only come because of the club's connection with death. Her friends' deaths.

"And I spent a sordid amount of money on it," he added. "I can't fault them for recognizing my unparalleled taste, and flocking here to revel in it."

Her lips curved into a smile, and she slanted a glance up at him. "Was it truly that much? Lilith claims you are the cheapest bastard she's ever known."

Pleased with himself for turning her thoughts from her grief, he said, "Agent Milton has a demon's tongue. I am not *cheap,* my sweet Savitri. I've an eternal retirement; I budget wisely."

Her throaty laughter pulled at already tight nerves along his skin. Her hip bumped against his leg as they rounded the corner to the entrance; her fragrance wafted around her. In her heels, she stood only a few inches shorter than he. So easy just to bend and press his mouth against . . .

He dropped his hand from her waist, clenched it into a fist. This was bloody ridiculous. A fruity perfume, and he had as much control as an adolescent pulling himself off on his sheets.

A huge vampire guarded the entrance and ran the guest list; he towered over Colin by his bald head, outweighed him by half. His muscles bulged through the tight black T-shirt. An intimidating presence, and one most vampires respected; but then, they were often fooled by appearances. Colin had deliberately chosen him for his resemblance in size and baldness to the nosferatu—but though the vampire was strong, Colin could have torn him in two with little effort. It was one of the advantages of Colin's transformation with nosferatu blood, instead of an exchange with another vampire.

And the taint Michael's sword had left in his blood had generated the other differences.

The bouncer's eyes widened—Colin usually didn't use the front entrance—and he quickly unhooked the velvet rope. "Mr. Ames-Beaumont."

The urge to dash inside, to find the nearest willing body and glut was almost overwhelming. "Mr. Varney, this is Miss Savitri Murray. She should be on the short list."

Her chin tilted up, her gaze leveled on Varney's features. It was difficult to tell human from vampire, but Castleford would have taught her to recognize the signs: the careful placement of the lips during speech; the slight perspiration in heated rooms or warm nights; abnormal respiration and reflexes. "What's the short list?"

"Full access, miss, including Mr. Ames-Beaumont's personal suite. No charge." There was more, but Varney didn't mention that any vampire who tried to drink from someone on that list would receive a visit from Colin. It hadn't happened yet; there were very few people this side of the Atlantic to whom he'd give anything for free, and Lilith and Castleford were the only other names listed.

A vampire would have to be a blithering idiot to attack *them*.

"Except for tonight." Colin led her forward, and descended the stairs. "You'll pay the cover and for your drinks." An auburn-haired beauty was going up; she glanced at him, then froze with her foot in the air and watched as he passed. "Do you know the Guardians' sign language?"

"No," Savi said, and looked back over her shoulder. "I hope she doesn't fall."

He suppressed his laughter with difficulty, and said in Hindi, "I'll walk with you to the bar; then I must leave you alone for a few minutes. Because you came in with me, you'll be a curiosity to the vampires inside. They may approach you. Don't ask them questions, don't talk to them."

"Why? Isn't the point of all this that I'm seen?"

"You'll be seen, sweet Savitri." But he didn't want them to have any more of her than that.

And hopefully, once he'd fed, his need for more would also fade.

❧

It was inelegant, perhaps even ill-mannered, but Savi eschewed the straw and gulped straight from the glass. Lime and salt, sour and sweet. And cold—she couldn't get enough of it.

Delayed reaction from the flight? Her breath fogged the inside of the tumbler. Heat from the mass of bodies?

Perhaps he'd been too stingy to pay for air conditioners.

She fished out a cube of ice, sucked it into her mouth. The bartender glanced at her. Another vampire. Colin had been right; they'd all watched as he'd taken her hand and led her through the club. As he'd dropped a quick kiss onto her forehead.

Like a little girl. A little sister. She'd known what it was: a display of protection. Because Hugh had saved Colin's sister, the vampire felt obligated to guard Hugh's adopted sister in return. She should have been grateful. Perhaps she would have, if she didn't feel so restless, as if she'd suddenly been caged.

It was a familiar feeling, but it usually didn't make her angry.

She crushed the ice between her teeth. Why was it so fucking hot in here?

She lifted her hand and gestured for another, asked for a water to accompany it. The wounds on her palm had almost completely healed over; only a lingering stiffness remained. She examined the thin pink lines on her fingers. The blood sped healing—is that what allowed them immortality? Accelerated regeneration or cell replication, with no degradation over time?

But wouldn't their hair grow more quickly if it was replication? Did it simply keep existing cells in perfect repair, not speed the manufacture of new ones?

Why did it only heal humans when applied topically, or through a transfusion? And why was it safe? A transfusion would temporarily give a human some strength and healing ability, but it didn't last. Only through ingestion was there a danger—blessing?—of transformation.

Was it the act of taking it in and the choice to drink that provided the power, or the blood itself? Before Michael could transform a human to a Guardian, the human had to agree to the change; she'd heard the same was true of a vampire—the transformation didn't take well if it wasn't voluntary. Could blood recognize choice and free will?

The blood*lust* supposedly did—except for the free will of the vampire it controlled.

She felt Colin before she saw him; he stood next to her, leaning gracefully against the bar. His expression was unreadable, his gaze hooded. Even in the dim lighting, she could see the slight flush on his skin.

She'd seen it before.

Lifting her glass, she took another long drink. Licked the

salt from the rim, from her lips, and forced a bright smile. "The redhead on the stairs?"

His mouth tightened, but he gave a slow nod.

She arched a brow. "You must lose a lot of clients if the ones you feed from leave bleeding."

"She wasn't. And I don't often feed here; I prefer the hunt. Pursuit offers a challenge." He looked away from her toward the dance floor, his mouth pulled down in a grimace of distaste. "When it is readily available, it is merely scavenging."

Her chest squeezed painfully. She'd not only been available; she'd thrown herself at him. "So the aristocrat surveys the un-washed masses, and finds them lacking," she murmured.

And she was just a brown little girl.

"They have their use during revolutions, but there is no rebel-lion here. Only a mess of conformity." His gaze met hers again. "But I do not care if they bathe, Savitri, as long as they bleed."

The glass was slick with condensation; she wiped her palm across her forehead, hoping to ease the heat with cold and wet. "I thought, because of—" She paused, switched to Hindi. He probably didn't want anyone to overhear that he couldn't create other vampires. Surely his impotency embarrassed someone like him, and she wouldn't prick his vanity again. "Because of your *incapability,* that you couldn't heal me. I was wrong."

He contained his emotions too well to interpret his response. "Yes. You also believed Castleford when he confirmed your as-sumption that I was gay."

It had been easier; a woman had little defense against a face like that—except to believe it couldn't be hers. But she'd been mistaken in that, too. Gloriously mistaken, until it had turned into something . . . painful.

"Did she tell you what you wanted to hear?"

A mocking smile. "She screamed it."

She nodded, drained her glass. "I'm going to go dance." Sweat out some of the heat boiling within her. Feel someone's touch on her skin.

Anyone's but his.

❦

She'd known better.

Before her family had been destroyed by a few bullets, Savi had been surrounded by stories—her mother had loved them.

Both surgeons, her parents had limited time dedicated to Savi and her brother. But in those rare evenings when her mother had been home, fairy tales and fables had been standard bedtime fare.

The music drowned out the voices of the men dancing with her, but she could still hear her mother's voice clearly—one of the advantages of a memory like hers.

. . . and the girl came across a cobra curled up against the freezing night air. The cobra begged her to stop and carry him in her pocket until the sun rose in the morning, but she refused. "You will bite me," she said. But the cobra promised not to. "I will die here; if you save me, I will treat you as a friend." The girl was too soft-hearted to let him freeze, and so she picked him up and put him in her pocket. She'd taken not two steps before she felt his fangs against her breast. "Why?" she cried, her voice weak from the poison. "You said you would not!"

"It is my nature," the cobra replied, "And you knew what I was."

Cold hands clasped her hips, pulled her back to gyrate against her. Vampire, but not Colin's hands. His were warm. He could walk in the sun. He was beautiful and charming.

She'd thought if she offered her blood to him, she wouldn't be hurt by it.

She should have known better.

Frigid fingers drifted beneath her shirt, along the curve of her waist. It felt fantastic. Her skin was tight, burning, and his hand trailed over her stomach like a block of ice. His cold form rocked against her back. His erection. Perhaps he could cool her from inside, make her forget . . .

But no—that was one of the drawbacks of her memory. Her mother's screams, forever captured. Her brother's tortured, bubbling breaths. Her father's silence.

And Colin's fangs buried in her throat, desolation and horror tearing through her mind as her body shuddered beneath his.

He'd done it to teach her a lesson—and, by god, she had learned. Her brain had gotten the message.

Her body had not.

She was on fire. Alcohol hadn't dulled it, water hadn't doused it. She hated being drunk; she couldn't think.

A shiver wracked her when his fingers slid higher. Her nipples drew tight beneath the silk.

"You're so hot," said the rough voice behind her.

Like a demon. Averaging 106.7 degrees Fahrenheit, 41.5 degrees Celsius, 314.65 degrees Kelvin. Or did he mean it in that you're-sexy-come-home-with-me way? Didn't he have a partner to share blood and a bed with? Perhaps he was one of those vampires whose partner had been killed by the nosferatu.

Vampires didn't drink from humans, not unless they intended to transform them. If that was what he offered, why not take him up on it? She was going to eventually anyway.

He could turn her, and she would live forever.

Clammy lips touched the back of her neck. Cold, wet—like the nosferatu. *Oh, god.* This wasn't what she'd promised Nani. She ripped out of his grasp, staggered forward.

Colin caught her. He hadn't been there a moment before; she was certain of it. She'd seen him at his table, where he'd spent the whole of the night. Watching her.

She hadn't known he could move so quickly.

His arm circled her waist, his chest hard and warm against hers. He didn't look at her, but over her head. His jaw clenched in a tight line.

Behind her, the vampire babbled incoherently.

"He didn't do anything," Savi said quickly. She'd seen that expression on Hugh's face once, when Lilith had come home with a knife wound across her chest after a fight with a vampire. Had Lilith not already killed it, Savi was certain Hugh would have left the house and not come back until he'd done the same.

But this vampire didn't deserve to pay for her mistake, her stupidity, her drunkenness. How to convince Colin?

Trying not to slur, she said, "Your lips are beautiful."

He flinched, and lowered his gaze. "You bloody foolish chit. You think to manipulate me?" he said through gritted teeth, but his eyes softened as he searched her features, as he inhaled her breath. "Christ. You're completely foxed."

"Deep in my cups," she agreed, nodding.

He blinked. After a long moment, a smile teased the corners of his mouth. "Sweet Savitri—what have you been reading?"

She needed to stop looking at him; surely he was worse for her brain than alcohol. But the firm curves of his upper lip were extraordinary—the dip in the center looked as wide as her forefinger. She reached up to test it.

"I had a phase about five years ago. I read about lords and

ladies. Waltzes. Did you waltz?" The faint stubble was rough against her fingertip; a perfect fit.

Colin gripped her wrist, pulled it away and slid his hand down to clasp his palm against hers. "Yes." His other hand settled over her hip. "Toss him out," he said to someone behind her. "Clear them all out."

And he swept her off her feet.

She didn't know how he did it; though past closing time, dancers still bumped and ground across the floor—yet he twirled her through them without touching a single person. She couldn't keep up or match his steps; he lowered his forearm to cradle her bottom. Then he lifted her against him and glided.

"Oh my god," she said. Lights and colors whirled around her.

"Focus on my beautiful lips, Savitri, lest you become dizzy."

"And cast up my accounts?"

"Yes," he said, laughing; how could she *not* to look at his mouth when he did that? At his elongated incisors, the sharp white line of his teeth. But safer than looking at his eyes and risk seeing the wholehearted, almost boyish delight that had so captivated her in Caelum.

The sound of his amusement rumbled through her, combined with the heavy beat of the music. He wore cologne, a masculine fragrance so light she'd not detected it before. Notes of orange and papaya and sandalwood. She buried her face in his neck, wrapped her thighs around his lean hips.

"Oh my god." His cock was thick and hard beneath his trousers, nestled between her legs. Another perfect fit; she remembered all too well how perfect.

She could come just from this.

"It didn't work," he said in Hindi. He sounded almost apologetic.

She was burning, burning. Just like Polidori's. "What didn't?"

"The woman from the stairwell. Acting the ass at the bar, that you would put distance between us. It seems I can protect you from everyone but myself."

Her body went rigid; her eyes flew open. *I don't always have control.* He'd tried to regain it by feeding, but that had been hours ago. How thin was it now? Her heart pounded. "You were lying at the bar?"

"No. But a gentleman can tell the truth without being cruel, if he wishes it." He slowed next to his table, and eased down onto the sofa without letting her go. Her knees sank into the cushions. His arm across her lower back trapped her hips against his. "Do not mistake me for a kind man, Savitri."

She wouldn't. Not again.

"What are you going to do?" She pushed at his chest.

"Taste you." He cupped her jaw. His thumb smoothed across her cheek. "Only your mouth, and only if you agree."

Tension coiled through her stomach, arousal and fear. And heat. He was a fever inside her, a sickness. "What if I don't?"

"I'll carry you to my suite and do it there." The apology dropped from his tone. He'd set his course; he would follow it. "I don't intend to take your blood, Savi. I simply want—*need*—to taste you." His chest rose and fell beneath her hand. "I think I will die if I do not."

She wouldn't believe that; only poets and horny teenagers did. But her gaze dropped to his lips. "Just a kiss?"

"Yes." With gentle pressure, he urged her nearer. "A sword lies behind the wall panel; the spring is two inches above the sofa, one foot in."

A strange offer. Did he think she would need it? But if he lost that much control, she'd have no possibility of defense.

She'd had a better chance against the nosferatu.

Her palms slid over his shoulders, up to curve around the back of his neck. Her fingers buried in the hair at his nape. So thick and soft.

"This must be because I'm drunk," she whispered as she lowered her mouth to his. "I know better."

So did he.

New in the "dark, rich, and sexy"*
Guardian Series from

MELJEAN BROOK

DEMON BLOOD

In an effort to save his people, the vampire Deacon betrayed the demon-fighting Guardians. Now he lives only for revenge. But Rosalia is in love with him and willing to fight by his side—even if she has to stand against her fellow Guardians to save him.

New York Times bestselling author Gena Showalter

penguin.com

NOW AVAILABLE
FROM *NEW YORK TIMES* BESTSELLING AUTHORS

Charlaine Harris, Nalini Singh, and Ilona Andrews

AND NATIONAL BESTSELLING AUTHOR

Meljean Brook

MUST LOVE HELLHOUNDS

Four original novellas from today's
hottest paranormal authors!

In these hound-eat-hound worlds,
anything goes...and everything bites.

FEATURING:

The Britlingens Go to Hell

Angels' Judgment

Magic Mourns

Blind Spot

penguin.com